Émilie's Voice

A NOVEL

Susanne Dunlap

A TOUCHSTONE BOOK
Published by Simon & Schuster
New York   London   Toronto   Sydney

TOUCHSTONE
Rockefeller Center
1230 Avenue of the Americas
New York, NY 10020

TOUCHSTONE and colophon are registered trademarks
of Simon & Schuster, Inc.

For information about special discounts for bulk purchases,
please contact Simon & Schuster Special Sales at
1-800-456-6798 or business@simonandschuster.com.

Designed by Melissa Isriprashad

Manufactured in the United States of America

1   3   5   7   9   10   8   6   4   2

Library of Congress Cataloging-in-Publication Data
Dunlap, Susanne Emily.
Emilie's voice : a novel / Susanne Dunlap.
p.   cm.
1. Women singers—Fiction. 2. France—History—Louis XIV,
1643–1715—Fiction. 3. Charpentier, Marc-Antoine, 1643–1704—Fiction.
4. Composers—Fiction. I. Title.
PS3604.U5525E45 2005
813'.6—dc22   2004063694

ISBN 0-7432-6506-8

For Cassandra and Chloe,
who learned to sing with their feet

Émilie's Voice

One

*What seems like generosity is often no more than
disguised ambition, that disdains little interests
to achieve greater ones.*
François, Duc de La Rochefoucauld, Maxim 246

One day in April 1676, the sound of laughter drew Madame de Maintenon to the window in her apartment at the château of Versailles. Below her, half a dozen ladies wearing bright-colored gowns clustered around one who was dressed all in white, a velvet blindfold covering her eyes, her blond hair brassy in the spring sunlight. The ladies turned their blindfolded companion around and around, singing a rhyme as they did, until she looked like a yellow-crowned stamen in the center of an enormous silk blossom. Madame de Maintenon—known as the widow Scarron to her enemies—uttered a *tsk* of disapproval and was about to turn back into her room when she noticed a gentleman behind a yew hedge, peeking at the game through the branches. When the rhyme ended, all the ladies scattered like petals, leaving the one with the blindfold staggering and laughing, alone against the emerald grass. The gentleman stepped out from his hiding place. He moved gracefully, and with a regal air. The blond-haired lady, dizzy from her game and unaware of his presence, stumbled into him as if he were nothing more than a shrub, or a servant who wandered into her path. The gentleman removed her blindfold with a gallant flourish and, in front of the other ladies, kissed her. All of them stopped in their tracks and curtsied deeply.

The widow Scarron closed the shutters abruptly. But the sunlight crept in anyway between the louvers and painted bright streaks across her austere parlor, which was furnished only with a few wooden chairs, a bookshelf, and a gilded prie-dieu. She knelt there and started to pray, beating her forehead rhythmically with the heel of her hand as her lips formed the familiar Latin phrases in a low, constant mutter. After a quarter of an hour, the sound of fingernails scratching on her door interrupted her. Emerging slowly from her deep concentration, she stood and said, "Come."

A middle-aged footman entered and bowed. "Monsieur de St. Paul is here, Madame."

"Show him in, François."

St. Paul walked past the servant, not waiting to be summoned. He flared his nostrils at the simplicity of the room, then set his features in a practiced smile. "Madame de Maintenon. To what do I owe the honor of being asked to attend you?"

"Monsieur de St. Paul, I understand that you are in debt."

The smile left the count's lips. He reached into his waistcoat, took out a gold snuffbox, and helped himself to a generous pinch.

The widow Scarron did not wait for him to answer. "There's no point denying it. And I would not have asked you here if you weren't. I would like to offer you a way to change your situation in life greatly for the better."

St. Paul sneezed loudly and dabbed his nose with a lace-edged handkerchief. "I am all attention, Madame."

"Are you aware, Monsieur de St. Paul, that the king's confessor has threatened to deny His Majesty communion?"

St. Paul shrugged his shoulders almost imperceptibly.

"This is a serious matter, Monsieur. His Majesty is God's chosen representative to lead the people of France, and he must not be diminished in their eyes. I think we both know who is responsible for his unfortunate weakness in these matters." Madame de Maintenon turned her head toward the window. The sound of laughter still filtered up from the garden.

"It will not be so easy, Madame, to turn the king from *that* path."

"Nonetheless," Madame de Maintenon said, looking St. Paul directly in the eyes, "we must try."

Late that same afternoon, in a humble workshop on the Bridge of Commerce—one of the bridges laden with buildings connecting the Île de la Cité with the quays on the right bank of the Seine—Émilie Jolicoeur sat on the floor and leaned against the leg of a large worktable, building fairy castles out of the curled shavings of maple and spruce that were scattered around her. Her father, Marcel, focused all his attention on wielding a small, sharp knife to make the final adjustments to the bridge of a violin. It was a commission, for the composer Marc-Antoine Charpentier. This was an important job: Monsieur Charpentier was a fine musician and a member of the household of Mademoiselle de Guise. In the few years since he returned from Italy, he had already made a stir in the capital. If he liked the violin, many people would hear of it, and more work would surely follow.

"Émilie!"

Émilie's mother yelled down the three flights of stairs that separated their apartment from her husband's workshop at street level. Émilie did not answer her.

"Didn't you hear your maman?" asked Marcel. He stood from his task and stretched. The setting sun radiated from around his body, which blocked some of the light from the window that looked out over the river toward the Pont Neuf. He was about to try out the violin to see if it sounded as good as he hoped it would.

"Please, Papa, just let me stay to hear you play." Émilie used the tone of voice that she knew would get her what she wanted.

Marcel met his daughter's eager gaze and could barely suppress a smile. "For a minute, but on one condition. You must sing while I play."

In her haste to get up from the floor, Émilie banged her head on the edge of the worktable.

"You are too grown up now to sit on the floor like a child," said Marcel. "If your maman has her way, soon we will have to find you a husband!"

Émilie pursed her lips in a mock pout. "I don't want to leave you, Papa, unless I marry someone who can make violins just like you."

"So, you want to be poor and have to work hard all the time like your mother?" Without waiting for his daughter to reply, Marcel took up a bow and slowly stroked it across the A string of the violin, making a round note that vibrated and swelled until it filled the crowded space.

When Émilie was an infant, she had slept in a cot in the workshop while her mother ran errands. She began to use her voice to match the pitches she heard in the cradle even before she could talk. When she was a toddler, Marcel would play little tunes for her to mimic. Émilie's ear was acute, and her ability to reproduce a sound almost uncanny. This private exchange between father and daughter had been nothing more than a game at first. But as she grew older, Émilie's voice grew too. Marcel had come to think it very pretty and would find excuses to have her sing to him. She sang nursery rhymes and folk songs in a clear, sweet tone. Nothing pleased him more than to hear her quiet tunes while he worked. He loved to have her sing along while he plucked at or drew a bow across the strings of a newly completed lute or pochette or viol or violin.

Of all the different instruments her father made, Émilie liked violins the best. She loved the warm, sad sound they made, and tried her hardest to make her voice sound just the same. But it was too young and light, too childish to match the subtle richness of gut strings and carefully aged and varnished woods. At least, it had been every time before.

But something extraordinary happened that day.

Émilie closed her eyes and opened her mouth, and the sound she produced was every bit as strong, every bit as rich, as the note Marcel played on the violin he had just finished making. At first Émilie did not hear herself. She only felt the way the sound resonated in her entire body. It was so wonderful, so freeing, to let the music stream out of her, as if she had bottled it up her whole life and was just waiting for it to escape, that she did not notice that her father had stopped his playing, and that the rich tone that washed over the other instruments and set their strings quivering in sympathy came from between her own lips.

"Émilie!"

She stopped singing and opened her eyes. The ghost of the sound she had just been making still reverberated around her. Her father had a strange look on his face.

"I didn't know you could—can you do that again?" Marcel laid the violin down gently on the workbench.

Émilie sang the pitch she had heard before, opening her voice as far as it would go and putting her whole heart into that one, beautiful note. Then, when she could do no more with it, she moved to other pitches and fashioned a little tune with them. When she sang higher, the sound of her voice became sweeter, more intense. Lower, it opened out like a flower. The feeling was entirely new to her. It was not like the singing she had done before. It came from somewhere else. Something, she was not quite certain what, had happened. Perhaps it was because of the beautiful violin, a copy of an Italian instrument that Monsieur Charpentier had brought back with him. Or perhaps not. Whatever it was, it had changed her voice forever.

Marcel tried to say something, but when he opened his mouth, nothing came out.

"Shall we go upstairs to dinner?" Émilie asked.

Marcel nodded, put his tools away, and followed his daughter up the three flights of stairs to their apartment on the top floor.

"What kept you! The soup will be spoiled," Madeleine Jolicoeur said, standing like a narrow stone pillar in front of the table that occupied the very middle of their apartment.

"Don't be cross," said Marcel. "I kept her. She was singing for me."

"Well, she can just sing for her supper then!"

Madeleine turned to stir the pot on the fire. Émilie fetched the wooden bowls from the small cupboard near the chimney and stood and held each one as her mother dished out the potage with a huge wooden ladle. Then from the same cupboard she brought a cutting board, a knife, and a round loaf of bread to the table.

"Her place is here, learning how to make the dinner, learning how to keep a house. You let her stay down there, and why? She is not a son, she cannot take over your business and make violins. She is fourteen. Old enough to marry, and what does she know?"

Marcel did not answer but sat down to his meal. Émilie sat as well, but she barely noticed what she did. Her mind was busy with wonder about the voice that had burst out of her just minutes before. Still, she lifted her bowl to her lips repeatedly and drank the soup until it was gone, hardly tasting it on the way. All the time she did so, she gazed out through the small window under the eaves that faced west. From where she sat, all she could see was the pale blue sky, but she knew that, if she were right at the window, she would be able to see the Louvre, the great palace that belonged to the king, in the distance.

"What are you gawking at?" Madeleine had caught Émilie staring at nothing.

"Mama, why doesn't the king live at the Louvre?"

"I don't know. They say it's not finished. Maybe it's drafty."

"Where does he live then?"

"St. Germain mostly. And Versailles, more and more, so they say."

Mother and daughter cleared up after dinner while Marcel sat in the only armchair and smoked his pipe. Then when the fire died down, they all went to bed, Marcel and Madeleine to their curtained enclosure on one side of the room, and Émilie to her narrow cot on the other.

Two

Nature creates talent, but luck makes it work.
Maxim 153

The next day, about a mile from the Atelier Jolicoeur, the young composer Marc-Antoine Charpentier clasped the top of his long conductor's stick and rested his chin on his knuckles, propping up the weight of his weary head. He sighed, lifting his eyes to take in his surroundings. Three enormous crystal chandeliers hung from the ceiling at regular intervals, swathed in white muslin like elegant spiders' nests. The furniture—all of it in the most ornate style, with gold and ormolu decoration, rare veneers in delicate marquetry, and Italian marble tops—was covered with linen sheets. The parquet floor, known throughout Paris as a superb example of the craftsman's art, was dusty and dull. Without the glow of candles, the great salon of the Hôtel de Guise was positively drab. Marie de Lorraine, whose titles included Princesse de Joinville, Duchesse de Joyeuse, and Duchesse de Guise (making her entry into a room sound like a whole parade of nobility), had not yet arrived from her retreat at the Abbey of Montmartre. Without the mistress in residence, no one did more than the minimum work required to keep the place from running down altogether. And were it not for the upcoming fête, Charpentier would have no reason to venture into this part of the great house, but as composer in residence would work quietly in his own comfortable apartment, churning out devotional music for the princess's mourning over the loss of her nephew Alençon, last of the great line of Guise.

It was spring, but there was still a distinct chill in the air. Charpentier was rehearsing the house musicians, and all six members of the ensemble rubbed or blew on their hands whenever they were not actually playing. Often they cast irritated glances in the direction of the empty fireplace. Charpentier did not know how his viol players could move their fingers, and as he stood before them in silence, he reminded himself to be patient.

Chill or not, it was necessary that they be at their best for the fête, which was to take place in a week. "Really, gentlemen, it is not so very difficult," he said, trying not to sound as irritated as he felt. "It is only necessary to play the notes as written and leave the embellishment to Monsieur du Bois. We must give him an opportunity to show off the new violin." A murmur of disgruntled acquiescence went through the band. Charpentier began to beat the time again, *one*-two-three, *one*-two-three. It was better than before. He let them continue, while his mind wandered. He imagined that he was seated at a harpsichord on the stage of the Guénégaud. Before him was a huge cast of singers and twenty musicians. There was beautiful scenery, with machines to change it between the acts. The costumes were rich and varied, and the voices . . . The music swelled and ebbed; sometimes the drama moved the audience to tears and sometimes it made them laugh. When it was over, the crowd roared with rapture. And then, just when he felt invincible, just when he was certain he was poised for great success, he turned, and—

"Monsieur Charpentier?" It was Alexandre, the leader of the ensemble. They had finished the minuet, but still Charpentier marked the beat, lost in thought.

Charpentier cleared his throat and smiled sheepishly. "Thank you, gentlemen. I think that will be all for today."

With undisguised relief, the members of the orchestra gathered up their instruments and left the room. Charpentier took the sheets of manuscript paper from the music stands and made his way back to his own apartment in another wing of the house. He was grateful that the princess, who had ties to his family that went back many generations, had offered him employment when he returned from his travels abroad. He had hoped for a court appointment, but none was forthcoming. Jean-Baptiste Lully, the court composer, saw to it that none but he received the favors of Louis XIV. It was Lully who reigned over music in France, in the name of the king. Charpentier had heard that he had his own handsome quarters at Versailles and St. Germain, and a large hôtel of his own in Paris. Somehow, while Charpentier was away in Italy, this voracious—and talented—composer had achieved a stranglehold on music in the capital and wherever else the king happened to be. He had even persuaded His Majesty to issue a proclamation limiting the number of musicians anyone could use in a performance, so that only Lully himself could mount an opera.

These bitter thoughts followed Charpentier all the way to his apartment. Although his quarters were ample and his duties light, Mademoiselle de Guise's beneficence did not extend to considering him anything more than a glorified servant. But that was only what Charpentier expected. In Mademoiselle's household, almost every musician was also a valet, or a maid, or a cook. Even in Italy, where music was the prince of all the arts, composers were merely pieces of property, like paintings or jewels. He was fortunate to be required only to compose and perform, not to polish the silver or open the doors.

Italy. The thought warmed Charpentier while he sipped his hot soup and gradually shed the bone-snapping chill of the morning's rehearsal. He could so easily conjure up the astounding voices he had heard in Rome, where the castrato reigned supreme. Men who were not men, who had undergone painful mutilation to retain their boyish high voices, were the most sublime singers in the world. Something about the unnatural prolonging of that temporary voice gave it a poignancy that was unmatched. The best of the castrati could sing with more control, sustain notes longer, and sing with more power than even the finest natural soprano. No one in Paris came close to producing such a sound. Yet the French considered a castrato an offense against the grand design of God—especially now that religion was so popular at court.

When Charpentier finished his dinner, he searched through the untidy pile of papers on the spinet and found the parts for his cantata, "Flow, Flow, Charming Streams." It was time to return to the ballroom to rehearse the singers. There were only three of them, as Lully's ordinance dictated. Only enough to entertain a party. Not enough to sing an opera.

⁓

As Charpentier approached Marcel's atelier in the middle of the afternoon a few days later, still brooding over the disappointments of his career, he heard something unusual. At first he simply folded it into the processes of his imagination, assuming that he had become so obsessed with the idea of finding the perfect voice that he had developed the ability to imagine it in his head. But as he drew nearer to the luthier's workshop, Charpentier realized that what he heard was no fantasy.

He walked into the Atelier Jolicoeur and removed his hat. Émilie was in her customary place, on the floor amid the wood shavings, and so Charpentier could not at first see the source of this extraordinary voice. He looked questioningly at Marcel, who put his tools down quickly.

"Good afternoon, Monsieur," Marcel said. "Émilie, say hello to Monsieur Charpentier."

The singing stopped abruptly, and Charpentier's attention was drawn to the side of the worktable, where he saw a young girl whom he knew to be the luthier's daughter unfold herself from the floor. There was a faint blush in her cheeks and she looked down. The sunlight that streamed in through the window made the wisps of her fair hair glow like a halo. Her voice, which had sailed out onto the street so pure and strong, now merely whispered an embarrassed greeting. Her awkward curtsey made Charpentier smile.

"You've grown, Mademoiselle Émilie," Charpentier said.

"Why don't you run and help your mother prepare the soup for dinner?" said Marcel.

Without a word, Émilie skipped off to the door at the back of the workshop. Charpentier could hear her running up the stairs, a perfect decrescendo. And then he stared at the space Émilie vacated for a long while, certain that it had all been a trick of his imagination.

"The Amati copy is finished, Monsieur," said Marcel.

"Yes, yes," Charpentier said. "I'm sure it is lovely. But I'd like to speak to you about something else." Charpentier looked toward the door that led to the Jolicoeurs' apartment. He could not believe what he had just heard. It was a voice in a million, and all the time it had been only a mile away from him where he worked at the Hôtel de Guise. Suddenly it did not matter how skillfully the luthier had crafted his violin. It was not the product of his hands, but the product of his marriage that interested Charpentier now. And so he turned the conversation away from the violin and toward the luthier's daughter.

Three

We always love those who admire us,
but we don't always love those we admire.

Maxim 294

By the time Marcel came up for supper, Émilie was bursting to find out how Monsieur Charpentier liked the violin. She had strained her ears to hear him try it out, but no sweet tones wafted up the stairs. Émilie wondered what they could have been talking about for all that time. Something told her when she left that she was really still down there, that they were even—possibly—talking about her. The way the composer looked at her unsettled her deeply. She could hardly meet the gaze of his lively gray eyes. So when her father walked through the door, she ran to him, ready to ask for some explanation. But he just smiled and patted her on the head, turning away from her before she had a chance to ask her question.

"Did Monsieur Charpentier come for his violin?" asked Madeleine.

"Yes. We'll talk about it later," responded Marcel, as he kissed his wife on both cheeks.

Émilie sighed and helped her mother put the dinner on the table. Once they were all seated, she plucked up her courage to ask her father about the violin. "Didn't he like it? Monsieur Charpentier?"

"What? The violin you mean. Yes, he did," said Marcel, without elaborating.

"I did not hear him play it," she said.

"No," said Marcel, between mouthfuls of potatoes. "But he paid his money nonetheless."

Émilie knew enough about the process of making and selling violins to realize that this was very unusual. The only way to tell if a violin was any good was to play it. But she did not know what to say, or how to question her father, without seeming impertinent. Before long they finished their dinner, and then all retired with the dying fire. But Émilie knew she would never be able to sleep. *We'll talk later* usually meant that her parents had something to say that they did not want her to hear. Those words were a sort of code that she had long since learned to interpret. The first time, she had heard her mother crying over her last, lost infant. Another time, she had heard her parents discuss whose son might make a good match for her when she reached the marriageable age of fourteen or fifteen. And then there had been the time when she had heard her father try to convince her mother that the expense involved in making violins, a new instrument that was not yet popular with the gentry, would pay off handsomely in the end. So although her eyes sprung open every time she tried to close them, Émilie made an effort to pretend she was asleep, forcing her breathing to be louder and more regular, and moving now and again as though she were deeply asleep and dreaming. Yet all the time she was completely awake, listening for that important conversation they did not want her to hear.

After what seemed an eternity, but which was probably only half an hour, Marcel and Madeleine began to speak in whispers.

"Monsieur Charpentier has offered to give Émilie instruction in singing," Marcel said.

Émilie almost gave herself away by gasping but quickly turned the sound into a deep breath, like those sleepy sighs she sometimes heard her mother utter in the very depths of night.

"And how much does he think he will charge us for this? I suppose he wants his violin for nothing!"

"No, he does not. As I said, he paid me for it, in cash. I think it was a sort of pledge," Marcel said.

After a pause, Madeleine said, "I cannot do without her, you know!"

Émilie could not hear them for a moment or two, but soon they spoke again in whispers she could just discern.

"Think of the opportunity for our daughter! She has a very great gift, and she could better herself, performing in the great hôtels for the rich. There is money to be made."

"Better herself? A pretty young girl of no family to speak of and no fortune? I know what she would become! She's a good girl. I do not want her spoiled."

"This is too important to decide in a moment. Let's see what happens after tomorrow."

With that, the conversation ended. *Monsieur Charpentier wants to teach me to sing properly, so that I may entertain the wealthy in their fine houses in Paris!* Like a chant, the thought echoed in her head. Émilie fell asleep dreaming of rooms full of cakes, silk gowns, and glittering jewels.

When she awoke the next morning, Émilie leapt out of bed, ran to her mother, and threw her arms around her waist. "Good morning, Maman!" she said.

Madeleine gently disengaged her and turned away. "No time for that. It's a busy day today," she said. Then she attended to the delicate process of making the tisane, the herbal concoction they drank every morning that, so Madeleine believed, was the way to ensure a long and healthy life.

Marcel was already sitting at the table, looking as though he had not slept well and staring into the fire that crackled and popped noisily in the sleepy household.

"Will you go for a walk with me today, Émilie? To deliver Monsieur Charpentier's violin?" he asked.

"I thought Monsieur Charpentier took the violin yesterday," she said.

"I have to make one or two adjustments this morning," he answered.

Émilie smiled at her father. Of course she would go. From that moment, she could hardly sit still, she was so excited about this alteration in their daily routine. She knew it must be related to her parents' conversation in the middle of the night before. Otherwise there would be no need for her to go along. Her mother would never let her take a walk with her father instead of staying home and helping her with the chores. Mostly Émilie was only allowed to go out when there was some great celebration, to see the magistrates in their costly robes, or to watch displays of fireworks over the Hôtel de Ville. At those times all Paris was out, dancing around bonfires, the city itself dressed up for a holiday. But most days it was just hard work. And today was Tuesday, which was laundry day. Even better. Émilie would be excused from the most grueling chore of the week.

Once the breakfast things were cleared away and the floor swept, she grabbed her cloak from the peg by the door, flew down the steps to the workshop, and stood in front of her father, trembling and expectant. She waited for him to set aside his tools and remove his leather apron so that they could go for their walk. He washed his hands in the basin, picked up Charpentier's violin, which he had wrapped in cloths and tied with string, then motioned Émilie to follow him out the door.

"Where does Monsieur Charpentier live?" asked Émilie.

"Somewhere very grand," Marcel answered, smiling at his daughter.

The beauty of the morning, with its clear blue sky and fresh, frisky breeze, suited Émilie's mood exactly. Always staying within ten feet of her father, she found ways to gambol like a fawn as they made their way through the streets of Paris. They crossed the Place de Grève, and Émilie was too happy to notice the workmen cleaning up around a scaffold that had been used for a public execution only the day before. Father and daughter both stopped and made the sign of the cross before St. Gervais–St. Protais, after which they continued down the rue St. Antoine, a street that was wide enough for Émilie to spread her arms like a bird and skip ahead of Marcel, without risking injury from the crush of passing fiacres and sedan chairs. From time to time she would stop and whirl around like a windmill, laughing gaily. But she had to stop when they turned up the much narrower rue du Chaume.

"Émilie!" Shortly before they arrived at the Hôtel de Guise, Marcel called his daughter to him. "You must act like a young lady," he said, smoothing back a few wisps of her hair that had shaken loose from her plait when she was skipping ahead. "You don't want Monsieur Charpentier to change his mind, do you?"

"About the violin?" she asked.

Marcel laughed. "I have a surprise for you. But you must be a very good girl to deserve it."

"A surprise?" she asked, almost forgetting that she was not supposed to have heard her parents' conversation the night before. But Émilie suddenly looked around her and noticed that the surroundings had changed. "Does Monsieur Charpentier live near here?" she asked. There were no mean little artisans' cottages in this neighborhood, or rows of houses squashed together and divided into small apartments for the working folk, but fine buildings, with grand entrances that led to cobbled courtyards, with walled enclosures that hid private gardens. She could see the blossoming trees poking above the high stone walls.

After passing beneath a magnificent arch, she and her father entered a courtyard. A footman who stood at attention by the door stopped them.

"We are here to see Monsieur Charpentier," Marcel said.

The footman looked down his nose at them. "Use the servants' entrance, if you please. It's on the rue des Quatre Fils."

Marcel smiled ruefully at Émilie. "I suppose Monsieur Charpentier assumed I would know."

They found the door easily enough, just around the corner on a tiny side street. It was only a simple wooden one, and there was no footman on hand to sneer at them. A kitchen maid, her hands wet and soapy, answered their knock.

"Could you tell Monsieur Charpentier that Marcel and Émilie Jolicoeur are here to see him?" Marcel asked, removing his cap.

"Tell him yourself," the maid said. "Down the corridor and up the stairs."

Émilie grasped her father's hand. It was cold and sweaty. Nonetheless, he led her on in the direction the maid indicated. It seemed as if they walked a mile before they came to a staircase. Once they reached the top of the stairs, they were faced with a new dilemma. Which way, and which door was Charpentier's apartment? Marcel scratched the top of his head. Émilie squeezed his hand.

From far down the corridor and around a corner came the sound of light footsteps approaching. Marcel drew himself up and cleared his throat, ready to ask directions of whoever it was who came into view.

To Émilie's delight, it was a very pretty young woman, dressed in what seemed to her to be the height of fashion. Her gown was silk, not homespun, and her hair was done up in curls and ribbons. When she saw the two of them standing at the end of the hallway, she stopped in her tracks.

"Excuse me, Mademoiselle," said Marcel, bowing slightly.

The lady walked toward them. "What have we here! Did you lose your way to the market?"

Émilie blushed. "We are here to see Monsieur Charpentier," she said.

By then the young lady was right next to them. She exuded a light scent of roses, but when she was up close, Émilie could see where her gown had been mended and patched, and she looked not much older than Émilie herself.

"Do you dance?" asked the lady. Émilie shook her head no. "Do you play?" she asked.

"No," said Émilie. "I sing."

"Ah," said the lady. "Then you must follow me. I'm Sophie Dupin. Sometimes I dance, but mostly I take care of the princess."

So this elegantly dressed young lady is a servant, thought Émilie. Perhaps I, too, will wear such beautiful clothes!

Émilie and her father followed Sophie through the corridors. She chattered constantly as she led them, winding around and doubling back on themselves. Eventually they arrived at a door.

"Isn't this where we started?" asked Émilie, noticing the staircase.

Sophie laughed. "Just knock on the door," she said, and then tripped away from them, giggling.

"Well!" Émilie said, cross that Sophie had played a trick on them. But she soon forgot all about it when Monsieur Charpentier opened the door and greeted them warmly.

"Won't you sit down?" Charpentier motioned them to take their places in two upholstered armchairs, whose comfort was beyond anything Émilie had ever known. He rang a little bell, and one of the kitchen servants brought them tea and cakes. Émilie stared at the cakes, trying not to lick her lips and swallow too obviously.

"Please, Mademoiselle Émilie, allow me." Charpentier carefully selected the most delicious-looking treat and placed it on a small plate, which he handed to Émilie.

"Say thank you, Émilie! Monsieur Charpentier will think you were brought up as a savage!" Marcel cast a stern glance in his daughter's direction and then smiled nervously at Charpentier.

Charpentier laughed. It was a light, musical laugh, not like the hearty guffaw of her father. "Monsieur du Bois is eager to try the new violin . . ."

While Marcel and Charpentier talked of the fine instrument that the luthier had laid upon the table when he entered, Émilie let her eyes wander over the room. This place was so different from the Jolicoeurs' apartment on the Pont au Change. Here there were shelves with books, a musical instrument with a keyboard, and a desk piled high with lined paper and ink bottles and quills, some of the sheets bearing what looked like dancing dots and dashes. Although Émilie had spent many hours and days in her father's workshop, his customers never brought music in with them, and her father could not even read words. The divan in the corner must be where Monsieur Charpentier sleeps, she thought. It had linen sheets on it, and a thick, woolen blanket. Monsieur Charpentier's quarters were more luxurious, but not cleaner than their apartment. The only place that looked truly tidy was a shelf that contained several notebooks, carefully labeled—although because Émilie could not read, she did not know what they were. Otherwise, everything seemed in a complete state of disarray.

"Mademoiselle Jolicoeur, I want you to be fully aware that what you are about to undertake will not be easy," Charpentier said, drawing her attention back to the center of the room.

Émilie had no idea what Monsieur Charpentier was talking about. She had been so busy looking that she had neglected to listen. She naturally assumed they were still discussing the violin, but clearly the subject had changed.

"Monsieur Charpentier would like you to become his student," explained Marcel, who knew his daughter's ways well enough to understand that she hadn't been paying attention. "He proposes that you should come here every day early in the morning, and he will teach you to use your voice, to read and write, and to read music. He will also see that you are given instruction in comportment and dancing. If this goes well, he will one day allow you to entertain the guests at the salon of the Duchesse de Guise, where you will sing his songs before the ladies and gentlemen."

Émilie smiled. Nothing seemed more fabulous to her than that she should be able to come to this delightful place every day, and spend her time singing and learning to be ladylike, surrounded by beautiful sights, sounds, and smells.

"Then I gather, Mademoiselle Émilie, that you agree to come?"

Émilie looked at her father.

"You must decide," he said.

"Yes. Yes, I do agree." Émilie could barely speak, she was so excited. It was a wonderful, frightening thought, to do something so completely different from anything she could possibly have imagined. And yet she knew that she wanted it, more than she had ever wanted anything before.

They left after Émilie consumed three more cakes and a dish of tea. She was convinced that God must indeed have singled her out for special blessing, and she decided she would sing a prayer to him every night for giving her the voice that had so miraculously opened this door before her.

Marcel, having seen more of the world than had his only child, knew that there were perils ahead and that it would take the strongest of wills to avoid them. He wanted to trust Charpentier, and yet the composer was a man. Marcel saw how he looked at Émilie. He did not share his wife's certainty about the fate that awaited his daughter if she became a singing ornament in the salons of Paris, but he knew that her innocence would be short-lived in that setting. Although she was still young, Marcel could see that Émilie would be beautiful, and beauty, talent, and poverty combined usually produced one thing: a courtesan. Innocence was a great treasure, to be sure, but people as poor as he and his family could not afford the luxury of protecting it beyond its time.

Four

Passion makes a fool of a wise man and
makes a wise man of a fool.
Maxim 6

"That woman must be stopped . . . She continues to lead the king down immoral paths . . . He flaunts his unlawful love before the court and the world . . . His Majesty does not yet realize it—he is too blinded by love—but such actions put everything—everything—in peril."

St. Paul went over the widow Scarron's words in his head as his carriage bumped along the rutted roads to Paris. She wants to get rid of Montespan. Well, so do half the women in France, if the truth be told, but no one had yet succeeded. He had been charged with an almost impossible task, St. Paul thought. It was no simple matter to turn the king's attention away from the wittiest, most intelligent, most beautiful woman in Christendom. And supposing he achieved this extraordinary feat? Then what? Then the widow Scarron might step in and take her place—no, the idea was too absurd. Yet the void would be filled, of that St. Paul was certain.

First, he thought that it might be a good idea to try to dig up some scandal on Montespan. It shouldn't be too difficult. He was going to visit his godmother, the Duchesse de Guise. She was no partisan of the court, and if he were going to hear anything really damaging about the king's mistress, he might well hear it there. And besides, his finances were in a more than usually disastrous state, and he could normally cajole the old lady out of a few louis. It was worth the risk of going to Paris and being accosted by his creditors. It would do him no harm to get away from court for a while too. He could think at the Hôtel de Guise just as easily as at Versailles—perhaps more easily, without the constant pleasures and distractions of the court to woo him, and with his belly full of his godmother's famously ample provisions.

He had agreed to the widow Scarron's terms most reluctantly. In exchange for his services in arranging the events that would deflect the king from Madame de Montespan, she would ensure that he would receive a generous pension. It irked him to be subservient to someone who had been born in a prison, although her father was of an ancient family. Despite himself, he could not help admiring her intelligence and wit, the qualities that had helped her overcome her failings to become the governess to the king's illegitimate children, but there was something sanctimonious about her unwavering piety. St. Paul had grown up inside the court, and this early training had taught him not to trust anyone who seemed to be sincere.

Athénaïs de Rochechouart de Mortemart, otherwise known as the magnificent Madame de Montespan, was altogether a different sort. She should have been queen, St. Paul thought, if her parents hadn't bartered her off in marriage at a young age to that idiotic Marquis de Montespan. He wondered if she knew that the widow Scarron—the woman who used to be her closest friend—was now plotting so desperately against her. St. Paul was more than willing to take the opportunity the widow Scarron offered him, assuming that he would be able to claim some support and compensation for his trouble along the way. But what or who could possibly distract a man with such legendary appetites from the marquise? She had swept in, practically annihilating her predecessor, the demure Duchesse de La Vallière. If there was any weakness at all, any chink where one might find a place to drive a wedge, it would be within the character of Madame de

Montespan herself. She had one flaw: her temper. If he could find a way to make her use it to her detriment, then there was the faintest glimmer of hope that they might be able to succeed.

But first, St. Paul thought, it was necessary to eat, drink, and pay his tailor. As his carriage drew up to the door of the Hôtel de Guise, he adjusted his features into a suitably obsequious smile, straightened his brocade coat, and prepared to spend a boring day playing cards with his elderly godmother.

∽

What Émilie did not realize when she agreed so readily to becoming Monsieur Charpentier's pupil was that learning how to sing would be only one of the tasks the composer would set her. Parisian society was elegant and sophisticated. The ladies and gentlemen were well read, appreciated art and music, knew how to dance the minuet flawlessly, and possessed sharp wits and knowledge on a vast variety of subjects. For Émilie to make her mark in that setting would require more than just a pretty voice. Half of every day was, therefore, devoted to other lessons: dancing, drawing, elocution, etiquette, and—most difficult of all—reading.

At first, when Charpentier realized Émilie found the reading and writing so daunting, he tried to make it a game. He would reward her with cakes and tea if she could learn the words he set her and use them in sentences. The results were not spectacular. When the lesson did not end successfully, Émilie stared longingly at the treats she was to be denied, until Charpentier relented and let her have them anyway. He could not bear it when her radiant smile faded, when her eager, dancing eyes turned away from him and tears gathered beneath her lashes.

It was another matter altogether when they turned to Émilie's singing lesson. Sometimes the look that spread over Émilie's face when she was lost in the music almost took Charpentier's breath away. That, and the magnificent sound that gave him chills, made him forgive her just about everything else.

And there were a few things to be forgiven. Émilie had never met an adult who was so eager to please her, who, for fear of losing her trust, did not discipline her. At first she was a little suspicious. But it did not take long for her to realize that in Charpentier's apartment, she was the one with the power.

"I'm not sure I feel like reading today," Émilie said, when Charpentier's insistence that she attend to a passage from a small book of children's stories was beginning to annoy her.

"Are you unwell?" Charpentier asked, immediately putting down the book with such an expression of concern that Émilie could not help laughing.

"I'm sorry, really, I feel fine. But I truly don't want to read anymore. When can I sing?"

Charpentier looked at Émilie from across the table. "I too wish that you could sit here and sing to me all day long. But that is not what will give you success, not that alone. I don't know what else to say to you to convince you that this is very, very important. It is worth the effort."

"My mother said it is idle foolishness to teach me to read, that I won't need to read in order to keep a household and raise children." Émilie knew she was testing Charpentier, knew in her heart what he would say to that, but she wanted to hear it from him.

Charpentier leaned forward. "If you do as I ask, you will not have a life like your mother's. You will be admitted to the highest circles. You will be showered with costly gifts. But most of all, you will spend your life perfecting the art that God meant you to practice, or he would not have given you such a voice."

Charpentier's look melted Émilie's determined resistance. He had eyes like deep, clear pools on an overcast day. Émilie opened the book in front of her and began to read aloud to Charpentier. There were several words she did not know, but he helped her along. In an hour she made it through the entire story, which took up three pages.

"That's more like it, Mademoiselle Contrary!" Charpentier said when they finished.

Émilie could not help smiling. She had read a story, all by herself. Well, almost.

Charpentier smiled his glorious smile at Émilie, and it sent a little thrill through her. She answered with a smile of her own, and the faintest tinge of a blush. "Is it time to sing yet?" she asked.

Charpentier rose and went to the spinet.

Émilie stood and stretched, thankful to be finished with the chore of reading. She took her accustomed place and began to sing to her teacher's accompaniment.

The composer watched and listened as his student put her voice through its daily exercises. She had made great progress. But there was still something holding her back, something he had not managed to convey to her that would unlock everything her extraordinary instrument could do.

"That is tolerable, Mademoiselle Émilie, but your breathing is not right. You are not giving yourself the support you need to reach those notes and sustain them. Breathe from here." Charpentier stood up and placed his hand on his abdomen, just below his rib cage.

Émilie put her own hand on her stomach, and breathed in and out a few times.

"No, it is still too shallow. You have the capacity. Here." Charpentier came over to Émilie and placed his own hand just below her waist. "Now breathe, and move my hand."

Émilie did as she was told. Charpentier pressed against her so that she had to push to make her stomach expand. He could feel her pulse right through the gathers of her homespun skirt.

"Now sing."

Émilie's voice soared through the room and seemed to push at the boundaries of the small space.

"Yes, you have it." Charpentier let go of her suddenly and stepped back to his seat in front of the harpsichord. "Now, let us try an air." He began to play, concentrating on the movement of his fingers over the ebony keys. He did not dare to look up at his student for fear she might notice that his simple gesture, his touch, had unnerved him.

"Please, Monsieur Charpentier," Émilie said when she finished the air. "Can we try the duet again?"

"You mean *may* we try the duet?"

"*May* we try the duet again?"

She mimicked the tone of his voice so perfectly that Charpentier laughed out loud.

"All right," he said, and then dug through the sheets of paper scattered around his feet for the piece she meant.

Charpentier's beautiful, high tenor voice blended particularly well with Émilie's rich, pure soprano. At first he had sung exercises with her, paralleling her scales a sixth lower to help her develop greater security with her pitch. She enjoyed this so much that they began to sing simple tunes together, until finally he wrote a duet for the two of them. He placed the music on the stand and stood next to her. Although Émilie memorized the words and music almost the first time Charpentier taught them to her, she leaned in close as if she were reading them off the page anew. Charpentier did not touch his student, but as they sang, every once in a while the music seemed to carry them to the same place, and the distance between them vanished altogether. The sounds they made collided in the room, beating against each other to become more than just two distinct voices, to become something else, something larger and more exquisite. When they finished, neither of them moved for a few seconds. Then Émilie looked at Charpentier.

He caught her gaze for only a moment. "I think you've worked hard enough for one day," he said, turning away immediately. Neither of them said anything else while Émilie put on her cloak and went out the door.

Émilie walked a little more slowly than usual on her way home that evening. It was cold, but she did not feel it. She did not even mind very much when a fiacre rolled through a puddle and splashed her. She still felt the warm pressure of Charpentier's hand on her stomach. She still heard their voices curling around each other, blending and touching. This intimacy warmed her all the way through, although she did not really understand why. She wanted to turn her steps back toward the Hôtel de Guise and sing again, but she knew it was time for dinner, and that her parents would worry if she did not come home.

When at long last she arrived at the Pont au Change, Émilie let herself into the workshop with her latchkey and found her way across it in the near dark. The fire had been doused about an hour earlier when the light went, and Marcel could no longer see to do his meticulous work. Odd how much smaller it looked to her now, she thought. She still loved the smell of varnish, and the faint outlines of unfinished musical instruments hanging from the ceiling and covering the walls exuded a certain potential for beauty. Sometimes she wished she lived down here, surrounded by all these curving shapes, instead of upstairs, where everything was plain and square. At the Hôtel de Guise, everywhere one looked was beauty. All the rooms were made to delight the eye. Even Charpentier's humble apartment was draped with curtains and had beautiful Aubusson carpets on the floors. Émilie knew it was unfair to compare her parents' little apartment with the home of a princess, but each day the contrast became more stark, and each day she walked home a little more slowly, postponing the moment when she must return to her old life.

Five

*To be a great man, it is necessary to know
how to profit from luck.*
Maxim 343

Early in the morning about a week later, there was a knock on the door of the Atelier Jolicoeur that was loud enough to hear all the way up on the top floor of the building. Madeleine was busy clearing up from breakfast, and so Marcel went down to answer it. He returned with a letter in his hands.

"What could it say?" asked Marcel. "We shall have to take it to the market to have it read."

"No, Papa! Let me try to read it myself!" said Émilie. She looked at the writing on the outside of the folded paper. "It's for me! and it says, '*Son al-tesse* Mademoiselle de Guise requests the honor of the' something . . . 'the presence of Mademoiselle Émilie Jolicoeur in her s-s-salon, December eleven, at six o'clock in the evening.'"

Marcel watched his daughter struggle over the words on the page. He was astounded. She could read. This fact obscured for him the even more astounding one that she had been invited to the most glittering salon in Paris. When she finished, Émilie danced around the room with joy, her exuberant movements filling every inch of space in their tiny apartment.

"I shall need a new dress, Maman!" Émilie said, breathless.

"There, what did I tell you, Marcel? Nothing but expense. And for what? We have no money for this dress. You shall have to stay at home with us." Madeleine's voice was sharp and she closed the cupboard door so hard that the dishes inside rattled.

Marcel watched the light go out of his daughter's face as if someone had thrown a bucket of slops over her. Never did he feel more sorry that his business did not thrive, that he could not provide more material comforts for his family. He shot a look at Madeleine and met her implacable gaze. "Surely there is something we could do without, just so Émilie could have this opportunity?"

"What could we do without? Supper?" Madeleine faced her husband without flinching.

"I could sell something, maybe one or two of my tools."

"No, Papa!" Émilie ran to him and took his hand. "It's not so important. Maybe I don't need a dress to go."

"What, and be laughed at by those idle folk?" Madeleine walked over and stood very close to her husband.

Marcel could feel her anger leap across the space that separated them. She blamed him for their poverty, he knew. He had taken a great risk with violins, an instrument that was not yet popular with his usual customers, at a time when things were just starting to go a little better for them.

"It does not matter," Émilie said. *"Au revoir."*

Silently Marcel accepted Émilie's kiss and watched her put on her cloak and leave the apartment; he wondered what she would say to her teacher.

Émilie had to pick her way slowly to the Hôtel de Guise that morning because the cobbles were coated with a thin layer of ice. Her slow progress gave her time to think of how she might break the news to Charpentier that she would be unable to perform at the princess's salon. By the time she arrived, she was frozen through and still did not know what to say.

"Good morning, Mademoiselle Émilie!" Charpentier said when Émilie walked through the door, shivering. "Come over to the fire and warm yourself. Did you receive anything by messenger today?"

Émilie untied her cloak and hung it on the peg by the door. She did not want to tell Charpentier her news. She could read the mischievous excitement in her teacher's eyes and was sorry she would have to spoil everything. "Yes, I had an invitation, from Mademoiselle de Guise. But," Émilie paused. "I cannot go."

"Why ever not?" he asked.

"Because I have—because my parents—" Émilie bit her lip and looked down at the floor.

"What is the matter?" asked Charpentier, taking a step closer to her.

Émilie could feel his presence, could feel the warmth of his gesture even before the hand he reached out to her touched her chin, lifting it so that she would have to look into his eyes. "Because I simply can't!" she said, turning around quickly so that she would not have to face her teacher.

She heard Charpentier clear his throat. "That is too bad, Mademoiselle Émilie, because I had decided, in honor of your hard work and perseverance, that we should take a trip to the dressmaker's today, and order you a silk gown, appropriate for such a grand event." Émilie turned back to him. He was smiling. "It is a gift, from me."

She wished that she could run to him and throw her arms around his neck. He had made her so happy. But he was not her father; he was her teacher, and so she stood where she was and tried to think of something to say. The best she could do was "Thank you, Monsieur."

"And so I understand that you will, after all, attend the princess's salon?"

Émilie smiled.

"Well, what are you waiting for? Put your cloak back on. We'll take a fiacre and be back in time for your singing lesson!"

*   *   *

Charpentier felt a little glow of warmth that he had been able to provoke such a reaction of pleasure and gratitude in his student. While they walked to the stand to hire a carriage, Charpentier thought back over his conversation with Sophie, the pretty maid who had led Émilie and her father just a little astray when they first came to the Hôtel de Guise, concerning which dressmaker to engage for the purpose of making Émilie's first silk gown.

"You wish to buy a gown for a lady?" The tone of her voice, and the look in her eyes, had disconcerted Charpentier.

"It's for Émilie."

"Ah! The little songbird! Have her lessons been progressing well?" A smile played at the corner of Sophie's lips. But she must have sensed his embarrassment, because without teasing him further she recommended a dressmaker in a different part of the Marais, on the other side of the rue St. Antoine.

Charpentier still felt vaguely ill at ease about buying Émilie a gown. He understood that it must appear strange for him to take such an interest in a young girl on the brink of womanhood. But he could not worry about that now. After a short walk, they arrived at the carriage stand. When he saw Émilie's eyes shining, Charpentier realized that she had probably never ridden in a fiacre before. The idea that he was giving Émilie such an experience, introducing her to the simple pleasure of being transported without effort from one place to another, made him forget all about the uncomfortable conversation with Sophie. He did not stop to question himself as to how much pleasure the sight of her fair skin, clear blue eyes, and pale blond hair gave him. All he knew was that they would have an outing, that they would drive through the beautiful, snow-frosted streets of Paris as if they had no cares.

It was difficult going on the icy, muddy roads, but despite that, Émilie would not have wanted to walk. There was something rather nice about sitting next to Charpentier, and she didn't mind at all when a sudden lurch of the carriage threw her against him and he gently righted her and smoothed down the warm rug that he had wrapped over her legs. Émilie felt very high up, and from this vantage point everything looked quite different. The winter sun glinted off the snow, nearly blinding her with its brilliance and casting enchantment over even the humblest objects. She shamelessly peered in all the shops they passed, catching glimpses through small, frosty windows of merchants smiling and haggling, showing off their costliest wares. A few hearty souls had spilled out onto the street despite the cold and were warming their hands on makeshift fires. The arcades in the Place Royale were as busy as ever. Cold weather didn't seem to deter those with money to spend from seeking ways to part with it. Since she had no money of her own and had only ever entered a shop with her mother for the purpose of purchasing something absolutely neces-sary, this spectacle was a treat. There were glove makers and milliners, carpet weavers and importers of porcelain, shops devoted to ladies' fans made of lace and ivory and painted and jeweled, ironmongers who made cooking pots and door knockers, silversmiths and gold-smiths, tea shops and confectioners. The smell of bread baking at the boulangerie reminded her that she had left her home that morning without finishing her breakfast.

If only my father could see me! she thought. And then she thought of him, alone in his atelier. Émilie's smile faded when she pic-tured Marcel without her there to keep him company. She wished, at that moment, that she could be in two places at once, that she could stay as she was before, and yet fly forward into the world to greet whatever new adventures it held.

After about twenty minutes of lurching and jostling, Émilie and Char-pentier arrived at the little boutique not far from the river that Sophie had recommended, where an elderly woman who seemed to sprout brass pins from all over her body greeted them and led them into a room that was draped with rich brocades, cut velvets, cloth of gold and silver, and delicate voiles. Émilie's eyes wandered over the rows upon rows of ribbons and laces, from the simple to the almost inconceivably grand. She tried to imagine a room full of people dressed in all these elegant materials. The idea that she would be one of them, wearing a gown made of silk and trimmed with lace, almost took her breath away. She could hardly stand still long enough to be measured accurately. But when Charpentier told her she could choose what sort of gown to have, Émilie looked as though she might cry.

"But how can I?" she asked. Everything looked so beautiful, she wanted it all. For a moment she wondered if she could have a dress made of a tiny scrap of every piece of cloth in the store. If she had to choose one or two, she would not be able to have the rest. Émilie had the feeling that not only was this the first time in her life she could choose a fine dress but it might be the last. The responsibility of getting it just right, of squeezing the last drop of pleasure from the experience, oppressed her.

"Is there not a color you prefer? Do you like flowers?" offered Charpentier, trying to be helpful.

"No," she answered, "I mean, I don't know what I prefer." Just then Émilie's eye rested on a bright scarlet velvet, the kind of material one might see on the seat of a fine carriage. Charpentier, noticing the look in her eyes, glanced at the dressmaker in alarm.

"Perhaps, Mademoiselle, a pale color would look best with your beautiful fair hair and pink cheeks," the woman said, pulling out a delicate lilac moiré for Émilie's inspection. Émilie looked beseechingly at Charpentier.

"You might prefer a pale blue, which would match your eyes," he offered. The dressmaker bowed politely and retrieved an elegant, ice blue silk damask, and quickly hid away the scarlet velvet. After considerable debate and consultation, it was decided that the manteau should be constructed of this stuff, and that the petticoat should have a small flower design in blue and rose, an intertwining lattice of luxurious silk. This difficult decision took well over an hour.

When the proprietress then began to pull out laces and ribbons to show Émilie, her head started to ache with the idea that she must once again choose. Charpentier saw that they might never finish if he left it entirely to Émilie, and so he selected a few trimmings that were not too expensive—much to the disappointment of the dressmaker. All that remained was to choose the ribbons for her hair, since a pinner, which would envelop her head and wrap around her throat, would be too cumbersome for a concert.

Among the many pretty ribbons the dressmaker brought out was one of deep blue cut velvet, about two inches wide. It had a pattern of roses stuck on a meandering, thorny stem. Émilie touched it, stroked it, and held it to her cheek. It was the most beautiful thing she had ever seen.

"We'll take a length of that too. You can wrap it up for today," said Charpentier. The lady curtseyed, smiling. It was one of her most expensive trimmings.

Charpentier saw how his little student's eyes lit up when she realized she was being allowed to have the coveted ribbon right then and there, and he suddenly felt a pang of regret. Was he so certain that this life he had planned for Émilie was the best for her? Could she not have spent her gift singing for her own family, without having to make the leap from one world to another?

"You are not pleased?" asked Émilie as she turned to Charpentier. His face was pensive, and he wore a slight frown.

Charpentier tried to shake himself out of his melancholy mood, for Émilie's sake. "Of course I am pleased. But you do not need any finery to be the most beautiful girl in all Paris." Charpentier rose suddenly from the stool he had occupied for the duration of their visit and turned away. "It's time we were leaving."

"The dress will be delivered in five days' time," the dressmaker said, after Charpentier signed his name in her big ledger book.

Just as Charpentier was helping Émilie into her cloak and bidding adieu to the dressmaker, the door to the shop opened, letting in a blast of icy air and a bundled-up young woman. Her nose was quite red from the cold, and she was so covered up that it was almost impossible to tell who she might be. Only a curl of strawberry blond hair that teased itself out from beneath the hood of her cloak might have given her away, if Charpentier had noticed. It was Sophie, who, knowing exactly where teacher and pupil would be, decided to time her own visit to collect a black crape gown for Mademoiselle to coincide with theirs. She was consumed with curiosity about what might happen on their excursion. She soon realized that they had not seen her, and therefore she decided not to make her presence known. Sophie turned away from them, pretending to occupy herself with some laces in a corner. She had seen enough, however, to give her a little thrill. Charpentier had tied the bow of Émilie's cloak in a protective, concerned manner. Sophie would be able to regale the servants with a very juicy bit of gossip.

Émilie and Charpentier left the shop, somehow managing to find a carriage to take them back to the Hôtel de Guise. The crowds had thinned a little, the winter sun had dried the cobbles so that the horses did not slip so much, and the trip was faster: it took only about ten minutes. Although Émilie would forever remember the magic of the journey to the dressmaker's that day, she could not have told anyone a single thing about the trip back.

Charpentier stole a glance at Émilie when she was turned away from him. He noticed the hint of a smile tugging at the corners of her mouth. Émilie had changed. How did it happen? Charpentier had some idea of his own role in the process, but he had not expected that in some critical way the tables would be turned. He was a little afraid of his own creation.

Perhaps it's for the best, he thought. He knew that Émilie would soon spread her wings and leave his protection; he only hoped that she would carry him with her at least part of the way to artistic success. What a rare treat for the guests of Mademoiselle de Guise, he thought, a little sadly. The scene was set, indeed, for the most brilliant of débuts.

Six

*The glory of men must always be measured by
the means they have used to acquire it.*
Maxim 157

Émilie could hardly believe her eyes. The image in the mirror looked back at her strangely, so familiar and yet completely different. Who was that elegant young lady in the blue silk gown, with her hair draped over her ears in cascades of curls? Surely more had changed than simply her outward appearance. It just wasn't possible that this creature she could not take her eyes off was the same one who used to sing to her father as he built violins in his workshop. It seemed that more than a number of months had passed, and that she was much farther than a mile from her home. The weeks of hard work were like a dream. She was almost dizzy with excitement. All her efforts—to polish her voice, to learn to read music, and yes, to learn to read words on a page—were about to pay off.

That is, if she could get over this one small problem.

"You cannot wear these shoes with this dress!" Sophie, who had developed a soft spot for the young singer and had volunteered to help Émilie get ready for her big début, stood back with her hands on her hips and a frown on her forehead and scolded her. She had already spent hours doing Émilie's hair, threading the lovely, velvet ribbon—the one Émilie had chosen at the dressmaker's the other day—through the poufs and curls she had stuck in place with sugar syrup. Now she discovered that the only shoes Émilie owned were rough leather boots.

"Perhaps I don't need to wear shoes," Émilie said.

Sophie looked at her as if to say, "How can you be so naïve?" and then whirled around and left her alone in the room.

Émilie shivered. While Sophie was there helping her dress and gossiping about the guests, it was possible to think only of how she looked. She could focus on the way the silk caught the light of the candles when she turned, and how the blue velvet ribbon set off her pale hair so becomingly. But once she was on her own, the reality of what was ahead began to dawn, and Émilie started to think about her coming performance. She so wanted to do well, for Monsieur Charpentier's sake. The thought of her tutor reminded her that she should warm up her voice, and so she began, slowly and quietly at first, moving from note to note, up and down the scales and arpeggios, gradually pushing higher and higher and lower and lower. She tried to remember everything he had taught her, about how to breathe, how to make the music live. Émilie paused to clear her throat. That was when the young gentleman, who appeared out of nowhere and now stood in the doorway, started clapping.

She jumped.

"Charming," said the stranger, who was elegantly turned out in a yellow velvet coat with gray petticoat breeches. His light brown hair fell in curls around his shoulders, and he would have been handsome, if it weren't for the fact that his eyes were of so pale a gray that they looked almost unearthly. He did not introduce himself, and Émilie wondered how a guest had found his way to this private part of the building. As he turned to leave, the gentleman almost bumped into Sophie.

"Well, well! Mademoiselle Sophie, if I am not mistaken?" the stranger said, inclining his head just slightly.

Sophie glared at him, not bothering to curtsey. The gentleman patted her on the cheek and then left.

"Who was that?" asked Émilie.

"Only Monsieur de St. Paul. He's Mademoiselle's godson. He comes here when he wants something from her. He's always turning up in the oddest places. But never mind that, I've found you some shoes." She smiled triumphantly as she removed from beneath her manteau a pair of the most beautiful satin slippers Émilie had ever seen, pale blue with a delicate flower pattern embroidered with little jewels and seed pearls on the toes. She tried them on. They fit her perfectly.

"Where did you get them?"

"It would be better if you didn't know. Just remember to bring them back before you leave. I could get into trouble if you don't!"

Émilie was about to protest that she didn't want to be the cause of any difficulties, and that she'd rather go barefoot than get Sophie in trouble, but at that moment there was a polite tap on the door. It was Charpentier. When he saw Émilie, the words of greeting that were on their way out of his mouth stumbled over themselves and came out as nonsense.

"What he means to say is, you look absolutely lovely," said Sophie, laughing.

Émilie curtseyed to her teacher and smiled. He held out his arm, pausing for breath before arranging his thoughts in an orderly line again.

"Will you do me the honor, Mademoiselle Émilie, of accompanying me to the salon of the Duchesse de Guise?"

Whatever idea Émilie had of the luxury that surrounded Charpentier at the Hôtel de Guise was completely transformed the moment the composer led her into the grand salon all decorated for a party. Although the sun had set two hours before, the great hall with the staircase was ablaze with light, the effect of thousands of candles, in sconces and chandeliers, and torches held aloft by liveried servants. About two hundred guests already milled around, and there was a sea of vibrantly colored silks, miles of lace, and jewels that caught the light and refracted it into showers of brilliant, multicolored points. Although it was December, there were fresh flowers everywhere, from Mademoiselle's hothouses in the country, and their scent made Émilie almost dizzy with its richness. Servants passed around trays of glasses filled with wine, and in one room there was a long table that overflowed with fruits and dainties. Charpentier whispered to her the names of several of the more illustrious guests, but she was so awestruck that she barely heard a word.

Before Émilie knew where she was, Charpentier had led her into the grand ballroom, which was strewn with small groups of ladies and gentlemen. Gone were the dust sheets, and every surface gleamed with polish. He nodded politely to several people he passed but did not stop, instead taking Émilie directly to Mademoiselle de Guise herself. The princess was seated at the center of the liveliest group. Although she was quite elderly and dressed in the light gray of mourning, she was bedecked with jewels and her hair was dyed black and done up in the latest fashion. Émilie thought she had kind eyes.

"Mademoiselle," said Charpentier, with a low, courtly bow, "may I present Mademoiselle Émilie Jolicoeur."

Émilie curtseyed deeply, as she had been taught. Charpentier nudged her and whispered, "Close your mouth."

"Monsieur Charpentier tells us that you can sing, Mademoiselle Émilie," said the grand lady. "Perhaps you would relieve the tedium of my discourse by favoring us with a selection?"

The ladies and gentlemen around the princess looked Émilie up and down with frank curiosity, waiting for her to take her place by the harpsichord. Émilie was a little embarrassed by the scrutiny, but the familiar sight of Charpentier seated at the keyboard calmed her. He played the introductory measures.

"What a dear little creature!" a woman standing near the princess said, quite loudly considering that the music had already started.

Émilie began her song, an air that Charpentier had composed specially for the occasion.

"Rather small, though, don't you think? Do you suppose she powders her hair? It's so fair!" a gentleman whispered audibly.

Émilie continued, wishing she could stop her ears so that she would not become distracted. Her tentative beginning was not forceful enough to cut through the chatter. Her voice felt pinched, as if she couldn't get enough air to hold the notes. With panic rising into her chest, she looked over to Charpentier, who smiled at her and mouthed the word *breathe!* at her. Émilie closed her eyes and tried to pretend she was all alone. Her voice grew and soared through the room, blossoming into its fullest beauty.

All fell silent. Even the servants ceased their constant rushing to and fro. To Émilie, it felt as if the room had fallen away, and she floated on a white cloud in a clear, blue sky. By the time she opened her eyes at the end of her song, she hardly knew where she was anymore. The sight of the crowd around her, completely motionless and watching her intently, astonished her. Then as if some secret signal had been given, the assembled company erupted in applause and shouts of *"Brava!"* and *"Bis!"* Émilie was at first startled, then pleased, and Charpentier smiled at her and then rose and kissed her hand.

Mademoiselle's guests expressed their appreciation loudly and long, except for one person: St. Paul stood in a far corner of the room, the faintest suggestion of a smile on his face. His arms were folded across his chest, and he leaned against a pillar, watching as his godmother kissed Émilie on the cheek and pressed a small velvet bag into her hand. Soon after, the nobleman left, unnoticed by any of the other guests.

Émilie sang a few more times over the course of the evening, and the audience was enchanted. She wished that she and her tutor could have performed their duet, but he refused, saying that he did not want the guests to hear any voice but hers that night. When it was time for her to go, at one in the morning, Mademoiselle de Guise sent for her own coach to take her home, with its four black horses, its footmen in livery, and soft, velvet cushions. Émilie felt very grand.

Monsieur Charpentier held the door open for her and she climbed into the carriage. "I'm very proud of you," he said taking her hand for a moment. The gentle pressure of his fingers sent a little thrill through her, and Émilie looked down in confusion. It was then that she noticed the borrowed slippers, still on her feet. She paused for a second knowing that she should go back and return the shoes to Sophie, but she didn't want to spoil the moment. It was something, to be handed into a vehicle that had been summoned just for her. Until they heard her destination, the footmen would think she was a fine lady. For just a moment, she believed it herself.

I can return the slippers tomorrow, she thought, as the coach lurched forward and finished its arc around the courtyard, and then passed through the gate and turned left onto the rue du Chaume.

Before long, Mademoiselle de Guise's carriage stopped in front of Émilie's door. The footman helped her out, and Émilie saw him sneer at her humble surroundings. She was determined not to let him ruin her evening, so she walked to her door with her chin held high.

When Émilie thought about that moment months later, she felt ashamed that she had been so proud. If she had not been concerned about what Mademoiselle's servants thought, about what they would tell the other domestics at the Hôtel de Guise when they returned, she would have walked carefully, looking down, and she would have seen the large puddle that lay directly in her path to the door. But because she did not do so, Émilie stepped right into the middle of it, breaking through the thin film of ice that had formed over it once the sun went down. Émilie drew her breath in sharply. For an instant she balanced with her other foot in the air, trying to find a way to step clear of the puddle. But dry ground was too far away, and she ended by standing with both feet in two inches of freezing cold water, which her long skirts quickly wicked up, soaking her to the knees.

"Damn!" she whispered. She heard the coachman snicker. Trying to act as if nothing had happened, Émilie sloshed the rest of the way to the door, longing to turn around and stick her tongue out at the impudent servants. She fumbled for her key, which she had hidden in her bodice, not wanting to look like a housekeeper with it dangling around her waist, and so it was somewhat awkward to retrieve. When at last she got it, the lock on the door stuck. "Damn, damn! Just open, will you!" Émilie's feet were so cold she could no longer feel them. But after a moment or two the door finally gave way. She slammed it behind her and leaned against it, listening to the sound of coach wheels and clopping hooves slowly dying away, struggling against the urge to cry. The borrowed slippers were surely ruined—not to mention her beautiful gown, a precious gift from Monsieur Charpentier.

Émilie walked through the dark workshop, leaving wet footprints behind her and picking up the fine wood dust with her heavy, dragging skirts. She opened the door to the stairs at the back and began the long climb.

When at last she arrived and let herself in, the fire in the grate had only a glow of forgotten warmth in it, and her teeth chattered audibly. Both Marcel and Madeleine were asleep, but not deeply. It was her father who awoke first and parted the curtains around their bed.

"How was it—" he began, stopping at the sight of her. "Émilie, child! You are cold!"

"I'll be all right. I just want to go to sleep," she said.

Marcel's exclamation roused Madeleine.

"Did they pay you?" Madeleine sat up in bed and beckoned Émilie to come closer.

Émilie's throat felt a little scratchy, so she didn't want to talk. She was so tired it felt like an enormous effort to walk across the small room to her parents' bed. When she got there, she simply dropped the velvet bag of coins into her mother's outstretched hand, then returned to her corner and let her damp dress drop to the floor. As she stepped out of the gown, Émilie saw the extent of the damage to the slippers and could no longer hold back her tears, which trickled down her cheeks, picking up color from the rouge Sophie had so expertly applied to them hours before. Her lovely evening was spoiled. Émilie slipped under her blanket, but not before she had unthreaded the pretty ribbon from her hair and tucked it under her pillow. By the time Marcel came over to make sure her covers were warm enough, she was already in a deep, exhausted sleep.

"You might have asked her if she had a good time," Marcel said to his wife when he climbed back into bed.

"Better that she didn't. I don't like it, all this mixing with the wealthy folk. It won't do for her to be getting ideas. She'll only be hurt in the end."

Marcel sighed and turned over. He wondered why Madeleine was so hard on her only surviving child. She seemed to take no interest in Émilie's talent and never even asked her to sing. He thought perhaps his wife was too afraid to become attached to their daughter, after losing so many other babies. It seemed a shame, as though she were cheating herself out of the one consolation of life. But there was nothing he could do to change Madeleine. And they were happy in their own way. Perhaps tomorrow she would let Émilie talk about all the fine clothes and jewels and tell them how the guests had clapped and fussed over her. Then maybe Madeleine would be able to take some joy in her daughter's triumph.

The next morning, when Émilie failed to be roused by the noise of logs being dropped onto the fire and the smell of breakfast, Madeleine went to prod her into action.

"Oh, let her sleep a little longer!" Marcel begged.

"What? Just because she was out making merry with the rich folks to all hours, she should lie in bed all day?" Madeleine asked. "Come on, time to be up!" she said, clapping her hands as she marched over to Émilie's bed.

But Émilie didn't so much as budge. Madeleine nudged her

daughter in the shoulder. "Émilie, wake up! It's a beautiful day, and breakfast is waiting."

Émilie's eyes opened halfway but did not see.

"Marcel!" shouted Madeleine. She noticed beads of sweat on Émilie's forehead and realized that she was unconscious with fever. Marcel came running.

"Émilie! Émilie!" They shouted and rubbed and patted, but all Émilie could say was "Shoes . . . shoes." Without knowing the manner in which she had come by the slippers, which Madeleine found on the floor by her bed, soggy and water-stained, the two parents quickly came to the conclusion that she blamed the inadequate footwear for bringing on the fever.

"Damned flimsy—! If that Monsieur Charpentier has murdered my girl—!" Madeleine's face was pale and her eyes bright.

Marcel was beside himself, but he realized that his wife must feel even worse. She had been so unkind to Émilie the night before. He continued to rub Émilie's wrists and call to her, trying to rouse her out of her delirium.

Madeleine picked the slippers up off the floor. They were a mess, and no substitute for Émilie's practical leather boots, although she could see that they must have been very beautiful once. No wonder she's caught her death, she thought. They must have made Émilie walk home in the cold. Madeleine was about to hurl the offending footwear into the now blazing fire when she noticed that the pattern on their toes was defined by tiny jewels that had been sewn carefully in place. She paused in mid-gesture. Madeleine looked to see that her husband was completely engrossed in trying to rouse Émilie, then took the slippers to her workbox, swiftly cut out the jeweled bits, and tucked the precious scraps away beneath the coils of thread. Then she threw what was left of them onto the flames.

Marcel's efforts to get a response from Émilie were futile. He approached his wife, who stared absently into the fire, watching it flare up in magenta and blue as it gobbled the delicate satin.

"I cannot wake her. I'll fetch an apothecary," he said, already putting on his cloak.

Madeleine reached up and took down a pot that was on the wooden mantelpiece. It was where they kept what money they had for emergencies and to buy items they could not barter for. Out of it she took the velvet bag Émilie had given her the night before. Madeleine's rough fingers untied the silk cord that held it closed. She upended the bag. The shiny, irregularly shaped yellow disks, stamped on one side with the image of a young King Louis XIV, clinked softly against each other as they poured into the palm of her hand. Madeleine stared at them for a moment. She had never held gold coins before.

Marcel scooped the money up, charged down the steps, and flung open the door to the street, in the process nearly crashing into a very well-dressed gentleman who had his fist raised in preparation to knock.

"Out of the way! My daughter is ill!" Marcel gasped, too distraught even to ask the stranger's name.

"Mademoiselle Émilie?" asked the gentleman.

Marcel nodded and was about to push past him, but the visitor stood his ground. "Monsieur Jolicoeur, if I may be of service. I have it in my power to procure the very finest physicians. Come with me, if you will."

"Who are you—begging your pardon, Monsieur?" Marcel asked, finally noticing that the caller was a person of quality.

"I am le Comte de St. Paul, godson of Mademoiselle de Guise," St. Paul answered with a flourish of his hand.

"Then you heard Émilie sing last night?" Marcel shifted his weight from one foot to the other and looked past St. Paul, afraid of delay but eager to hear something about his daughter's triumph the night before.

St. Paul smiled. "Yes. A rare talent. But we are wasting time."

He gestured for Marcel to climb into his coach, and the two of them took off toward the right bank.

When Marcel and St. Paul returned about an hour later with three bearded men who, she was told, were His Majesty's own physicians,

Madeleine was nonplussed. "We cannot afford their fees!" she whispered to Marcel, knowing that the money she had given him earlier would never cover everything.

Marcel shrugged. "Monsieur le Comte is the godson of Mademoiselle de Guise. He insists that we are not to trouble ourselves about the cost, that it will all be taken care of."

Madeleine narrowed her eyes, and went to prepare a fresh bowl of vinegar water. She and her husband watched as the physicians laid on poultices and compresses and measured out drops of mysterious liquids from ominous-looking bottles.

"What are you giving her?" Madeleine asked. She did not like to relinquish the nursing of her daughter to these strangers.

"Only something to help her rest," one of the doctors answered.

The other one uncovered a bowl with leeches, shiny and black and squirming.

Madeleine recoiled at the sight of them. "Must she be bled?"

The doctor did not look at her but turned to St. Paul. "This room is very small. Perhaps you would clear it of distractions?"

"Well, I—" The color rose into Madeleine's cheeks when she realized they were pushing her out of the way.

St. Paul took her by the elbow and steered her in the direction of the table. "I think the best thing you could do is make us all a nice tisane."

Marcel stood silently by the fireplace, his brown leather clothes almost blending into the wooden walls. He could not bear to watch the doctors examine and then bleed his daughter. "Will she be all right?" he asked St. Paul.

"The doctors must watch her closely. I think it would be best if we left them to their purpose."

Madeleine tried to occupy herself by making a tisane, and Marcel reluctantly retired to his atelier. He realized he was completely incapable of contributing anything more to Émilie's well-being, and their apartment was so small, he felt as if he could not move around it without bumping into someone or something. But down in his workshop Marcel found it hard to concentrate on what he was doing. He kept imagining Émilie there with him, peeking up at him every once in a while from beside the table. Sometimes he even thought he heard her sing, but it was just the wind whistling through the cracks in the walls.

The doctors stayed around the clock. They had brought their own candles, and they refused Madeleine's offers of tisane and bread. St. Paul came to visit again the next morning. When he was there, Madeleine became a little nervous, and blushed—things that rarely happened to her. They had let this elegantly turned-out nobleman into their home and were suddenly on the most intimate footing with him. It seemed indecent, and yet somehow thrilling. When he arrived, St. Paul greeted her with a smile and gazed deeply into her eyes, before bowing over her hand and kissing it. Madeleine brought the best chair over to Émilie's bedside for him to sit in, and she stood next to him. As they spoke in whispers, St. Paul let the back of his hand accidentally brush against Madeleine's thigh, and when he stood to confer with her about Émilie's health, he placed his fingers lightly upon her shoulder.

Within a day Madeleine's initial distrust of St. Paul evaporated. She was not accustomed to such attention and regard. Compared to the discreetly refined sensitivity of the count, Marcel's gruff affection seemed coarse and common.

∽

The grass in the garden was brown and crisp with frost. It crunched beneath St. Paul's feet as he walked to a secluded corner to meet the widow Scarron. She was already there waiting for him, her black garments stark against the crisp landscape. She stood with her back to him and spoke still facing away.

"What, I wonder, could possibly necessitate such uncomfortable secrecy?" She turned and extended her hand to St. Paul, who took it and bowed over it, not even touching it with his lips.

"I have news that will warm you," he said rubbing his own gloved hands together.

"Speak."

"Let me first ask you, what is the king's greatest passion?"

"Monsieur de St. Paul, it is too cold to play games." Madame de Maintenon turned away and prepared to leave him.

"This game, as you call it, could be the answer to our prayers."

"Are you a devout man, St. Paul?"

"As devout as most," he answered.

"Which is to say, not at all. Pray then, do not make light of the sacred practices of our Holy Church."

St. Paul prepared to speak, then thought better of it.

"You had better state your business."

"Very well." The count took a step or two closer to Madame de Maintenon. "I shall answer my own question. The king's passion is music. What if I were to say—I mean, I must tell you that I have found a voice in a million, a true novelty, a voice—"

"Is she pretty?" interrupted Madame de Maintenon.

St. Paul thought for a moment before answering. "She is only a child."

The widow Scarron looked at him. "Ah," she said. "I think you had better tell me more."

St. Paul stretched out on the narrow bed in his tiny apartment at Versailles. His boots were filthy, but he was too tired to take them off.

"Jacques!" he yelled. But no one came. "My head!" St. Paul groaned aloud to the empty room. It was very quiet, but he could hear distant voices, perhaps in the kitchens on the floor below.

He was hungry. At the moment, unless he managed to arrive at his godmother's in time for lunch or dinner, or happened to be in attendance upon the widow Scarron at a mealtime, he was unlikely to get much of anything to eat. His uncle was abroad and had closed up the Paris house to save money, and St. Paul had gone through everything he had. Short of selling his clothes, his personal effects, his carriage, or his horses, he had no means of getting cash. Mademoiselle de

Guise had given him twenty silver écus the night of her soirée, but he had used them up paying the court physicians and buying little presents to curry favor with the girl's mother. It was a gamble, but this time, St. Paul thought, it would all pay off. He had nothing more to lose; half the moneylenders in Paris were hounding him. If something did not go right soon, he might have to flee to England. It was annoying, to be born with a title and position and have a father who was so fond of gaming that he wagered his son's inheritance. When he sobered up and realized what he'd done, the old count had jumped off a bridge into the Seine.

St. Paul was only eight years old at the time. For the next ten years, the boy and his mother lived with her brother, a prosperous banker in Paris by the name of Goncourt. But when his sister died and left him to find a career for her then eighteen-year-old son, the banker had the effrontery to suggest that the young gentleman might be useful in his business. More than that, he utterly refused to give him any money unless he earned it.

"Damn it, Jacques! Where the devil are you?" St. Paul sat up slowly and swung his legs over the side of the bed. He reached for the almost-empty beaker of wine, which he tipped up and drained into his mouth, licking out the insides with his tongue. St. Paul felt deep within him that he was made for something greater than this meager existence, and that the way to get what he wanted was not by sitting at a desk in a bank. He was convinced that he could secure a profitable position at court, that he would prove himself to be not only useful but indispensable. There were not many at Versailles who were smarter than he was. Even the widow Scarron, he thought, was not fully aware of his abilities. Soon, however, she would be in no doubt, despite her reticence. If everything went well, that little girl's voice would open doors for him as if by magic, and Madame de Maintenon would see to it that the king rewarded him handsomely.

And then, perhaps, he might live in a decent house of his own, instead of the tiny room in this rabbit hutch of a palace. And Jacques would come when he was summoned, he could order food and wine whenever he liked, and his headache would at last go away.

*   *   *

As Charpentier walked up to the Atelier Jolicoeur the day after the princess's soirée, he could not help thinking how silent it seemed. There was something all wrong about it, and it confirmed his worries that something had happened to prevent Émilie from coming for her lessons that day. The door was unlocked, and so he entered the workshop without knocking. Marcel was deeply engrossed in varnishing a lute. Charpentier cleared his throat.

Startled, Marcel looked up. "Monsieur Charpentier! I am happy to see you."

"Where is Émilie?" asked the composer without returning Marcel's greeting.

Marcel put his brush in a bowl of solvent, wiped his hands on his apron, and came out from behind his worktable. "She is upstairs. She is ill. Although out of danger now, they tell us."

Charpentier took a step back, as if the news had struck him physically. Somehow, he did not expect this. "Ill? Can I see her?"

"I'll see if she is awake," answered Marcel. "Madeleine!" he called up the stairs. There was no response, and so he turned back to Charpentier. "I don't know what is keeping her. The young gentleman is here, though. Perhaps that is it."

"Young gentleman?"

The sound of Madeleine's hurried steps coming down the flights of stairs from the apartment interrupted Marcel's explanation. His wife appeared in the doorway, a frown on her face.

"If she is ill, Émilie must have the best care," said Charpentier, preparing to climb the stairs.

Madeleine blocked the way. "Monsieur Charpentier. Forgive me, but I don't much feel that your care is what is best for my Émilie!" she said, lifting her chin and smoothing her apron.

"I don't understand," said Charpentier, turning to Marcel for an explanation.

"Keeping her up to all hours, making her walk home in the cold and wet. No wonder she was at death's door!" And with that,

Madeleine turned and slammed the door in Charpentier's face.

"How can she think . . ." Charpentier was too stunned to say more.

Marcel shrugged. "I told her you were not to blame, but she won't hear it."

"You mentioned a young gentleman. Who is here?"

"Monsieur de St. Paul has been so kind as to take an interest in Émilie's recovery," answered Marcel, looking down at the lute he had been varnishing. "He came to congratulate Émilie yesterday and was good enough to bring His Majesty's own physicians to attend her."

"But—" Charpentier was about to ask Marcel how he could have let that slimy opportunist into his home, when he realized that the couple could have no idea that St. Paul was anything other than a rich man—godson of Mademoiselle de Guise, no less—with some interest in their daughter. He needed to think about what to do. He wanted to know how ill Émilie was, whether she was being properly cared for. But it was clear that he would not get that information just now. "Please send my wishes for a speedy recovery to Mademoiselle Émilie," Charpentier said, then bowed and left.

Try as he might, Charpentier could not understand what he had done to deserve Madeleine Jolicoeur's enmity. He had taught their daughter music and singing for no fee at all, bought her a gown that cost him a great deal of his own money so that she could perform with dignity at one of the most illustrious salons in Paris—he had done nothing but try to help her. He did not like to think that the woman harbored ill feelings toward him, and he thought of returning and demanding an explanation.

But his cold reception by Madeleine was not the only thing that weighed on Charpentier's mind. Marcel said that St. Paul had brought His Majesty's own physicians. It was an extravagant gesture for the sake of a young girl from a poor family in Paris. And he knew St. Paul. He had no money of his own but played on his godmother's generosity whenever he needed cash. Her lack of relations made her overly indulgent, and usually he succeeded in wheedling substantial sums out of her. If St. Paul was being generous, it was because he saw some potential gain for himself. That was what really bothered Charpentier. He was certain St. Paul could not care less about Émilie herself.

And if Émilie had a fever, it could easily affect her throat, ending her career before it really began. And yet, barred from seeing her, Charpentier could do nothing about it. He knew a doctor who had made a special study of the throat and the vocal cords. If only the Jolicoeurs would allow the doctor to consult, just to be sure that nothing had harmed Émilie's voice.

He thought he would give Madeleine time to cool off and then return and ask to be permitted to see Émilie. Charpentier was haunted by the picture of Émilie lying ill. But she was just a student, he reminded himself. More talented than most, but perhaps he would find another.

When he arrived at his apartment in the Hôtel de Guise, Charpentier kicked aside the mess of manuscript sheets scattered across the floor of his study, found a bottle of wine and a cup, and poured himself a glass. Then he sat in his chair and stared into the fire until the sun went down.

~

By the end of a week, Émilie's condition did not appear to be improving any further. She still spent most of her time in a deep sleep and was virtually incoherent whenever she surfaced from her stupor.

"I think a change of air is what the doctors would advise," said St. Paul, perched uncomfortably on the edge of a wooden armchair, sipping tisane from a small earthenware bowl.

"I do not wish her to leave." Marcel stood at the side of the fireplace, gazing into it. "Not without seeing Monsieur Charpentier."

"The doctors would be able to continue caring for her night and day. As it is, they are now wanted at Versailles and can no longer give

Émilie the attention she requires. You'll see, she'll recover much more quickly there."

"How can we keep her here, when the count is making such a kind offer? You have seen how these great men pay such attention to her," Madeleine said, approaching her husband. "And what has that singing teacher to do with anything? If he had been more careful of Émilie, she might not have gotten sick in the first place."

Marcel was silent for a long while. Charpentier had returned day after day, and Madeleine had steadfastly refused to let him see Émilie. Although his wife clearly had her reasons, Marcel was uncomfortably aware that they owed the composer some explanation at least. But he had to make a decision, and Madeleine clearly wanted to acquiesce to St. Paul's wishes. Marcel saw St. Paul shift a little and wince, the wood of the chair hard against his slender frame. "When would she return?" he asked the count.

St. Paul smiled. "Whenever she likes!"

Marcel stared down at the floor. He could think of no more excuses to hold out. "Well, if you really think it would be best."

The matter was settled. To seal the bargain, St. Paul gave Madeleine a purse full of copper coins and a surreptitious pat on the behind, and Marcel the promise that Monsieur Lully, the court composer, would purchase five of the Atelier Jolicoeur's best violins for his famous ensemble.

About a week after she had fallen ill, Émilie was carried, still semiconscious, to St. Paul's coach, where she was tucked into a corner and transported to Versailles. She was not in a condition to see her mother and father waving as the coach drove away over the bridge and across the Île.

That same evening, Marcel stood at the end of the bed in which his daughter had so recently lain, hovering between life and death. Madeleine had wanted to take away the linens and turn out the straw, wishing to eradicate the sickroom smell from her home, but he would not let her—not yet. He imagined his daughter beneath the blankets, her head cradled on the pillow, her blond hair darkened by perspiration, cheeks stained with the unnatural roses of illness. While he was lost in this private reverie, he saw something poking out from beneath the pillow, something dark. He drew closer and realized it was a bit of fine cloth, which he teased out from its hiding place. It took him a moment to recognize it as a length of velvet ribbon that Émilie had shown them the day that Charpentier took her to the dressmaker's. Marcel remembered how his daughter's eyes had shone when she took the ribbon out of her pocket. It was exquisite, but Madeleine had refused to look at it. Now it was crushed and matted and almost unrecognizable. Without telling Madeleine, Marcel tucked the ribbon in his pocket.

Seven

One is never so happy, nor so unhappy, as one imagines.
Maxim 49

The widow Scarron's black silk gown rustled as she strolled around her sitting room. When she reached the window, she paused for a moment and looked out over the now barren gardens. "So, Monsieur de St. Paul, you have brought her here."

"As we arranged, Madame." St. Paul bowed.

"And Monsieur Lully has been instructing her these few weeks now."

"Of course. He agrees with me. Her voice is simply unequaled." St. Paul took a pinch of snuff.

"I looked in on her dancing lesson yesterday. She is very young, as you said." Madame de Maintenon was often described as handsome rather than beautiful, with her strong, placid features and dark brown eyes. She had a way of speaking that made her seem very intimate, and yet wholly separate from the world. There was something in the tone of her voice and the expression on her face that conveyed great humility and boundless pride at the same moment. It had taken her all her life to develop this extraordinary ability to act so that her financial inferiority and her spiritual superiority were apparent in equal measures at all times. It was what had helped her triumph over the almost insurmountable adversities of her past, a past that included being born in prison, marrying a brilliant but impoverished writer, becoming a widow at a young age, and being given charge of the infants who were the result of the king's immoral activities. Through an astounding process of personal alchemy, she had become the most respected—and the most feared—woman at court.

St. Paul paused to indulge in a hearty sneeze. "That is the beauty of it. A child, really."

"Yes, that is fortunate. And her parents? Were they difficult?"

St. Paul smiled. "I know how to handle such people. It was only the matter of a few gifts, a few promises. And your idea, to make her appear more dangerously ill than she really was by using the drops to keep her unconscious—"

Madame de Maintenon turned her head abruptly and looked at St. Paul over her shoulder, her eyes hardening into coals that hid sparks in their midst. "I know nothing of this! And I wish to know nothing, Monsieur le Comte, however clever your solution to the problem was."

St. Paul's smile froze on his face. "Of course, how foolish of me."

"She will require careful handling. It is important that the child be properly groomed to be the very embodiment of music. It is this alone that will raise her above the commonplace."

"That will not be so difficult. After all, what could be more exalted, more pure—or more pleasing—than music?"

"Plato, Monsieur de St. Paul, had something to say about music that it might well instruct you to read. The only truly pure music is that to be heard at the entrance to the gates of heaven. However, on this imperfect earth, the child will do."

St. Paul sniffed. "It might be wise to have someone watch her closely at all times."

"François is keeping an eye on her. He is a loyal servant. I pray you inform me of Mademoiselle Émilie's artistic progress so that we may determine the best moment to introduce her voice to the king."

Madame de Maintenon put her hand out to St. Paul, who took the hint that he was being dismissed, kissed it, and left.

~

The sky Émilie saw through the tall windows of the Salle de Bal was hung with clouds that looked as though they could not decide whether to unleash rain or snow. Émilie pulled her shawl more closely about her shoulders as she waited for Monsieur Lully to instruct the harpsichordist concerning which piece would form the subject of her lesson that day. She had made a miraculous recovery almost as soon as she arrived at Versailles, and she had started her lessons with the court composer the next week.

But Émilie did not like Lully much. He was older than Charpentier, and fat. His clothing, although very luxurious, was always a little creased, as if it had been worn too many days in a row. He also had a mildly unpleasant odor about him that was not entirely masked by the rose water he sprinkled on himself, and his smile never enlivened his heavy-lidded eyes.

"*Attention,* Mademoiselle Émilie," he said. At the beginning of every lesson, Lully set her off to warm up like a windup mechanism and then walked around the room, not seeming to pay any attention to her at all. In the month that she had been working with the court composer, Émilie felt she had gained little. He showed her tricks and devices, and encouraged her to develop her highest notes rather than explore the deep riches of her middle range, as Charpentier had. Although Lully had already written some very pretty airs for her to sing, Émilie did not care for them much, and singing them gave her no joy. They did not seem to fit her voice quite as well as Monsieur Charpentier's did, and she could not imagine singing with Monsieur Lully—even if he could sing, which he could not. His raspy baritone warble made her cringe the first time he demonstrated a new ornament for her.

While she continued, Émilie turned to look out of the windows once again. She watched a small army of gardeners plant blossoming flowers in the beds close to the château. When the frost made them wilt a few hours later, the gardeners would come and dig them up again and replace them with new flowers from the acres of hothouses. She thought it utterly absurd.

Émilie had no definite idea of how she came to be at Versailles. She remembered opening her eyes while she was still in her bed on the Pont au Change and seeing St. Paul hovering over her, with an older gentleman who she now realized was probably an apothecary or a surgeon. She thought that she was having a terrible nightmare, that she would wake up and it would all be over. Even after trying very hard to remember what had happened to her, the best she could do was recall being moved down the stairs. She thought it might have been her father who carried her, but she could not have said for certain. When she finally woke up, it was to find that the world had changed around her, and that the strangely aloof nobleman who had surprised her when she warmed up for her début at the Hôtel de Guise was suddenly a regular inhabitant of her daily life. He told her that her parents had not wanted the worry of caring for her while she was sick, but it hurt her that they would say such a thing.

As she continued her voice lesson, Émilie focused her eyes nearer so she could see herself reflected faintly in the uneven glass panes of the enormous windows. Her pale blond hair was set off by a dark blue silk day gown, fitted sleekly in a bodice that ended a few inches below her natural waist, from which yards of fabric flowed before being caught up in places by little gold satin ribbons to reveal a paler blue satin petticoat beneath. It was richer by far than the gown she had worn to the princess's salon. She thought for a moment about her début at the Hôtel de Guise. And then she thought of the ruined satin slippers. Émilie stopped singing. She hoped Sophie had not gotten in trouble. If only she could find some way to tell her what had happened.

"Mademoiselle Émilie, *encore*!" said Lully from across the room.

Clocks began to chime. It was eleven in the morning, and soon Monsieur Dubuffet would arrive to give Émilie her dancing lesson.

Lully took out a large pocket watch and looked at it. "Until tomorrow," he said, with a small nod.

Once the distant din of the timepieces died away, it was so quiet in the palace that Émilie could hear the footsteps of Lully and the accompanist fading for several minutes.

Monsieur Dubuffet was late. Émilie strolled around the room. The only sound that broke the stillness was the *pit-pat* of her own soft-soled shoes on the parquet floors that had been polished to a glassy sheen. After a few minutes Émilie could resist the impulse no longer. Since no one was watching, she stood at one corner, then ran as fast as she could to the middle of the room, where she stopped running and let herself slide, skating all the way to the opposite corner. She smiled and barely contained a little shriek of delight. A moment before she reached the other wall, hands outstretched so that she would not crash, a door that had been made to match the paneling so exactly that it was almost invisible opened. Through it came not Monsieur Dubuffet but François, Madame de Maintenon's trusted servant. Émilie had been introduced to Madame de Maintenon when she first arrived, and the lady would glide in and out like a wraith every now and again, appearing at the most unexpected moments. Émilie was afraid of her.

"Monsieur Dubuffet begs your pardon, Mademoiselle, but a slight indisposition renders it impossible for him to attend you for your dancing lesson this morning." François, who had witnessed Émilie's youthful mischief, only just managed not to smile.

The exaggerated formality of speech practiced by everyone at Versailles, from the loftiest of courtiers to the lowliest of servants, made Émilie want to laugh. A breach of etiquette was deemed more serious than a capital crime and, so she heard, forgiven less easily by the king.

"Where are you from, François?" she asked, smoothing her hair into place and doing her best to look dignified.

"From Paris, Mademoiselle."

"What are your people?" she persisted.

François stood stiffly with his hands clasped behind him, ready to bow and retreat at any moment. The veteran servant walked with a slight bend at the middle, as if he were saving himself the effort of straightening up entirely because he would soon enough be required to fold over again. This creased way of standing made him look quite old, but he was not above middle age. "My father was only a humble blacksmith, Mademoiselle."

"Then I am no better than you, François, for my father is only a humble luthier. Can't we be friends?"

François shifted a little nervously from one foot to the other and glanced around him.

"I think we're alone here. Everyone else has gone out hunting!" said Émilie, trying to put him at ease. It was François himself who had told her that the king was so passionate about stag hunting that all the courtiers, whether they wanted to or not, went on the hunt with him.

"Mademoiselle, humble you may once have been, but you have been chosen to be elevated to a different class, and you must seek your friends among those who are much better than I." He bowed again and was about to retire, when Émilie's entreaty stopped him.

"Please wait, François. They do not care about me. They only take care of me because I can sing. Have you heard me sing, François?"

"No, Mademoiselle Émilie," he answered, preparing to withdraw again.

"No! Don't leave," she begged, and then, before he could protest, she began to sing a little folk song, one that reminded her of Paris.

Émilie started out quietly, but before long the generous tones of her voice filled the large, vacant space of the Salle de Bal. Everything she consciously withheld from Lully's music she poured into that simple ballad. She fixed her eyes on François, pinning him to his spot with her song. As she warmed to her performance, Émilie ornamented each verse more and more lavishly, so that by the seventh and final one, she enhanced the contours of the melody with her own twists and turns, with spine-tingling flourishes and astounding feats of vocal gymnastics.

François had never been the focus of anyone's attention in this way before in his life. In fact, he possessed the capacity of being almost invisible when he chose to be, and it was this quality that had caused the widow Scarron to single him out as her eyes and ears at court. She was not a wealthy woman, but her influence had made his life in the king's retinue as comfortable as anyone's. He had a private room that was ample, warm, and well-furnished, and he ate not with the domestic servants but with the personal valets and maids, many of whom were from good families in straitened circumstances. In exchange, he made it his business to be in a position to know the sordid affairs of everyone who ever got close to the king, and to report back to Madame de Maintenon. Of all the tasks his mistress had ever given him to perform, spying on this young singer was certainly the most pleasant. She did as she was told, and was too young and innocent to make it likely that he would ever have to burst in upon some intimate scene "by accident," or intercept some poison-pen letter destined to stir up trouble among Louis's intimates. Émilie, who was barely more than a child, was like a fresh breeze blowing through the château. And here she was, singing for him. He had never heard anything more lovely in his entire life.

When the song was over, François made Émilie a low bow but this time did not turn to leave.

"Can we be friends now?" she asked, suddenly seeming like a little girl again. For a moment François wondered if the girl really knew what she was asking. It would be useful to have her confidence, but something in him shrank from abusing it in such a way. There was no way to deny her, however, especially when agreeing would so easily suit the purposes of Madame de Maintenon.

"It would be my honor," answered François. "I fear it is too cold to walk in the gardens. Would you like me to escort you through the château?"

As Émilie and François strolled aimlessly through the public reception rooms of the great palace, she talked about her father, her mother, making violins, and mending by the firelight.

"My father makes the best stringed instruments in Paris, you know," said Émilie. Her eager smile faded and her lower lip began to tremble.

Oh dear, François thought. He was supposed to make sure she

was content, so that she would not cause trouble or try to leave. "Please don't cry, Mademoiselle," he said, holding out to her a large, white cambric handkerchief. He watched her wipe her eyes and then blow her nose into it. Then he had an idea. "Would it make you feel less lonely, Mademoiselle, to write to your parents?" A correspondence might be just the thing. A girl at her age would undoubtedly pour out any secrets upon the page, especially one so unused to the treachery of court. Thus he could remain acquainted with everything she was thinking without even having to ask.

Émilie's face brightened for a moment and then clouded. "They cannot read."

"Is there no one you could ask to inquire after them, and who would bring them your news?" Having once hit upon this clever stratagem, François was unwilling to give it up at the first hurdle.

"I could write to Monsieur Charpentier!" said Émilie. "He could go and read my letters to my parents." And then, she thought, she could also explain to him about the shoes and get him to tell Sophie how sorry she was.

François stopped in his tracks. This wasn't quite what he expected. "Is there no one else? Really, anyone else would do." They had reached the Ambassadors' Staircase. He looked around quickly and then steered Émilie into a little antechamber that would not be quite so public, where their voices would not resonate so dangerously.

"Why?" asked Émilie.

How was he to explain the complicated factors and nuances that led to being out of favor at court? For that was precisely Charpentier's position. Yet if the musician was really the only person Émilie knew who could read, perhaps there was a way to make it work without really being disloyal.

"Monsieur Lully fears no one so much as Monsieur Charpentier. You see, word of his great talent has reached Versailles, and he is the only one who stands a chance of displacing the court composer. Monsieur Lully has tried to convince the king that Charpentier is not to be trusted, that Charpentier was a traitor."

Émilie's already large eyes grew immense at this. "How could anyone believe it of him?"

How indeed, François thought. The poor man was only guilty of being talented. "He went away to Italy for some years. And now he works for the Duchesse de Guise, whose family has always been a threat to the throne. Although these things prove nothing, to his enemies they are, shall we say, suggestive?"

"I suppose, then, for you to take a letter to Monsieur Charpentier would not be wise?" Émilie inquired.

François bowed his head to think. Émilie's eyes filled with tears again.

"There, there, Mademoiselle! Perhaps there would be no harm . . ." François made a decision in that moment to take a chance. Madame de Maintenon might not approve. But she wasn't in the habit of questioning how he came by the information he transmitted to her. "If you would permit me, I will make some enquiries, and then let you know tomorrow if there is a way to manage it so that a letter can be delivered to your friend."

"Oh, thank you! A thousand times!" Émilie went down on her knees before the astonished François, who waved her up nervously.

"As I said, I shall inquire. But remember, I promise nothing."

⁓

Jean-Baptiste de Lully—he insisted on the *de,* even though his claim to it was tenuous and based on a distant relation in Italy, the place of his birth—had been brought to court as a mere boy to entertain the Grande Mademoiselle, the king's first cousin, and teach her Italian. No one paid much attention to him for several years, until one day when a young King Louis XIV discovered the extent of Lully's talent entirely by chance. Someone heard the young lad playing the violin in the kitchen quarters, and after that, his rise to position of favorite was meteoric. Luckily for Lully, he was also smart enough to know when to switch loyalties, and so as soon as the Grande Mademoiselle was in disgrace after the Fronde, he made sure to attach himself to the king's retinue. Once in place, he set about pleasing his powerful patron until he became nearly indispensable to France's great monarch.

"Pierre!" Lully called when he reached the door of his comfortable apartment on the ground floor of the château shortly after he finished trying to teach Émilie, who had been thrust upon him by Madame de Maintenon, the right way to sing.

The door opened, and a lithe valet of about seventeen bowed and ushered him in. "Monsieur de Lully, would you care for a cordial?"

"No, I just need to rest a bit before I attend the king," Lully sighed, as he sank into an upholstered chair and put his feet up on the stool that Pierre brought over to him. He closed his eyes when the young man removed the tight, high-heeled shoes he wore and began to massage his feet. "You are too good to me," he said. "Come, sit by me here."

Pierre shifted his position so that he was by the side of Lully's chair, and then leaned his head upon the composer's knee. Lully stroked his blond curls.

"I am heartily sick of being used to further the schemes of that woman!"

Pierre turned his head to look up through his long lashes at Lully. "What woman?"

"Who else could I mean? The widow Scarron, of course. Daily she seems to rise in the king's esteem, and he doesn't even notice how she's manipulating him."

Pierre turned and put his hands on Lully's knee, then rested his chin atop them. "What has she done now?"

Lully traced the contours of the valet's face with his forefinger. "She has foisted a young singer upon me, a little younger than you, I imagine! A girl with a very pretty voice, but still untrained. She was a protégée of that upstart, Charpentier."

"And now you have got her, *n'est-ce pas?*" Pierre smiled.

"You're a smart lad! Yes, indeed. And I may be able to make something of her, if she is not pushed along too fast. But mark my words, Pierre, she is not here merely to sing. Madame de Maintenon must have plans to dangle her before the king."

"Ah, so she must be pretty."

Lully lifted Pierre's chin and gazed into his eyes. "If you like that sort of pretty, I suppose she is." He bent toward the servant, who rose up higher on his knees to meet him. Just before their lips touched, there was a loud knock upon the door. Pierre stood quickly and smoothed down his satin uniform and Lully sat back in his chair. "Go and see who it is, Pierre," Lully said, loudly enough so that whoever was waiting would hear.

The boy opened the door to a black-liveried servant of the widow Scarron. "Madame de Maintenon wishes to see you, if you are free to attend her."

Lully said nothing for a moment, then kicked the footstool out of the way and stood up from his chair. "I was taught never to keep a lady waiting. I shall come in half an hour."

The servant bowed and left. As soon as Pierre shut the door, both he and Lully burst into peals of laughter.

~~~

After a week of being turned away by Madeleine from seeing Émilie, Charpentier decided it was better to give Madame Jolicoeur some time to cool off before renewing his attempts to get his pupil back. He threw himself into his work, trying to put Émilie out of his mind. But even so much feverish activity did not prevent him from dwelling on the fact that his talented pupil had been taken away from him, and for no apparent reason. The last time he went to the atelier, Marcel had told him she was making a good recovery, although still unable to stay awake for very long, and Charpentier was concerned that perhaps she might have had a relapse. So he decided to return to the workshop on the Pont au Change and make one last attempt to see Émilie, so that he could begin the process of persuading her parents to allow her to return to her lessons. He did not think that Marcel shared his wife's feelings that Émilie's illness was his fault, and so Charpentier hoped that perhaps a little effort would mend things. He was fully prepared to have to convince them all over again that it was in Émilie's best interest that she continue to study. The key was to see and talk to Émilie. If only he could do that, he knew he could persuade her, and Marcel was not likely to stand in his daughter's way.

Charpentier knocked on the door of the atelier and Marcel let him in.

"I have come to see Émilie. She must surely be better now, and you must know that I did not cause her illness."

Marcel did not meet his eyes. "She is not here, Monsieur."

Charpentier staggered backward as if he had been struck. "You can't mean . . ." he said.

"Oh, no, Monsieur! I am so sorry. Émilie is still alive, and completely recovered. She has just gone away."

It took a moment for Charpentier to adjust to this news. At first his relief was so great that he wanted to embrace the luthier. But then there was this other information. She was not there. There was a quiet emptiness in the atelier, and Marcel was not his usual cheerful self. "Where is she?"

The luthier put down the knife he was still holding and wiped his hands on his leather apron. "She has gone to Versailles."

"Versailles? Why on earth?"

"Monsieur de St. Paul said they would be able to look after her there, and she would have lessons with Monsieur Lully."

Lully. There it was again, that name that stood between Charpentier and all his fondest ambitions. It was simply too much. "And you believed him? Do you know what kind of a place it is to which you have sent your only daughter?" Charpentier raised his voice. Although making a brilliant début at court could assure anyone's future, it was also a dangerous place, especially for pretty young girls.

Marcel was not practiced at hiding his feelings, and his eyes revealed that he not only understood Charpentier's implications but was deeply troubled by them. "But Monsieur de St. Paul was so kind, so concerned about Émilie. And she will have many opportunities to advance herself. What could be the harm in that?"

Charpentier was a little sorry he had frightened Marcel, who, after all, was only trying to do what he thought best for his daughter. If only they had let him in to see her! If only he could have spoken to

Émilie, could have found out what she really wanted. "I am only speaking from what I have heard from others. Perhaps it will turn out all right for Émilie. They may truly take care of her, because of her extraordinary voice." Charpentier did not hold out much hope that Émilie's remarkable talent would protect her for long. But he could not help feeling for Marcel, whose expression only became more pathetic with everything Charpentier said to him. "What do you hear of her?" asked Charpentier, forcing himself to appear more calm. "Does she like Versailles?"

"As yet, we have heard little." Marcel pushed some curls of wood around with his boot, making them into a shape on the floor. "But Monsieur de St. Paul promised to stop in and bring us more news by and by."

Charpentier remembered that the luthier and his wife could not read and therefore must rely on a visit from some intermediary to find out how Émilie was doing. When he realized that this was probably the first time Marcel had been separated from his only child, Charpentier softened. It must have cost the craftsman a great deal to agree to part with her in the first place. But he could not rid himself of the sinking feeling that Marcel and his wife would never see their daughter again. And whose fault was it anyway? It was he who had brought Émilie to the attention of the nobility by presenting her at the princess's salon. He could not blame Marcel for being taken in by St. Paul. All he could do now was to demonstrate his friendship by continuing to take an interest in Émilie. "I would be grateful if you would send word to me if—when—you hear anything of your daughter," Charpentier said, bowing to Marcel and taking his leave.

Once on the street Charpentier walked not back to the Hôtel de Guise but instead onto the island in the middle of the Seine, the ancient heart of Paris, to wander around the market near Notre Dame. It was winter, and so there were no flowers in the open-air stalls, only beautiful caged birds. People scurried and jostled and went about their business, stopping occasionally to stare at a particularly exotic specimen. Having once gauped at these refugees from distant shores, they all continued on their way, hardly breaking their conversations to register the divine miracle that created such a vivid rainbow of colors.

To Charpentier, the human voices sounded harsh and loud. Even the laughter of children was shrill and unpleasant to him. Only one sound could satisfy Charpentier's hungry ear, and it was out of his reach for the foreseeable future. Still he wandered through the marketplace searching for something, anything that might take its place. His eyes combed the cages, some large and ornate, others tiny. He watched a young blade buy a bullfinch for his lady love, and followed them with his eyes as they walked away laughing merrily. Charpentier was almost ready to give up his search when, all at once, almost out of sight, a very old woman with only one bird in a cage caught his eye. This bird was not splashed with vibrant colors like the parrots and canaries that had been borne on ships from the tropics to Paris. It was mostly brown, almost plain, but with a knowing eye that peered out at Charpentier from between the bars of its simple cage.

"Does it sing?" he asked her.

"She does not like the cage. At home, I let her out, and then she sings."

"So your nightingale is not for sale?"

"No, not for sale." The old lady reached into a satchel and pulled out a crochet hook and the end of a ball of yarn, and started to work her gnarled fingers so rapidly that the fabric she created seemed to flow magically from her hands.

"Then why do you bring her here?" Charpentier asked.

"For company."

He looked closely at the bird, which seemed rather aloof from its surroundings. "She doesn't seem to care about the other birds."

"Not her, Monsieur, me! I like the company!" The old lady started to cackle, and everyone within earshot turned to look.

"Perhaps I can change your mind?" Charpentier suggested, taking a purse full of coins out of his waistcoat.

The crone paused in her laughter long enough to weigh the

purse in her hand. After a moment she gave it back to Charpentier, and said, "*Non,* Monsieur. There is not money enough for my nightingale."

He looked at her and nodded his head. At that moment Charpentier understood not only why the lady would never part with her special bird but why being separated from Émilie had made him feel so entirely bereft. Everything was suddenly clear. Whatever else happened, he must find a way to get his student back from Versailles. Now all that remained was to figure out how.

Eight

Jealousy is always born with love,
but it does not always die with it.

Maxim 361

Madeleine looked around with satisfaction at the new lodgings. Her eye rested on the louvered shutters that kept the heat in during the winter and shut out the glare of the sun in the summer. One of them was not pushed completely open. She adjusted it, then stepped back and admired her handiwork. Taking pride of place in her parlor were two armchairs with cushions on them. These she moved slightly, so that they were at exactly the same distance from the fireplace, in which a comforting blaze leapt and crackled. Checking to see if the maid was occupied in the other room, she slipped her foot out of her leather shoe and ran her toes over the needlepoint rug on the floor. Then she smiled.

Madeleine had fought for this move. She was tired of living in tiny, cramped quarters under a roof that sometimes leaked and through which the heat from the fire seemed to evaporate in the winter. When she married Marcel, she had thought his trade would bring them prosperity. But he was too slow and meticulous at his work. Although they were not exactly destitute, life was a constant struggle.

And just when Madeleine thought she might find a suitable match for her daughter, and there would be one less mouth to feed and at least Émilie might have a hope of a better life, all this nonsense about singing came up. Of course, if she had known what it would lead to, Madeleine might not have been so reluctant to send Émilie off to study with Charpentier. Because she had to admit, it was this alone that had changed their circumstances almost overnight. Every once in a while her unkind treatment of the composer pricked her conscience slightly. But what if Émilie had died? That she recovered was no thanks to him. And now that Émilie was at Versailles, commissions poured in to the Atelier Jolicoeur. Royal favor was like a lodestone, attracting prosperity. Marcel had taken on two apprentices just last month to keep up with the work. Still, he had been reluctant to leave their old, one-room apartment.

"How can you wish to stay here!" Madeleine had shouted, exasperated by her husband's stubbornness.

"But there are only two of us now. Why do we need more space?"

"It isn't just the space. Look at this place. It hardly keeps the weather out. We are wealthier now, and I want to have a maid. With a separate kitchen, she could sleep in a corner by the fire, or just come in early in the morning. And we could invite people, in the evening— perhaps even play cards." Madeleine was starved for leisure after all her years of hard work. It did not seem much to ask.

After a few weeks, Marcel gave in. But he refused to move his workshop, and so life, for him, changed little.

But Madeleine did not need Marcel's constant presence to enjoy her newfound leisure. She drew herself up to her full height of five feet and patted her hair lightly. The sugar syrup crusted here and there, and she rubbed the strands together to flick the little crystals off. Then she walked to the edge of the carpet and lifted a corner of it.

"Girl! Come here!"

The maid was only twelve years old, but she worked hard, and they didn't have to pay her very much.

"I told you to beat the carpet. Look at the dust!"

"Sorry, Madame!" she said with a little curtsey.

"Never mind. Tomorrow will do." Madeleine was expecting her oldest friend, Hortense Bougier, to come and drink tea with her shortly. There would be no time to struggle with the rug, and despite her show of superiority, she would probably help the maid do it the next day. She took some pleasure in showing the young thing the right way to keep a house, as she would have done for Émilie.

The maid returned to the kitchen to prepare tea, and Madeleine wandered around her parlor aimlessly. She was not used to free time. Then she remembered her embroidery frame, and the packet of silk threads she had bought in the market. It would look good for her to be seated there, starting some pastoral scene to replace the plain covers on the chair cushions, when Hortense arrived.

"Beg pardon, Madame."

"What is it, girl?"

"There's someone to see you."

Madeleine expected Hortense, and so she did not rise from her chair. When St. Paul walked into the parlor instead, she stood so quickly that all the threads in her lap landed in a jumble on the floor. It would take her hours to untangle them.

"My dear Madame Jolicoeur," he said, bowing over her hand and brushing it with his lips. "How snug you are in your new home."

"Monsieur le Comte, you honor me." Madeleine knew she blushed, and it annoyed her. She had a gnawing sense of guilt when she remembered how things had been when the count was there every day, so concerned about Émilie. They were usually alone in the apartment; Marcel stayed in his workshop. She still had a delicious memory of the count whispering in her ear, his lips just touching occasionally and sending a thrill right through her. "Would you like some tea?" She motioned him to sit in Marcel's chair and waved her hand at the maid, who vanished into the kitchen.

St. Paul reached into his waistcoat and took out a small package, wrapped in paper and tied with a silk cord. "Just a token, for our friendship." He placed it on the table, then perched himself on the very edge of the chair Madeleine had directed him to.

"And how does my daughter?"

"She is fully recovered, I am delighted to say. Is that not a new gown you are wearing?"

Madeleine ran her hands proudly over the silk. They were not so rough now, and did not catch on the smooth fabric as they used to. "I had it made. The silk was left over from the ball gown of a marquise. There was almost enough for a dress—only the sleeves are of flax." Her nervousness made Madeleine rattle on.

Once she had exhausted the subject of her dress, Madeleine had no idea what to say to St. Paul. They sat facing each other from the two chairs on opposite sides of the room for a minute or two. The count smiled in her direction but did not appear to be looking at her.

They both stood and spoke at the same moment.

"I'm afraid—" "Would you like—"

"It grieves me that I cannot stay longer to enjoy your company. I must call on the Duchesse de Montpensier—a frightful bore, but I'm sure you understand," said St. Paul, bowing again.

Madeleine curtseyed, and the nobleman left, just as the maid entered the parlor with a tray bearing two tea dishes and a little jug of milk.

"Take it away!" she snapped, sending the girl back to the kitchen. Once she was alone, she opened the package St. Paul had left behind. It contained a lace-edged silk handkerchief that concealed three bright, silver coins. Madeleine stared at the gift for a moment or two, then walked to the fireplace. She put the coins in the earthenware pot that held their savings, and then threw the handkerchief onto the fire.

The next time St. Paul came, he brought her a small wooden box that contained a silver thimble, and after that it was a bit of lace tied around an ivory spindle. They were always objects of some value, but never anything worth enough to sell or to make a material difference in their lives. His visits were brief and awkward, and Madeleine never knew what to say to him now that they did not have the common ground of Émilie's illness. She did not really know why he continued to come, and she began to suspect that he was using her. But for what? It made no sense to her, and so she tried to dismiss her uneasy feelings.

~

For a few weeks after the salon, Sophie's life at the Hôtel de Guise returned to its normal pattern of mending Mademoiselle de Guise's gowns, doing her mistress's hair, and entertaining her with gossip about court that she picked up from the lady's maids in other households whose mistresses came to visit the princess. Sophie had a wicked sense of humor, and she knew how to tell a story and derive the most entertainment from it. At first Émilie's failure to return the slippers did not worry her very much. She assumed the girl would bring them when she came for her lessons with Monsieur Charpentier. But time passed, and there was no sign of Émilie. Sophie was annoyed at this apparent breach of trust, but she did not expect Mademoiselle de Guise to notice that one was missing from among her dozens of pairs of shoes. The princess usually wore black these days anyway, since the death of her nephew.

In this, Sophie was correct. But she failed to estimate how intently a young housemaid, Mathilde, was looking for an opportunity to discredit her so that she could step into, literally, Sophie's shoes.

"Madame Coryot," began Mathilde, some time after Émilie had been whisked away to Versailles, "they're missing, her slippers."

"Whose slippers? I don't know what you're talking about." Madame Coryot, the housekeeper at the Hôtel de Guise, was busy settling the accounts. At first she had no idea what the girl was referring to and was about to put it down to the odd ways of a country lass and dismiss her, but Mathilde was insistent.

"They were her prettiest, and I don't want anyone to blame me for something I didn't do."

"What didn't you do, girl?" asked Madame Coryot, impatient that the housemaid was speaking in riddles. And she didn't like to see the lass's dirty fingernails and her slovenly appearance, both of which had kept the young thing from advancing in the household.

"It's that Sophie! I saw her take Mademoiselle de Guise's jeweled slippers the night of the party, and they're still not back in her cupboard."

"How did you get into Mademoiselle's armoire? Sophie keeps it locked. . . . Perhaps she was taking them to be mended," said the housekeeper, who had many more important things to do in preparation for the princess's return to another retreat at Montmartre.

"She wasn't. Come and see for yourself."

Madame Coryot was forced to resolve the issue, and to her dismay, discovered that the maid spoke the truth. The armoire had been left unlocked, and the slippers were nowhere to be found. She sent for Sophie.

"What's this I hear about Mademoiselle's satin slippers? And why wasn't the armoire locked?" asked the housekeeper, thinking that Sophie probably had a perfectly reasonable explanation.

"I was doing my mending. I leave the wardrobe open so I can get in and out easily. And the slippers—I'm sure I don't know what you're talking about," Sophie answered, with a black look in the direction of the housemaid.

"Perhaps you've forgotten. You apparently took a pair of the princess's slippers to be mended, and have neglected to bring them back."

"I know nothing about this matter." Sophie turned her nose up and folded her arms just beneath her ample breasts.

"Nonetheless, the slippers are not here."

Sophie was thinking fast. "Perhaps Mathilde took them herself, just so she could blame me. As you see, there are times when I leave the cupboard open."

Madame Coryot shifted her attention to Mathilde. "Well, what have you to say?"

"I did not! It's you who's always giving yourself airs. Probably wore them yourself and ruined them!" Mathilde shrieked at Sophie.

Before she could stop the words from escaping her mouth, Sophie yelled, "You bitch!"

"Sophie! I'll have no such behavior in this house. What if Mademoiselle should hear you? Profanity is strictly forbidden here. Whatever has become of the slippers, I cannot leave this outburst unpunished. I expected more from the princess's personal maid. Put your hands upon the desk."

Madame Coryot took up a willow switch that she kept for purposes of disciplining the staff and began caning Sophie.

As soon as she felt the sting of the switch, Sophie jumped away from the housekeeper. "Don't you dare touch me! I am Sophie Dupin! I have powerful friends!"

This was too much for Madame Coryot, who wished that Mathilde was not there to witness Sophie's impudence—better yet, wished the matter of the slippers had never been raised. "Then you may rely on your powerful friends to give you the means to live. You are dismissed from this household." She rang for a footman.

"Don't bother to throw me out. I wouldn't stay here if you begged me!" With that, Sophie left the Hôtel de Guise.

Why didn't I just tell her the whole story? Sophie berated herself as she strode out into the cold January afternoon. The answer to that was simple enough. She should never have taken the slippers and would probably have been dismissed for that act anyway. All she had wanted to do was help out poor Émilie, who, like Sophie, had been given a chance to make something of herself despite her humble origins.

She probably doesn't have a temper like mine to get in her way, Sophie thought. It was stupid of her, she knew, to forget one of the primary rules of the household—a household where many things more immoral than profane language went unpunished, because they were hidden beneath a surface of carefully polished gentility. Sophie's anger and frustration at herself propelled her through the streets of Paris. *If only that silly little Émilie had brought the shoes back like she told her to!* Perhaps she should go back and find Monsieur Charpentier, ask him where Émilie was and what happened to the satin slippers. It did seem odd that the singer just vanished after the soirée. Everything she heard from the servants indicated that Émilie had had a huge success. If the truth were known—but no, the fact would remain that she, Sophie, had borrowed the princess's shoes without permission and had used foul language in front of the housekeeper.

And now I'm homeless, Sophie thought.

Because the truth was, she had no friends. She had, in fact, come to the Hôtel de Guise under a bit of a cloud. Her ambitious father, a low-level clerk, realized several years before that his pubescent girl was developing the kind of physical characteristics that might get noticed at court, thus giving him the possibility of obtaining some sinecure—if she struck a nobleman's (or even the king's) fancy. It was not an unreasonable ambition: many had founded their hopes on less.

He had a friend of a friend who secured Sophie a position at Versailles as a lady's maid to Louise de La Vallière, the king's official mistress at that time. Once installed in the opulence of the court, Sophie developed a taste for a life of ease and luxury. She soon learned that her curly, strawberry blond hair and effusively curvaceous body were irresistible to men. Even the unnaturally long waistlines of fashionable gowns could not hide her proportions, and the off-the-shoulder court dress preferred by Louis made the amplitude of her bosom all too apparent. She was not taken by surprise when one day she was summoned to attend the king in his bedchamber late the next night. Having already tasted the delights of the flesh with one of the courtiers, Sophie was not afraid to be so honored by the king.

But what to Sophie was a naughty frolic was to others a matter of life or death. At the time when Louis XIV was eyeing Sophie for a night of fun, the Marquise de Montespan had begun her campaign to win him away from Louise de La Vallière, and she was damned if she would let some bookkeeper's daughter deflect her from her purpose. On the morning of Sophie's assignation with the king, one of the kitchen staff was bribed to put something suspicious in her food. Sophie had a healthy appetite and did not notice any difference in the taste of her soup. She felt queasy all day but was determined to go through with the rendezvous, afraid to let the opportunity slip by. By the time she arrived in the king's bedchamber late that night, Sophie was green. She took one look at His Majesty in his silk shift and promptly vomited all over him.

This was too much for the king, and the pretty maid was ordered to pack her bags and leave. Madame de La Vallière (who had no idea what had happened but who suspected some treachery) felt sorry for her and gave her a letter of introduction to Mademoiselle de Guise. As far as this venerable lady was concerned, anyone who vomited over her power-hungry cousin was welcome in her establishment, and so Sophie joined the household, where she had remained these five years.

Sophie stopped at the corner of the rue des Blancs Manteaux. People rushed past without noticing her. Snatches of conversation came and went as she stood and tried to figure out what to do next. She hugged herself for warmth. Foolish not at least to go and fetch her cloak, she thought. Sophie continued walking. Just as easy to think and move at the same time.

Who would take care of Mademoiselle? She was so sad after her nephew died. Sophie thought about going to find her father, to beg for shelter. But his last words to her echoed in her mind. "All you had to do was be there, and you made a mess of it. No daughter of mine could be so stupid!" He would not hear her side of the story. She did not go to look for him again after that. No, her father's house was not an option.

"Eh! Mam'selle!" A gruff voice spoke when Sophie slowed her quick march to nowhere. She looked around. A sailor leaned against the wall of a tavern, obviously having already had a belly full. Sophie sniffed at him and continued walking.

Not ten feet beyond that point she heard another man's voice. "Ten liards for a good fuck!"

Ten liards. That was a decent amount of money. She did not earn that in a month at the Hôtel de Guise. She'd only have to do it once or twice, just to get herself on her feet . . . Sophie turned to look at the man who had made the offer. He was old, with a gray beard that had yellowed at the edges. He had only a few teeth left in his grinning mouth. He was already fishing his small penis out of his pants, and licking his lips in expectation.

Sophie glanced up and down the street. There were few passersby. "In advance," she said, then she walked to where the man waited. He reached for her breasts, but Sophie stood just out of his grasp.

"You're a hard woman!" he said, then he used his free hand and his teeth to untie a leather pouch and pour the promised payment on the cobbles at his feet. "But I'm a hard man!" he said, lunging for her before she finished picking up the money.

This encounter was her first, but not her last. The stinking men, whose drunken embraces she endured in corners of taverns and in ill-lit alleyways, disgusted her. Yet she did not think of herself as a whore. She was able to shut off some part of her and accept her fate, counting the coins she amassed day by day.

After a time Sophie learned the ropes enough to attract a higher class of clients. She knew the ways of the court and the gentry and was quick-witted and entertaining. Word spread among the gentlemen who roamed the Paris streets looking for a good time that Mademoiselle Sophie could be counted on to provide one. Gradually her life improved. Her quick thinking and luck made it unnecessary for her to join a "stable" or to stay in a whorehouse surrounded by other prostitutes, most of whom died before reaching their fortieth birthdays, either from the English disease, at the hands of inept abortionists, or at the hands of men who thought that women who forfeited their virtue also forfeited their right to live. For Sophie, disease and death were unthinkable. She had to stay alive and well if she were to succeed in her plan. She was determined to set the record straight, to reclaim her position and move on in her life.

It was only a month or so before Sophie had saved up enough money to rent a squalid room in a house on the wrong side of the rue St. Antoine, where she could actually sleep alone if she wanted to.

"The cat comes with the room," said the old landlady, a pipe hanging from the corner of her mouth. "Rent's due in advance."

Sophie gave her enough for the first month, then shut the door on her. She was alone at last. Well, almost alone. There was the cat. A mangy-looking, orange-striped tom who dug his claws into the straw of the bed and glared at her. It was the only place to sit in the small room, whose other furnishings consisted of a washstand and bowl and a tiny cracked mirror. A piece of dirty linen hung across the window, which faced an alley that ran with sewage. Sophie sat on the bed. The cat opened his mouth and hissed.

"We have to share, you and I." Sophie stared hard into his yellow eyes. "Is there a devil in there? Yes, that's what you are. Monsieur le Diable. We shall get along just fine, I think." After two minutes of an unblinking gaze, the cat looked away. Sophie felt that her first victory was auspicious.

Nine

*The greatest ability consists in knowing
the price of everything.*
Maxim 244

Charpentier dropped the sheets of music on the table in his study and walked to the spinet. He sat on the bench and picked out a tune that he had composed for Émilie, one that she had sung at her début. Despite his determination to find a way to bring Émilie back from Versailles, he had been able to achieve nothing. He had no connections at court, and all his inquiries had led him up blind alleys. Émilie might as well have been transported to China as transported fourteen miles away. Charpentier was so lost in his own thoughts that it took him several moments to hear the polite tapping on his door.

"Come!" he said, as he straightened up and picked up a quill that was on the floor by his feet.

"Monsieur Charpentier," said the valet with a bow. "This letter just arrived for you."

"Put it on the table," he said, without looking up.

The valet looked at the pile of papers strewn across the surface, shook his head, and placed the letter on a footstool nearby.

Charpentier assumed it was some instructions from the princess and left the note where it was so that he could return to his daydream. He thought about what might have happened if Émilie had not gone away, if he had been able to present her in a new opera. He'd have found a way to get around Lully's restrictions about musicians. And then he would have become famous, and the king would command a performance, and his fortune would be assured. And then, once he had made his name, and Émilie was a little older, who knew what might happen?

The sun set, and Charpentier found himself sitting in the dark. He stood up and stretched, added some fuel to the fire to bring it back to life, and lit a candle. Then he remembered the letter. He thought he'd better read it, but when he looked where he had told the valet to put it, it was not there. Charpentier searched through the whole pile of music, but still no letter. He looked everywhere near the desk, even turning out the drawers, until the floor was completely strewn with music paper. He was ready to give up the search when he noticed the footstool that was tucked almost out of sight next to his chair and saw the note resting on it.

The handwriting was vaguely familiar, but he could not place where he had seen it before. Charpentier opened the letter and looked at the signature. "Émilie!" he cried out loud, and then lit another candle, sat in his chair, and read.

> *Mademoiselle Émilie Jolicoeur requests that Monsieur Charpentier, who lives at the Hôtel de Gise, should read this leter.*
>
> *I don't much like it here. I miss everyone. My parents should know that I am well. We must take great care. I need to tell you something important! I wish we could sing together.*
>
> *Émilie Jolicoeur*

Charpentier could not stop smiling. Émilie was well! She thought of him, and wrote a letter! The poor grammar and bad spelling gave him a lump in his throat. Suddenly all her little characteristics and mannerisms came flooding back to him. He rang for a servant. A moment later a valet arrived.

"I received this letter earlier," said Charpentier, almost out of breath. "Who delivered it?"

The valet looked at it and shrugged his shoulders. "One of the footmen answered the door."

"I need to send a reply, by the same courier. Do you think you could find the footman?" Charpentier pressed a shiny coin into the valet's hand.

"Certainly, Monsieur," he replied, and then bowed out of the room.

Charpentier looked closely at the letter. It bore no official frank and looked as though it had been crushed, perhaps hidden away, before it reached him. With no date, he could not tell how long ago it had been written. Perhaps this correspondence was secret. He would have to be careful, until he discovered the whole story. He would find a way to get a letter to Émilie without anyone's knowing. And so Charpentier fished through the mess of papers on his floor to find a blank sheet and penned a note to his former pupil. At last he might discover what had happened and perhaps start the process of getting her to return to Paris.

～∾～

For a while, Sophie was generally too occupied with earning a living and trying to save up enough money to dig herself out of her current living situation to do much about remedying the debacle with the slippers. And surviving on the streets was proving more difficult than it had seemed to her at first, because the house she used for her more reputable clients demanded more and more money from her each time she availed herself of the lodgings there. In addition, she found that in order to attract better clients, she needed to upgrade her wardrobe a bit.

But despite this business, Sophie kept her ultimate goal clearly in mind. At first she thought it would be an easy matter to return to the Hôtel de Guise and quiz Charpentier about Émilie's whereabouts, find the girl, and get the slippers back—or at least get her to provide some kind of explanation to Madame Coryot so that Sophie's good name could be reclaimed, possibly even her position in the Guise household, if the housekeeper was willing to overlook her unfortunate outburst. But she tried twice to gain access to Charpentier, and both times was practically thrown out on her ear by one of the footmen.

"So, you think you're better than I am, do you?" Sophie shrieked the second time, when Gaston, the young lad whom Mademoiselle had brought up from the country when he was an adolescent, pushed her roughly out the servants' entrance. This rude treatment made her furious, but when she stepped back and realized the extent to which her recent life had changed her outwardly, she began to realize that she could expect little more. No more the pert, saucy lady's maid, Sophie was now quite obviously a denizen of the night, wearing clothing and face painting that announced her trade all too clearly to any who passed. Her one decent gown had had to be cut and tied up to get her the first few customers, and she had not seen a need to change a successful tactic. And Sophie did not want to spend any of her hard-earned money for finery that was unrelated to her lucrative new trade.

Dressed thus, she would not be able to gain access to Charpentier at the Hôtel de Guise. So she had taken to following the composer discreetly, looking for an opportunity to approach him where he would not be too startled and where they could have a quiet conversation unobserved by any nosy gossips. The opportunity presented itself as Monsieur Charpentier hurried along the rue St. Antoine in the middle of a pleasant afternoon. The crowd miraculously filtered away for a few moments, and Sophie decided to seize the moment.

Charpentier was so deeply engrossed in thinking about what Émilie had written in her last letter to him, and how to respond to her with sensible advice that might help her survive in that snake pit they called Versailles, he did not notice he had been followed for quite some time. At first the figure kept her distance. But as Charpentier turned onto the rue St. Antoine, she shortened the space between them until she was within arm's reach. The young woman tapped him on the shoulder. Startled, Charpentier looked around. He frowned when he saw this creature of the streets and pushed her away, assuming she was just looking for a customer.

"Bah! Monsieur Charpentier!"

The woman spat out his name. Charpentier halted in his tracks and looked again. There was something familiar about the reddish-blond curls and the fullness around the lips. But the whore's face was so covered with paint and her clothing so outlandish that he could not make her out. How did this person know his name? He did not patronize her type.

"Where is she, Monsieur Charpentier? Where are they?"

The whore was trying to steer him into a small alley. Charpentier looked around him for a policeman. "Stand back!" he yelled. "I know not of what you speak."

As if he had said some magic words, the creature stopped in her tracks and let him go. He rushed away from her, relieved to have been spared any more embarrassment, but as he went, he heard her yell out after him, "I curse you! I, Sophie Dupin, send a thousand curses upon your heirs!"

"Sophie!" Charpentier cried, suddenly realizing who this whore was. But by the time he turned to look for her, she had whirled around and run off, melting into the monochrome, workaday crowd. What did she want of him? He knew, of course, that she had been dismissed, and was mildly curious about why. She had certainly changed. For a moment an image of Émilie flashed through his mind. He shivered. Surely she was not in danger of sinking to such a low state. She was too young, he hoped, even to recognize flirtatious advances. But what if she had no choice? What if she was being corrupted in that place where sexual favors were simply part of the social commerce? Until that moment, Charpentier had not allowed himself to imagine the worst. He had kept his most specific fears at bay, hiding behind his trust that Émilie's essential innocence might protect her from any more egregious transgressions. Now, however, he was not so sure. He quickened his pace back to his apartment, determined to find some way to get to Émilie, to warn her. He did not want to ruin her chances of a brilliant career at court, but he was desperate to protect her from harm. Yet in his heart Charpentier knew that Émilie's were not the only interests he had in mind.

Sophie's hope of getting a straight answer and civilized cooperation from Charpentier vanished with his response to her approach. She had thought he was a nice person, kinder than most. Yet he could not see beyond her appearance any more than could the lackeys at the Hôtel de Guise. That left only one course open to Sophie. She would have to discover for herself what had happened, and make the wrongdoers pay for her shame. Although she still had no idea where Émilie had gone, and whether the slippers were still in her possession, Sophie made an important decision. Rather than try to vindicate herself, she would redirect her energies toward another goal: revenge on Émilie and Charpentier, the two people she held responsible for her downfall.

And so Sophie became Charpentier's shadow, whenever her business would spare her, and spent as much time as she could looking for clues in his actions and habits that would lead her to Émilie. When he was in his apartment at the Hôtel de Guise, she stood patient watch over the servants' entrance, making mental notes of who came and went, and what hours Charpentier chose for his own comings and goings. It was while she was engaged in this dogged watching that Sophie stumbled on her first bit of information about Émilie's fate.

It was a beautiful, unseasonably warm afternoon. Business was not brisk; the burgeoning spring gave people thoughts of love more than lust. The birds burst their guts with song all day and well into the evening, and Sophie fairly hated the sound of them. She harbored malicious thoughts about the sparrows who sang outside her window and woke her each day at an indecent hour, wishing that Monsieur le Diable could be trained like a hawk to hunt on command. Her mind was busy imagining how she might subdue the cat as she idled across the street from the side entrance of the Hôtel de Guise, watching out of the corner of her eye for anything unusual while she pretended to cut her fingernails with a small knife.

"I have a letter for Monsieur Charpentier that I must give into his hands only."

Sophie looked up from her task. Just by the servants' entrance, a letter dangling from his hand, stood a lad who looked too young to be a clerk and too old to be a page from some other fine house. He had that air of someone who did not belong anywhere in particular, and yet he had been entrusted with some important message for Charpentier. It could be a legal document, she thought. But the letter had no official seals and ribbons. Sophie's curiosity was aroused. She simply had to know what communication that mysterious piece of paper contained before it reached Charpentier's hands. She swiftly tucked her knife away and sauntered across the street.

"Young man," Sophie said, loosening the tie of her blouse to reveal more of her bosom, and exaggerating the sway of her hips as she drew closer to the lad. "I'm a friend of Monsieur Charpentier. I could give him the letter."

Sophie let her large breasts brush against his arm. The boy's eyes nearly popped out of his head, and he swallowed audibly.

"Come here for a moment," she said, "I have a special hiding place for a letter, and I need you to put it there." She drew the messenger into the alley across the way. Once out of sight of the passersby, she loosened her blouse a little more and exposed one of her breasts. "Wouldn't you like to taste it?" she said, taking the letter out of his now trembling hands and guiding his head toward her bosom. She reached down with her free hand to the lad's crotch. He was as hard as a rock. After one or two squeezes, he doubled over in ecstasy, and Sophie quickly hid away her tits and the letter, then scampered off toward her room, laughing at the poor fellow's helpless confusion.

It amused Sophie to turn the tables every once in a while. In her present line of business, she sometimes lost sight of her own power of seduction. It was having to sell herself, to compete so brazenly with the other girls, that made her forget that, if she chose, she could reduce a man to a jellylike heap. Somehow the shoe was on the other foot, and the person with the money was the one who was in control. Sophie could see some similarities with the process of trying to advance at court, but the gloss of luxury had made it all seem less vulgar.

Although at Versailles she did not learn what it was really like to be a whore, Sophie acquired many other useful scraps of knowledge, including how to unseal a letter, read it, and seal it again so that no one would know it had been tampered with. In her room, after sliding the warmed blade of her pocket knife under the wax seal, she unfolded the paper and cast her eye over the childlike writing. "How did that bitch manage to get herself to Versailles!" she exclaimed. She read on. Émilie's letter contained nothing particularly important. It was only an account of a music lesson, and it mentioned that she was going to take part in a masquerade. At the end, though, Sophie thought she detected a note of warmth:

> *I miss our lessons so much. I wish I was in Paris again, but they will not let me leave. I only have one friend here, his name is François.*
>
> *With love,*
> *Moi*

Sophie had to restrain herself from tearing the paper into shreds. If she had had any doubts before that Émilie deserved to be punished for betraying her kindness, they were all gone now. Not only had the vixen stolen a pair of valuable slippers and been the cause of Sophie's dismissal from a position that suited her, but she was no doubt poised to reap the rewards of being the new flavor at Versailles. Sophie threw the letter on her bed and walked around her tiny room ten times in succession, breathing deeply and clenching and unclenching her fists. When she had worked off enough of her violent anger and felt it was safe for her to handle the letter again, she sat on the edge of her bed and examined it closely. Clearly Émilie and Charpentier had been carrying on a secret correspondence for some time. The fact that the letter itself contained nothing particularly damaging was irrelevant. It had already occurred to her that the composer's interest in Émilie might have been more than professional, and Sophie was convinced she could use even a faint whiff of scandal to ruin both of them, if she chose to. But for now she decided simply to keep an even closer watch on Charpentier, to see if this exchange of letters continued, perhaps to try to disentangle the route the correspondence took from Paris to Versailles and back again. Sophie knew, from her own time at court, that to succeed, any scheme had to be very carefully planned and executed.

When Charpentier received the letter the next day from a different young delivery boy, he had no idea anyone's eyes had seen it other than Émilie's. He pressed his lips to the untidy handwriting, not realizing that it was the scent of Sophie's body, not Émilie's, that he inhaled.

Ten

The spirit of most women fortifies their folly
more than their reason.
Maxim 340

Madame de Maintenon rose slowly from her deep curtsey, as if reluctant to forgo the pleasure of abasing herself before the king.

"Come, Madame, you know that we are friends. There is no one here to see you standing before me!" Louis held out his hand to assist the widow Scarron to her feet. They were alone in an almost hidden corridor of the palace, and they walked together slowly, heads toward each other, deep in quiet conversation.

"Forgive me, sire, but I must speak." Madame de Maintenon always prefaced her remarks to the king in this way. It gave her the deepest thrill to know that speaking to him honestly—or as honestly as she dared—was a privilege she had won through careful stratagems and a patient campaign of calm strength. Unlike the royal mistress, she took care never to be insistent, never to raise her voice, never to demand recognition or privileges.

"You know that I count upon you to do so," said the king, stooping a little lower to hear his companion's words.

Madame de Maintenon cleared her throat and continued. "Now

that you need even more help from the Almighty to prevail in the Low Countries, I believe it is imperative that you look to your salvation." She referred to a recent dispatch that informed the king that, contrary to all he thought, things were by no means over in Belgium, and he may soon be forced to lead a campaign there again.

"I am always mindful of such things, whether I am at war or at peace. I attend mass every day, and under your tutelage I have come to understand the requirements of the pious life much more thoroughly," the king said, with a little bow of his head in recognition.

The widow Scarron returned the bow as if almost overcome with gratitude. "Understanding them, and acting upon them, are two different sides of the same coin," she said. "You have a queen—"

The king interrupted her. "And I have done my duty by her! I have fathered heirs to the great throne of France, and she wants for nothing, including my respect."

Madame de Maintenon turned a corner, leading the king onward but appearing only to have wandered as though she were following a train of thought. "You know that your confessor does me the honor of hearing my own confession," she said. "And he has alluded to me of late that his conscience is troubled by administering the sacraments to a king who, although great beyond measure as a monarch, refuses to curb his appetites as a man."

Louis's face darkened. Madame de Maintenon thought for a moment she had gone too far and rapidly began to think how she might soothe the king. She paused, and in the silent interval she could hear clocks chime eleven in the morning. With a swift glance around she checked their location. They were in the corridor just behind the Salle de Bal, and soon Émilie would begin her lesson with Monsieur Lully. She stopped walking so that they would not pass beyond that place without hearing the young girl's voice, which had been the object of this conference all along.

"As divinely appointed sovereign, surely I was given these appetites to exercise them!" Louis said.

"Or, if you will forgive me, to overcome them?"

At that moment, Émilie began her vocal exercises. The king

stopped and cocked his head. The walls of the château were quite thick, and so it sounded as though the voice were coming from somewhere very far away, not from the chamber on the other side of the wall where they stood.

"Your Majesty?" Madame de Maintenon said, with an expression of curiosity on her face.

"Who is that?" Louis asked.

"Who is what?" answered the widow Scarron, pretending not to know what he was talking about.

"Can't you hear it? That voice? I've never heard anything so beautiful!"

Madame de Maintenon smiled. "Perhaps, sire, that is the voice of your own conscience, for I hear it not."

She turned and commenced walking back in the direction of the king's apartments, trying not to hurry, but hoping that they would be out of earshot before Lully began instructing the young singer and the illusion would be destroyed by the sound of his irritating, nasal whine. The king seemed unwilling to tear himself away from listening, but Madame de Maintenon knew he was too polite not to escort her as she walked, and so after a few more minutes of strolling through the corridor they could no longer hear Émilie.

As they continued their conference, the widow Scarron tried hard not to smile with satisfaction. Her plan had worked to perfection. The king was agitated and thoughtful when she left him. And tomorrow, when he saw Émilie in the fête, the next step in her plan would be complete. Then it would only remain to orchestrate the final coup that would persuade the king that his affair with the Marquise de Montespan was divinely condemned.

At that moment, Madame de Maintenon still believed that her motive was pure, that it was her duty to turn the great monarch of France away from the path of sin, to make him be once more an example to his people of piety and justice. She was far more adept at reading the secrets of other hearts than those of her own.

* * *

The day of the fête dawned. Almost before she got out of bed, Émilie could tell that it was going to be hot, although it was only the beginning of May. Her skin prickled with a light sweat, and she threw the covers off with relief. The cold wooden floor of her room felt pleasant on the soles of her feet. She stood in just her muslin slip, looking out of her window at the slightly hazy sky above the opposite wing of the château, waiting for Marie to bring her morning tray. In a few moments a gentle scratch on her door announced the quiet young maid's arrival.

Émilie skipped over to let her in. She turned the key and the mechanism of the lock disengaged with a satisfying clunk. It made her feel safer to be able to lock her door at night, although she had nothing of value to protect—unlike many of the courtiers, who kept stashes of costly jewels in their tiny rooms.

Marie placed the tray on her little desk, curtseyed, and left.

"Thank you!" Émilie called after her. So far Marie, who took care of all her intimate needs from bringing her clothes to emptying her chamber pot, had not said a word to her.

Tucked in next to her dish of hot chocolate, Émilie found a note.

Mademoiselle Émilie,
    Please attend your costume fitting at 9 o'clock, in the Salle de Vénus.

A little thrill of excitement went through her. Today she was going to take part in a masquerade that was to involve the entire court. At last she would see the king. She imagined him taller and grander than anyone else in the world. Too bad she was not going to sing for him. Monsieur Lully said that the fresh air might damage her voice. Still, it seemed bizarre to Émilie. They'd brought her here and worked with her, taught her mountains of notes and made her memorize volumes of words, spent hours training her in movement and pantomime, and the first time she did anything in front of the king she was to be the centerpiece in an enormous tableau vivant. She would neither move a muscle nor make a sound for most of the thirty minutes she would be on display.

Although she had very little to do, Émilie's task in the masquerade was not exactly easy. She had practiced her pose, which was not the difficult part (although she thought it might be a little tougher to hold it for the required half hour while perched on the top of a fifteen-foot ladder). The hardest thing, she thought, would be not to perish of boredom out there doing nothing.

Émilie knew better than to be late for an appointment at court, even if she subsequently had to wait for someone else to arrive. And so, when she heard the distant clocks chime the appointed time, she found her way to the Salle de Vénus. This was her chance to try to get used to her costume. Not only was it to be made entirely of feathers, but, she had been informed, she was to be naked from the waist up.

"Mademoiselle will be magnificent!" the smiling costumer had said, looking for all the world like the guardian of the gates of heaven, standing in front of a sea of mostly white feathers. "Mademoiselle must not be ashamed! Such a beautiful young body. She will be *très artistique*!"

When Émilie began to cry at the idea, they summoned François. "It is nothing to be ashamed of, Mademoiselle Émilie," he told her. "Every morning, the king and queen dress before scores of courtiers. And you see, on the ceiling, all the naked women? It is only art. You will be like a sculpture, like the fountains in the garden."

Émilie calmed herself but decided she would not tell Charpentier about her costume in her next letter. If word ever got back, her mother would be furious.

When the moment arrived for the celebration, Émilie was quite accustomed to being half exposed. She did not feel entirely like the same person, and so it was not so difficult to put aside her modesty. And besides, from her perch atop the ladder she could see a great exodus from the château, platoons of courtiers streaming out of every door, flowing down the steps to the garden, a splendid, glittering, human mass. They swarmed over the sets that the workmen had labored all the night before to build, and which they would demolish entirely later that day. By tomorrow, no one would ever suspect the event had taken place at all.

The royal fanfare was sounded, signaling the start of a procession of such magnificence that Émilie was completely awed. She had a glimpse of it coming past on its way to parade before the king, a full mile of richly arrayed courtiers on horseback. The platform upon which she was seated on the ladder, with children and domestic animals gamboling below her, was hidden behind an immense curtain that had been rigged to a sort of frame. At precisely noon, this curtain was to be drawn aside to reveal the tableau. Émilie was then expected to remain absolutely still while an ode, written specially for the occasion by Monsieur de La Rochefoucauld, was recited. At its end, she was to climb down gracefully, take two of the putti by the hands, and step up to a point about ten feet in front of the king before curtseying and then backing away.

Émilie had practiced her descent from the ladder several times on the days before the masquerade, but not in costume, and not atop a platform that was already eight feet off the ground. She was a little anxious but felt confident that she would be able to maneuver her feathers without a misstep. But matters were complicated by the warm weather. After only a few minutes in position, Émilie felt the perspiration gathering beneath her feather skirt and trickling down the backs of her legs to her bare feet. There was no way for her to reach them to scratch what was soon an almost unbearable itch. Although she did not suffer as much as the courtiers who had added so many heavy layers of jewels to their normal habits, soon the heat made Émilie feel a little dizzy.

Despite her growing discomfort, she managed to strike her pose before the curtain was pulled away, and the gasp of pleasure the tableau provoked was sincere. It was the image of pastoral beauty: angelic children, sheep and goats that had been washed to snowy whiteness, and quantities of colorful flowers, atop which sat Émilie, looking like a cross between a bird and a goddess about to ascend to the sky. The perspiration had added a sheen to her skin that made her almost glitter. Émilie longed to be able to look at the king, but she had been warned not to change her pose until the very end.

For the first fifteen minutes, Émilie was fine. She ceased noticing the tickle of sweat, but the glare of the sun (which she was forced to confront because her eyes were to be cast upward) and the heat made her feel increasingly shaky, and the world started to revolve around her slowly. A dull pounding in her temples gradually drowned out the sound of the actor, who savored every syllable so that the king would be sure to appreciate the delicacy and finesse of his expression. A few moments before he finished reciting the ode, Émilie began to feel that she was in danger of falling off her ladder. She feared greatly not only the harm to herself that would result, but the possibility of crushing one of the infants, all children of servants and workmen, who played so innocently beneath her. She held out as long as she could, then decided she could no longer risk waiting.

Just before the last, adulatory line of the ode, Émilie gingerly started to negotiate her descent on the ladder. The rungs of the ladder had become slippery despite having been rubbed with resin. Émilie stepped very cautiously, but on the fourth rung she lost her footing. She could feel the skin being scraped off the top of her left foot as it shot through the ladder. She grabbed the vertical poles. The ladder swayed from side to side, but her grip was strong through sheer desperation, and she managed to counterbalance the movement. The result was that, rather than float delicately down from her aerial perch, she found herself suspended, hanging upside down, her swan feather skirt around her ears, revealing her derrière most unbecomingly to the royal party. In that moment, Émilie wanted to die.

A horrified gasp escaped the crowd. There was a great clicking and whirring of fans as ladies opened them suddenly and agitated them, more to prevent anyone's seeing or hearing them laugh than out of a sense of modesty. All Émilie could think of was that she had not had time even to glance at the king, and now here she was, not exactly showing him her best side.

To the shock of all, King Louis stood up from his seat and swept the crowd of courtiers and servants with his gaze. "Won't one of you help the poor girl?" he asked, and then commenced laughing heartily.

Within seconds François had leapt upon the stage and disengaged Émilie's foot from its caught position. He righted her, but her head-dress was a shambles. Émilie did not know what to do, so she removed it, gave it to one of the children, and then made the deepest, slowest curtsey she had ever managed. She did not look up. She couldn't bear to see the king's expression.

The curtain was hastily drawn across again, and the festivities continued. Émilie, however, was rooted to the spot. She did not know how she had been able to descend to the floor and rise again in her curtsey despite the pain in her ankle.

"Come, let me help you back to your room," said François, supporting her under her elbow.

"No!" cried Émilie. "I can't."

"Why not?" he asked.

"It's my foot. I can't walk. And . . ."

"And what, Mademoiselle?"

Émilie did not answer him but looked down at the floor. François followed her eyes and saw the blood that had trickled down from between her legs. The servant blushed.

"I'll fetch one of the maids, and a surgeon," he said.

Eleven

One often passes from love to ambition,
but one seldom returns from ambition to love.
Maxim 490

The king's first view of Émilie had precisely the effect that Madame de Maintenon had planned on, although she had hoped it would have been accomplished with more decorum. Louis began to make discreet inquiries about the young cygnet who had fallen off her perch.

"I am very pleased, Monsieur de St. Paul, with Mademoiselle Émilie's progress," she said.

St. Paul pretended to yawn. "I knew you would soon see the many ways in which the young thing might entertain the king."

"Ah, but simply entertaining the king is not very difficult."

"You seem to imply that this project took no effort—nor, might I add, expense—on my part," said St. Paul, his voice betraying more than he wished of pique.

"The expense, I imagine, you intend to recoup. The effort—what effort has there been, after all? It is Monsieur Lully who instructs her, and François who looks after her. All you did was bring her to Versailles in your carriage! And now that she is here, you have no more expenses on her behalf."

"What if I had not seen her at my godmother's salon? Where would you be now!" The count was becoming annoyed.

"There would have been other ways," she said, walking to the window of her sitting room and looking out over the gardens. It was so hot that the landscape seemed to duplicate itself just above the horizon. No ladies cavorted on the lawn today. She closed the shutters and plunged her room into near darkness. "Do not worry yourself, Monsieur le Comte. If all goes well, you will be amply rewarded for your troubles. But the real question is how to take the next step. What must Mademoiselle Émilie do to secure herself in the king's regard so that I may continue with my plan?" Without looking at St. Paul, she went to her bookshelves.

"You mean *our* plan, do you not, Madame?"

She smiled. "Of course, how foolish of me."

St. Paul took his handkerchief out of his pocket and wiped the perspiration off his face. The widow Scarron never misspoke, and so he suddenly had the distinct impression that she had not told him everything. From what she had originally said, he thought that the idea was to replace Madame de Montespan, who had become rather too powerful and public, with someone whom they had in their power and could manipulate as necessary. Now it seemed that she had something else in mind. This powerful lady had promised him advancement, and he knew she could procure it. But if she did not trust him, he could not trust her. He would have to be very cautious. "I am here to do your bidding," he said.

"I thank you, Monsieur." Madame de Maintenon ran her fingers along the spines of the books, and chose one seemingly at random. "But instead, let us do Monsieur Quinault's bidding. Or at least, let Mademoiselle Émilie do it." Madame de Maintenon opened the volume and traced the lines on the page with her forefinger. "According to Quinault, she must offer to give her life to save her husband. Then we shall see—if she plays her part well, she shall be redeemed by the gods."

"Of course. How clever of you. Let her sing in an opera. It is the story of Alceste, if I am not mistaken? The king will be utterly enchanted. I shall inform Monsieur Lully right away. Is there any-thing else you wish me to do?"

"I will call for you later, when we see how things go." The widow Scarron punctuated her last phrase by snapping the book shut. She extended her hand to St. Paul, who bent over it, and then left.

～

"She is not ready! She has no finesse!" Lully's face was almost purple with consternation. First, the widow Scarron had persuaded him not to let Émilie sing during the fête, which would have been the perfect opportunity for her to do something easy and charming for the king, and now she wanted him to give the girl one of the most demanding stage roles he had ever written!

"Do you question the judgment of the king? It was, after all, his command," St. Paul lied, examining his fingernails for a few moments before speaking once again. "And so, you must make her ready by the day of the performance. There is time enough, I think!"

Lully knew that this wish was never expressed by the king. He was accustomed to receiving his sovereign's orders directly but he did not want to disabuse St. Paul of the belief that his lie had worked. No, this was the work of the widow Scarron, he was in no doubt whatever. She was up to something, that he realized. It did not matter to her whether the performance itself was perfect or not. Music was not her forte, not like the Marquise de Montespan. He had composed *Alceste* for the pleasure of the king's official mistress in the first place, and she had such taste, such esprit. This gesture was in some way intended to lash out at Madame de Montespan, and he, by being forced to comply, would alienate one of his greatest allies at court.

He also knew that, whatever his feelings about the matter, he would never dare to confront His Majesty. Madame de Maintenon was too well liked, and he could see where things were headed. He had no choice but to accede.

"All right, Monsieur de St. Paul, I shall commence rehearsals on the morrow."

"Perhaps I'll pop in from time to time and see how you're coming along," said St. Paul with a smile of triumph.

"Only His Majesty is permitted to attend rehearsals."

St. Paul paused on his way out the door of Lully's apartment. "Oh, did I forget to say? His Majesty won't be able to come to any rehearsals. He is much too occupied with the distressing news from Belgium. In any case, he knows his part. And he would prefer to be surprised on the night of the performance."

Lully ground his teeth and stared at the door through which he saw St. Paul's back disappear. He shook his head. The girl's voice was pretty, there was no mistaking it. But to perform a major role required so much more than that. It could be an utter fiasco, and then he, Lully, would have let the king down. Never had his productions been anything but magnificent, perfect in every detail. He must talk to Quinault about rewriting the book a little. Such a young creature would never be believed as a matron with several children. At least he could retain Mademoiselle St. Christophle, the best singer in his troupe, as the Spirit of the River Seine in the prologue. St. Paul only mentioned the role of Alceste herself, and she does not enter until Act I. And then he would have at least one lead singer he knew he could count on to get the production off to a good start.

"La Christophle will be furious!" Lully said aloud to his empty study.

∽

Émilie opened the hidden door that led to the Salle de Bal very slowly. Already gathered in the room were about a dozen people she did not know, whom she had never seen before. Realizing that her jaw was clenched and the muscles in her face tight and unnatural, she forced herself to relax: she would have to sing before long. Everyone looked so big, so much older than she. She smoothed her dress down and checked to see that her hair was not messy, then stood as tall as she could and joined the others in the center of the room.

"I am Émilie," she said to a young woman who looked to be only a little older than she was, and who was standing a little off to the side. "Pleased to meet you."

Before the girl had a chance to answer her, Lully walked in and clapped his hands. "Attention!" he barked. "Today, we begin an enterprise that the king has commanded. We are to perform, out of doors, the tragedy of *Alceste,* two months from today, on October the fifth."

A murmur passed through the assembled crowd, and Émilie saw several of the singers smile and nod to each other.

"I shall announce the roles and would like each of you to come forward and stand by me when I have read your name."

Lully went through almost the entire cast, including the chorus of soldiers and the ballet dancers. He paused for a moment when only Émilie and one other woman were left standing on one side of the room. "In the role of the Spirit of the River Seine, Mademoiselle St. Christophle."

The lady stepped forward. "The River Seine, and Alceste, at your service, Monsieur!"

The other cast members laughed, but Lully continued with his eyes fixed on the paper he held before him.

"As Alceste, Mademoiselle Émilie Jolicoeur."

Émilie walked over to take her place among her colleagues. But instead of the subdued chatter that had greeted all the other announcements, there was complete silence. Émilie knew nothing about the way things worked in an opera troupe, that young singers normally had to put in a couple of years singing the small roles before they leapt to stardom. She did not realize that Lully had instantly made her a pariah among the rest of the players, who, one by one, turned their backs on her.

Émilie bit her lower lip to stop herself from crying. She wanted to run from the room and hide away, not be the focus of everyone's attention. If this was what it was like to be in an opera, she never wanted to do it again. At least, not one of Monsieur Lully's. Monsieur Charpentier would never let something like this happen to her, she was certain.

∽

The late-summer trees had begun to look as if they were growing tired of being green, and here and there a bright scarlet or yellow leaf dotted the foliage. Soon it will be autumn, Émilie thought somewhat sadly as she nodded back and forth in a sedan chair in time with the footsteps of the servants who carried it. She was on her way to visit the Marquise de Montespan at Clagny, a journey of only about a mile, but she wished she were on her way home. Autumn in Paris was her favorite season. She loved to be all snug indoors with the wild wind whistling around the roof of their house, and the restless water of the Seine sloshing against the stone supports of the bridge far below. It was on those nights that her father would tell a long story that sent a frisson of fear through her body, a story about dungeons and desperadoes, of treasonous princes and poisonings. All three of them would stay up late, past the time when the fire went out, and every slam of a door that was caught in the wind would make them jump with delighted terror.

The summons to attend the king's official mistress had come just after her rehearsal the day before. François brought it to her. Madame de Montespan was still the most powerful woman at court, she had been told, although there were rumors that Madame de Maintenon was edging her out of the king's favors. Émilie saw the marquise once in a while in the evening, at the queen's card parties, when she, Émilie, was summoned to be decorative and helpful, picking up ladies' fans when they dropped them or beckoning servants to replenish glasses of wine. The Marquise de Montespan was always the most magnificently dressed and still very beautiful after several childbirths. She looked more regal than the queen herself but was never unnecessarily unkind. She even asked Émilie to sing for her someday.

"Be careful," François had told her. "She did not get to her position through an excess of virtue."

"Why does she want to see me? Do you think she'll ask me to sing?" she asked him.

"Who can say? But her summons must be obeyed, as surely as a summons from the queen. Now let me see how you look." François stepped back to admire Émilie's gown and coiffure, over which Marie had taken special care that morning.

As she made her short journey dressed like a lady of rank, Émilie suddenly wished that Charpentier could see her. She was embarrassed to think how childish she was when she had gone for her lessons every day. He would be proud to see how elegant, how calm she had grown. She had written to him and told him about singing the role of Alceste, and he wrote back, so happy for her and full of advice. She read the letter several times over before burning it, as she had all Charpentier's others on François's advice. It always pained her to do it. The paper with Charpentier's handwriting on it was her only connection with the world outside Versailles. There were days when she thought she might die if she did not receive a letter from her mentor—her friend. Émilie could tell that he worried about her, and she could also tell that he wished she would come back. He wished, even, that she had never gone away. She would reassure him that Lully's music, although very skillful, was not the equal of his, and that she would never enjoy singing it as much. Émilie longed to be permitted to sing one of the airs Charpentier had written for her. Even more than that, she longed to sing their own, special duet.

Émilie's memories were interrupted when the servants deposited her chair abruptly at the bottom of a long flight of marble steps leading up to the door of the miniature Versailles that was in view of the full-scale version where Émilie now lived. She knew that if she were a little more important, they would have carried her all the way up and into the very room where her hostess awaited her. As it was, they stood by, immobile. She struggled somewhat awkwardly out of the chair, exposing her ankles in the process.

Although from the outside Clagny resembled Versailles, as soon as Émilie walked through the door, she could tell she was in an altogether different place. As in Versailles, there were parquet floors, marble columns and statues, and beautiful hangings and pictures, but the ceilings were lower. And because the rooms were not as deep, the light from the windows illuminated them better, but it was filtered by gauzy silk curtains that waved languidly as she walked by and stirred up the peaceful air.

The footman led Émilie past the formal reception room, with its thronelike, red-velvet-upholstered armchair at one end and tapestry-covered tabourets lining the walls, then ushered her through a small door into a more intimate chamber. Madame de Montespan's private sitting room was not awe-inspiring and monumental; it was large and luxurious, filled with a vast quantity of soft, silk- and velvet-upholstered furniture that beckoned one to recline. Silver salvers of sweets were placed so that they were never out of reach, and the sunlight that washed in through the sheer drapes seemed to hang, tremulous, in a state of near extinction. In the corner a musician played the lute quietly. Because he was somewhat hidden behind all the furniture, the music seemed to arise from nowhere, to be distilled from the atmosphere, and once created, it was absorbed into all the yielding surfaces of the room. Madame de Montespan also had her own magnificent suite of rooms in the chateau of Versailles, but it was a measure of the king's regard for her that he had built this jewel of a home for her practically on his own grounds. Those who were less charitably inclined implied that Louis built it so he could have an occasional rest from his volatile and demanding mistress.

Émilie closed her mouth suddenly, realizing that it was hanging open when she walked in. Never had so many of her senses been assaulted in so delightful a way at the same time. It took her a moment to realize that some of what seemed to be upholstered furniture was actually motionless footmen, stationed here and there with the function of holding a tray of chocolates, or a sconce containing a candle, at the precise location necessary for someone's possible need, should he happen to be sitting or standing in a certain place. Émilie half expected that the chairs themselves would suddenly sprout arms and legs and beckon her—an image that was both amusing and terrifying.

It was not until she spoke that Émilie noticed Madame de Montespan.

"Come closer to me, *mon enfant,*" she cooed.

Émilie approached her cautiously.

"Come now! I won't hurt you, child. Come and sit by me."

The marquise patted the space next to her on the divan, most of which was covered by her rich, damask gown. The setting was perfect, and although Émilie had admired the marquise's beauty before, for the first time she really understood the lady's capacity to enchant.

"Why are you frightened? You must know that I am your friend." With this statement, the marquise lifted her feet off the sofa and sat upright, making more space beside her. Émilie obeyed and perched on the edge of the divan. The scent of Madame de Montespan's rich perfume wafted toward Émilie every time the marquise made a gesture. She took Émilie's hand and began to stroke it.

"Sing for me," she said, sounding like a sulky child begging for a treat.

"What, now, Madame?" asked Émilie.

"Of course!" she answered, letting just a hint of irritation creep into her voice. "My lutenist can accompany you." Madame de Montespan smiled very, very slowly.

The control she had over her facial muscles fascinated Émilie. Just the slightest shift of her eyes brought a little Moorish footman, whose skin was the color of the ebony keys on Monsieur Charpentier's harpsichord, to Émilie's side. He bowed to her, and gestured toward the musician, whom Émilie now saw on the other side of the room.

The lutenist stopped playing the moment the marquise asked Émilie to sing. He waited for her to walk the distance from the sofa to the corner where he sat with the lute cradled in his lap. With a little pang of homesickness, Émilie noticed that it was not one of her father's. She also noticed that the musician smiled serenely and stared somewhere off into the distance.

"What will you sing?"

His question caught Émilie off guard. He had not turned toward her when he spoke, and all at once she realized that he must be blind. She whispered to him the name of an air by Lully, and he strummed a few notes of accompaniment. Then Émilie began to sing.

"No, no, no! Not that one!"

Émilie had barely let one note escape from her mouth when she was interrupted by the marquise.

"Sing me something from *Alceste*." Her expression was almost pleading, beseeching. The abrupt change in tone from one sentence to the next made Émilie's head spin. And besides, she was not supposed to sing the music from *Alceste* for anyone. No one was even meant to know that she was going to perform the role, outside of Lully, St. Paul, Madame de Maintenon—and the rest of the cast, of course.

"You see, it's *my* opera. So it's only right that you should sing it for me."

For an instant Émilie wondered who had betrayed the secret they had all been sworn to keep. But with so many in the cast, and footmen always hovering around, it seemed logical that word would spread. And besides, she did not see how she could say no to Madame de Montespan, and so Émilie did as she was told.

When the song was finished, there was total silence in the room. Émilie looked in the direction of the marquise, whose face was turned away. One of the footmen approached his mistress cautiously and held out a silk handkerchief, which she took and applied to her eyes. Émilie saw her draw a deep breath before she turned and spoke.

"I have been watching you closely. Yes, you are indeed a talent." In one languid movement, she shifted her position on the divan to make even more room at her side. "Come back and sit here," she commanded, but not without kindness in her voice. "You are very young." She watched Émilie walk back across the room. "I can see what they are doing. I see it all. I was there, at the masquerade. You are very pretty."

Madame de Montespan's eyes traveled up and down Émilie's body. She shivered to remember the feeling of being so exposed on that dreadful day. But the marquise ignored her discomfort and continued to speak. Soon Émilie became mesmerized by her face. Watching it was like watching clouds skitter across the sky on a windy day. In that moment Émilie thought she had never seen a more beautiful woman.

"I must tell you something that may cause you distress," said the marquise, her expression darkening. "You have been brought here to help a certain woman—I shall not dignify her with the title of lady—destroy me." She paused.

Her comment shocked Émilie. It jarred against the soothing atmosphere of the room. She had no idea how to respond, and so she said nothing.

"Yes, what can you say? I feel it is my duty, my obligation, to warn you that the perpetration of her designs upon me will result in your destruction too." Madame de Montespan held perfectly still at the end of this statement, keeping Émilie's eyes locked in her gaze. "My spies inform me that they have plans to put you in the king's bed, which is the way that they propose to supplant me, so they imagine . . . You blush! And I dare say you hardly understand why. Well, no matter. Others have failed, and you will too."

Émilie was horrified. The stern look on the marquise's face gradually subsided and was replaced by one that seemed to close off all communication between them for a moment.

"They have miscalculated, however, and the result will have no effect upon my position with the king. And once they realize this, you will have outlasted your usefulness. That is a very perilous position to be in at court."

A wave of mild nausea swept over Émilie. It had never occurred to her that there was any reason at all beyond music that she had been brought to Versailles. How could she have been so naïve? There was danger all around her, and she had failed to notice it. Émilie had a momentary image of herself as a little mouse, being toyed with by a well-fed cat. She began to realize that human beings were passed around like chips at a gaming table at Versailles. Madame de Montespan seemed to imply that she, Émilie, was merely currency, that it was all she had ever been since she arrived at court.

"I can see that you are alarmed. But have courage, *ma chérie!* I have a plan to extricate you from this unappealing prospect," said the lady, "and I think you will find it greatly to your liking. It involves, among other things, a reunion with your *'Cher Maître,'* Monsieur Charpentier."

At the mention of this name, Émilie sat up just a little straighter. It did not escape her notice that Madame de Montespan used a term for Charpentier that could only have come from a perusal of the letters that were supposed to have been completely secret.

"I thought that would please you!" said Madame de Montespan, a note of triumph in her voice. "In order to achieve this object, I must ask you to follow my instructions precisely and to maintain utter secrecy, for your own sake if nothing else."

Émilie cast her eye around the room at the six or seven servants who stood placidly waiting for instructions.

"You need not mind them!" The marquise gestured vaguely in the direction of her staff. "They would not dare breathe a word of what passes within my boudoir."

Émilie looked to see if her comment had had any effect at all on the people who were so cavalierly included in her sweeping comment. Either she spoke the truth, or Madame de Montespan's footmen were so adept at concealing their true feelings that they could have chosen careers on the stage. From all Émilie had seen, servants were a fickle lot, requiring little more than higher wages to persuade any one of them to switch allegiance. She did not know what could possibly induce those at Clagny to behave any differently.

"Ah, young love! I know it. I have loved and been loved as no other before me. Fortune, power, glory—all these are nothing when compared to love. Do not throw it away for an hour of notoriety."

Émilie was confused. What did any of this have to do with love? She was very fond of Monsieur Charpentier, to be sure. And she counted the days between letters, and compared everything that Monsieur Lully told her to what her former teacher had told her, usually to the detriment of Monsieur Lully. But was this love? And if it was, why did it matter to Madame de Montespan?

"Imagine how it would be to return to the man you truly love, the man who taught you what it was to live, to breathe, to sing!"

Émilie let this thought trickle into her heart and, once it was there, turned it over and over. She remembered the feeling she had when she and Monsieur Charpentier sang together, a feeling powerful and yet unnameable, and the memory warmed her from her scalp to her toenails. She closed her eyes and conjured up the sensation of Charpentier's hand pressing against her abdomen, and the way he would not look at her when he sat at the harpsichord, and the way he did look at her when he had come to escort her to the fête. It all seemed to make sense now. Of course she was in love. As she listened to Madame de Montespan outline what sounded like a very risky plan, she was powerless to move, speak, even think for herself. The plan involved a daring rescue in the middle of the night after her début as Alceste. The marquise promised that she would take care of bringing Monsieur Charpentier into the scheme. She had certain knowledge, so she said, that he was just as attached to Émilie as she was to him.

"Is he?" asked Émilie, forgetting to address the marquise with her proper title.

Madame de Montespan pushed a little tendril of hair back behind Émilie's ear. "Poor child, you really are naïve. Don't you know what power you wield? All that beauty, and that voice as well. You could have anyone you wanted."

Émilie blushed deeply. What was this beautiful lady implying? "But I don't want anyone," she said, not knowing what else to say.

"No, of course not. You don't want just anyone, you want him."

By the time she sent Émilie on her way back to Versailles, the Marquise de Montespan knew that, despite the hazards, this young girl would do anything she asked of her. Years of experience taught her to recognize when she had made a conquest, and little Émilie Jolicoeur was in love. Perhaps not with her, but with the idea of love that she had made so enticing.

Madame de Montespan was particularly pleased with herself when she went to the queen's apartments that evening to play cards. She sent for Émilie, and the ladies persuaded the girl to sing an air. As each listener was enfolded in the rich, thrilling sound of Émilie's voice, the marquise thought she could detect greater depth and power in it even since earlier that day. And for this she accepted some of the credit, quite happy to partake of the imminent triumph of the most remarkable creature at court.

Twelve

‿‿◦‿‿

There is no disguise that can hide love for long when it is
present, or give the appearance of love when it is not.
Maxim 70

One warm September Sunday, as Charpentier walked home from the
Church of St. Louis, where he had just directed the music for High
Mass, he noticed that a private coach, small but very beautiful, kept
pace with him and stayed near him all the way through the streets of
the Marais. When he was about a block away from the rue des Quatre Fils, he heard the horses quicken their pace just a little until the
vehicle drew up level with him. The coach window lowered. A
woman's gloved hand rested on the top of the door. It was dark
within, and he could just see the suggestion of her profile, shrouded
in veils.

"Monsieur Charpentier," the woman called to him. He approached.
"Do not come closer. I have a letter for you, from someone who
wishes to help you." The woman held a folded piece of paper out to
Charpentier. He reached from where he stood and took it from her.
"I shall return exactly one week from today for your answer," she
said. Before Charpentier could say anything, the driver clucked his
horses to a trot, and the coach departed.

Charpentier examined the note he held in his hand. The paper was very heavy and fine. He opened it and read.

Monsieur Charpentier,
I have reason to believe that your little music student is in peril of losing her innocence at the hands of the mighty. I have spoken to her about this danger, but she is sworn to secrecy, so she will not speak of it in her letters to you. For reasons of my own, I wish to help you remove her from this situation. Before I can tell you my plan, I need to know if you would be willing to act swiftly and without concern for your safety. Please give your answer by this same courier one week hence.

The letter was not signed. Charpentier felt the blood race to his fingertips. For the past months he had temporarily put aside his notion of reclaiming Émilie, ever since she wrote and told him that she was to sing the role of Alceste in Lully's opera. This was too big an opportunity to squander; Charpentier felt he must trust Émilie's innocence and better nature to protect her from any scandal at court. His letters to her were always full of advice, including any information he could pick up from the other servants at the Hôtel de Guise about who to watch out for and who was harmless. He was relieved to hear that Lully, although unscrupulous, was hardly likely to have designs upon Émilie's person. And nothing in Émilie's letters to him had given him any cause to think there was anything that was troubling her beyond a little homesickness.

On the other hand, Émilie had been at Versailles for almost nine months. Even over the brief time he had worked with her, she had matured. Without any fresh input to give him a new impression, Charpentier's memory of Émilie was frozen in time. All at once he realized that she could be in much more danger now, the result of nothing more than the normal course of nature. It was clear that leaving matters as they stood might spell disaster. Yet if Charpentier took Émilie away from Versailles, neither of them would ever be able to return. All his dreams of a court appointment would end, and Émilie's career would be destroyed.

"Monsieur Charpentier, are you quite well?" It was old Robert, one of the footmen, who sat by the servants' entrance polishing some silver when the composer arrived at the Hôtel de Guise, hardly realizing that he had continued to walk.

"Yes, I'm fine," answered Charpentier.

He went to his room and sat for a long time. As the sun set, and the walls turned golden and then red, Charpentier came to understand that he must not put ambition above what was right. But it was this, the deciding what was right, that caused him some difficulty. Was it right to leave Émilie to her fate, an innocent all too vulnerable to the unscrupulous forces at court? And was his desire to rescue her from some indistinct but ominous fate more self-serving than he wanted to admit?

In the end Charpentier decided that Émilie was still too young to defend herself against the intrigues at court. If he did not think that the effort would prove unsuccessful and probably ruin any future attempt he might make to bring Émilie back to Paris, he would have rushed to Versailles immediately. But with neither the means nor any definite proof that she was in imminent danger, he judged it prudent to be guided by whatever insider it was who claimed to have a plan to avert disaster. And so Charpentier wrote his affirmative response, saying that he would go along with the plan no matter what it entailed, and carried it with him for days until he finally delivered it into the same gloved hand that reached out of the same small coach that followed him home from St. Louis the next Sunday.

∾

In addition to Émilie's letters, over the next few weeks Charpentier received three more from the mysterious woman. That it was a woman Charpentier assumed, as much from the delicacy of the sentiments as the scented paper. The scheme she outlined was relatively simple: Charpentier was to come for Émilie at eleven forty-five at night on October the fifth. She would be ready to flee with him, waiting by a door to the right of the Cour de Marbre. So long as no one found out about the plan, it should go smoothly. Émilie was under the watch of the servant François, but her general compliance, so the anonymous informant told Charpentier, had lulled her guardian into a false sense of security.

It was fortunate in some ways, Charpentier thought, that he had not been called upon to rush off to Versailles the very next day. Mostly the delay gave him time to prepare for Émilie's return. It was difficult to know what to do with her once she was back in Paris. He could hardly bring her back to the Hôtel de Guise, and he had been told in one of the letters that Émilie should not return to her parents' home, since that would be the first place she would be sought. The only answer was to engage a room for Émilie somewhere discreet and quiet. He had asked a valet at the Hôtel de Guise for advice, since he had no idea about these things, making up some story about a sister of his coming from the country. The servant suggested an address south of the rue St. Antoine, in an area that was a little run-down, he said, but private and cheap. Charpentier found the house and secured the lodgings for Émilie, feeling a little sheepish about the whole process. He did not like the way the landlady looked at him, assuming, he was certain, that he was simply looking for a place in which to carry on a love affair.

∽

"Did you know, Madame, that Mademoiselle Émilie has been to see la Montespan more than once?" St. Paul and Madame de Maintenon strolled in a secluded part of the garden at Versailles. He had just arrived to deliver his weekly report on Émilie's progress and development.

"Is that so?" she said. "It does not surprise me."

"Should we not keep a closer watch over her?"

The widow Scarron fingered the pearl rosary that hung around her neck. "I don't think that is necessary. I have everything under control. François keeps me well informed."

St. Paul thought for a moment. "The marquise might try to

remove her from court. She was there, at the masquerade. She saw how the king—"

"I don't think she would dare. The king would suspect her immediately. Too many other so-called rivals have been, shall we say, encouraged by Madame de Montespan to leave court."

St. Paul stepped on a large black beetle that crawled over the grass.

"And what is more, Monsieur le Comte, His Majesty is now departing once more for the Low Countries to lead his armies," said Madame de Maintenon.

"No doubt with the marquise in tow!"

"I hear not. He has specifically asked that she remain behind. Her health is delicate, apparently."

St. Paul thought about this. Montespan would be in a foul temper over such a slight. "Which gives us time to prepare Mademoiselle Émilie even more fully for her encounter with the king," he said.

Madame de Maintenon fixed St. Paul with an unflinching stare. "Sometimes I am amazed, Monsieur, that a gentleman with your instincts can still be so naïve. I believe you have only partly understood my intentions. My goal is not simply to unseat the marquise, who is hardly worth my consideration, but to save the king by teaching him that there are greater pleasures than the gratification of the senses. The girl is my instrument, in all senses of the word. In any case, putting a guileless young peasant in the way of losing her innocence would not distract His Majesty from the considerable charms of Madame de Montespan. The king is not so easily amused for more than one night."

"I see." But St. Paul did not see. His fears were confirmed. He was no longer fully informed of the widow Scarron's plans. He knew as well as anyone how treacherous a place the court of Versailles could be. It was a very uncomfortable feeling, to be on the receiving end of some clever deception.

"My motives are of the highest, and the end I seek will result in the moral salvation of the greatest king ever to live. Such a noble project requires extreme measures." The widow Scarron did not so much raise her voice as intensify it. The effect was chilling, and it avoided all risk of being overheard.

"How extreme?" he asked.

Madame de Maintenon seemed to grow inches taller before St. Paul's eyes, drawing herself as upright as her spine would go and lifting her chin. "This is a matter of state. It justifies any action. Once you have done my bidding, you must leave the next step to me. I will send for you when I need you. Good day, Monsieur de St. Paul."

The count departed feeling chastened, and angry. The woman is mad, he thought. What could she be up to? She thinks she knows everything, but if she teases His Majesty with some new toy and then does not allow him, in some fashion, to gratify his desire, the king won't thank her!

By the time St. Paul arrived at Lully's study, where he had gone at the bidding of Madame de Maintenon, he was incensed. Bursting in without knocking, he surprised Lully, who jumped away from his valet, whose clothing was in a slight state of disarray.

St. Paul took in the scene with one sweep of his eyes, deciding in an instant to store up the information it gave him for use if he ever needed it. "The sketches for Mademoiselle Émilie's costume," he demanded, holding out his hand.

"Whatever for?" Lully covered up his discomfiture by acting irate. The valet bent quickly over a pair of shoes on the floor and began polishing them with a handkerchief, as if this had been his innocent occupation when St. Paul barged in.

"Madame de Maintenon is concerned. We do not want a repetition of the fiasco at the masquerade," he said.

"I might remind you, Monsieur le Comte, that the ladder—and the costume—were your idea!"

St. Paul ignored him. "The sketches, if you please."

With reluctance, Lully produced the drawings for Émilie's costume for Alceste. It was the usual thing, very heavy and ornate. Lots of jewels and gold thread.

"Thank you," said St. Paul. "This will do." He departed, a little smile on his lips as he closed the door behind him.

"This will do! Who does he think he is?" Lully asked Pierre, who dropped the shoe on the floor and then began to massage the composer's shoulders. Lully sat on the divan and closed his eyes. "You'd better stay away for a while," he said to the youth, who kissed him on the forehead before quietly slipping out the door.

⌒

From one of the high windows of the palace, Émilie could see a corner of the garden that was somewhat overgrown, a little wilderness where the ladies seldom walked, especially when the ground was damp from a recent rain. Whenever she could escape from François's constant vigilance, she tried to reach this haven before anyone discovered she was missing. Usually she was intercepted on her way and gently guided back into safer territory. But on this day François was occupied with other things, and everyone was preparing for the visit of an ambassador, so she actually managed to attain her goal. She thought when she was there that she was probably far enough away to sing something without being heard. She could, at last, sing one of Charpentier's airs.

Émilie began her song, trying to keep her voice small so that it would not sail out over the landscape and creep into the open windows of Versailles. She looked away from the magnificent edifice that loomed behind her, and that she had come to feel was almost a prison, and sent the tones of her voice into the countryside. No one actually locked her in or tied her up, but she had no access to a carriage, and even if she wanted to make the trek back to Paris on foot, she did not know the way. It would hardly do to ask. All her questions about going home for a visit had been met with silence or evasion, as if no one could understand why anyone would want to return to a humble workshop when she had the opportunity to live at the greatest court on earth. And then there was this impossible-sounding scheme that Madame de Montespan had told her about. Why it was necessary for her to flee so furtively, in the middle of the night after her début, she could not figure out. It would be so much easier just to go home for a visit. Then she could decide whether to come back or not. She knew that if she ran away without permission, she would have to sever all ties with Versailles, and no matter how appealing Madame de Montespan made the idea of being with Charpentier again, she wasn't entirely certain that was what she wanted.

To chase away these confusing thoughts, Émilie sang. Before long the birds began to chime in. The gardens at Versailles were full of rare and exotic creatures that had been captured in other locations and then brought to the park to entertain the courtiers and the king with their gaudy plumage and their unearthly songs. There seemed to be quite a concentration of them, there in that carefully landscaped wilderness. Although they remained generally out of sight, it pleased Émilie that they blended their songs with hers, and when she tried to imitate them, they sometimes answered back. Wouldn't it be wonderful, she thought, if I could tell that nightingale to go and sing a message to Monsieur Charpentier?

Émilie was quite lost in this fantasy, imagining that her spirit and that of her former teacher could meet somewhere in the air, and that they could sing together again, and trip over the clouds to arrive back in Paris, when François cleared his throat behind her. She jumped.

"I apologize, Mademoiselle," he said with a bow, "but your presence is requested by the ladies. They would like you to sing them an air while they drink their tea."

"Can't one of the other singers do it for once?" Émilie asked, vexed at having to end her pleasant reverie.

"You know that there is no one who sings as you do. Now that they have heard you, only your voice will do."

"I should be flattered, I know. But why is the king never there when I sing?"

"I don't know. I think perhaps Madame de Maintenon wants to prepare a wonderful surprise for His Majesty, so that he will hear you for the first time in *Alceste*."

"Why is everything so calculated here, so planned?" Émilie kicked her foot into the ground, sending a little clod of grass and dirt scattering over the wildflowers.

"I cannot say, Mademoiselle."

"Cannot, or will not? François, who should I ask if I may go home for a visit?"

"You mean *whom.*" François thought for a moment or two. "I believe that Madame de Maintenon would be the person who would have it in her power to grant you that."

"Do you think I can go to see her?"

François looked away from Émilie. "It can be difficult to arrange. As tutor to the king's . . . children, she is much occupied. And when she is not attending to the education of others, or advising the king, she is generally at prayer."

"Oh, never mind, François. If it's so difficult . . . I'll race you back to Latona!"

Before François could protest, Émilie lifted her skirts and started running toward the fountain. He chased after her, partly for fear of being admonished for not keeping a close eye on his charge, partly because he liked to run and seldom had any excuse to do so. Émilie's silvery laugh faded into the distance as he did his best to catch up.

Thirteen

Virtue is just as useful to self-interest as vice.
Maxim 187

The morning of her birthday, September 18, Émilie awoke in a petulant mood. She had taken care during the previous weeks to mention to François that she was about to attain her sixteenth year and had dropped little hints to everyone—even St. Paul—whenever she got the chance. She had written of it in a letter to Charpentier, trying not to make it too obvious that she wanted him to acknowledge it in some special way. But all morning no one said a word, and no messenger brought her a crisply folded and wax-sealed letter with that telltale, elegant scrawl. She had her singing lesson just as usual and could barely bring herself to utter a sound, she was feeling so upset.

"Ah, *mon Dieu!* Where is your voice?" Lully strode up and down the room with his hands clasped behind his back and then stopped. "You are ill, perhaps?"

Émilie shook her head no, and sang again, trying to do better.

"That is more like it, Mademoiselle Émilie. There is no room for temperament here. You are too young, and too easily replaced."

Lully's comment was cruel, but Émilie knew it was true. She wanted to say, "And why don't you replace me then?" But in her heart she knew that the idea of singing the role of Alceste had grown on her, and that she would have been very sorry to lose the opportunity now. So she sang with more effort, more feeling.

When the lesson was over, Émilie stayed and gazed out of the window at the remnants of a mist that gradually burned off in the brilliant sunlight. The gardens were deserted, so there was no one to watch. In the distance a thin wash of high clouds clung to the horizon.

"*Ahem,*" said François. Émilie jumped before she realized it was just her friend. "I am here to escort you to Madame de Maintenon, who wishes to extend her felicitations on your sixteenth birthday." At that, François held out a small parcel to her. It was wrapped in plain paper with a bit of silk cord holding it shut. The bright look on his face told Émilie that this was his gift, not Madame de Maintenon's.

She opened the parcel, making no effort to hide her pleasure that François had indeed understood her hints. It contained a paintbrush and a few watercolors.

"Oh, thank you, François! For this, and—for arranging things!" exclaimed Émilie, embracing him. He patted her on the back and gently pushed her away.

"Now, we must go to Madame de Maintenon."

Although Madame de Maintenon was a constant, looming presence, Émilie had only ever seen her with other people in the room. She knew that the lady kept an eye on her through François, and she had some inkling that it was Madame de Maintenon who, through St. Paul, had worked to bring her to Versailles. But it still mystified her why this important and severe lady might have an interest in someone as insignificant as herself. Unlike the Marquise de Montespan, she did not seem to have any particular sensitivity to music or to enjoy the sound of Émilie's voice. She usually left the room when Émilie sang at the ladies' card parties.

And yet here Émilie was being granted a private interview. It was quite an honor. The gossip Émilie heard as she circulated around the card tables was that even if her beauty did not equal that of Madame de Montespan, and even if the king still went to Madame de Montespan, his official favorite, in the afternoon for a private "conversation," it was Madame de Maintenon to whom the king really listened. So Émilie, determined not to squander her opportunity to be granted a visit home, prepared her request as she went, trying to think of the most deferential way possible to broach the subject. She thought perhaps of intimating that her father was ill and she needed to see him. Something told her that she would need more than just homesickness as an excuse to be allowed to make the trip.

The memory of her interview with Madame de Montespan was still fresh in her mind, so Émilie prepared herself for even more grandeur in the apartments of the incoming favorite as she followed François through the inner corridors of the château.

But nothing at Versailles was ever as one expected. By the standards of the court, Madame de Maintenon led an austere life. There was little furniture within the small suite of rooms she inhabited. An ornate crucifix was the only ornament that interrupted the surface of her barren white walls. In the center of her sitting room, attired in simple black, the widow Scarron stood out more imposingly by far than if she had chosen to bedeck herself in a rainbow of jewels and silks. Although Madame de Maintenon had a reputation for piety and good works, this cold setting made her seem rather sinister. Émilie could not help seeing her as a spider at the center of an invisible web, waiting for her prey to enter and not moving a muscle. Her two attendant footmen, instead of blending into a rich background, stood out against the white walls like flies she had already stunned and wrapped in silk to be enjoyed at a later time.

"Mademoiselle Émilie Jolicoeur, the king sends you his felicitations on the attainment of your sixteenth year."

Émilie curtseyed deeply and rose. How could the king have known it was her birthday? And why would he care? She was so taken aback that she failed to notice that Madame de Maintenon did not invite her to be seated.

"In a few weeks, you will take part in a very important state occasion. Monsieur de St. Paul informs me that you progress satisfactorily in your rehearsals for the role of Alceste. The king has commanded the performance, and I am pleased to hear that you undertake it with an air of seriousness and decorum. But your role on the stage is only one part of the service I shall ask you to render to the Crown."

She paused. Émilie thought that what she had said sounded like a well-rehearsed speech. Her face, which most people described as handsome rather than beautiful, was serene and unmoving. Her eyes and her hair were dark, her skin of a pale olive cast. Even the light that smoldered in her brown eyes seemed to be carefully controlled. She moved with dignity rather than grace, and if the occasion did not require it, did not move at all. Her entire essence was the very opposite of the graceful mobility of the Marquise de Montespan.

"Later on the evening of your performance, I have reason to believe that the king will confer upon you a great honor, one that you would never deserve were it not for your peculiarly beautiful voice—a gift you owe to God alone."

If her voice was so beautiful, Émilie thought, why did Madame de Maintenon never stay to listen to her? Émilie did not take her eyes off the widow Scarron, who walked slowly around the room, looking at the spines of the books on her shelves as if seeking inspiration there for what to say next. Her black gown sucked in the light that poured through her windows so that she became a focal point of negative space.

"Today your father has been granted a pension to be the official luthier of the king—" Émilie's gasp of pleasure interrupted Madame de Maintenon's recital for only a moment. "But there is a much more important task ahead for you. For what I am about to say I demand the utmost discretion on your part. Should you be tempted to make capital of the knowledge you will receive, I might remind you that favors can as easily be taken away as granted."

Émilie lowered her eyes and bowed her head.

"The king has hitherto been under the sway of principles that are less than godly. Those who would ingratiate themselves to him have done so by seeking to supply his every pleasure. These people are the enemies of his salvation."

Émilie waited for her to continue, waited for her opportunity to bring up her request to visit her family.

"On the evening of your performance as Alceste, there will be a grand feast and ball. After this, you will be summoned to the king's bedchamber. He will have eased his troubled mind—a mind much occupied by matters of state and by the necessity to lead his armies against his enemies—by becoming enflamed with wine, and this will cause him to desire the pleasure of amusement with the leading lady of the ensemble who performed for him that afternoon. In a mere man, this would be a weakness—regrettable, but of no great moment. In a monarch, it is something with much more serious implications."

This conversation—or rather, lecture—did not so far present any opportunity for Émilie to make her request to be permitted to visit her parents. But that was not the only disquieting element of her encounter with the widow Scarron. The lady appeared to have some purpose in mind, and that purpose had something to do with Émilie's being ushered to the king's bedchamber in the middle of the night. This, thought Émilie, was precisely what Madame de Montespan had warned her about.

"I beg your pardon, Madame," said Émilie, "but why would *I* be asked to attend the king in his bedchamber?"

Émilie's question stopped Madame de Maintenon in her tracks. "Surely you cannot be unaware of such things? You are old enough, I think, to understand the ways of the world." For the first time since Émilie entered, the widow Scarron looked her full in the face. She did not say anything for a few moments but stared hard, as though by doing so she could pierce through Émilie's skin. "I see that you have remained an innocent. That is a rare accomplishment in such a place as this, and I congratulate you on it. However, that fact changes nothing."

Émilie wished that François had remained in the room so that she could ask him later what it all meant. Her head was aching with confusion about where she fit in to the elaborate mosaic that was called the court. She thought she was just a hired entertainer, the latest novelty who was fed and clothed in exchange for being constantly available to help the courtiers while away the long hours of attendance upon the king and queen. But here was the person whom everyone acknowledged would soon be the most powerful woman in the realm telling her that she was there for some other reason. Worse still, it appeared to be a reason that had been foretold by the other powerful lady in the court, one who was the avowed enemy of Madame de Maintenon. So she was to answer the king's summons to his bed-chamber late at night after the performance of *Alceste*. What next?

"You must go to the king's apartments as though you intend to oblige him in his every desire." Madame de Maintenon approached Émilie until she was so close that Émilie could feel the warmth of the lady's breath on her ear. "But, God willing, you will not be required to make the ultimate sacrifice of your virtue. I cannot tell you more at the moment, but you must trust that events will occur that will turn the king's attention away from you, and in doing so, away from all such earthly temptations."

Madame de Maintenon took a step away from her and said, "Tell me, do you know your rosary?"

The question, spoken in a normal tone of voice and therefore quite loud compared to the near whisper of her previous sentence, caught Émilie off guard. She squeaked out an affirmative reply.

"Let us say it together. Come, kneel by me." Madame de Main-tenon took Émilie's arm and drew her toward the prie-dieu. Her grip was strong, like the claw of an eagle.

"Hail, Mary, full of grace . . ."

Émilie's knees hurt by the time they finished. To her surprise, imme-diately after they ended their litany, Madame de Maintenon fastened an exquisite string of large pearls around her neck.

"Pearls are for purity," she said.

"Please, Madame," Émilie groped for words. "There is something I would much rather have than pearls."

Madame de Maintenon stood back and lowered her eyelids just a little, hardly enough to be described as narrowing her eyes at Émilie.

"I would like, please, to be able to bring the news of his pension to my father in person."

The widow Scarron let out her breath as if she had been holding it while Émilie spoke. "I'm afraid that is impossible at the moment. You simply cannot be spared from court. And although your filial affection does you credit, you must understand that you have left that world behind."

Émilie lowered her eyes and curtseyed. She wanted to ask Madame de Maintenon if she had any family living that no one would allow her to visit, but she already knew that the lady was an orphan as well as a widow. Émilie could not think of another question that might hurt her; she wished she could yank off the pearls she had just been given and throw them in the widow Scarron's face.

As soon as the door to Madame de Maintenon's apartments closed behind her, Émilie stormed off to her room. When she arrived, she slammed the door and locked it, then picked up the book of essays she was trying to read and hurled it across the room. It made a mark on the wall. She paced back and forth, chewing on her finger-nails and muttering to herself.

"Why me? What do they want from me?" She stopped suddenly and sat down at her desk, took a sheet of paper and dipped her quill into the ink pot. Instead of writing anything, she scribbled on the sheet, tearing through it and leaving ink spots on the wood beneath. The wish to destroy something was so strong that she thought of rip-ping her beautiful gown to shreds. But she knew she would get in trouble. Instead, she bit the sides of her thumbs until they bled, and pounded on the surface of the desk until her fists were bruised. *"I hate you!"* she screamed, and then burst into tears.

∾

Once Émilie was gone, Madame de Maintenon sent the footmen away and sat at her desk. She picked up a quill but did not write. Sometimes it helped her think, just to hold the quill in her hand. After a few moments of contemplation, she reached for the bell but did not pick it up. Instead she drew a sheet of paper out of the desk drawer and dipped the quill in the ink. For several minutes only the sound of scratching against paper broke the stillness of her room.

When she finished writing her letter, Madame de Maintenon folded and sealed it, then rang the bell. It was answered almost immediately by a footman.

"Deliver this to François," she said. The footman took the note, bowed, and left.

Alone again, the widow Scarron knelt at her prie-dieu. The instructions she just sent to François, if they were ever intercepted, could send her to prison. She had told him to ask the wine steward for a particular vintage to serve to Émilie late on the night of her performance. This "vintage" was their secret signal for lacing a fine claret with sublimate, a slow-acting poison. By the time Émilie arrived in the king's apartments, she would be very ill indeed, possibly near death. Madame de Maintenon picked up her rosary, knitted her fingers together, and began to pray. "Dear Lord, give me the strength to carry through this plan, and forgive me for the harm I may cause to an innocent creature. It is for a greater good, for your glory. I shall bring you a prize worthy of immense sacrifice. I shall bring you the soul of a king. Amen."

Fourteen

If one judges love mostly by its effects,
it resembles hate more than friendship.

Maxim 72

When Charpentier arrived at the Atelier Jolicoeur one fine September afternoon riding a magnificent destrier, passersby stopped and stared. The horse was far more beast than one needed simply to get around Paris comfortably. Charpentier left it stamping and fretting, tied to the post outside the workshop on the Pont au Change, while he went in to share his latest letter from Émilie with Marcel. He knew it was a slight risk to let the luthier know that he and Émilie exchanged letters, but it seemed cruel not to do as Émilie asked him and convey news between the family members, separated for the first time in Émilie's life.

"She will make her début in a week!" he said, scanning the paper for details that might be interesting to the luthier. Charpentier explained that it was a great honor for Émilie to be cast in the lead in one of Lully's *tragédies lyriques,* and that it was very good for Émilie's career. He described the grandeur of the role itself, explaining how Alceste consented to be sacrificed for the sake of her husband, and for her magnificent gesture was brought to life again by the gods.

"Hah!" exclaimed Marcel. "No woman would do such a thing. If she did, she would be a fool. For what man, in his heart, could ask it of her, if he truly loved her?"

Charpentier listened with only half his attention. His mind was racing with all that was ahead of him. He wished he could share his secret with Marcel. The luthier would be happy to know Émilie was coming back to Paris. But, then, would he be happy to know by what means, and for what reason?

"And does she eat well still?" Marcel asked.

"She does not often speak of the food. But she does not complain, so that must mean something!" Charpentier was eager to give Marcel any morsel of information that would set his mind at rest.

"What of the fine ladies and gentlemen? I know my wife would like to hear some of the gossip."

"Émilie does not repeat gossip to me. I expect she's too young to hear much of it. Sometimes she sings to entertain the ladies at cards, and she says that their gowns are very fine and that they wear many jewels." By now Charpentier was fabricating news simply to feed Marcel's desire for information about the life his daughter was leading. "And it sounds as if they keep her very busy with her lessons. She is learning to draw now."

Marcel looked into Charpentier's eyes. "Does she say when she will come home to visit?"

Charpentier looked away. He longed to tell Marcel the truth, but he dared not. "No, she mentions no visit. I think it is difficult. She has no one to bring her, and she must do as they say." He folded up the letter and tucked it into his waistcoat. "I must leave you now," he said to the luthier.

The two men walked out to the street. "Good-bye, Marcel."

"God speed, Monsieur Charpentier." Marcel held the reins of Charpentier's horse close to the bit so that the composer could mount. He continued to gaze at Charpentier, as if he were waiting for him to say something more.

But Charpentier simply looked around at the crowd, whose eyes were drawn to the beautiful bay horse, smiled at Marcel, and trotted off in the direction of the Hôtel de Guise.

As he let the horse take his leisurely way back to the rue du Chaume, Charpentier's mind was occupied with everything that was ahead. He wanted to shout from the rooftops that soon he would have Émilie back, soon he would once again be able to hear her magnificent voice sing his music.

But no sooner did he feel this uncontrollable elation than in the next instant he was assailed by doubts. It all seemed so fantastic, so unlikely. Perhaps it was a trick, and they were both being used. Charpentier hoped that there was nothing out of the ordinary about the dangers Émilie faced. Many a pretty serving girl had caught her master's eye, but once removed, was soon forgotten. Yet in his heart he feared there was more to the entire thing than he could see from his vantage point in Paris. Émilie was pretty, but it was her voice that caused him alarm. When she gave herself to the music, when she let it take her over, she became a vessel for something beyond the notes themselves. She was possessed, she became another being, and to witness this transformation was to be transformed oneself.

More than anything, Charpentier wanted his music to possess Émilie again. The thought of Lully's music passing through Émilie's body and having this effect on her drove him nearly mad.

As often happened at these distracted moments, Charpentier began to form in his mind the contours of a melody. It would lie in the upper middle range of the female voice, the range that suited Émilie best. He would find a text, a poem, and then work melody and words until they fit each other as if they had been conceived in the same moment. Then he would write the air down in his notebook with others of its kind. There it would remain, unperformed like all the songs for *haut dessus* he had composed since Émilie left, waiting for her to come back and bring them to life. They were his gift to her voice.

Sophie found out very little from reading Émilie's letters to Charpentier. Her dogged surveillance of the composer yielded much more, however. She knew that something was going to happen soon. It was too easy to read the signs. To begin with, she had seen Charpentier take a letter from the hand of a lady in an unmarked coach, and then noticed Charpentier's subsequent restless and preoccupied behavior as he moved about the city. It was obvious to her that some scheme had been hatched. She had not yet discovered the exact day, time, or manner of the event, but she counted on her near invisibility to give her a certain advantage, and Sophie was quite confident that she would be one step ahead of the composer whatever course he planned to take.

The biggest clue that something was soon to happen came when one day Sophie followed Charpentier to a livery stable, and heard him instruct the groom to make sure his horse was well fed, clean, and ready to be ridden in three days' time, at nine in the evening.

That was it—the information she had been waiting for. Charpentier had bought a horse and was going to carry Émilie away, she thought. Sophie wondered who was pulling the strings from Versailles. Clearly this was the final result of those letters from some unknown hand. She wished she were better informed about court matters. In her present mode of life, it would be difficult to get gossip from ladies, who were usually much more on top of things than men. But some of the men she knew were close enough to the inner circle to supply, quite inadvertently, vital facts. She knew, for instance, that the king went less frequently to Madame de Montespan's boudoir these days and that he was often to be seen in deep conversation with the governess, Madame de Maintenon.

Sophie returned immediately to her room, forgoing her afternoon take to spend the next few hours figuring out the most effective way to ruin Charpentier's plans. She decided fairly quickly that the best thing to do would be to alert someone at Versailles about the impending abduction. The trick was to write something revealing without identifying herself so that she could send it to Versailles and avoid any personal risk.

> *To the attention of . . . ,*
> *A person who wishes you well in your endeavors seeks to inform your ladyship/lordship that a certain young singer is carrying on a secret correspondence . . .*

She stroked the bottom of her chin with the stiff, pointy feathers on the end of her quill, looked at what she had written, then took the paper and crumpled it up, tossing it angrily on the floor. Around her dainty feet were half a dozen dried-up orange peels, two empty wine bottles, and a quantity of similarly crumpled balls of paper. She sat on the edge of the bed in her stays and stockings and leaned on an old wine barrel she had fashioned into a makeshift desk.

"It just doesn't sound believable!" she said aloud to Monsieur le Diable, who narrowed his eyes and purred a little more loudly, while he lounged next to her and languidly dug his claws into the straw of the bed. "What do I know, after all? They've been so goddamned clever!"

Now that she had the final bit of information she needed—a time and a date—all that was necessary was to write the letter, and Sophie would foil an abduction that doubtless involved Émilie. Why was it so difficult to find the right words?

"What if they don't believe me?" And then there was the question of whom to send it to. She knew that if she addressed her letter directly to the king, it would probably never reach him, and if it did, he would dismiss it as some vindictive misinformation. And if she sent it to Madame de Montespan, there might be other hazards. She had heard that the king's mistress was spending more and more of her time at Clagny, and she feared that news might take a while to filter through to her, so she might not act as quickly as necessary. Besides, if there was any chance that Émilie could engage the king's affections,

Madame de Montespan would quite likely prefer the abduction to succeed.

"I know!" Sophie said after a pause, taking up her quill with renewed enthusiasm. In a few short minutes she had written what she knew was the letter she would send.

> To the attention of Madame de Maintenon,
>   Your pretty songbird has plans to fly away. Watch for a man on a large bay horse, around midnight, on the fifth.

Although Sophie had no idea whether the stern, devout widow Scarron had anything at all to do with Émilie, she thought the odds were even that she might be interested in preventing a defection from court, especially if what Sophie had heard was true, that the widow was working her way up in the king's esteem and would do anything to oust Madame de Montespan.

Sophie put down her quill and stood up. Her elbows cracked as she stretched her soft, white arms over her head and yawned. When she brought them down, she scraped her knuckles on the rough plaster. If she stood sideways to the window, there was hardly an arm span between two of the walls of her room. Sophie remembered the vastness of Versailles. How she loved to dance in the Salle de Bal! It was there that the king had noticed her. But she had no illusions. She would have ended up doing exactly what she was doing now, only in finer clothes and in more elegant surroundings. And yet that would still have been something.

After carefully sealing the letter with a nub of sealing wax she had borrowed from a notary with a penchant for being spanked, and a hot ember from the tiny stove in the corner of her room, Sophie leaned the finished missive up against the mirror, then got down on her hands and knees and looked beneath her bed.

"Yecchhh!" she said. Monsieur le Diable had deposited a half-eaten mouse carcass there. No wonder it smelled so bad! But although she preferred to be clean, tidy, and organized herself, she left this place dirty on purpose, to discourage nosiness in her land-lady. Tucked under the boards of her bed was a little leather pouch, which Sophie gently released from the groove that held it fast. She untied the drawstring of the pouch and emptied its contents onto the rough woolen blanket.

"Five, ten, twenty-five, forty!" Sophie counted with satisfaction. It was enough to purchase a fine dress, rent a better room, and make a fresh start. Sophie weighed the sealed letter in one hand and her hoard of coins in the other. She could forget all about Émilie and Charpentier if she wanted to. She could leave them to the luck of their own folly and walk away from this degrading life she had been forced to pursue for more than six months. Sophie had decided that instead of returning to a life of service, she would become an actress. Drawing herself up and adopting a regal air, she opened her mouth and began to sing a comic song. Her voice was husky and rough, but she could carry a tune. She stood and tried to mark the steps of a dance in the tiny space of her room. When she finished her performance, Sophie placed herself so that she could see almost her entire body in her little mirror. She ran her hands over its firm, youthful contours. All she needed was stays and a decent dress, and she could pass for a fine lady. Her present cir-cumstances were only temporary. "I could have stopped any time before this. I had three proposals of marriage, I did!" she said to Monsieur le Diable once more, who opened his eyes wide suddenly, as if he did not actually believe her.

Sophie gathered up her treasure and hid it away again. Then she picked up the letter and fanned her face with it as she stared out of her window. Why should Émilie not have to suffer the conse-quences of her actions? she thought. Sophie noticed that the sky was becoming dark. Time to go out on the streets and earn a little more money for her nest egg. After she put on a dress that was hiked up very high on one side, and a cloak that she could open to reveal the leg the dress did not cover, Sophie put the letter in her pocket. She decided to let luck be her guide. If she happened to see the valet she knew who was acquainted with a groom who, in exchange for a little sex, could get the letter to Versailles by tomorrow, then she would send it. If it remained in her pocket by the end of her night's work, she would burn it and think no more of the wretched slippers. She patted Monsieur le Diable on the head, then walked out of her tiny room into the cool autumn night.

Fifteen

Hypocrisy is the homage that vice pays to virtue.
Maxim 218

The ladies were all gathered in the queen's apartments playing cards. Even though she knew that the Marquise de Montespan had become her husband's acknowledged lover, Queen Marie-Thérèse could not give up the pleasure of the company of the most beautiful woman at court. It was the only way, indeed, to ensure that the ladies attended her in the evening, since everyone followed where Montespan led. Although she did not much like knowing that she had lost her husband's affection, the queen had no desire to languish alone. And besides, her taste for gaming was indulged most willingly by the courtiers.

Her command of French was still somewhat patchy, and so the queen did not understand that her foreign ways and unattractive appearance made her a laughingstock in society. The marriage was the result of a political alliance; there was little passion on the side of the king. He did his duty and fathered several children by her, but Marie-Thérèse was deemed to have no style, no esprit. In the cruel world where the ability to turn a phrase was the ultimate measure of social value, she was fair game for any jest or scheme. Only her estranged husband, ever chivalrous toward all ladies, treated her with any respect. He had just returned from a successful campaign in Belgium, and was feeling particularly kindly disposed toward her. She was in an excellent mood.

And so the most shocking things happened right under the queen's nose, and she was none the wiser. That evening was no different.

"I need you to arrange for some money to be sent to someone in Paris." Madame de Montespan spoke to one of her own ladies-in-waiting, who stood next to her at the card table the night before *Alceste*. Her eyes were ablaze with the pleasure of winning enormous sums from the queen, which she would return to her later. It was not seemly to take advantage of poor Marie-Thérèse's hopeless inability at cards.

"How much?"

"One hundred louis!" It was the queen, who overheard the lady and assumed she was asking her the amount of her wager.

"Twenty louis," murmured Madame de Montespan, smiling across the table at the queen. "One hundred and ten," she said aloud, and the queen licked her lips, preparing to bet again. The marquise opened her fan and spoke behind it to her lady. "See that it gets to the Hôtel de Guise tomorrow."

St. Paul, who attended the evening at the behest of Madame de Maintenon (who never wagered, considering it immoral and wasteful), walked past the queen's table just in time to hear the tail end of Madame de Montespan's aside. After completing his circuit of the room, he slipped away unnoticed.

Madame de Maintenon was already in her nightclothes, and had finished her hour of prayer before preparing to sleep, when she heard the scratch at her door.

"Who is it?"

"St. Paul. I must speak with you. It's urgent."

The widow Scarron put on her black shawl, then unlocked the door. "You had better be quick. No one must see you here at this hour!"

"I heard something, just now. La Montespan is sending money to the Hôtel de Guise. I think it must be for the musician."

"The musician?"

"The one who receives Mademoiselle Émilie's letters."

"But François told me there was nothing important in the correspondence."

"There hasn't been. They must have some other way of communicating. I fear, Madame, that they are planning an abduction. I think it will take place after the performance tomorrow night."

Madame de Maintenon lit another candle, bringing her small room into a little less obscurity. "Thank you for telling me this, Monsieur de St. Paul." She held out her hand to the count.

"But Madame, we must do something!"

"You have performed a great service to me, and to His Majesty. Thank you."

There was nothing for St. Paul to do but to kiss her hand and leave.

Once she was alone, the widow Scarron went again to her priedieu and knelt. Her features, so often in a state of tense concentration, relaxed. If what St. Paul said was true, the matter was conveniently out of her hands. No longer would she be forced to risk discovery as the person who had taken extreme measures to deny the king his pleasure, nor even the one who had chosen a method that would be sure to implicate Madame de Montespan in that occurrence. The marquise had played right into her hands. Tomorrow she would reverse her instructions to François—provided St. Paul's suspicion proved to be true. She could find a way to make the moral lesson just as strong, even if the king did not hold the dying object of his passion in his arms.

"Thank you, my Lord. You have truly heard the desires of my heart." Never had Madame de Maintenon's prayers been more sincere.

St. Paul returned to his chamber on the lower floor of the château in a state of disbelief. He had been dismissed by the widow Scarron again! And after bringing her such important information.

"Monsieur, allow me." Jacques, the retainer St. Paul had inherited along with his father's debts, held his hands out in readiness to help him undress.

Lifting his arms to the side to facilitate the process, St. Paul asked, "What is it, Jacques, that the king desires more than anything in the world?"

"It is not for me to say, Monsieur," he answered, easing the count's heavy brocade coat off his shoulders and down his arms.

"Precisely, good fellow. But supposing," St. Paul continued, lifting his chin so the valet could untie the knot of lace and remove his collar, "one were to make a lucky guess. And that then," St. Paul turned to allow the valet to untie his breeches, "one were able to supply it in a manner that would be unforgettable to him. What do you think might happen?"

Jacques smoothed out his master's clothes and laid them on the chair. "Then the king must surely be extremely grateful."

"Exactly." The valet approached St. Paul with his nightclothes. The count held out his hand to stop him, as if he had heard a voice from far away. After a moment, he said, "Jacques, dress me."

The valet's arms dropped and his mouth hung open for just an instant before it snapped shut. "Yes, Monsieur," he said, and then carefully unfolded each item he had removed from his master only moments ago and helped St. Paul back into his clothing.

When the process was complete, St. Paul instructed his servant to let anyone who asked know that he had gone to Paris to visit his godmother. Then he snuffed the candle with his fingers, leaving Jacques in the dark when he closed the door of his room.

～

The next morning Madame de Maintenon summoned François.

"Madame." He bowed deeply.

"I had a visit from St. Paul last night," she said. "He tells me that there may be an abduction after the performance. Do you know anything about this?"

François went hot and cold at the same time. It had been his idea to promote a correspondence between Émilie and Charpentier, and he had carefully vetted all the letters. Did he miss something that he should have reported to his mistress? He knew that, just as she had the power to make him comfortable and secure for the rest of his life, Madame de Maintenon could also manage the reverse. "I swear to you, Madame, that there was nothing in the letters that indicated this possibility."

The widow Scarron brought her eyebrows together almost imperceptibly so that only the hint of tension was visible in her brow. "And there have been no other letters? You are certain?"

"None, Madame. I don't know how to prove it to you, but the girl is incapable of plotting, of that I am certain."

"I believe you, François," she said. "I just wanted to know for sure. You are clear about your instructions?" she asked.

"Yes, Madame," François said. He was altogether too clear. He had become quite fond of Émilie, despite knowing where his interest lay. Her candor and innocence had taken some getting used to, but now he generally believed what she said, and knew that she considered him her friend. If there were any way to avoid delivering the tainted wine, he would have leapt at it. Any way, that is, except putting his own head into Madame de Maintenon's metaphorical noose.

"Remember, you are not to take her to the king's apartment a moment before the appointed time. And once she is there, you must wait for her outside His Majesty's door. I have reason to believe she will not remain for very long." Madame de Maintenon walked to her window. "Thank you, François. And now, would you please tell Monsieur de St. Paul that I wish to see him?"

"I beg your pardon, Madame, but the count is not here."

She turned. "Not here? When did he leave?"

"Sometime last night."

"Do you know where he went?" she asked.

"To his godmother's, in Paris."

"Thank you. You may go."

François closed the door behind him.

"Fool!" said Madame de Maintenon to her empty parlor. His actions seemed to confirm that he was no longer trustworthy. Certainly she had more cause to believe her faithful servant, whose future rested securely in her hands, than the opportunistic Comte de St. Paul. Still, it was vexing. Her dangerous plan was not to be altered after all. The widow Scarron sat at her desk and began reading her morning correspondence. The frown she wore persisted for the rest of the day.

Sixteen

Usually one praises in order to be praised.
Maxim 146

In her heart, Émilie knew she could do it. She knew she was ready to enter fully into the role of Alceste, to breathe the tragic heroine's sufferings and triumphs into life and lay them—whole, deep, and round—before an audience. While the outcome of her own drama was far from certain, Émilie wandered around in Alceste's dilemmas safe in the knowledge that the opera would go well. This was one thing that being at Versailles could not change. No matter what intrigues they tried to create around her, the moment of performance itself was completely inviolable.

Surrounded by the rest of the cast, Émilie marked her part on the wooden stage that had been erected over the black and white marble surface of the courtyard, walking through the positions and gestures that would accompany the notes and words that her heart knew and had long since made her own. The costumers were busy making the final adjustments to the splendid robes she would wear, and at one corner of the stage, Lully coached the chorus of soldiers, who had to look as though they were doing battle while they sang.

Over in another corner, the corps de ballet—which was composed entirely of men, whether they were meant to be fairies or demons—was trying to figure out how to translate the leaps and turns they had practiced indoors to this capricious, damp surface. Monsieur Dubuffet yelled "Soft knees!" every few minutes, so that his words began to sound nonsensical. Émilie watched Monsieur Chicanneau try to execute an *entrechat quatre;* when he landed, his feet went out from beneath him on the slick floor. He ended up on his behind. The others laughed but extended their hands to help him stand. Émilie knew that if she fell, no one would pull her up again.

Her eyes left the group of dancers and returned to Lully, who now instructed Mademoiselle de La Garde concerning where she should walk during her big scene with Monsieur Langeais. Lully was so different from Charpentier. Although Émilie knew that her former singing teacher craved a court appointment and had ambitions to be more well known and successful, she could not imagine him in this setting. He was too honest and open—at least, he appeared that way to her. Here no one said what he really thought, and she had come to understand that it was hazardous to take anything at face value. Every day she heard courtiers contradict one another behind each other's backs, all jockeying for a position close to the king in a court where being invisible was worse than being dead.

The attitudes of the courtiers seemed to infect everyone at Versailles. The singers in Lully's troupe, for instance, were unyielding in their refusal to accept Émilie because she had jumped the queue, had usurped a prize place where royal notice was guaranteed. And Lully himself—propinquity had not improved Émilie's opinion of the composer. He had a secretive air, and she particularly disliked the pretty valet who followed him about like one of the queen's lapdogs. Sometimes, simply out of loyalty to Charpentier, Émilie wished she could withhold her finest singing from Lully's music for *Alceste.* But once she started, she became the character whose words she sang and could no longer hold back the overwhelming flood of emotion that possessed her. Whatever his personal vices, Lully had an unerring instinct for the rhythm latent in the words, the shifting, breathing meters, and the expressive lines, and the resultant airs were too adept for Émilie to mishandle. Despite her wishes, the sound that emerged when she opened her mouth ennobled the music to a degree that even its composer had never imagined before.

All at once a commotion began in the downstage right corner. It seemed to Émilie as if all the singers and coaches and dressmakers were stalks of wheat, and a wind had arisen out of nowhere that bent them, in a wave, to the ground. The instant before the wave reached Émilie and carried her with it, she saw the cause of this phenomenon. It was the king, resplendent in golden robes embroidered with diamonds. The stage cleared for his passage, and he took his stately way through the midst of the players. Lully came forward to greet him.

"It is Apollo, come to bless our endeavors," said the composer, with a deep, reverent bow.

To Émilie's amazement, the king put one hand on his hip and with the other gestured to the crowd of actors, and then began to sing the lines of the god Apollo from the tragedy:

> Today, the light will be taken from your eyes;
> There is only one way to prolong your fate!
> Destiny promises to return you to life,
> Only if someone else will offer to die in your place.
> Do you know if there is someone who bears you perfect love?
> His death will gain him immortal glory:
> To commemorate his sacrifice,
> The arts will build a magnificent monument in his honor.

The members of the orchestra quickly shuffled their sheets of manuscript paper to find the place in the score where the king had started singing, but because he began without them, he chose the key that was most comfortable for his voice, and it was not the one in which the part was written. The clash was excruciating. Lully gestured to the orchestra to stop playing. But Louis had a decent voice and certainly appeared most godlike. When he completed his *récit,* from the first act of the opera, in which the sun god descends to tell Admète how to avoid the fate that has been written in the stars, wild applause and loud bravos erupted from the crowd.

"Your Majesty," said Lully, bowing again, "your musical instincts are so fine, so superior. Could you give me the note you commenced with, so that I may rewrite the key which I so mistakenly chose? I can see that the music does not achieve true grandeur when it is pitched too high."

A scribe hurriedly appeared from nowhere and wrote down the note the harpsichord matched as the king sang it once again, then scurried off to recopy all the orchestra parts in the few hours remaining before the performance.

So that was it, Émilie thought. She had often wondered why the role of Apollo was only marked by one of the older singers. The king himself was to perform. She wondered how he knew the part so well. She suspected that perhaps he had sung it before.

After the rehearsal was over, Émilie made her way slowly back to her room. The voices of Madame de Maintenon and Madame de Montespan echoed in her head, arguing back and forth with each other.

"You must go to the king's bedchamber and throw yourself on his mercy," said the voice of Madame de Maintenon.

To which Madame de Montespan countered, "Don't be such a fool! Take your chance now, and go away with Monsieur Charpentier. Then you will be free."

But then the widow Scarron would crowd in again, saying, "If you do not do as I say, your soul will be eternally damned, and the king will not have his chance of salvation."

"If you do not do as I say, you will be the cause of my destruction and forfeit any chance of happiness in your life." Madame de Montespan's argument, even in Émilie's imagination, tugged at her heart almost irresistibly.

"God will punish you if you do not do as I tell you!"

Madame de Maintenon always had the last word in these imaginary arguments. It was difficult to refute the claims of the Almighty.

Émilie was frightened. Whatever action she took would provoke the wrath of one of the ladies, either of whom was powerful enough to make things very unpleasant for her as a result. She could not decide what would be worse: to find herself alone with the king for God knew what purpose, or to be caught in the act of trying to escape, and therefore condemned for some unspecified time to the horrors of Pignerol or the Bastille—or worse. More than anything, Émilie just wanted to close her eyes and then open them and find herself back at home on the Pont au Change.

~

Fourteen miles away, St. Paul walked back and forth in front of the servants' entrance of the Hôtel de Guise, stewing about the way Madame de Maintenon had used him. He had gone to a great deal of trouble and expense and put himself in some peril of losing whatever ground he had gained at court by allying himself exclusively with a woman who, however astute, was not yet in the position most coveted by any lady. It was a great risk to turn from Madame de Montespan. She was more adept than anyone else at plunging a knife into her enemies' backs.

When he revealed what he felt was certain evidence that La Montespan had been working to remove Émilie from court, St. Paul expected Madame de Maintenon to fly into action. Instead it appeared that she was content just to let the girl slip away from them. It made no sense at all. Everything they had talked about depended on inserting Émilie into the king's bed. How else was she planning to put a wedge between His Majesty and Montespan? And getting rid of Montespan was the idea, at least of that he was certain.

"The woman has lost her mind," St. Paul muttered. And with that possibility, he imagined his future no longer looking as rosy as it once did. Madame de Maintenon could as easily plunge him into obscurity as assist him to great fortune. He did not like being in a position where he was not in control of his own fate.

There was only one answer. He must take control again, even if it meant turning Madame de Maintenon against him. The groundwork had been laid. It was up to him to make sure that Émilie ended up in the arms of the king, and now it seemed that the way to do so was to prevent an abduction. St. Paul was prepared to take whatever measures were necessary, no matter how extreme. He ground his teeth as he paced. In his mind he enacted a scene where the widow Scarron apologized to him, acknowledging the brilliance of his foresight, the ingeniousness of his plans. At the end of his recital, he always imagined the king entering, and Madame de Maintenon telling His Majesty how clever he, St. Paul, had been. Then Louis would demonstrate his gratitude by endowing him with rich lands and a post that carried with it a handsome pension.

St. Paul's carriage was stationed around the corner, out of sight. His coachman, who only remained in St. Paul's employ because he was owed a king's ransom in wages and did not want to relinquish altogether any hope of getting them, watched the main gate. St. Paul was certain that Charpentier planned to act that day: if the couple waited, it would be too late. After tonight, what would be the point? The deed would have been done; Émilie's flower would have been plucked. He assumed that Charpentier's motives were, like everyone else's, base and self-serving. What other reason would the composer have for kidnapping Émilie and bringing her back to Paris if his ultimate aim was not to take her into his own bed?

He took out his pocket watch. It was only three in the afternoon, and his stomach growled audibly. Just at that moment a ragged young boy skipped by.

"You there!"

The boy stopped.

"Come here. I won't hurt you."

He approached St. Paul but stayed just out of the count's reach.

"How would you like to earn a few liards!"

"No way! I know your type!" The boy started to run off.

"It's not what you think, and I'll make it a silver écu."

The lad, who could not have been above ten years old, stopped again. A silver écu was a great deal of money. "What do you want?"

"I only want you to go and get me some bread to eat."

"Why can't you get it yourself?"

St. Paul thought for a moment. "I'm waiting to see someone very important, and I must stay here."

The boy shrugged. "I'll get you some bread."

"And a bit of cheese. And some wine. This should be plenty." St. Paul tossed the lad a few liards, barely enough to purchase a loaf of bread.

"I thought you said I was to get a silver écu."

"When you come back with the food."

"How do I know you'll pay?" the lad asked.

"I'm giving you money now, aren't I?"

For much of the day Charpentier stayed in his apartment and tried to keep his mind off the coming evening. He tidied up his papers and organized the parts for his new cantata, which was already neatly recorded in one of his notebooks. However chaotic the rest of his life, Charpentier was scrupulous about keeping his notebooks in order and dated. It was his legacy to the world, since he feared by now that he might never achieve the notice that would result in fine printed editions of his works. Even this comforting exercise, though, could not keep his mind off what was ahead. It had been almost a year since he had seen Émilie, and his image of her had simplified in his memory, had become distilled to the essential features: pale blond hair, light blue eyes, a build that was slight and straight, and a voice that, when it was raised, made everything else about her fade into the background.

For the twentieth time since breakfast, Charpentier mentally ran over the list of things he had arranged. His horse was to be saddled and ready at nine. He had a dark cloak in which to wrap Émilie so that she would not be cold on the midnight ride from Versailles to Paris. The key to the room was in his pocket. Charpentier had to force himself not to think about Émilie sleeping in the bed. Every so often, he picked up a letter that lay atop his desk, and read it again.

Monsieur Charpentier, all is arranged. You are to come to the Cour Royale, and look for a small door at the right side of the Cour de Marbre. Mademoiselle Émilie will meet you there at precisely a quarter to midnight.

Every time he cast his eye over the lines, Charpentier was filled once again with doubt. It seemed altogether too easy. Who would want to help them like this? Where was St. Paul? As the person who had taken Émilie from her family, he must have some vested interest in keeping her at Versailles. And then, Lully might not want to let her go. Having had the use of her voice for one of his lyric tragedies, he had undoubtedly come to understand what a jewel he possessed.

But all these worries were not powerful enough to obscure the image of Émilie seated behind him on the saddle, her arms about his waist. Together they would slice through the air that divided Versailles and Paris, their bodies and that of the horse cleaving the distance that had separated them for nearly a year. He wanted the black night to stitch itself back up behind them as they passed, hiding all trace of their path. Émilie did not belong to the court, she belonged to his music. She belonged to him.

∽

Émilie at last reached the door of her chamber, which she was very surprised to notice was standing wide open, with a cool breeze flowing through it. She walked in and saw a man's legs dangling into her room from the windowsill, his torso seated precariously on the outer edge of the window frame. Next to him on the outside was a long ladder that had been leaned up against the building from the Cour de Marbre, a ladder upon which another man perched.

"That's those three all set," said the workman whose body was half in and half out of Émilie's room. He wiggled forward and jumped down to the floor. His hands were filthy, and his pockets were full of nails and a hammer.

"I beg your pardon," said Émilie, not knowing how else to react.

"Hello, Mademoiselle," the workman said, tugging on the hair above his forehead. "All done now. Had to put the torches up on the roof for the performance," he explained as he left the room and shut the door behind him. Émilie went to the window and looked out. The ladder outside was being moved along to the next dormer, while the workman who had clung to it crept along the gutter to the next window, looking very much in fear of his life. She followed his gaze down to the courtyard below. The stage and scenery covered most of the marble squares, but they were still visible here and there. No one would survive a fall from such a great height.

Émilie felt as if she needed to remind herself just to breathe in and out. She moved slowly and deliberately, afraid to break the silence around her. One little noise, and she would forget everything she was supposed to do that evening, and be unable to go on. What she required was complete peace, utter concentration.

At some point when she was at the final rehearsal, a servant had left on her washstand the face paints Émilie would need to transform herself into Alceste. There they stood, in a neat row: kohl to outline her eyes, rouge for her cheeks and lips, and powder to make her face white and masklike. On a wooden stand that looked like a faceless, severed head was an enormous wig, shot through with jewels. It was still too early to start dressing, and so Émilie paced slowly around her room, the words she was to sing circling around her head, all out of order.

Admète has had my heart since my earliest childhood . . .

When marriage and love are in such close agreement . . .

How can the heavens permit the hearts of Alceste and
    Admète to separate like this?

O God! What a horrible spectacle!

Her heart started to race. What was her first line? She could not remember it. She couldn't breathe. She went to her window and opened it wide and inhaled the fresh air deeply. Émilie closed her eyes and thought of Charpentier. Gradually her heart slowed to a normal pace, and she ceased feeling as if her blood were racing through her veins and trying to get out through her fingertips or the soles of her feet. She had no idea how much time had passed, but after a while, she heard a light scratch on her door.

"Come!"

Marie entered and tried to curtsey, although the heavy costume she carried made it almost impossible. Without saying a word, she laid the jeweled robe across Émilie's bed, and then helped her apply her makeup, tied back her hair so that she could settle the heavy wig on her head, and then guided her into the costume and laced her and sewed her into it.

After about half an hour, when the feat of transforming Émilie from her everyday self into the character of Alceste was nearly complete, Émilie stood completely still before the mirror. There before her was Alceste. Just behind her, looking at her with a curious expression, stood Marie. There was something disturbing about this scrutiny. Émilie realized that if anyone had asked her, she would not have known the color of Marie's eyes, because she had never before looked into them. Marie herself prevented it, thought Émilie, by always looking down, or looking away as soon as she could. But now, here she was, staring at Émilie as if she longed to say something. Marie's eyes were hazel, Émilie noted. The servant's lips parted slightly.

"What is it?" Émilie asked, turning. But by the time she faced her, Marie had adjusted her expression again. She dipped a curtsey and left abruptly, leaving Émilie thinking that the image she had seen in the mirror was stolen from some other place, no more than a ghostly suggestion of a soul. Marie had been about to speak. Something stopped her. Émilie wished she knew what, and why the maid never dared say a thing to her.

～

"Monsieur de St. Paul!"

St. Paul looked up, hoping it would be the young boy with his food, but realized that the lad would not have known his name. It was his coachman, a burly, streetwise fellow who, in addition to the virtue of discretion, possessed the even more useful virtue of brute strength.

"I've been sent to find you."

"Did you see our friend?" By now St. Paul was weak with hunger. The child had obviously decided to cut his losses rather than risk being stiffed. St. Paul had to admit it was a good decision on the boy's part.

"No, but your godmother returned from visiting and invites you to tea."

"Damn." Although the idea of tea, preferably accompanied by some cakes, was very appealing, St. Paul was afraid to end his vigil.

"I am a little acquainted with a housemaid here, and she might be prevailed upon to let us know if our man makes a move to leave," said the coachman.

"You're a good fellow. If you could arrange it while I do the honors with Mademoiselle?"

The coachman bowed, then knocked on the door to the servants' entrance. St. Paul walked around to arrive in style at the front gate of the hôtel.

~

After having conducted Émilie back to her room to rest before the performance, François went through the letters and parcels addressed to Madame de Maintenon that had arrived in the afternoon coach, sorting them into "personal," "confidential," "business," and "not worthy of consideration." She received literally hundreds of entreaties a day, for everything from prayers to valuable gifts from the king. And, with her increasing power and influence, there was always the possibility that someone would try blackmail, or even, heaven forbid, poison. More than one courtier had been sickened by handling a letter that had been impregnated with some venom.

The letters from individuals whose identities he knew François did not open. But those from strangers, or that looked at all suspicious, were fair game. That afternoon he found one that struck him as very odd. It was in an unfamiliar hand and had traces of dirt on it that were different from those of rough handling en route. His first thought was to protect Madame de Maintenon from the importuning of a petty blackmailer. He took the letter to his own small chamber, warmed the wax seal, and slipped the blade of a knife underneath it. When he read the note, François put his hand to his heart.

Your pretty songbird has plans to fly away . . .

He read it again. Its meaning was quite clear. So there was a plan, after all. Or at least, someone wanted the widow Scarron to believe that there was. But he did not know what difference it could possibly make to Madame de Maintenon if someone were scheming to abduct Émilie. Her plan, as he understood it, meant that there would probably be no point. Or if the abduction occurred before he served her the tainted wine, then the girl would be out of the way in any case. Either Émilie would die in possession of her virtue and go straight to heaven, or someone would carry her off right under the widow Scarron's nose.

After some thought, François decided that it would be better to hand Émilie's fate over to chance. He liked her, and if it was possible for her not to perish, then all the better. He held the letter over the candle flame and watched it disintegrate into ash. What was the use, in the circumstances, of ruining his position with Madame de Maintenon by letting her know that he was not possessed of all the secrets at court?

∽

Émilie did not have to appear on stage until scene six of Act I— which followed a long prologue designed to heap adulation on King Louis. So she waited inside the palace, in the dark, looking out of the French doors two floors below her own room onto the Cour de Marbre, which had been transformed almost beyond recognition. From her vantage point, she could see the struts and buttresses that held the scenery in place and the twenty or so stagehands who worked the pulleys that set the gears in motion to move the huge wooden structures; the scene would be changed no fewer than five times in the course of the evening. The opera was just like the rest of life at Versailles. It was all blown out of proportion and ridiculous. People pretended to be what they were not. And yet, there was the music . . .

Waiting there, inside the château, Émilie could hear the orchestra and singers only when they were quite loud. Little snatches she recognized would reach her ears from time to time. Her heart began to beat fast, and she felt as if she were going to faint. In her costume, she could not sit down. François waited there with her: he had come to conduct her downstairs, and she had asked him to stay.

This is what it's like to be nervous, thought Émilie. She never recalled being nervous before. She took a few deep breaths, and then quietly, with her mouth closed, worked the muscles in her throat slowly over a few easy exercises. Her trembling gradually ceased. She did not know if it was the breathing or the power of her own will, but she knew she would be able to do her part.

The grinding, squeaking noise of gears going into action startled Émilie, and she realized that the scene was changing from a mythical land of pleasure fed by the principal rivers of France, to the seaport of Thessaly, and that those on stage were celebrating the marriage that was supposedly taking place behind the scenes between herself and her beloved Admète. Very soon she would be called to step out in front of the audience, in front of every single one of Louis's devoted, ambitious courtiers, and justify the time, effort, and money that had been expended to foster her vocal development. Oddly, she was no longer afraid.

The moment arrived. François held the door open for her and the orchestra's jaunty snap made her heart leap with excitement. The heavy costume forced Émilie to walk tall and with determination. She lifted her chin and strolled to the center of the stage. She could hear the approving murmurs ripple through the audience. Then she opened her mouth and sang.

Her voice blended with that of Monsieur Clédiere, who until that moment had utterly refused to look into her eyes when they sang their love duet. What Émilie did not realize was that in that instant, when she gazed at Monsieur Clédiere, she saw and heard Charpentier. Clédiere's tenor was not as close a match for her voice as Charpentier's high tenor, but it hardly mattered. Love and admiration lit her from within and gave her voice a warmth and truth that transcended the artifice of the tragedy she enacted. The entire audience was enraptured.

The music carried Émilie over all her fears and doubts, and she entered into it so fully that, at the moment when she realized that her husband must die, the musical phrases were punctuated by sniffs in the audience. And there were actual sobs when the image on Apollo's monument became hers, announcing that she had sacrificed her own life to save that of her husband.

When the tragedy was over, the applause and shouts of *"Bis!"* from all quarters were unrestrained. The effect on the king, who had never before heard her sing, was profound. Émilie had noticed that when he came on stage to sing the role of Apollo, he fixed his eyes upon her without wavering. At that moment she felt that she could have wielded great power over him, or over anyone present. But the impression was fleeting, and when the crowd began to move toward the palace to go upstairs and enjoy the feast, Émilie began to feel like herself again.

Before she could join the festivities, she had to change out of her costume and stage makeup in an anteroom just off the courtyard. A court dress had been provided for her, and Marie awaited to assist her out of the heavy costume.

"Mademoiselle Émilie! *Comme vous êtes charmante!*"

A lady-in-waiting accosted Émilie as soon as the door to her dressing room was opened. Émilie did not know how more than a dozen courtiers had managed to reach that place, which was right behind the stage, before she did.

"Please, Mademoiselle, accept this gift from me." An elderly gentleman with only half his teeth proffered a delicate sugar rose to her. Just as she was about to thank him and take it, another woman bumped into him. He dropped the confection, and it disintegrated into a mess of sugary fragments.

"I'm so sorry!" said Émilie, but the gentleman she wanted to apologize to had already been elbowed out of the way by the woman. She was fat, middle-aged, and sweated profusely.

"Mademoiselle, if I could only have a moment of your time, tomorrow, in private." She grasped Émilie's hand. Émilie could feel the imprint of something hard in her palm.

"Shoo! Shoo! Mademoiselle Émilie must change her clothes!" It was François desperately trying to stem the flow of courtiers, who now overwhelmed the tiny space. He had little success. Émilie realized that privacy was not highly valued at Versailles: King Louis did almost everything in full view of the world. Nonetheless it shocked her that when it was clear that she had made a successful début, no one would leave her alone. Even while she had her arms above her head so that Marie could lift the costume off without damage, they swarmed around her. One elderly gentleman actually ducked under the skirt with her to give her a gold locket and pay her extravagant compliments. She tried tactfully to push him away, and he backed off, becoming once more part of the crowd that pressed in on her.

Émilie started to feel light-headed. She knew that the sudden attention had nothing really to do with her, only with what she might be able to get if she were ever in a position to influence the king. To influence the king! The idea was absurd. It made her want to laugh out loud. She asked François to try once more to herd the crowd of spectators out of the room, promising that she would soon join them at the festivities upstairs. With some reluctance, they all departed, and François shut the door on them and leaned against it, exhausted.

Once she was on her own, Émilie began walking around and around in a little circle, at first slowly, but then faster and faster until she was almost running.

"What is the matter, Mademoiselle Émilie?" said François. "You have had such a great triumph, and the king is much pleased with you. You see how everyone praises you!"

"Oh, François, I don't know what to do!" Émilie burst into loud sobs.

"Please, Mademoiselle Émilie! Stay calm!"

François fluttered around her helplessly, offering her his handkerchief and looking at the door. He had no idea how to deal with such hysteria. The contents of the note he had destroyed earlier that day weighed on his mind, as did his instructions from Madame de Maintenon. He knew why Émilie was so disturbed. And yet he wondered if she truly realized what a dangerous game she was playing. If she did not appear in the king's apartment as arranged, she could be charged with treason. Her failure would not technically be illegal, but it would be a simple matter to trump up charges by accusing her of passing court secrets to an informant outside. The widow Scarron was fearsome when thwarted. Émilie did not have friends powerful enough to prevail on the king's sense of honor. François had seen it happen before, and now, if the abduction succeeded, it would be difficult to persuade his mistress that it had not been arranged through the secret correspondence that he, François, had facilitated. Émilie was not the only one who could be endangered by her actions.

François tried once again to calm Émilie, but before he could approach her, something extraordinary happened. She stopped crying suddenly and became very still. Her eyes, almost painfully open and vulnerable most of the time, had lost their expression, as if the flame that lit them from behind had been extinguished. François, although relieved that she was no longer sobbing, was a little frightened.

"Shall we go to the party?" he asked, motioning Émilie toward the door.

She smiled at him. "It's all right, François. I'm quite calm now. I realize what I must do. But it can wait until afterward. Shall we?"

Émilie led the way out the door with François following behind, proud but sad. She looks taller, and very beautiful, he thought. She has grown up since she came to Versailles.

Seventeen

One more often commits treason through weakness than through any intention to do so.

Maxim 120

St. Paul was so hungry that it took little convincing on his god-mother's part to make him stay for dinner and cards. They made an odd pair: the aging dowager in black silk and heavy jewels, and the young courtier in bright yellow brocade, a red sash, and high, red-heeled shoes. The princess was small and seemed almost to have to reach up to play her cards. St. Paul was on the tall side and curved over the table like a bird of prey. He was a little thinner than he liked to be, but that was because he was never quite certain when he would next enjoy a proper meal.

"*Excusez-moi,* Mademoiselle, but I have a note for Monsieur de St. Paul."

The housemaid who was a friend of St. Paul's coachman gave him a folded piece of paper. He opened and read it.

"I am very sorry, Godmother, but urgent business calls me away."

"What a pity," she said, holding her hand out for St. Paul to kiss.

"*À bientôt.*" He bowed and departed.

St. Paul's coach waited for him outside the front gate. "Where did he go?" he asked as he climbed in.

"North on the rue de Grand Chenier. He was walking."

"Let's catch up to him, but stay enough behind so that he does not see us."

"Yes, Monsieur le Comte."

Trusting his coachman to spot Charpentier, St. Paul reached beneath his seat and pulled out a wooden box. He released the catch, lifted the lid, and ran his fingers lightly over the polished wood and chased gold handles of an exquisite pair of dueling pistols. He had been tempted to sell them a few months ago, when his godmother was away and he was feeling the pinch of poverty rather severely, but he was glad he had withstood that urge. Although he might not have to use a pistol, it was best to be prepared. With a firm grip, St. Paul lifted one of the flintlocks from its velvet cradle. Then he grasped a little round brass knob and raised the lid of a small compartment between the depressions that housed the pistols, and removed from this cavity a delicate gold powder horn. Balancing the pistol carefully on his knee with one hand, he measured out a quantity of the black powder and poured it into the muzzle. Then he replaced the powder horn and took out a round lead slug and a little piece of linen. He spat on the linen, and placed the ball in its center. Wrapping the cloth around it, he pushed the missile into the end of the muzzle. Once it was securely seated, he reached back into the pistol box and removed a slender ramrod, which he used to push the linen-wrapped slug home until it sat firmly on its bed of gunpowder. That accomplished, St. Paul rested the pistol carefully on his lap, raised the frizzen, lowered the hammer, then added a few grains of priming powder from a slender gold tube to the flash pan. The coach jolted as it stopped. Some of the fine black powder spilled. "Damn!" St. Paul whispered, cautiously tucking the loaded pistol in his sash before dusting the grains off his yellow breeches.

"Charpentier is inside," whispered the coachman, who leaned down from the box and spoke into the open window.

St. Paul nodded to him and climbed out of the coach. "Pull just ahead there, a little out of sight. I'll wait for him to come out and persuade him to join me."

The coachman did as he was told, and St. Paul stood to one side of the stable door. He drew his pistol out of his sash, cocked it, and stood at the ready.

〜

The public reception rooms of the château had never been so beautiful. For the first time since she had come to Versailles, Émilie did not feel diminished by her surroundings. She was part of them, and yet distinct: a mural come to life; a marble statue animated. She blended with the air, thick with the smoke from thousands of candles and torches. It was her natural element, this rich soup of perfume and body odor, food and burning fuel. She dove into the atmosphere and swam through it, flashing and sparkling like an exotic fish in a pond, smiling, smiling.

Émilie ached with tenderness when she beheld the gorgeous plenty of the Salle d'Abondance and the Salle de Vénus. She could see beyond each delicate morsel of food, every one a perfect product of culinary art, to the hundreds of laboring hands that had produced it.

The Chambre du Billard glittered with the forced gaiety of people losing money and pretending not to mind. In the Salle de Bal dancers so skilled and controlled in their movements that they looked as if they were made of wax performed a stately minuet. And in the next room, ladies fanned themselves and yawned at card tables set up around the state bed, the scene of the birth of all the royal children. Émilie had a vision of the queen, screaming with the pangs of labor, blood-soaked sheets clenched in her fists, while all around her courtiers laughed and told secrets.

All eyes followed the ingénue as she glided from room to room. Some even called out to her or touched her on the arm or face as she passed, but she did not notice. She looked out on everyone from somewhere else, protected, secure. Even François's furrowed brow and occasional questions and comments did not penetrate her cocoon.

It could have been years or a moment ago that she had sung her heart out upon the stage. She paused in the midst of her progress to look out over the three fountains, playing exuberantly in the torch-lit garden. The autumn wind tossed spray irreverently at a few brave pedestrians, who scurried away from this unwelcome benediction. Arching jets of water created sparkling, fluid architecture, as ephemeral as it was miraculous, the backdrop to a living stage set upon which the drama of court life was constantly rehearsed. But none of that mattered now. Émilie wallowed in a state of delicious oblivion, letting herself imagine that it all happened magically, that no vast system of hydraulics was necessary to make the water flow against its will, but that some sprite had enchanted the entire acreage of Versailles, and that she too had been caught in the spell, frozen in time and space.

~

When Charpentier arrived at the stable, the groom was nowhere to be found and his horse dreamily munched hay in his stall, more ready to settle down for the night than to spring into action.

"Hey there!" At the sound of his voice, the horse lifted his head suddenly. After a moment Charpentier heard a shuffling and a loud *"Ssshh"* from the direction of the hayloft. "Where are you, boy? I need my horse!" A stifled giggle filtered down from above his head. He scrambled partway up a ladder to see where it came from.

There, sprawled amid the bales in a state of undress not easy to remedy quickly, was the young groom, and with him a common prostitute. Because she faced away from him, Charpentier did not notice that it was the same whore who had announced herself to him as none other than Sophie Dupin, but he realized that no matter what he did, the lad would not be fit to help him with his horse for some minutes. So without a word, he climbed back down, fetched the tack himself, and did his best. He was not accustomed to the job, and although he knew what to do, it took him much longer than it should have. He lost twenty precious minutes in the process as he grappled with his horse, who had caught the mood of urgency and would not stay still.

Once he was finished, Charpentier leapt onto the beast even before he left the stable.

St. Paul saw the doors fly open, and he lowered his pistol to take aim. Charpentier galloped out at full speed and sent pedestrians scurrying as he wove through the evening crowd of coaches that clogged the rue de Grand Chenier. St. Paul pulled the trigger, but instead of a bright flash and a loud explosion, there was only a soft click.

"Damn!" he said, and then yelled out, "You there! Stop!"

He thought he saw Charpentier look back. His only consolation was that if Charpentier kept going at that rate, the man's horse would expire before he reached Versailles. He was going too fast to catch by driving a carriage, and they would never get around the other vehicles that inched along the road. St. Paul tucked his pistol in his sash again and ran to his coach. "Unharness the horses!"

Before the coachman was off the box, St. Paul started slashing at the traces with his knife. The coachman lifted the harness off one of the horses. "You'll never manage sir, there's no saddle!" he yelled.

St. Paul ignored him and quickly knotted the long rein he had cut over the horse's nose, leapt on his back, and kicked the beast. The coachman watched as his master followed the path that Charpentier had taken. Once St. Paul was out of sight, he tried to arrange what was left of the harness so that the remaining horse could pull the coach.

～

Émilie arrived in the throne room. At its center sat Louis, in a red velvet armchair on a platform, surveying the scene around him with satisfaction. He was by far the most magnificently dressed of all the company, and his large wig added to his height. He was a very handsome man, with a bearing that left not a soul in doubt that everything the eye could see happened because he willed it. Beside him, Madame de Maintenon gave orders to servants, already more in command than the queen, who played cards in another room and was losing heavily to the Duc d'Orléans, so everyone whispered. Louis caught sight of Émilie straightaway and leaned to say something to the widow Scarron. She came forward to greet Émilie, her face full of meaning.

"The king would like to hear a selection from *Alceste*."

She did not wait for any sign of assent from Émilie but turned immediately and gestured to the servants to bring in the harpsichord. Lully himself followed it in and then took his seat, prepared to act as accompanist. Everyone in the room went completely silent; no one dared not attend to that which held the interest of the king. For one evanescent moment, Émilie imagined herself back at the Hôtel de Guise, about to make her début. There she had had to sing out to be heard above the noise of conversation, and had, by sheer force of her beautiful voice, startled the entire company into raptures of applause and admiration. Here she looked around at the absolutely still and silent courtiers, smiled, and began to sing, very quietly.

At the end of Émilie's performance came the muted approbation of gloved clapping. Louis smiled at her, then turned and spoke into a man's ear. It was Colbert, the finance minister, who left the room for a moment and returned carrying a black velvet box about six inches square. He presented it to Émilie. She looked at it, puzzled. François, who had stayed as close by her side as he dared, nudged Émilie and bowed deeply. She took his cue and curtseyed, then backed away and left the room.

Once she was out of sight of Louis, Émilie had the sensation that someone had let all the feathers out of her magical cushion. What before had seemed warmly enveloping now felt so close that it abraded her. The noise of the crowd hurt her ears, the brilliance of her surroundings was like needles in her eyes. Her feet were so sore that every step was agony, and it was with difficulty that she kept from crying again.

François saw her wilt and realized that she was so weak that she might drop the velvet box the king had just given her. He put his hand beneath her elbow and supported her, letting her lean on him all the way back to her chamber. He understood that she might lose heart at the prospect of what was to come later that night. He wished he were in a position to comfort her.

"Why don't you open your present?" suggested François when he opened the door of her room, thinking that perhaps a beautiful bauble would distract Émilie from her agitation of mind. He felt sorry that such a sweet young creature had gotten herself mixed up in all these schemes. François placed the box on Émilie's little writing table, then bowed to her and closed the door behind him as he left.

When François had gone, Émilie wandered slowly to her desk and picked up the velvet box. It had a gilt clasp with a single pearl embedded in filigree that had been designed to resemble a bird's nest. She teased the mechanism with her fingers until it disengaged, and lifted the lid. Cradled there in a bed of satin was a magnificent diamond brooch in the shape of bird. Its mouth was open, and its throat extended. She lifted the precious object out of the box and held it before her, letting the light from the candle glint and fracture into thousands of tiny points on the walls of her room. The brooch was like nothing she had ever seen before, and yet it made her immeasurably sad. The bird was trying to sing, but since it was only a piece of jewelry, it could not. Émilie was about to replace the bird in its silken nest when she noticed that the folds of satin concealed a small piece of paper. It was a note addressed to her.

Mademoiselle Émilie,
The king requests a private performance in his chamber at half past midnight tonight. François will conduct you thither.

Émilie did not recognize the handwriting. Not that she imagined for one moment it was the king's, but she knew that Madame de Maintenon had not written it. She also knew that her performance would not involve any singing at all, although she wasn't entirely clear concerning what exactly losing her innocence would entail.

Midnight was still over an hour away. Émilie took off her court dress and laid it across her bed. Then she walked to her window. The latch stuck when she tried to open it. When it finally gave way, the casement crashed against the outer wall of the palace, and one of the tiny panes shattered. Clouds scudded across a bright, moonlit sky, although the moon itself was out of sight, on the opposite side of the château. Directly across from her window, on the other wing of the château, one or two of the torches that had been fixed up high still glowed, half-heartedly competing with the moonlight. Below, the shiny surface of the Cour de Marbre was again exposed, the stage having been dismantled as quickly as it had been assembled. The black and white squares seemed to move and heave with the constantly changing cloud shadows.

Past and future fell away. Now was all there was. It was comforting, in a way, to know what she had to do, before a different choice was forced upon her. Émilie turned away from the window and walked back to her desk, where she sat, perfectly still, and gazed unseeing toward the night sky.

Eighteen

It is easier to be wise for others than for ourselves.
Maxim 132

"I am expecting an important message from Paris this evening." On her way to bed after the celebration that night, Madame de Montespan addressed the guard who stood outside the door of her apartments in the château. "It will come by messenger on horseback. Please make certain that he will be allowed to pass by the gate, sometime around midnight, I believe."

The guard bowed and walked to another guard a little farther along the corridor, who then walked to the next one and so on until the message reached the sergeant who was posted to keep watch over the main gate. By the time it arrived at its destination, Madame de Montespan was in her bed, drifting off to sleep. Satisfying to be able to help an insignificant person and harm her most detested rival at the same time, she thought, as she let herself sink into the luxurious comfort of silk sheets and goose down pillows. Besides, she was almost certain she was pregnant again. And Louis was becoming more and more fond of the children they had together. He had just agreed to allow her to bring them to court. Another baby was sure to cement her position.

*   *   *

Every so often Charpentier looked behind him to see if he was being followed. Sometimes the wind carried the sound of pounding hooves in the distance, but he could not see anything. Still, he was afraid to slacken his pace. He had no idea who it could be that called after him like that as he left the stable. Who would have known of his plans?

He guessed that he was about halfway to Versailles. The horse was already foaming at the mouth, and sweat gathered in white streaks on his flank. Charpentier decided he had to ease up or he might kill the animal. He slowed to a canter. It was hard to see the road anyway; the moon kept vanishing behind the clouds, and he had to traverse deep countryside to get to the little village that had once been the site of only a humble hunting lodge. He had never been to Versailles before. Charpentier had followed the directions he was given but was still anxious in case he had not taken the right road. The fact that it was the most well-kept highway to the southwest of Paris reassured him, however. Best not to dwell on it, he thought, and instead went over the other arrangements as he rode. A parcel had arrived earlier that day that contained twenty louis. The note said to use them if he needed to bribe the guards. He had tucked the pouch of coins hurriedly in his sash; now he let go of the reins with one hand to feel if it was still there. It was.

After half an hour, St. Paul's satin breeches wore through from rubbing against the sweating horseflesh beneath him. He was in agony. The horse, accustomed to pulling a carriage rather than being ridden, was not a smooth mount, nor was he particularly fast. St. Paul lost sight of Charpentier even before he left Paris.

"Damn it all to hell!" he reined in his horse, which was willing enough to take a rest, and dismounted. They were miles from anywhere and hadn't a hope of being able to stop Charpentier from carrying Émilie away.

Just off the road St. Paul saw a chestnut tree with a boulder beneath it. He could sit there and wait for his coach to catch up to him. At least, he hoped that the coachman had followed. What a fiasco!

As soon as he slid off, the horse, unused to being ridden so hard, put his head down and commenced tearing up what was left of the grass. St. Paul limped over to the boulder he had spotted. He tried to sit on top of it, but his backside was so sore he could not endure it, and so he settled for the soft ground, using the rock as a back rest. He removed his pistol from his sash and examined the firing mechanism. The priming powder was still in the pan. The flint was dull. He closed his eyes. He thought for a moment that perhaps he would be able to stop the couple on their way back to Paris, but in the dark he did not trust his aim—even if he were able to sharpen the flint enough to make a spark. It would not do to kill the girl by accident. At the rate Charpentier was going, St. Paul figured it would be at most two hours before he passed this way again. He yawned and let his head lean back. Within minutes his jaw fell open and his breathing was loud and regular.

∽

The moon had moved across the sky and now seemed to hang just over the slate roof of the old château. It beckoned Émilie, a magnetic disc of light, pulling her off her stool, drawing her slowly toward the window. With her eyes fixed on it, she climbed up onto the casement. In her hand she clutched the jeweled bird the king had given her.

The cool breeze caressed her face. Her own voice rang out and echoed in her head, singing the words of Alceste that Quinault wrote and Lully set to music.

Ah, I would do anything to save my true love!

The sound she imagined was more beautiful than anything she had ever heard. She let it engulf her, let it drown out all other noises. Soon she could see the wind pushing and pulling the clouds into fantastic shapes, but she could no longer hear it. Below her was the Cour de Marbre. Somewhere, she was aware of clocks chiming and an insistent pounding, dull, like fists against wood, but very far away. She focused her mind out and over the black and white pattern of the marble below. When the wind was at its wildest, and the song in her head had reached its zenith, Émilie let go of the window frame, spread her arms wide, and balanced on the sill. While she stood there feeling almost drunk with freedom, memories of the hours of singing with Charpentier and visions of her days in the workshop with her father crowded into her mind. She felt her eyes sting, and the moon seemed to swim in front of her. Émilie blinked hard. She would miss both of them in heaven, she thought, more than they would miss her on earth.

∼

A guard stopped Charpentier as soon as he entered the Cour Royale.

"You there! What's your business?"

"I have a message, for . . ." Charpentier forgot what he was supposed to say and began to fish for the purse full of coins at his waist.

"Ah yes! You're expected. Dismount please, sir."

"I beg your pardon?"

"Nobody rides into the Cour Royale except the king."

With relief, Charpentier slid off his exhausted horse and then led him on toward the door where he expected to find Émilie waiting. He tried to be quiet, but every step they took echoed loudly off the walls of the palace. He looked over his shoulder. There was nobody there, although he was still certain he had been followed from Paris. A noise from the direction of the château made him turn around suddenly. He put his hand over his horse's nose, signaling for him to be quiet, and then listened. Nothing.

Charpentier stepped slowly forward and his horse whinnied quietly, restless and tired. After three or four steps, he heard the sound once more. Again Charpentier stopped. But all he could hear was the roar of the wind in the autumn trees. In the Cour de Marbre, remnants of the earlier performance, in which Émilie had no doubt enthralled her audience, were still scattered around—a piece of scenery, meaningless and flat without its neighbors, and the orchestra's stools and music stands not yet taken indoors. A few sputtering torches cast a faint, uneven light that made the black and white marble squares shimmer and dance. He tried, for a moment, to imagine Émilie singing there, but the wind had picked up, and it whistled around the stone palace and whooshed through the dry-leaved trees, drowning out everything he heard in his head.

Something was wrong. Although the atmosphere was alive with the restless night breezes, there was not the faintest sign of humanity anywhere. He was neither early nor late. The clock had struck the three-quarter hour almost at the moment he dismounted. But the door to the right of the Cour de Marbre was shut, and all was utterly quiet, except for the occasional snorting of his horse, and Charpentier's own pounding heart. It was time to make a move, regardless. To delay might spoil everything. So he tossed the horse's reins over a post and grabbed the spare cloak he had brought for Émilie, then ran to the door and flung it open, hoping to find her waiting just on the other side. The sudden movement sent a rat scurrying away. It had been nibbling at a dead mouse that was right against the door. No doubt it was this that had pushed it open slightly and made the noise Charpentier had heard. His precipitate entrance not only startled the rat but also awoke a young servant who had nodded off on the floor a little away from the door with a sputtering candle next to him.

"Where is she!" Charpentier, with unaccustomed force, grabbed the lad by the shoulders and lifted him into a standing position.

"That way!" the frightened lackey squeaked, pointing to the door that led to the stairs. "Two flights up, at the end of the hallway."

Charpentier let go, leaving the boy rubbing his arms, and charged down the hallway and up the stairs. When he emerged at the top, he saw a servant at the end of the corridor, standing at what he assumed was Émilie's door. He heard the sound of breaking glass and was vaguely aware of the splash of some liquid on his hands as he threw all his weight against Émilie's locked door, splintering the hinges away from the frame.

"Good God!"

He bounded across the room in two steps, reaching his arms out to grab Émilie, who was balanced precariously on the window ledge. As he pulled her back in, he felt her body go limp. She had fainted. Charpentier swirled the cloak around her, scooped her up, and carried her out past the servant.

Panic seemed to give him wings. With strength he did not know he possessed he mounted his horse with Émilie in his arms, and they galloped through the gates as the guard called after them. Charpentier kept riding. He looked back once or twice, but no one followed them. Émilie was still slack against his chest, and he rode with one arm around her waist and the other controlling the horse. Émilie's head lolled backward so that her lips were within inches of his, and he could smell her sweet breath. She was still slender, he noticed, but taller and more womanly than when he last saw her. Charpentier clung to his former student, partly because he feared that she might slide off the furiously galloping horse, and partly because he did not want to let her go.

"We'll be there soon, my love," he whispered to the unconscious girl, and then he spurred the beast on faster and faster through the night.

$$\sim$$

François had arrived at Émilie's door about twenty minutes before midnight with a small tray bearing a carafe of wine and a single glass. He wished, more than anything, that there had been some easy way not to follow Madame de Maintenon's instructions. He knew the horrible fate that awaited Émilie if she drank the wine. François thought for a moment of "accidentally" dropping the tray. But the widow Scarron was canny, and she would not expect François to make such a mistake. It passed through his mind that he could drink it himself. But although he took no pleasure in harming others, François had no desire to harm himself either. As the hour drew nearer, he continued to hope that he would think of something, or that events would transpire that would solve the dilemma for him. If the note he intercepted told the truth, then someone would attempt to abduct Émilie that night. Abduct, or rescue, depending on how one looked at it. If not, then it was up to him, to give her the wine and take her to the king, or not. He stood quietly outside the door, listening closely for any sound, trying to read the silence for meaning, trying to find a way to resolve the predicament that he—and Émilie—faced.

François's thoughts were interrupted by loud noises from below, and he looked up just in time to see a stranger barreling down the hallway toward him, his hard-soled boots ringing against the wooden floor. Before he could say a word, the man—Charpentier, he assumed—shoved him aside, sending the wine spattering against the walls and the glass to the floor, where it shattered. The stranger rammed himself so hard against Émilie's door that the frame came apart.

There was no time even to utter a sound before the intruder dashed back past him, this time carrying the unconscious Émilie in his arms. Stunned into complete immobility, François heard the abductor take the steps two at a time, marveling that he did not lose his footing. The door to the courtyard slammed behind him, and then the hollow clopping of hooves on cobbles faded as they made their escape.

François shook himself out of his stupor and cautiously entered the room. Émilie's empty dress was draped over her bed. The window was wide open, and the cold night air blew in unimpeded. In that moment François understood what had actually happened. Charpentier had prevented Émilie from taking her own life. This was an outcome he had not foreseen, and it changed everything. He crossed himself and said a silent prayer.

"Heaven help us," said François to the empty room. There would have to be an explanation. If he raised the alarm, guards would chase after them, they would be apprehended, and then—anything could happen.

In the course of a lifetime at Versailles, François had seen everything. The most preposterous events seemed to be daily occurrences there, as if there was an unwritten law that life at court should be absurd and exaggerated. He looked at Émilie's window and pictured her standing framed by it on the window ledge, then just leaning forward and sailing out, to plunge into the courtyard below. It wouldn't have been the first time such a thing had happened. And why couldn't it have happened? Who else had seen Charpentier arrive? Who had seen him leave? Two, maybe three servants? They were easily bought.

François ran down the stairs to the door by which Charpentier had entered. The little page stood there still, looking confused.

"What happened here, lad?" asked François.

"Not sure really. A man, he grabbed me, and then ran upstairs, and came back carrying something that looked like a sack but I think it was a person."

The boy was very young, probably not more than eleven or twelve years old. "Listen to me," said François, taking the lad's chin in his hand and turning his face so that he could look directly into his eyes. "You saw no such thing. You were asleep in your quarters until I called you to come and help me. The young girl jumped out of her window and was killed in the Cour de Marbre. We moved her, you and I. We got a cart, and we took her to a far corner of the garden and buried her. And we cleaned up the blood in the courtyard."

By this time the lad's eyes were huge. "You want me to lie?" he said.

"That's right," said François. "I want you to lie, so that someone may live in peace and serenity. I don't think it's much to ask." François reached into his pocket and pulled out a shiny coin, which he gave to the boy. "Promise me," he said.

"I promise," the boy said, and then scampered off to bed.

Nineteen

Truth does less good in the world than the appearance
of truth does harm.

Maxim 64

The horse was clearly flagging on the return trip to Paris, and Charpentier was afraid that he had injured Émilie by handling her so roughly in his haste to get away. There was nothing to do but stop.

Charpentier pulled his horse up by a copse of trees, and walked him to where they could not be seen from the road. He gently slid off, holding Émilie close, then laid her on the leafy ground.

"Émilie, Émilie!" he said, patting her cheeks and rubbing her wrists.

She murmured and opened her eyes. "Am I dead? Did I go to heaven?"

"No, Mademoiselle. Only to Paris. At least, that is where we will be in about an hour, if you can manage to sit up and hold on for a little while longer."

"Monsieur Charpentier! I'm so glad to see you." She began to cry. Charpentier lifted her and held her to him for a moment. He could feel her trembling.

"We must get back on the horse and continue. I have a place for you to stay. Are you all right?"

Émilie nodded. Charpentier helped her stand. "Just let me see to the horse for a moment," he said, and then walked away from her to tighten the girth and check the horse's hooves for stones.

She was a little wobbly at first, but Émilie pulled herself upright, stretched, and breathed deeply. When she did this, she noticed something small, sharp, and bright stuck on the inside of her cloak. She reached into its folds and felt a hard, pointy object caught by a few threads on the lining of the wrap. It was the diamond bird brooch the king had given her a few hours before. Émilie looked toward Charpentier, but he was still busy, now lengthening a stirrup so she could remount easily. She wrapped her fingers around the brooch. She would tell him about it later.

"Come and let me help you up," said Charpentier. He lifted her easily onto the saddle and then mounted behind her. After readjusting the stirrup for his own leg, he yelled "Get on!" The horse, now a little rested, took off at a gallop.

Émilie leaned back against Charpentier's chest, feeling his arms enclosing her, muscles tensed to control the horse, and shut her eyes. The wind felt good on her face. She could already smell Paris.

∽

St. Paul's coachman approached the sleeping figure propped against a boulder at the side of the road. "Is that you, Monsieur de St. Paul?"

St. Paul shook himself awake. "What time is it?" he asked, leaping to his feet.

"It's two in the morning. I was afraid I wouldn't find you."

"What took you so long!"

"With only one horse, it was slow."

"Did you see anyone ride by, very fast, toward Paris?"

"No, I didn't—that is, only one horse, but not going very fast, because it was carrying two people."

St. Paul shook his head and sat in silence for a minute or

two. "Let's go on to Versailles. There's nothing else I can do now."

"Very good, sir."

"Where's the horse?"

"I think he's over there, enjoying all this grass. I'll get him, and we'll be on our way before you know it."

St. Paul was very happy to see the inside of his coach. This kind of excitement was not really in his line. He was annoyed at himself for failing to stop Charpentier, but it was only a temporary setback. He would find a better way. He would bring Émilie back to Versailles, with or without the help of Madame de Maintenon. He had tried it her way, and what was the result? Now the king would have no one else to thank but him. St. Paul looked at his ruined breeches and sighed. He had no more credit with the tailor. He would have to convince his godmother to advance him some cash.

∽

"You say she jumped," said Madame de Maintenon, who looked as if she had not been asleep when François knocked on her door.

"Yes. There was nothing I could do. By the time I was able to enter the room, it was too late."

"Thank you for coming and telling me first," she said, looking steadily at François. "Where is she now?"

"I buried her."

The widow Scarron did not take her eyes off François. "So soon? How did you manage it?"

François was certain she had seen through his lie. "I had help. A young page was nearby. And besides, you know, a suicide . . ."

"I think you had better inform the king." Madame de Maintenon let go of the line of inquiry, but François was under no illusion that she bought the story completely.

"Someone should tell the girl's parents," said François.

"Yes, her parents. Do you know them?"

"No, Madame."

"I shall send St. Paul when he returns. François," she said, and

François could almost see her mind at work during the pause in her speech. "François, did you give my instructions to the wine steward?"

"Yes, Madame."

"And what happened to the wine for Mademoiselle Émilie?"

"I am afraid I dropped the tray when I heard the noise that made me force the door of her chamber." François was certain he saw the widow Scarron breathe a sigh, almost of relief.

"You may go."

~

The door had certainly been broken in, and the window was still wide open. Apart from these two things, it looked much like the other little rooms in the great château. There was nothing in particular to distinguish it, except for the things on the desk: a set of watercolors and a velvet box. St. Paul was mildly curious about what was inside the box, although he imagined it was a gift from the king, very likely a valuable and utterly useless trinket. He picked it up and opened it. He was really not surprised to find it empty, except for a piece of paper, whose message was clear enough. If there had been anything of value in the box, he would have taken it himself and blamed one of the servants for stealing it. He glanced around the room for the object that the box should have contained, but he found nothing.

Altogether too early the morning after his unsuccessful adventure, St. Paul was called to attend Madame de Maintenon. She told him that Émilie had leapt from her window and killed herself, and that he was to go to Paris to inform her parents. He went directly from the widow Scarron's apartments to quiz his coachman about what he had seen the night before. The man swore that it was two people on a horse. Of course, it might have been a different two people. But at that hour? And on that road?

The palace guard, on the other hand, swore that no one had come through there before St. Paul himself in the early hours of the morning. Someone could have bought him off, though.

"Serves me right for leaving Versailles." St. Paul's voice sounded loud in the deserted room.

∼

"Oh, she'll see me!" Madame de Montespan said, sweeping past the footman at Madame de Maintenon's door.

"To what do I owe this honor?" said the widow Scarron, rising from her desk and curtseying to the marquise.

"You just couldn't leave well enough alone, could you!"

"I'm afraid I have no idea what you're talking about."

"The girl. You knew she was going to flee, didn't you? What did it matter to you?"

"My dear Marquise, exactly what do you insinuate?"

Madame de Montespan strode restlessly around the small parlor, her silk skirts swishing against the furniture. "Why did she do it? She had everything to live for."

"These are mysteries we must look to God alone to answer." Madame de Maintenon turned away from her visitor.

"God, or the devil! Be careful how you use your influence, Madame."

"Surely such agitation is not good for a woman in your delicate condition," said the widow Scarron.

"Yes, another of the king's darlings for you to teach. Make no mistake, that is your job."

Madame de Maintenon curtseyed. "So sorry you could not stay longer and enjoy a cup of tea."

"I wouldn't dare drink tea that you had prepared."

"I thought that sort of thing was more in your line."

Madame de Montespan left the room as suddenly as she arrived.

∼

When St. Paul made the journey to Paris the next day to inform Marcel and Madeleine, he said nothing of the velvet box with its note, and its lack of an object he knew must be very valuable. He told them only what he had been told: that François had found a discreet spot within the garden of Versailles to lay their daughter to rest. Marcel broke down immediately, but Madeleine maintained her composure. St. Paul admired her restraint.

Émilie, as she had been, effectively ceased to exist.

Twenty

There is only one genuine kind of love,
but there are thousands of copies.
Maxim 74

Three days had passed since Émilie's dramatic exit from Versailles. She departed, as she often mused, exactly as she had come: more or less unconscious. Now she was in a small apartment, spending much of her time entirely alone. Charpentier told her they were still in the Marais, but what did it matter? He had forbidden her to go outside.

"What if someone recognized you? It could be dangerous—for both of us."

"You mean I cannot walk home to see my father and mother?"

Charpentier looked at her and sighed. "Promise me, for now, you will not go outside. Lucille will see to your needs. If you want anything, anything at all, just tell me."

"When can I go about the streets again?"

"When the danger is past," answered Charpentier, in a tone of voice that had signaled to Émilie that there was no point in pressing the issue further. He had been her teacher before, but it irked her that he took command so completely. How was she to know whether it was best to follow his instructions or whether he too was trying to use her in his own way? The world seemed to have undergone a strange transformation since the night of her début at Versailles. Nothing felt certain anymore.

Charpentier had taken care to provide clothes for Émilie and brought her books to read and a deck of cards. Émilie had learned a simple game of solitaire at Versailles on those evenings when she was required to attend the card parties, when she would watch the ladies wager huge sums of money against each other with a kind of desperation. Now she began to understand why, when everything else in life seemed to be in the control of others, trusting to pure chance might have its allure.

When she was not singing, Émilie's favorite occupation at Versailles had been drawing and painting. The drawing master was a kind old soul who was nearly blind, and he complimented whatever she did. Charpentier said that he would bring her paper and paints too, so that she could amuse herself during the many hours she would have to spend without him. Émilie was not completely alone all day, though. Lucille, the maid, came for a few hours, to tend the fire and bring Émilie food—delicious, simple food instead of all the rich delicacies that were the usual fare at court—and see to her daily wants. Charpentier himself stopped in for an hour or two each evening. He had to continue his life at the Hôtel de Guise as if nothing had happened and so could not spend the days in Émilie's company.

With so many empty hours between visits, she had ample time to reflect upon what had happened to her. They had arrived in Paris in the dead of night. Charpentier sat with her until she fell asleep in the comfortable bed in the tiny apartment. By the time she awoke several hours later, he had returned, looking refreshed.

"Tell me everything," she said.

Charpentier filled her in quickly on the events of the night before. Émilie shivered when she realized that if he had not arrived when he had, she might have fallen out of the window and would really be dead.

"What shall we do now? Do they know I am here? What about Mesdames, and François, and St. Paul, and the king?"

He reached into his waistcoat and withdrew a letter from his inside pocket. "They all believe that you fell. This was waiting for me when I went back to the Hôtel de Guise this morning." He showed Émilie the note that had arrived at dawn that day. It said that the king had been informed of Émilie's death, and that if Charpentier valued his or her life, he must ensure that she was never again brought before the royal notice. The note was not signed.

"So, I am dead after all," she said.

For a moment Émilie was aware of an enveloping silence, as if the world had fallen away, and all that was left was herself, perched atop a lofty peak that was surrounded by clouds. She was far away from everyone, including Charpentier. No one could know, she was certain, how it felt to find oneself erased from so many minds. She shook her head from side to side, just to bring herself back to the present. Then she turned toward Charpentier.

"Don't you see what it means?" she said.

"It will not be so bad! They will leave us alone. I can show you the music I have written. You can sing for me."

Émilie gazed steadily at him. She felt her eyes stinging and could not stop the tears that burned in them. She knew, after her triumphant début, that anyone with any connection whatsoever to the court would recognize her voice the instant it was raised in song. Her face they might forget, but her voice—never. She understood that as long as she and Charpentier must avoid the notice of the king, she must not sing.

"Ah," Charpentier said, the light fading from his eyes. "I see. How stupid of me. Of course." He walked over to the window. Émilie could see his shoulders droop. After a moment or two he turned and came back to her bedside.

"So, that's how it must be. It doesn't matter, to me. Really it doesn't."

Charpentier took Émilie's hand in his and stroked it. Although she realized that it was meant to be comforting, his gesture only irritated her. Émilie wanted to scream out loud, but she was too tired, so she lay back and turned her head away. Charpentier lifted her fingers to his lips, then departed in silence.

* * *

Now the lonely hours yawned before Émilie, who found herself counting each day off as if she were serving out a prison sentence. Although she was no longer confined to the château and grounds of Versailles, she was a captive still, this time in solitary confinement, with the boundaries of her world tinier and more restrictive than they had ever been. She never thought she could possibly miss anything about her life at court, but she did miss contact, however superficial, with other people. She missed François and his quietly sensitive responsiveness to her every need. She missed the silent Marie, who took care of her without a word of complaint. She missed running through the corridors or the garden when no one was looking. She missed disliking Lully, and being fussed over and petted, even if there was always some unstated motive behind the attention. She missed being part of the world, whatever that world was.

Lully drew himself up to his full height and tried to suck in his belly. He was dressed in his finest clothes, having arrived to go over with the king the plans for an upcoming celebration. When he felt he looked his best, he cleared his throat and tapped lightly at the door. Colbert's voice called to him to enter.

"So, my friend, will you have a new ballet for me?"

The king was in a good mood. He had just recently discovered that he was to be a father again.

"Yes, Your Majesty, a ballet. Will you take part? There is a wonderful role for you."

"Alas, my dancing days are at an end. Madame de Maintenon advises me that it does not become a monarch to appear upon the stage."

Lully was not certain, but he thought he saw a knowing look pass between the king and his finance minister.

"And how much, Monsieur de Lully, will this new production

cost?" Colbert asked. He had his ledger books open on an enormous table at the right height for standing.

"That is impossible to say, Monsieur. We must maintain the utmost quality. The king's festivities cannot be seen to be anything less than perfect." Lully glanced in the direction of the king for corroboration.

Louis turned to Colbert. "Monsieur Lully speaks the truth. However, I believe that he may be able to make some economies, now that we no longer have the expense of the young singer to bear." The king cast a meaningful look at Lully.

"Yes," he said, "a great pity that such talent should perish." Lully understood that this was his monarch's way of punishing him for whatever role he might have had in provoking Émilie's suicide. He would have to bear some of the expense himself. This was vexing, to say the least. He had his heart set on some new tapestries for his town house in Paris. And Pierre had asked for a pretty little bauble, a gold buckle with rubies and pearls. He had been so sweet and comforting lately, Lully hated to say no.

The king smiled. "Let us have a grand bower. I see thousands and thousands of roses . . ."

"And perhaps there can be a chorus of pages, to cast flower petals before the king. I believe there is one in particular who has a fine voice?" Colbert waited for Lully to answer.

"I do not know whom you mean, Monsieur," he answered.

"Strange," said Colbert, smirking, "I have heard that you give private instruction to one young fellow at all hours of the day and night."

Lully's response caught in his throat, and he pretended to cough into his handkerchief.

"I hope you are not suffering from a cold," said the king, leaning back in his chair away from the court composer.

"No, Sire," Lully answered. "It was only the slightest tickle. But I believe you will not be disappointed with the spectacle or the singers who will next perform before you."

Lully remained closeted with Louis and Colbert for the remainder of the afternoon. By the time he left, he was furious and had made a mental note to discover who had betrayed him so infamously to Colbert. In those few hours he had discovered not only that his fortune was to be diminished because of Émilie's demise, but that he must take somewhat greater care with his personal proclivities, or he might find himself accused of a crime that not even the king would dare forgive. Fortunately, he knew that his wife would back him up. She was a fool, but she was loyal, and she liked the life to which his influence at court entitled her. She spent almost all her time in their house in Paris, never questioning her husband's right to have his personal valet in attendance night and day. A pity, really, that he could not return her esteem in equal measure.

$\backsim$

"Émilie," began Charpentier just before he was going to leave her one night and return to his celibate quarters at the Hôtel de Guise.

"Yes?" She stopped leafing through the book of poetry he had brought her and that she was too lazy to actually read and looked up at him from where she sat on the rug in front of the fireplace. "What is it?" she asked.

"I just think, it's time we made a few changes."

At last, thought Émilie. "You mean, I can go out now?"

"Well, not exactly, but if we make this change, I think you will be safer, and then soon you may start to appear in public again." Charpentier fidgeted with the lace on the edges of his cuffs.

Émilie was puzzled. He looked distinctly uncomfortable and would not meet her eyes. "I don't understand," she said.

All at once Charpentier turned his gaze full onto her, grasped her hands, and pulled her to her feet. The book that was in her lap tumbled to the floor. "Émilie, I think we should get married."

"Why?" Émilie blurted out the question before she could stop herself, and immediately regretted it.

Charpentier stepped back from her, pushed his wig back slightly and scratched his scalp, a familiar gesture that brought a smile to Émilie's lips. She reached for his hands again. "Do you love me?"

He was silent for a moment or two, his eyes traveling over her face as if looking there for confirmation. "Yes," he said.

The look on Charpentier's face made Émilie want to hold him like an infant, it was so full of uncertainty and fear. "Well then," Émilie said, lowering her eyes, "perhaps we should."

Charpentier took Émilie's face between his hands and drew her forward to him. He kissed her, very gently.

Émilie felt the touch of his lips, warm, moist, and light, on hers. Something gave way inside of her, and she felt a tingling in regions of her body that were far from her mouth. It was a pleasant sensation. She let his kiss continue as long as he cared to press his mouth to hers. Émilie knew that they should get married, knew that it would happen even if she had not enjoyed Charpentier's kiss so much. There was the matter of propriety, after all. Despite the fact that no one was aware that she was living there at a man's expense, unchaperoned, in an apartment in a part of town where women of ill repute set up house-keeping four or five times a day, Émilie realized that the arrangement was not entirely *comme il faut*.

"And what about you?" asked Charpentier, after he had stopped kissing Émilie, and the two of them simply stood there, searching each other's eyes.

"Me?" she asked.

"You know," he said. "Are you happy? About getting married?"

"Of course I am!" Émilie wanted to give him the answer she knew he was looking for. But somehow, just then, she could not. It would have been so simple, just to say those three words, to surrender herself completely to the idea that they would never be separated again, that her soul was bound to his for all eternity, but something held her back. She was grateful to Charpentier for not asking in a way that would force her to say it when she needed time to understand what it all meant. The reality of her situation, the carrying through of the scheme that Madame de Montespan had concocted ostensibly to help Émilie return to the man she loved, had opened her eyes. What she had felt before was yearning, infatuation, desperation. Consenting to be married was one thing. Admitting to being in love was something else altogether.

*   *   *

The wedding was set for three days later, at midnight.

"I feel like a criminal," Émilie said as they went over the arrangements.

"Nonsense! You're not doing anything wrong. You have never done anything wrong."

Émilie was not so sure. She had never told anyone about the evening slippers, not even Charpentier. Somehow committing her misdeed to the permanence of pen and paper was too frightening, and so she did not relate the story of their demise in her letters, as she had intended to. And Charpentier still did not know about the diamond brooch. It remained hidden, wrapped in a handkerchief, in the little cabinet that contained her personal belongings. When he was not there, she sometimes took it out just to look at it. It was her only link with a life that seemed now to have been no more than a dream. She would ponder for hours at a time the idea that everyone she knew at court presumed that she was no longer alive. She had in her possession the only evidence that might prove them wrong, and it fascinated her.

"We'll have to do something about your hair, for a while at least."

Émilie shook herself out of her reverie and tried to attend to all that Charpentier said.

"We'll try a wig, just to be sure."

"But I still don't understand why midnight," she asked, having followed her own train of thought despite her attempt to pay attention.

"I've told you before. We need to do it when there will be no one in the church."

Émilie feared, from something he said, that Charpentier had laid down large sums of money to keep the records hidden. He had gone over everything several times, but try as she might, she could not keep it all straight in her mind. Every time she asked him about it, she hoped that the circumstances had somehow magically altered, that there was no more need for secrecy. But his answer remained always the same. He explained to her that she was not to be "Émilie Joli-coeur," but "Marcelline Sansvoix"—only for a few hours, because she would return to the apartment as Marcelline Charpentier. That was very difficult for her, losing her name. Émilie could not accustom herself to the idea. Charpentier promised her he would still call her by her given name when they were alone. It was only necessary for the sake of the parish register that she not be Émilie.

The court of Versailles seemed a lifetime away at that moment, and yet it loomed like a threatening presence over everything they did. Émilie tried to picture what was happening at each moment in her absence, and only then realized how much her existence there had been centered upon her own activities. She had no idea what everyone else did while she was engaged in singing, drawing, reading, writing, walking in the garden, or learning fancy needlework. And yet, there were hundreds—thousands—of people, continuing what-ever occupations and business had previously taken up the hours of their days, as if she had never existed. Just as they would have if she had truly died. Perhaps François missed her; perhaps he was the only one whose life would be different without her there.

When she took Charpentier's name tomorrow, she would cease to exist again, or at least a part of her would no longer be, that part of her that identified her as the daughter of her father. There too, her parents' life would not change at all. She wondered who had told them that she died. It grieved her to think they would believe they no longer had a child. That would be the first thing she would do when she could. She would find a way to tell them that she was still alive. Being dead to everyone else was bearable. Being dead to her parents felt too real.

Twenty-one

*There is no passion where pride reigns more powerfully
than in love, and one is more often content to sacrifice
the peace of mind of the person one loves
than to sacrifice one's own.*
Maxim 262

Less than three blocks away from where Émilie waited in chaste
near-solitude to become a married woman, Sophie continued to
sell the rights of consortium several times a night. Circumstances
had made it necessary that she put her plans for an acting career
aside for a little longer. Although she had counted on being finished with her vengeful meddling by now and therefore able to
move on to a more respectable lifestyle, nothing had gone according to plan. She waited outside the Hôtel de Guise early the morning after she had waylaid the stable boy, hoping to be present
either when Charpentier returned disappointed or when the
bailiffs arrived to arrest him for his part in the plot. To her dismay,
neither of these events occurred. A courier came to the door with
a note just after Charpentier showed up at around dawn, the distracted elation in his eyes telling of the success of the previous
night's adventure. Sophie was smart enough to realize that some-

one at Versailles must have intercepted her letter before it could reach Madame de Maintenon. And clearly, interfering with the stable boy had not delayed Charpentier enough to spoil the abduction. If only she could have thought of some way to meddle with the horse. But she was afraid of horses and did not know what she might have done that would have rendered the animal unfit to ride.

So far, Sophie's actions had been determined by a combination of will and serendipity. There was no question that she felt badly used by Émilie and Charpentier, but without full possession of the facts, Sophie was not entirely willing to condemn them. Now, however, calamity was piled upon calamity, and her pride was stung. As far as Sophie knew, Émilie had been handed the life she herself had craved and then had thrown it all away by running off with Charpentier. It never occurred to Sophie that the successful abduction was achieved without Émilie's full cooperation. And yet she had seen enough of life at court not to assume that she knew everything. Therefore she felt that it was still necessary for her to guard her hand, to maintain whatever anonymity she had until she could arm herself with more information. The worst thing would be to go barging in somewhere and discover that she'd gotten everything entirely wrong.

So whenever work would allow, Sophie took the opportunity to wait for Charpentier at the Hôtel de Guise so that she could start following him again. After only two days, she managed to be there at the time he emerged, late in the afternoon. He carried a leather satchel under his arm and was far too preoccupied to notice her, and so despite his circuitous route—no doubt designed to prevent anyone's discovering exactly where he was going—she shadowed him all the way to the apartment in the Marais where Émilie was hidden. To Sophie's amazement, this was in the same part of Paris in which her own squalid room was located, although the house where Émilie was hiding looked nicer than hers. Not that she actually saw Émilie, but she knew that Charpentier was not the type to patronize a whore, nor was he likely to keep a mistress. In fact, from everything she had seen

of him at the Hôtel de Guise, she had once presumed he wasn't interested in women at all.

It happened that the house where Émilie was staying was known
to Sophie. Although she had never used it herself, other women
she'd spoken to on the streets named it as an ideal place to bring
high-class customers, who might be offended by the usual rundown
apartment. The landlady made a show of being respectable, but in
addition to renting rooms on a long-term basis (generally to the more
modest class of kept women), she was not averse to letting out for an
hour or two any that stood vacant, if those who wanted them looked
respectable enough and could pay.

For the moment, Sophie bided her time, waiting to see what the
couple would do next. She took to loitering near Émilie's room whenever she could, hoping to hear or see something significant.

It was not long before Sophie's patience paid off. The day after
she began her new vigil, she overheard Charpentier speaking to the
landlady on his way in.

"I'll want a closed fiacre, here, at midnight. Can you arrange it for
me?" She saw Charpentier discreetly slip a few coins into the landlady's hand.

"Easy as pie," she answered. "It'll be waiting for you, right
here."

Charpentier thanked her and went into the house.

That's an evening's wages out the window, Sophie thought. She
would have to be on hand to see what Charpentier intended to do
with this carriage so late at night. She would do her best to compen-
sate, then return at about eleven-thirty. It was more difficult to get
business early in the evening, before too much drink had made the
men bold and horny, but it was better than nothing at all. And there
was no question of her not being on hand to see what Émilie and
Charpentier would do.

By midnight, with only a few additional liards in her pocket,
Sophie was hidden in the shadows near Émilie's room, watching,

waiting. After a moment or two she saw the door of the house open, and through it came Charpentier leading a cloaked and hooded figure by the hand to the waiting coach. Sophie had not seen Émilie since the night she helped her prepare for her début at the Hôtel de Guise, but she had a clear, physical memory of the young girl. A year of growing, a long cloak, and a dark wig were not enough to disguise Émilie's way of walking, her gestures, her profile.

The coach traveled slowly to avoid making too much noise, so Sophie was able to follow them easily on their course through the winding Paris streets, taking little short cuts in order to keep up. In any case, the exercise did not tire her. It was time and energy well spent.

"Pardon, mademoiselle."

A man's voice spoke, and Sophie quickened her pace. She did not want a customer at that moment.

"Mademoiselle! Stop at once!"

Sophie, with a sinking realization that this was not a customer, stopped where she was. Doing her best to look respectable and fierce, she turned just as she heard the heavy footsteps about two feet behind her.

"Monsieur, may I be of service?" There before her was a police officer.

"What's a girl like you doing out here at this hour? And in a nice, respectable neighborhood like this?"

"I'm just going for my evening walk, to settle my stomach."

"Perhaps you've just eaten something that disagreed with you?" The officer leaned toward Sophie. She stepped aside quickly and he lost his balance, falling flat on his face. *"Putain!"* He spit the word out as though it fouled his mouth to say it.

Sophie looked around. She could still hear the coach wheels but had lost sight of the vehicle. She had to think of something. The policeman struggled to stand up.

"So sorry, Monsieur, but I fear I shall be ill at any moment." Sophie slid her foot in the way of the officer's so that he fell down again, cursing and spitting. She tried to run off, but he grabbed her ankle. His grip was very strong.

"I think you'd better come with me."

Marriage was something Émilie's mother had threatened her with when she did not behave. She had never thought of it as a desirable event. Although her parents were certainly not miserable, she was more aware of their affection for her than conscious of their feelings for each other. She had left home too young and too suddenly for her mother to have fully explained all that getting married involved. Émilie knew that she and Charpentier would sleep in the same bed together and that they might possibly have children, but the connection between the two events was not entirely clear to her. Added to that, the obscurity of the night, the lonely furtiveness of the excursion, only placed another layer of unreality on the whole event.

"You're trembling!" Charpentier held Émilie's hand.

"I don't know why I'm frightened. I know you will be kind."

Neither of them looked directly at each other, instead choosing to peer out of the coach windows as they rolled quietly along. When at last they arrived at St. Louis, having taken a deliberately circuitous route to the church that was only about half a mile from where Émilie lived, Charpentier helped her out of the fiacre.

"Wait here a moment," he said, leaving her halfway up the steps as he went on ahead to see that everything was in order.

Émilie stood where she was and removed her hood. A breeze had come up and chased away the mist that hovered at ground level. The buildings and streets were suddenly very clear, clean, and quiet, devoid of the constant bustle that normally enlivened them. Émilie filled her lungs with air that smelled of Paris, an unmistakable mix of baked bread, fish, and horse manure. She had not been outside since their arrival in the city a few days before. She looked up to the heavens and saw the remaining clouds being pulled away from the moon, and a few autumn stars twinkling weakly. Émilie let the moonbeams caress her face for just a moment, and then she looked toward the east and gasped.

There, illuminated for an instant, were the eight towers of the Bastille, silent and dark. Even in the daytime the compound was a heavy, threatening blot at the end of the rue St. Antoine. Émilie lifted her hood again as the clouds came racing back to conceal the moon. She turned to look for Charpentier, suddenly desperate for his touch. He walked toward her down the steps, smiling. She began to breathe again.

"Let me go! I haven't done anything wrong! I was just—" a female voice shouted, rupturing the stillness of the night.

Émilie looked at Charpentier with alarm. A policeman led a whore down the middle of the rue St. Antoine in the direction of the Bastille. She struggled and dragged against the rope he had tied around her wrists.

"We'll just let the magistrate decide in the morning, shall we?"

"Quickly," whispered Charpentier, taking Émilie's hand and pulling her up the church steps and into the sanctuary.

Inside, Émilie could still hear the prostitute's voice complaining and yowling against her captor.

"It's all right. I don't think they noticed us," said Charpentier.

"But the poor thing! Do you think he was taking her to the Bastille?"

"It's of no account. Look, here is Father Dominique."

The priest, who was a particular friend of Charpentier's, greeted them. The small group processed quietly up the long center aisle of the church, whose nave was lit only by a few candles, leaving it mostly in deep obscurity. But the darkness felt far from empty. Whether because of the echo of worship just finished or because she felt the presence of the souls of those who were commemorated in windows and tablets, it seemed to Émilie that a crowd thronged just beyond reach of the candlelight.

The rites were very brief. Émilie was relieved to mount the coach once again and return to her little safe haven, this time as Marcelline Charpentier. Yet despite her misgivings, something about the whole affair, now that it was accomplished, gave her a glow of pleasure. To be married was to be something else. To be someone else. To belong to someone else. To be a wife. To have a husband. Émilie threaded her arm through Charpentier's and leaned her head on his shoulder, letting the gentle motion of the coach soothe her.

He gave her arm an answering squeeze.

Twenty-two

*Those who are incapable of committing great crimes
do not easily suspect them of others.*
Blaise Pascal

Madame de Maintenon was alone in her sitting room writing letters
when the footman announced St. Paul. She was still extremely vexed
with him for his part in the disastrous events following the performance, and would have preferred not to see him. But as yet she was
uncertain how much the count really knew about her initial plan, and
thought it unwise to risk alienating him. The girl had died; that was too
bad, especially since the manner of her death did not have the dramatic
force she had hoped it would. At least her own hands were clean.

Madame de Maintenon had just finished folding and sealing a letter to Monsieur de la Rochefoucauld when St. Paul entered.

She stood and curtseyed deeply. "I am delighted to see you, Monsieur le Comte."

"Madame," St. Paul said. "There is some paperwork, for the
authorities. As a self-murderer, Mademoiselle Émilie must be
accounted for. What do you wish me to do?"

"I beg your pardon, but I was under the impression that François
had taken care of all the legalities."

"If a burial dispensation was to be given, it required the signature of the king."

Madame de Maintenon rose and turned away from St. Paul. "I think you should leave the authorities to me. I don't want to trouble the king if it is not necessary. He is much occupied at present. There is trouble once again in the Low Countries. Ask François to attend me here, and I shall discuss the matter with him."

"As you wish, Madame," said St. Paul, who bowed and left. As soon as he was on the other side of the door, he smiled broadly.

⌒

"What do you know about this business of the singer?" the king asked one morning when he was closeted with Colbert, going over the accounts. "St. Paul has been running around suggesting that all was not as it appeared."

"I know little about the matter, but I don't advise an investigation," said the canny finance minister, not looking up from the ledger.

"Oh?"

"It doesn't do to go turning over rocks. You never know what will crawl out." At that, Colbert made a hand gesture that was their silent code for Madame de Montespan. One could never be too careful. The king's mistress was not known for her forgiving nature, and if the singer's death just happened to remove a potential rival from court, then there was always the chance that something suspicious was going on.

"I see. Shame, really."

Louis intended that to be his final word on the subject. He had long ago learned to choose his battles, and he did not want to upset his pregnant paramour. There were many other pretty maidens at court who were all too eager to amuse him, although none, he had to admit, had such a voice.

But the matter of Émilie's death refused to stay sealed shut. One cold winter's day, Marcel Jolicoeur took it upon himself to deliver two violins to Monsieur Lully, who had ordered them months ago.

"What can this accomplish?" asked Madeleine, as she brushed off Marcel's best coat while the maid waxed his new leather boots.

"The violins must go to Versailles in any case. And I must do this, for myself. I cannot believe—" Marcel could not continue his thought.

Madeleine sighed. "Going there will not bring her back. And now, how do we know the commissions will continue? What about the money?"

"The fiacre will cost less than the silk for your dresses," said Marcel.

Madeleine said nothing more.

The luthier had never been so far away from his home before. The trip seemed momentous, despite the fact that he planned to be home in time for dinner. He watched the houses and churches become more sparse and finally give way to rolling fields and forests, dotted only by the occasional farmhouse or inn. After a time the village of Versailles appeared, and then, like a monstrous growth from the landscape, the immense château loomed ahead. Out here, stuck in the middle of nowhere, it looked more imposing than the Louvre.

Marcel instructed the fiacre to wait for him, and a footman led him to Lully's apartment on the lower floor of the château.

Lully was a little surprised to see Marcel but just as glad that he would have to take one less trip to the luthier's squalid little workshop to collect the violins for his ensemble. Still, he had to admit Jolicoeur's work was very fine. Almost as fine as the Italians'. They concluded their business quickly, but Marcel stood in Lully's study, curling the edge of his hat nervously in his fingers.

"I wonder, Monsieur Lully, would it be too much to ask—would you be so kind—"

Lully waited impatiently for him to finish his sentence.

"Could I see where she is buried? My daughter, I mean?"

"Of course, this is a natural desire," he said. "It was a terrible, terrible loss to art. Unfortunately, I am unacquainted with the exact location, you understand . . ." He paused, letting Marcel fill in the gap however he pleased, but with the knowledge that as a player, as someone who had dared to step upon the stage and perform for an audience, Émilie had fallen permanently from grace and could not be buried in consecrated ground. The fact that she was a suicide simply gilded the lily. "Pierre will fetch someone who may be able to help you, however. If you would be so kind?"

Lully sent his page off to find François while he tried to carry on a polite conversation with Marcel. He did not know what to say to the luthier, who did indeed look very sad. He himself was mystified by Émilie's actions. It made no sense for her to have done such a thing when she was clearly poised for great success—which was precisely what he told the widow Scarron when she asked to see him. Lully believed that Émilie's suicide was one unfortunate incident that Madame de Maintenon had had nothing to do with. She had sent for him and quizzed him about the singer's state of mind on the night of the performance. Lully was a little worried that she would try to blame him for the girl's rash step, although he did not know why she would think it necessary.

It really was a pity. Émilie had even surprised Lully with her ability to rise to the demands of the role. He was prepared to put Mademoiselle St. Christophle aside for good after the other evening. His one consolation about the whole thing was that Charpentier didn't have Émilie's voice at his disposal either.

Within a short while Pierre returned with François, who asked Marcel to accompany him for a walk in the deserted, winter garden.

Marcel let loose a torrent of recollections about his daughter. The memory of her was still fresh in his mind. Every time he looked around at their new comfort and prosperity, knowing that it had been bought at the price of Émilie's life, he felt as if there were bands wrapped around his heart that were being squeezed. At first he thought of giving up making violins. If it were not for the Amati copy he had crafted for Monsieur Charpentier, none of this would have happened. Émilie would have stayed at home singing for him, perhaps one day for a husband, and eventually for her children. But making violins was like breathing to Marcel, and so instead he lavished even more love and care on every one he produced.

"Were you with her at the end? Why did she do it?" Marcel's words were labored, squeezed out, as if it hurt him to speak.

"She was unhappy with her performance. She felt the king was displeased with her, and could not bear the disgrace." François looked away. He wondered if the luthier could tell he was lying.

Marcel nodded, working his mouth a little as if he wanted to say something else, but he simply shook his head. François led Marcel to a corner of the garden, not far from the village of Trianon, the same distant corner where Émilie often strayed when she tried to steal a few moments unobserved. The two men sat for a while on a rustic bench, each absorbed in his own thoughts. Marcel tried as hard as he could to imagine his daughter sitting by him on the bench. He almost felt like reaching for her hand, or stroking her golden hair, and when he closed his eyes, he could see the expression on her face. Marcel always imagined Émilie smiling.

François, on the other hand, could see much more than just the specter of the young girl he had helped to disappear from life. He could see that his action had only complicated what was already a very murky situation. Although he did not know it for a fact, François suspected that Madame de Montespan was involved in Émilie's disappearance and that Madame de Maintenon was not taken in by his story of her suicide. The entire tale would unravel with the slightest tug at a dangling thread, and yet everyone left it there in plain view. This was a very bad sign indeed.

The image of Émilie's father trudging slowly off to the main gate of the château, his strong shoulders bowed with almost unbearable grief, haunted François for the rest of the day and refused to go away when he tried to sleep that night. That and the thought of himself being carted off to prison conspired to make it impossible for the normally sanguine servant to have any repose. He shifted and fidgeted, punching the bed's lumps of straw into different shapes, but to no avail. At about three in the morning, François rose from his bed, lit a candle with an ember from the fire, and then sat down at his desk.

For the next two hours, François composed a letter and figured out a way to get it to its destination without its being discovered. Writing was the simplest action to take, and it would cut short the train of lies. Although there was no way to fix everything that had happened, it was entirely within his power to amend one part of the whole mess, and so that is what he did. He had to trust that the luthier would understand the necessity to maintain the secrecy concerning what had happened, to allow his daughter to remain dead to the rest of the world. Just before daybreak, when the movement of only a few menial servants broke the stillness of the enormous palace, François crept down to the kitchens to have a word with a certain scullery maid whose discretion he trusted, and the letter began its journey that very morning.

～

"Monsieur le Comte, if I may beg a word with you." Lully stopped St. Paul on his way back from Mass the morning after Marcel visited Versailles.

"If it is brief. I have much to do."

"Its brevity will depend upon you, Monsieur." Lully gestured in the direction of his study, and the two men walked there in silence. When the door closed behind them, Lully spoke. "I have one or two questions, about Mademoiselle Émilie's . . . demise."

Lully told St. Paul of Marcel's visit, and his own curiosity about how a young girl with such a bright future ahead of her could have taken so rash a step. "And then, there is the matter of the legalities surrounding a suicide. How is it that the servant François could simply dispose of the girl's body somewhere in the garden, like a beloved lapdog? And that no one, not even Madame de Maintenon, raised any objections to it? I was wondering, Monsieur le Comte, if you had any insight about these matters—as you seem at present to be so intimate with the widow Scarron. You see, she called for me, and I do not want her to be under any misapprehension about my role in the affair."

St. Paul was silent for a moment. It occurred to him that here was a potential ally in his new quest to get Émilie back to Versailles. He knew there was no love lost between Lully and Madame de Maintenon, and the composer would certainly be delighted once more to thwart his rival, Monsieur Charpentier. Added to that, St. Paul was in possession of secrets about Lully and his illegal proclivities that might act as security against any possible treachery on the composer's part. "Monsieur Lully, what would it be worth to you to have a voice like Mademoiselle Émilie's at your disposal again?"

"There was only one such voice. You were fortunate to find her in the first place. I doubt such good luck will be yours again."

"Ah, but I think you are mistaken. I have it in my power to bring Émilie Jolicoeur back from the dead."

Lully's eyes opened wide, then narrowed. "I think you must tell me what you know."

"I shall tell you, not because I want to gratify your wishes, but because I need an ally here at court." And, St. Paul thought, Lully's famously extensive personal resources would not go amiss either.

"I thought the widow Scarron occupied that position," Lully said.

"So did I, until recently."

Lully looked at the ceiling and thought for a moment, then turned his eyes back to St. Paul. "But there could be great risks. And what makes you think that you can trust me?"

"Shall we say," St. Paul answered, "that there are aspects of your life that would not withstand scrutiny." At that St. Paul let his gaze wander over to Pierre, who made a show of polishing Lully's perfectly immaculate boots. "Therefore I know that I may rely upon you to maintain absolute secrecy. We both have much to gain, I believe, and also much to lose."

Lully made a sucking sound with his lips and then let out a low whistle. "What do you want me to do?"

"I am never short of ideas, but I fear I am quite short of capital. And there are expenses . . ."

"All right, Monsieur de St. Paul. Perhaps you had better tell me your plan."

The count told Lully of his suspicions, of the planned abduction on the night of *Alceste,* and of his own failed attempts to apprehend the couple. "So you see, Monsieur Lully, where things stand."

It took Lully a moment or two to digest what St. Paul told him. After a brief silence, he said, "I am prepared to do whatever is necessary to bring Mademoiselle Émilie back to Versailles, so long as it will not compromise my own position."

"Oh, I hardly think it will. After all, we are only dealing with a peasant."

"A peasant, yes, but what of Charpentier?"

"What of him?" asked St. Paul. "He is only a composer."

"Do not forget, Monsieur le Comte, who is paying for this project." Lully drew himself up and pulled his waistcoat down a fraction of an inch over his paunch.

"And do not forget, Monsieur de Lully, who is pulling the strings." St. Paul looked once more in Pierre's direction. "But let us not quarrel. The first thing we must do is engage a spy."

"I am acquainted with a certain person who is particularly adept at seeing people without being seen. Shall I ask him to watch the Hôtel de Guise?"

"No, I think Charpentier will be too careful. Let us, rather, keep an eye on the Atelier Jolicoeur. It would not surprise me if Mademoiselle Émilie were unable to resist the call to visit her family."

The two men agreed and then parted, each of them certain he had the advantage over the other.

∽

One evening a few days later, just after the maid had cleared away the dinner dishes and Madeleine was preparing to work at her embroidery frame by candlelight, Marcel cleared his throat.

"I received a letter today," he said, walking to the chimney breast and reaching down his pipe.

"Oh? What did it say?"

Marcel waited until his pipe was lit and he had sat comfortably in his armchair before replying. "I don't know."

"Didn't you take it to the market to be read?" Madeleine was a little irritated.

"No. I didn't like to."

"Why ever not?" she asked, looking up from her work.

Marcel pulled the letter out of his pocket and held it out to his wife. Madeleine walked over and took it, turning it around in her hands, looking at the fine paper with the meaningless scrawl covering one surface.

"I was afraid. It looks important. If it was about money, I did not want the clerk to lie to me and make up some story about what is in the letter."

He had a point, Madeleine had to admit. You just couldn't trust anyone these days. "Still, you must find out what it says . . . Will Monsieur Lully come soon to collect his lutes?"

Marcel nodded his head. "Of course! He will be here in a day or two. I shall ask him to read it for me. At least I know I can trust him."

That settled, Marcel and Madeleine sat absorbed in their own worlds until the candle burnt down and it was time to go to bed.

～

Three days later, when Lully arrived, François's letter was nailed to the wall of the Atelier Jolicoeur, still undeciphered. After he and his patron had finished their business with the lutes, the luthier cleared his throat.

"Pardon, Monsieur de Lully," he said, "but I wonder if I could impose on your kindness. I have received a letter, and . . . you understand . . ." Marcel saw the puzzled look on Lully's face. Although he had never missed the ability to do so before, having never needed any knowledge that he could not carry around in his head, Marcel wished at that moment that he could have spared himself this embarrassment by reading his letter himself. He released the folded paper from its nail and held it out to Lully.

"What does it say?" asked the composer.

"That's just it. I do not know."

"Ah! I am so sorry. Forgive me. Of course I would be delighted to read it for you." Lully took the letter and cast his eye over it quickly.

Marcel waited patiently. Since he had no idea how long these things might take, he did not notice that Lully had read the document several times before clearing his throat and saying, "It says that there are some of your daughter's effects at Versailles, which François forgot to give to you when you visited the other week. They will be sent to you when a suitable messenger can be found. Indeed, had I known, I would gladly have brought them myself!"

Marcel thanked Lully and reached for the letter.

"If you would permit me to keep it, I can be certain to collect all these effects for you and bring them back when I come for the consort of viols." Lully held the letter by its edge, as if it were of little consequence.

The letter was no use to Marcel since he could not read it, and so he agreed. He was a little surprised that its contents were not more important, but he had no reason to assume that Monsieur Lully had not faithfully conveyed them to him. He would tell Madeleine all about it later on. It was a relief to know that it did not bear still more ill tidings.

Twenty-three

*True love and ghosts have much in common: they are
often talked about, but few people have ever seen them.*

Maxim 76

Émilie began to draw curling shapes all over the little picture she had
just finished sketching. She took her cue from the tail of a bird that
flipped upward with insouciance, extending and extending the line,
following the arc and then bending it and twisting it, and soon all the
white space on the paper was covered with arabesques. She held the
picture up at arm's length to examine the end result. The riotous effu-
sion of lines and spaces made her feel nauseated. She had to close her
eyes for a minute and think about the clear blue sky. Émilie thought
she had spent too much time indoors, and married life disagreed with
her, literally. She had lost all her appetite and was frequently in a bad
temper—although she tried hard not to be sharp with her husband.
Her only consolation was that, now that she had been married for a
while, she was no longer troubled by the inconvenient descent of her
monthly flowers.

Once her wave of nausea had passed, Émilie looked around her at
the home that she and Charpentier shared, and whose walls had
become the boundary of her life. Although they had traded her tiny

room for a larger apartment on the rue des Écouffes, and Lucille now came to them for the entire day, Émilie itched to go out of doors, to roam freely through the Paris streets. But it was too dangerous. Even if no one really cared about her, she knew that Charpentier's actions, if discovered, might ruin him. So she made the time pass as best she could and stayed out of sight of everyone except her husband and the maid, who had been trained to rebuff nosy neighbors and was rewarded handsomely for not gossiping.

Émilie picked up her pen and a fresh sheet of paper.

"Dear Marc-Antoine," she said aloud, writing the salutation at the top of the sheet. She stopped and ran her fingers over the words she had just written. Then she blushed, remembering the first time they were together, the night of their wedding. It was embarrassing, not knowing what to do. And it had hurt. Marc-Antoine had tried to be gentle, but there it was. By now she had grown used to it all, to the fact of his nakedness beside her in bed. In fact, she often welcomed it. Thinking of him, now, gave her an indescribably warm feeling, deep inside her. Sometimes she spent hours remembering what Marc-Antoine had said and done with her the night before. It made the time pass pleasantly when she was on her own.

Émilie sat very still, listening to the tick of the mantle clock her husband had given her as a wedding present. In the complete stillness, the ticks became almost deafening. The other day she counted them, from the time Marc-Antoine left until the time that Lucille returned from the marketing to prepare the midday meal. Six-hundred forty-seven thousand and sixty-three seconds. The exercise so enervated her that she fell asleep in front of the fire that afternoon.

"I wish you didn't have to go to work." Émilie's voice and the scratch of the pen broke the silence of the empty room once more. When Charpentier returned at the end of each day, Émilie drank from his experience like someone dying of thirst. He had had contact with the outside world; he had things to report on and joke about. She would sit on the floor at his feet and listen to him, making sympathetic noises and little comments that encouraged her husband to continue talking until it was time to go to bed, and then he would begin to do all the things she had learned to enjoy so much, before they finally fell asleep in each other's arms. Émilie crossed off the sentence she had just written, and instead wrote, "I wish that I could go to work with you." Then she crumpled up the paper and tossed it in the fire.

Émilie waited impatiently for Charpentier to return that night. When he walked through the door, she wanted to run up to him and throw her arms around his neck, but Lucille was still there, and she was not yet comfortable enough with her new relationship with her husband to be able to ignore the maid's presence.

"I've started on my needlework. I decided to work this picture." She held up one of her drawings, of a bird flying from an open window.

"Very good," he said, patting her on the head. Émilie blushed and glanced at Lucille, hoping she had not noticed this gesture. She did not like it when Marc-Antoine treated her like a child.

"What did you do today?" she asked, hoping he would begin his usual recital of frustrations and woes so that she could comfort him.

But instead he replied, "Oh, just the usual."

Émilie was surprised. She tried to make small talk, but every conversation she started dropped like a stone into the lake that suddenly yawned between them. They sat in silence for most of the evening. Émilie stitched her cushion cover, but it took a long time to do even a tiny patch. She interrupted herself dozens of times by looking up at Marc-Antoine, who sat and stared into the fire.

It was quite late, and Marc-Antoine had made no move to draw her into the bedroom. She yawned. "I'm tired," she said, when the fire became too low to give off enough light to work.

"You go to bed. I'll be in presently."

A hard lump rose from Émilie's chest into her throat. This was not right at all. They always went to bed together, facing away from each other as they undressed, and then slipping their naked limbs under the cool, soft linen sheets. There was a little game. It started with Émilie pulling the covers up to her chin and lying there like a virginal corpse, staring at the ceiling above her. After only a minute or two,

Marc-Antoine would reach over to her and gather her into his arms. The warmth of his skin against hers comforted her; it made up for all the hours alone, the endless stretches of time when she was assailed by doubts about what they had done. He would whisper silly endearments to her as he explored her body with his hands.

It was all wrong, to be in bed by herself. She left the candle burning and lay there, awake.

After about a half an hour, Marc-Antoine entered the room and began to undress. He sat on the edge of the bed, facing away from Émilie. He would not look into her eyes, which were still wide open, waiting. Before he finished undressing, he walked around to Émilie's side of the bed and snuffed the candle. When he climbed in next to her, she could feel that he still wore his shirt.

Émilie swallowed hard and tried to form words in her head so that they would come out sounding right when she finally worked up the courage to say something.

"Marc-Antoine?" she said. He turned toward her but did not answer. "Is something the matter?"

He rolled on his side, reached over to her and stroked her head, then leaned forward and kissed her on the cheek.

"We don't have to make love every night, you know," he said.

"We don't?"

"If you don't want to, you should tell me. I can't guess."

"Oh. I mean—" Émilie was confused. She thought she was doing what she was supposed to do. And she liked it. Did he not know? "I don't mind," she said, not knowing how else to tell him that she wished they would make love that night too.

"You don't mind," he repeated with a short laugh. "You don't mind."

They lay there in the dark, each staring into black nothing. Émilie wished she knew what had happened. Suddenly she felt she would die if he did not touch her, if she did not feel the slightly damp warmth of his hands on her skin. And yet she could not extend her own hand. She could not even make herself speak, or utter some word that would draw him to her. Wounded, Émilie rolled away from him and pulled her knees up, hugging them to her so tightly that her feet fell asleep before she did.

Émilie was stiff when she awoke the next morning. There was an empty space next to her. Marc-Antoine was already up, sitting in the other room, ready to leave her for the day.

"Won't you have tea?" she asked, trying hard not to cry.

"No, I have much to do. I won't trouble you. They'll give me tea at the Hôtel de Guise."

Émilie pictured herself running to him and wrapping her arms around his waist, begging him to forgive her for whatever it was that she had done. She was working up the courage and strength to ask him, again, what was wrong, when he rose, came to her and kissed her lightly on the cheek, and then left. The sound of the door shutting behind him released her from her stupor, and she ran into the bedroom, flung herself on the bed, and sobbed until she started to cough.

Charpentier walked more quickly than usual, pounding the heels of his boots into the cobbles so hard that they left little curved marks as he went. The night before was the first night since their marriage that they had not made love. He knew that if he had started it, everything would have transpired as usual. But he had been afraid that Émilie just went along with whatever he wanted, that she did not really love him. He was afraid that he had forced himself on her and that she simply lacked the courage to resist, to assert herself. He knew the conjugal rights were his, but the circumstances, the way they had married out of necessity—and she was so young, perhaps he really had no right. He tested her last night, to see how much she wanted to be with him, truly. And now it seemed that he was right. After all, what did he bring to her? Only furtive imprisonment.

Charpentier gradually slowed his pace, and when he reached the Hôtel de Guise, he did not go around to the servants' entrance but continued walking for another five minutes. He could not shake the image of Émilie's face that morning. His bride did not look bored or uninterested. If he really thought about it, really imagined her face when he left that morning, she looked hurt. Perhaps he had misjudged her. Perhaps she was too young to understand her own feelings. Perhaps he just needed to encourage her, to show her how he loved her, and not just the physical part. He stopped suddenly when he was almost at the Temple, turned around, and walked straight back home again. The musicians could wait.

Charpentier ran up the stairs to his apartment and flung the door open, an abject apology ready to burst from his lips. But he did not see Émilie in the parlor. From the bedroom, he heard a sound of someone being sick. He rushed in and saw Émilie retching into a basin.

"What's the matter? Are you ill?"

Émilie looked at him sadly. "I was so worried, and so sorry. I don't know what I did!"

Charpentier put his arms around her and cuddled her like a child. "It's all right. You didn't do anything wrong. I'm just a foolish man. Will you forgive me?"

Émilie looked up at his eyes and smiled. Suddenly a wave of nausea overcame her, and she rushed back to the basin.

"But Émilie! You are ill! Has this happened before?"

She nodded her head yes.

"I'm going to fetch a doctor."

"No, please!" said Émilie. "I feel better now, really!"

He looked at her for a moment, and the color returned to her cheeks. But still, he was concerned and insisted on sending Lucille to get the doctor.

"She's in perfect health," the doctor said after poking and prodding, putting his ear to Émilie's chest, and feeling her forehead to see if she had a fever.

Charpentier breathed a relieved sigh. "But then why?—"

The doctor interrupted him. "Which is a good thing, because in about five months, there will be another little member of this household. My felicitations to you both!" He beamed.

Émilie's and Charpentier's eyes met. At the same instant they rushed together and wrapped themselves around each other, leaving the doctor to let himself out.

∽

St. Paul gave his name to the footman outside Madame de Maintenon's apartment at Versailles. After a moment or two the servant returned.

"I regret to say that Madame is praying and may not be disturbed."

He looked at his pocket watch. "Nonsense. She never prays at this hour. Announce me."

Before the servant could protest, St. Paul pushed past him and entered the widow Scarron's sitting room. He found her with her auburn hair streaming down her back, wearing a black dressing gown that was trimmed with fur. She was at her desk writing letters. With a look she dismissed the footman.

"Ah, St. Paul! So good of you to call. I'm feeling much better now, thank you." Madame de Maintenon cleared her throat and coughed a little.

"Of course, that is the purpose of my visit. I thought you might need a little cheering up. I have some interesting news for you."

"Pray, be seated. I'm sorry I cannot offer you tea, but the servants are much occupied with bringing me my medicine." Another cough punctuated her speech.

"I trust this information will hearten you, and perhaps thereby speed your recovery."

"What information is that?"

"Only that Mademoiselle Émilie Jolicoeur still lives, and might be found by inquiring of a certain Parisian composer what he has done with her."

Madame de Maintenon stood and turned around quickly. She walked to her prie-dieu and looked up at the crucifix on the wall above it. "You toy with me, Monsieur de St. Paul. The girl is dead. She cannot come back to life."

"I submit, Madame, that she is not dead! We were duped, that is all. There was an ab—"

"I will hear no more!" Madame de Maintenon whirled around and glared at St. Paul. "I know not whence your 'information' comes, but it is absurd, it is macabre! Please do not trouble me further with this nonsense." She picked up a little bell and rang it peremptorily.

"As you wish, Madame, but I have proof," said St. Paul, and he retrieved François's letter from his pocket. "If I were you, I would question who around you I could really trust." He tossed the letter onto the floor between them and bowed before he turned and left, almost colliding with the footman who came in answer to the widow Scarron's bell.

～

Émilie rubbed her hand in a circle over her belly. It had not yet started to swell, but there was a firm fullness about it. She rocked back and forth slowly as she stood in front of the window, watching the world pass by in the twilight.

"When shall I be able to sing?" she asked. "Surely no one would mind if I just sang a little, to myself?"

"You must wait a while longer, now that we have to worry about the baby too," said Charpentier.

"But I'll lose all my agility! I was getting such high notes, at Versailles," she said, remembering, a little wistfully, the way the crowd cheered her when she sang *Alceste*.

Charpentier rose from his chair and stood next to Émilie at the window. "When you can sing again, I shall create such music for you!" He paused and stroked his chin. "Let me show you something." Charpentier went to the leather satchel that was next to his chair and withdrew a notebook. "This is only one of them. I have been filling them up, with songs for you. No one else shall sing them."

Émilie rushed to him and took the notebook from his hands, turning the pages and smiling. She traced the lines with her fingers and nodded her head. She could hear the music in her mind. "They are beautiful. Thank you!" Her eyes glowed. "How I wish I could sing them now."

Charpentier held out his hand for the notebook. "Not yet, my love."

She closed the volume and hugged it to her. "Let me just have this one, to look at now and again, and study, so that I know the songs when I can sing again."

Charpentier let his hand drop. "All right."

Émilie did not let go of the notebook all evening, and she placed it on the table next to the bed when they went to sleep.

The proximity of music, even cold and unrealized on the page, was a comfort to Émilie. But it did not lift her sinking spirits. When she felt particularly lonely and frustrated, she reached into the back of her dressing table drawer and drew out the little diamond bird, the morsel of Versailles that had attached itself to her the night of her escape. It glittered strangely in the otherwise modest surroundings. Charpentier still did not know she had it. She was afraid to show him; Émilie knew it was dangerous to keep it, but she could not let it go.

And then the idea that she would have a baby, be a mother, God willing, made her suddenly desperate to see her parents again. She longed to tell them. It gave her a cold feeling in the middle of her that they thought she was dead, especially when she was most particularly alive, alive for two.

Without really deciding to act, only letting her instincts carry her through, one especially desolate March day Émilie donned her dark wig and hooded cloak and quickly slipped out of the apartment. Lucille had laid the fires and tidied up and had gone out to do some errands and to visit a sick relative (or at least that is what she said she was doing, but Émilie suspected she was really going to meet a boyfriend). A fine, gloomy drizzle acted like a veil. Émilie was not the only person abroad who held her cloak tightly around her, and whose face was all but hidden from view.

Her feet felt the hardness of the cobbles beneath the soft soles of her indoor shoes. When the damp began to soak through, she remembered, with a guilty pang, that night more than a year ago when she had ruined a pair of slippers that were never meant to be worn outdoors and had ended up with a fever. That had been the start of her bizarre adventure, and so much had happened since then.

But soon Émilie forgot all about her feet, as her nose picked up the unmistakable scent of bread baking, and the smoky tang of leather from the glove maker's shop. She breathed the chilly, fouled atmosphere deeply, feeling it grate on her throat and slap into her lungs. Everyone on the street rushed to accomplish his business so that he could return to the comfort of a blazing fire, and no one took much notice of her slight figure, weaving along the streets, stepping aside to let coaches pass or to avoid a knot of people haggling over the price of a sausage.

Émilie wandered gradually southward, until she came to the Seine, just east of the Pont Notre Dame. Through the mist she could see the floating mills resting atop the greenish water. She heard rather than saw the pumps on the bridge, doing their work to make water flow to the fountains all over the city. She glided swiftly through the crowds, cutting through shoppers hurrying from place to place.

I must be careful. Perhaps I should turn around now and go home.

The words circled like plainchant in her head. But Émilie simply could not stop her feet from carrying her west along the quay toward the Pont au Change. She wandered past the fishermen spreading their catches out for the housewives to buy and paid no attention to the crowd that gathered in the Place de Grève to witness a hanging. All she was aware of was that just fifty feet ahead of her, tucked in next to the haberdashery on the west side of the bridge, was her father's workshop. She swore she could smell the wood from where she stood. Émilie knew that she must not get any closer, but for a moment or two she was suspended between coming and going. She did not know that her parents had moved to an apartment a few hundred yards away on the Quai des Mégissiers— Charpentier only visited the workshop and shared her letters with Marcel, and never having ventured into the apartment was not aware of the change. So Émilie imagined that nothing had altered since she went away. She pictured herself looking out of the window that faced west toward the Pont Neuf, making up romantic stories to fuel her imagination through the hours of helping her mother with the chores.

Émilie was so still and focused that she did not notice when passersby began to stare at her. Among the strangers who eyed her out of simple curiosity were two whose interest was more than passing. One of them was Hortense, her mother's best friend and someone who had known Émilie as a child. The woman's normally ruddy face went white, and she crossed herself three times before carving a wide path through the workday crowd in the direction of the Jolicoeurs' new home.

The other was the spy that Lully and St. Paul had placed in the vicinity of the Atelier Jolicoeur to watch for Émilie to respond to the ties of home and family.

After no more than a minute or two of gazing at her father's workshop, Émilie whirled around and hurried home again, not stopping to enjoy the sights and sounds, suddenly anxious to get back to the apartment before Charpentier returned and discovered her missing. On the way, though, and despite the fact that the sun was completely hidden in the mist, she had a shadow. It followed her almost to the door of her conjugal abode, where she was known as the reclusive Marcelline Charpentier, before slipping away to pass its intelligence on to its masters. Unaware that she had been followed, Émilie rushed into the apartment.

"Madame! Where did you go? You might catch a chill in this damp, and the baby!" Lucille scolded her as she removed the now very wet cloak from her mistress's shoulders.

Yet by the time her husband trudged wearily through the door two hours later, eager to return to the cozy warmth of his home, the cloak was dry and had been safely put away, and Émilie was engaged in working her embroidery, which was now nearly half complete. Charpentier noticed only that Émilie's cheeks were rosier than usual, that she looked healthy. He thought perhaps the worst was over for his pregnant wife, that there would be no more sickness in the morning, and that they could breathe a little more easily about the infant's health.

Émilie's inner turmoil, the powerful effect of seeing her home again after so much time, was nothing to the disturbance her appearance caused on the Quai des Mégissiers. After her sighting of the cloaked and wraithlike Émilie, Madame Hortense Bougier arrived chez Jolicoeur completely out of breath. She did not wait to be announced but burst in upon Madeleine, who was choosing between two bits of lace to embellish a new headdress.

"The saints preserve us!" exclaimed Hortense.

"What is it! Get a hold of yourself!" cried Madeleine, picking up a beaker of water and splashing it in the face of her agitated friend. Although not the politest of gestures, it worked, and Hortense's breathing slowed, the palpitations of her heart gradually eased, and she was able to explain herself.

"I've just seen a ghost! Or else, or else . . ."

"Or else what, for God's sake?"

"Émilie's alive!" Hortense practically exploded with the news.

Madeleine turned ashen. "That's impossible. They told us she was dead."

"Well, then, her ghost has come back to haunt us!"

Madeleine paced around the room, casting her eye over the upholstered chairs, the curtains, and the carpet, all evidence of the prosperity they now enjoyed thanks to Émilie's brief—but brilliant—career at court. There was no such thing as ghosts, so Madeleine believed. That Hortense had seen a real person she did not doubt. That it was Émilie seemed highly unlikely. "You must have been mistaken. You saw someone who looked like Émilie, that is all. How dare you frighten me so!"

"As God is my witness, there is no one who could possibly look so like Émilie. I swear it was herself!"

"Tell me exactly what you saw."

Madeleine poured a cup of wine for her friend and made her sit down until she was calm enough to describe everything. Émilie's mother listened patiently and asked few questions. When Hortense had finished, she sat in silence for several minutes.

"What will you say to Marcel?" asked Hortense.

Madeleine knew that the news would cause the most violent reaction in her husband, whose emotions were only just concealed beneath the surface of his life. It was still just an impression, just a possibility. No use getting his hopes raised only to discover that it was all a trick of the light, or a hallucination. And Hortense admitted that the figure she saw was almost entirely hidden by a hooded cloak. "I will say nothing to him. Nothing at all," Madeleine replied. "I would ask you to keep all of this to yourself for the present. Would you care for another cup of wine?"

Twenty-four

⮜⮞

*The vanity of others is insupportable only because
it wounds our own.*
Maxim 389

It had suited Madame de Montespan that Émilie was permanently
out of the way, although she was, truly, sorry that she had died. She
would have preferred a more romantic ending, with the young girl
being carried off in the middle of the night by her dashing young
lover—just as she had planned. But the end result was the same. The
singer was no longer a potential rival for the king's affections, and the
widow Scarron's plot had been foiled most effectively.

But one day, Madame de Montespan's usual network of informers
brought her surprising news. Émilie was still alive. Thank heaven that
the voice is preserved, she thought. It was necessary, however, to take
steps to ensure that others did not discover the singer's continued
existence and try to bring her back to court. The last thing she
wanted was to start all over again trying to get in the way of the widow
Scarron's plans. The marquise sent for François who, although she
knew he was one of Maintenon's spies, was also a particular friend of
Émilie's and might have more information that he'd be willing to
share with her for a price.

"So, I hear that Mademoiselle Émilie miraculously survived her fall from a great height."

François did not speak. The marquise addressed him in her formal room, seated in her velvet armchair.

"I confess, I am pleased that she did not perish. And I have no desire to see her returned to court." Madame de Montespan rose and walked toward François. He cringed slightly, as if he expected her to strike him. "My good fellow, you think because you are the widow Scarron's spy—I'm sorry, I mean footman—that I would demean myself by an assault upon your person?" She laughed her liquid, golden laugh. "Come with me."

She led François to her private study, a small room, furnished with an ornate escritoire and a few gilded stools. "No one will hear us in this place. You must tell me everything, because I alone can protect the young woman. I have heard that St. Paul is trying to bring her back, to finish the business he started with your mistress's help."

For the next hour François told Madame de Montespan as much as he dared.

"You say you wrote to the luthier? Has he been reunited with his daughter?"

"Alas, Madame. I made a terrible error. I remembered only after I sent the letter that the good Monsieur Jolicoeur cannot read."

"This is a complication. But it need not signify. Perhaps it is best he does not yet know of his daughter's whereabouts. We must remove her from Paris, before St. Paul finds a way to remove her from Monsieur Charpentier's protection."

"I do not understand, Madame, why the count wishes to do such a thing."

The marquise sighed. "Surely you cannot be so naïve. Don't you see that he wants to present her to the king? In these past months his Majesty has not stopped talking about the beautiful young singer and what a tragedy it was that she died. I'm sick to death of the topic."

"But what of Madame de Maintenon? Surely she cannot wish this to happen."

"You may serve Madame de Maintenon in this, or you may serve me. I do not know what that woman would do if she knew that Émilie still lived, because I do not know what she might have done had the girl not been carried off the night of her performance. I want to keep Émilie alive, but out of the way." Madame de Montespan leaned forward, fastening her bewitching eyes on François. "It's your choice. Keep Émilie safe and betray your mistress, or be loyal to your mistress and betray Émilie."

François wanted to tear his eyes away from this lady, but he was incapable of doing so. Perhaps Madame de Maintenon could be kept in the dark, and Émilie would be allowed to live out her days in peace. "What can I do?" he asked.

"I believe you have family in Paris?"

"Why, yes, Madame, but—"

"You must beg leave to go and see your father, who is very ill."

"But he died last year."

"Who knows this, besides yourself?"

François acknowledged that he had shared this personal news with no one at court.

"Go to Paris, then, immediately. Seek out Monsieur Charpentier, but take care that St. Paul does not know that you do so. Tell Charpentier to take his wife out of the city, to this place"—Madame de Montespan scribbled an address on a sheet of paper—"and leave her there. Oh, and give him this as well." She reached into a drawer in her desk and retrieved a leather pouch full of coins. "Quickly!"

François bowed and departed, taking the money and the paper with him.

∽

As the fields and forests gave way to scattered houses, and gradually to dwellings that were closer and closer together, François tried to remember the last time he had been in Paris on his own. It was when he was very young. From the age of ten he had been attached to the court, at first serving the Grande Mademoiselle and now the widow Scarron. He had generally traveled only between St. Germain and Versailles, with occasional sojourns at the rue Vaugirard to the south of the city proper when it was deemed prudent to get the illegitimate royal progeny out of sight. There were more buildings than he remembered, and more people too. The city was noisy—in part because more of the streets were cobbled than in the past, so that horses and carriages made a mighty clatter as they went about their daily business.

The route to the Hôtel de Guise took him over the Pont au Change. François saw the lute-shaped sign of the Atelier Jolicoeur as he passed. He wondered what Marcel had done with the letter, whether he had found anyone to read it for him. He would know soon enough. Undoubtedly the luthier would have been to see Charpentier by this time if he had. And François was afraid that it was only a matter of time before Madame de Maintenon discovered that he had switched his loyalties. It was a foolhardy thing to do, at his age, when he was so close to being taken care of for the rest of his days.

The carriage stopped at the servants' entrance to the Hôtel de Guise. François alighted and was led to Monsieur Charpentier's apartment.

"My name is François. I must beg leave to speak plainly with you."

Charpentier gestured toward the one chair in his study that was not covered with papers.

"Thank you, but I cannot stay long. I would prefer to stand."

"Perhaps you had better tell me your business." Charpentier felt the heat rise to his face. Without being told, he knew who François was. He had seen him, once before.

François looked around him nervously. "It is already dangerous that I had to come here. I have put myself at great risk. I would do so for no other person."

"But we have never met."

"I speak of Mademoiselle Émilie," he said.

"She exists no more." Charpentier turned away from François and pretended to be looking for something in the untidy heap of books and papers on his desk.

"I think we both know that she does. I was there when you came, that night after the performance."

"What do you want of me?" The composer stopped fussing with his papers and faced François. "And I tell the truth: there is no more Mademoiselle Émilie. She is now Madame Charpentier."

François took a step back. "Forgive me. Perhaps I misjudged you. I pray that she comes to no harm. But still, I must tell you."

"Tell me what?"

"There are interests at court who know she did not perish that night, and who will do anything—anything—to bring her back. I speak of le Comte de St. Paul."

"But why?"

François shrugged. "Why else? To please the king. To please the king, and grow wealthy."

Charpentier's legs suddenly felt weak. "What can I do?"

"You have an ally at Versailles, whose name I must not mention. You may trust this lady if for no other reason than that it is in her interests that Émilie *not* be returned to court. I bring you instructions, and some money with which to effect your escape."

Charpentier listened carefully to what he said. Things were worse than he imagined. It was dangerous for Émilie to remain where she was; in fact, it seemed likely that her whereabouts were already known. He wanted François to leave immediately, wished that courtesy did not require him to stay and listen politely, so that he could return to his wife, pack her into a fiacre, and send her into the country to escape St. Paul. But courtesy also required him to be sensible of the risk the servant had taken to warn them. "Thank you, my friend. You are very courageous to come and tell me this. I hope your kindness will not endanger you as well. If there is something I can do for you—"

"*Non,* Monsieur. Please do not consider yourself obliged to me. I act only on the orders of another. Good-bye, Monsieur. God speed Mademoiselle Émilie—Madame Charpentier."

～

Sophie was at her usual afternoon station, across the street from the house on the rue des Écouffes where Émilie and Charpentier lived, when she saw a doctor rush up to the door and enter. He was there for about an hour, and when he came out, his shoulders were bowed, and there was an air of defeat about him. She had no way of knowing whom he had gone in to see, but something told her that all was not well in the Charpentier household. Respectable doctors did not normally pay calls on prostitutes and the mistresses of clerks, who were the only other occupants of Émilie's building. A few moments later the Charpentiers' young maid emerged, carrying a basket full of linens and crying.

Could Émilie have died? Sophie thought she would have noticed something more, she had been so vigilant. Perhaps Émilie was very ill. She stayed where she was and waited to see if Charpentier appeared. After about twenty minutes she saw him run from the direction of the rue St. Antoine into the house, followed by the maid, whose basket was now empty. Sophie was desperate to know what had happened. She looked down at her scanty costume. After a few moments' thought, she headed toward her room a few blocks away. If Émilie was about to die, she didn't want to miss her final opportunity to confront her about the slippers. And for this visit, she thought she'd better make herself appear a little more respectable.

～～

It started that morning. Émilie awoke with a terrible pain in her abdomen. The baby, who had just begun to kick and move inside of her, was utterly still. She did not want to stir from her bed.

"You don't look well today, my love," said Charpentier, as he dressed to go to the Hôtel de Guise for a day's work.

"No, I'm a little tired. I think I'll just rest a while longer."

Charpentier kissed Émilie on the forehead and left.

For an hour or two, Émilie slept. She had horrible dreams. She saw St. Paul laughing at her and brandishing a pistol. Then Madame de Maintenon's mouth dripped blood. Finally, Marc-Antoine sobbed and sobbed, as if he had lost his soul. She awoke with a start, her abdomen in agony.

"Lucille!" she screamed. "Lucille!"

The maid rushed in. Émilie writhed on the bed, clutching her stomach. Lucille pulled the covers back and gasped. Émilie looked down. A large pool of blood soaked the sheets. "Run! Fetch a doctor, and Monsieur Charpentier!" she said, wishing she could die, anything to stop the pain.

Émilie had no idea how much time passed before the doctor was there. He stood by and felt her forehead, letting her body run through its ghastly business. When her spasms stopped, he lifted the sheet and examined her. "I'm sorry, Madame Charpentier. Your baby, you understand."

The pain in her stomach gradually subsided completely. She knew that she had pushed everything out, that all the blood and mess around her was what had been inside her, and now it was gone.

"I'll lift her while you remove the sheets," the doctor said to Lucille. "Take them to be burned. I'll stay and see that she's all right."

Lucille was pale. Her hands shook as she gathered up the blood-stained linens.

The doctor held Émilie in his arms. She could not take her eyes from the bed. There was something there. "My baby," she whispered, then she closed her eyes and turned away.

∽

Charpentier had just bid adieu to François and was already extremely agitated when Lucille burst into his study, shaking and crying.

"Oh, Monsieur!"

"Émilie! Is she—?"

"Thank the Lord, Madame Charpentier will be all right, she is just very weak. But the baby . . ."

Without waiting for her to finish, Charpentier grabbed his cloak and ran all the way back to the rue des Écouffes. He found Émilie exhausted and in some pain.

"Oh, Marc-Antoine!"

"Hush, Émilie, it's all right." He held Émilie and let her sob her heart out into him. Within moments his shoulder was soaked.

"I want—my baby—I want—to die!"

"There now! It's all right. You are well, that's all that matters. Hush, you must sleep now."

Bit by bit, Émilie's choking and weeping abated and she lay back against her pillows, exhausted. Charpentier sat on the edge of the bed and stroked her forehead until she closed her eyes. When she was fully asleep, he joined the doctor in the other room.

"Will she be all right?" Charpentier asked.

"There was not too much blood, so she should make a recovery. But she should not be moved for a week." The doctor handed a bill to Charpentier and waited politely while he counted out the coins to pay him.

"What about—children?" Charpentier stopped the doctor on his way out of the door.

He turned with his hand on the knob and said over his shoulder, "I wouldn't advise it. She was lucky this time, but who knows what might happen the next. And if she should go to term . . ." He did not finish, but nodded to Charpentier and then left.

Charpentier sighed deeply, then returned to the bedroom. He began to walk back and forth, every once in a while casting a glance in Émilie's direction. Her face twitched now and again, and twice she murmured something and then awoke with a start, only to fall asleep again the next instant. Charpentier felt his pocket. In it was the pouch full of money François had given him, and a piece of paper with the address far out in the country where he was supposed to send Émilie so that she would not be discovered. He had been told that he could not remain there with her. It would be too suspicious. But now everything had changed. Émilie was too ill to be moved right away: the doctor said a week. And he did not want to leave her alone with Lucille, who was too young to deal with any potential difficulties.

And with Mademoiselle's fête the next night, it would arouse suspicion if Charpentier left town suddenly. If they were to get Émilie away undetected, he must continue his life as if nothing were planned. That would mean leaving Émilie at home alone and unprotected. He had to think of something else, yet every idea led to a dead end.

"Beg pardon, Monsieur Charpentier, but there's a lady downstairs says to give you this." Lucille entered the room and handed Charpentier a pasteboard card. On it a small but confident hand had written "Sophie Dupin."

Sophie . . . Charpentier could not place the name. All at once he stopped pacing. Sophie! Of course! "Please ask her to come in."

Lucille stood where she was.

"Go on, do as you're told!"

The maid turned, shaking her head as she went down to the street door. "Won't even let me bring the landlady in for a cup of tea . . ."

Sophie had gone to some trouble to make herself look decent. She had washed the paint off her face, run a comb through her hair, donned a dress she had purchased in preparation for the end of her career as a prostitute, and doused herself in lavender water. Altogether she did not look too bad.

"What brings you to my home?" Charpentier greeted Sophie in the parlor, having closed the door to the bedroom so that she could not look in and see Émilie.

"Well, I, uh, I'm looking for a position, as lady's maid."

"A lady's maid? But as you know, I am a bachelor." Charpentier was aware that Sophie had been let go without references. And he remembered her approach to him on the street. He thought it odd that she should just turn up like this, although he could not blame her for wanting some other employment than that of prostitute. He wondered how much she knew.

"I beg to differ, Monsieur. Not only are you married, but your wife is a person who, you recall, is known to me. I have seen her. I know she lives here. But I am able to keep a secret."

Charpentier looked Sophie up and down, and then directly in the eyes. She drew herself up proudly and met his gaze without flinching. Could this be a solution to his temporary difficulties? "That does not mean—if it is true—that we actually need the services of a lady's maid. If I were to engage you in this post, what assurance do I have that I may trust you? I know that you were dismissed from the household of Mademoiselle de Guise. I never discovered why."

"My dismissal—there was a misunderstanding. Had I been able to tell the entire story, Monsieur, I do not think that it would have been I who was dismissed."

"Perhaps you'd care to tell me that story?" Charpentier remembered Sophie's kindness toward Émilie on the night of her début and thought perhaps she was telling the truth.

"I don't think it is important right now. If you do not need a lady's maid, I shall trouble you no longer." She turned to go.

"Wait!" Charpentier gestured toward a chair. "Please sit down. You were good to my wife once. I owe you some hospitality."

Sophie paused, then took the seat he offered. "My life has not been easy since we last met, Monsieur."

"We have little money. The wages would be very small."

"It has been difficult to find a position, you understand. In short, Monsieur, beggars cannot choose their relief."

"It just happens, Sophie, that you have come at a fortuitous time. I cannot help but place great trust in you. My wife is ill. She has suffered a—" He could not bring himself to say it. He had to turn away. "You see, until today, she was going to have a baby." Charpentier barely uttered the last word.

"I'm sorry, I have come at a bad time." Sophie stood.

"No, as I said, it's a good time. Please sit. We need your help. I too am a beggar of sorts. I have to tell you a long story, and you must swear never to repeat it." Charpentier sat down in the chair opposite Sophie.

∾

"So now what are we to do, Monsieur le Diable?" Sophie stroked the tom's chin. He purred loudly and closed his eyes. She had all the information she needed to put Émilie away for good, and to ruin Charpentier's career. She did not ask about the slippers. She had not been able to see Émilie at all, which was entirely understandable. Apparently she was still unwell.

In fact, Sophie had found out that Émilie had fallen ill once before, the night after the soirée at which she had made her début. It occurred to Sophie that it was this that had prevented the singer from returning the borrowed shoes. Yet whatever happened all that time ago did not change the consequences. She, Sophie, had been disgraced, had had to earn her living screwing dirty, greasy men who, nine times out of ten, really wanted to kill her. And she had been incarcerated for one revolting night in the Bastille, although the magistrate had let her go the next day (he was one of her customers). All because Émilie had repaid her kindness with, at the very least, disregard, if not malice.

Sophie decided she needed to sleep on the question. She stretched out on her bed, shoving to one side the cat, who growled at being displaced from the spot he had warmed up so thoroughly. Then she blew out the candle and tried to rest.

Twenty-five

It seems that nature has prescribed for each man,
from his birth, the limits of his vices and his virtues.
Maxim 189

Lully and St. Paul's spy easily discovered where Émilie was living, but
this knowledge was not yet converted to a plan that would succeed in
getting her back to Versailles. Other than François's letter, which only
proved that she was actually alive and had been carried off by Charpentier, there was no proof of any wrongdoing on Émilie's part, and
she was not important enough for charges of a political nature to be
trumped up against her. So once her whereabouts were known, the
two co-conspirators had to meet to discuss what they might profitably
do with this knowledge.

"For heaven's sake, man! This is unbearable." St. Paul covered
his nose with a scented handkerchief. The location of his conference
with Lully was the cellar where the garbage was thrown before being
removed from the vicinity of the château altogether, and the stench of
rotting flesh and vegetation (not to mention human feces from the
thousands of chamber pots emptied daily) was almost overpowering.
The locale had been Lully's suggestion. He well knew that there was
no other place in the palace of Versailles where they might stand a

chance of being able to discuss their business unheard by anyone else.

Trying not to retch, Lully outlined the situation to St. Paul. "I think we both . . . render invaluable service . . . His Majesty—" he said, turning to gag from the necessity of breathing in order to speak.

"Yes?"

"Our man knows . . . couple hides," he gasped. "Two possibilities. One—make Mademoiselle Émilie sing."

"And what would that do?" asked St. Paul, removing the handkerchief from his nose just long enough to spit out the words before gagging and covering it again.

"She would be recognized. Bring her back. But—difficult. Something else: a valuable trinket—missing," said Lully, drawing closer to St. Paul and forgetting to hold his nose against the smell.

"Go on," said the nobleman.

"If the girl has it—thief—and we can arrest her!" Lully was so pleased with himself that he almost shouted his last few words.

St. Paul hushed him, although there was no one anywhere near them to hear. He had almost forgotten about the missing gift. "What . . . look like?"

"A bird. Diamonds."

"Nowhere here?"

"They've searched. Gone." Lully turned and gagged again.

"We know where . . . but she never leaves."

"The maid. A bribe?"

St. Paul thought for a moment. "Possibly. Or landlady. I'll go, tomorrow."

As soon as courtesy would allow, the two men virtually ran away from each other to more congenial surroundings.

∽

François bowed to Madame de Maintenon as he placed her letters on the table near her desk. She was already busy writing replies to those from the day before, although it was only nine in the morning and others in the household were still asleep. Madame de Maintenon, Madame de Montespan, the illegitimate royal progeny, and an assortment of staff—including François—were on the rue Vaugirard in Paris. Although at Versailles the widow Scarron could minimize her contact with the marquise and concentrate only on educating her children, since Madame de Montespan had been sent away from Versailles, she had to accompany her. It was all in a good cause, however. The king's confessor had again refused to give communion to His Majesty and a woman who was living in sin—even though it was with the monarch. Every so often, when the public mood was particularly focused on morals, the Church would take a swipe at Louis's self-indulgent way of life. But when the furor blew over, things always went back to the way they were before. It was not easy to deny a king like Louis whatever he wanted. Madame de Maintenon knew this, and her desire to see him lead a more godly life was her principal motive for having tried the scheme with Émilie. Although it seemed as if it had ended in utter fiasco, she had information that might yet lead to producing the result she originally desired. But this time she did not enlist St. Paul's aid. She knew, in fact, that the count and Monsieur Lully were up to something. She also suspected that the marquise had something to do with it.

The widow Scarron was nothing if not patient, and so she bore her exile from court with fortitude. The unhappy band of travelers had only been at the house on the rue Vaugirard for a day or two and were just as likely as not to be recalled to Versailles at any moment. In the meantime, she decided to start her own subtle inquiries. She summoned François to attend her.

"François, I understand you paid a visit to Monsieur Charpentier a few days ago," said the widow Scarron without lifting her eyes from the sheet she continued to fill with words, in an apartment that differed from the one she occupied at Versailles only in its slightly smaller dimensions.

"Why, yes, Madame, I did."

"What business did you have with the composer?" She looked up, fixing him with her dark eyes.

François was caught unprepared. He rarely conversed with Madame de Maintenon, only arriving to receive instructions, and never thought that she would ask him such a question. "Monsieur Lully desired me to deliver a message to him. He was preparing to use too many musicians in Mademoiselle de Guise's fête."

"The king's ordinance only applies to public performances, François. I'm surprised you did not know that." She lay down her quill and stood, running her finger over the back of a chair and examining it for dust. "And it was not like you to go to Paris at all. You said your father was ill?"

"Yes, Madame."

"Extraordinary. And I thought he was already dead. Or perhaps this was your other father?"

François looked down at the ground.

"You had better tell me what your real business was. I fear you are meddling in something that is more dangerous than you know."

No, thought François, he knew just what it could all mean. "I am sorry to say, Madame, that I know nothing more than what Monsieur Lully told me. Perhaps he sought only to frighten Monsieur Charpentier."

"Very well, François. Although I am disappointed. I thought we understood one another."

She returned to her letters. François left the room silently.

∽

When Sophie first went to visit the Charpentiers, she really had no idea of proposing herself as domestic help. It was an inspiration of the moment, when she found herself confronted with Charpentier alone instead of both of them, or just Émilie. Once she left the apartment, she thought a little more carefully about accepting the post but could not see how it would hurt—although she had not entirely decided what she was going to do once she was installed in the position of lady's maid and companion to the person whom she still held primarily responsible for her own downfall.

Charpentier gave her a month's wages in advance so she could purchase more ladylike clothes. He also brought a cot into the apartment for her to sleep on. Everything was arranged very quickly, and

Sophie understood the need for speed once Charpentier had filled her in on what François had told him. But the haste and secrecy meant that Sophie had no chance to speak to Émilie until the day she took up residence with the family on the rue des Écouffes. Even then, she knew the residence there was temporary, as it was Charpentier's intention to move Sophie and Émilie out to the country as instructed by François as soon as his wife was recovered enough and the princess's fête was over.

The very day after Émilie's miscarriage, Lucille opened the door for Sophie, who carried a small parcel and had Monsieur le Diable tucked under her arm. He growled and hissed, his eyes wide with indignation.

"Monsieur Charpentier didn't say anything about a cat," said Lucille, backing away from Sophie.

"He must have forgotten," she said, pushing past the young maid. "Where does Madame do her toilette?" she asked, placing the cat on a stool by the fire and depositing her parcel in the middle of the parlor floor.

"I—I don't know."

"*Hmmph.* Of course. You are a housemaid." From somewhere deep inside her, Sophie's native snobbery emerged. It felt good to be superior to something, even if it was just a housemaid in a three-room household.

"I'm just off to the market," Lucille said, taking her cloak and walking out with her chin in the air.

Sophie looked around at the apartment. She ran her finger over the tops of the chairs and the mantelpiece. "*Tsk.*" With her handkerchief she flicked some dust off a stool and sat on it.

"Lucille?"

Sophie heard Émilie call out from the other room. She stood, smoothed down her hair, and prepared to confront the young woman whom she had tried to help more than a year ago, and who had repaid her kindness with thoughtlessness.

"Lu—" Émilie stopped in midword when she saw Sophie coming toward her. "Sophie!" She smiled and reached out her hand. "My husband said you were coming. I'm so grateful. And so ashamed."

Sophie stood just out of Émilie's reach and watched as she let her hand fall back onto the bed. "I am to be your lady's maid," she said, and then busied herself arranging Émilie's brushes and mirrors on the dressing table in the corner.

"My lady's maid—and my friend, if you can ever forgive me."

Sophie turned to look Émilie in the face. "I'm sure I don't know what you're talking about."

"The slippers. I should have come back that night, but I forgot, and then it was too late."

"And the next day?"

"I—I ruined them, I'm afraid. I stepped in a puddle. And then I was ill."

"Why didn't you tell anyone?" Sophie was in no mood to let Émilie explain her way out of the calamity that had wreaked so much havoc on her life.

Émilie thought for a while. "I don't know. Once I was at Versailles, it all seemed so far away."

"Well, there's nothing to be done now," Sophie said, turning back to her aimless straightening while she tried to think of what to do next.

"I'm still very tired. I'm sorry. I just need to sleep for a while longer."

Almost before Sophie turned around to face Émilie again, she heard her breathing become audible and uniform. Once she was certain Émilie was fast asleep, Sophie opened the armoire in the corner and looked through all Émilie's shoes, thinking perhaps she might find the missing slippers among them, and, when her search proved unsuccessful, opened the drawers on the dressing table and took everything out. She wasn't really certain what she was searching for, but it occurred to her that somewhere there might be some remnant, some note—something that would contradict the simple story Émilie had told her. If Émilie awoke while she was ransacking the drawers, she could say she was simply reorganizing things the way she liked them, so that she could find everything to help Émilie dress.

The first drawer Sophie emptied had only buttons and rouge in it. The second looked as though it was just handkerchiefs and other small items of linen. But when she reached deep into the drawer, she found something small and hard, wrapped in a hankie. She pulled it out and quietly unwrapped it.

Sophie gasped when she saw the diamond bird, and then looked at the bed to make sure Émilie had not awakened. The brooch was heavy and utterly magnificent. She had never seen anything like it before. While she stood there unable to take her eyes off the stunning piece of jewelry, Sophie heard the door at the street open and Lucille climbing the stairs. Quickly, she wrapped the treasure in the hankie and started to put it back in the drawer, then thought better of it and stuffed it into her bodice. The pin was not too large, and there was plenty of room there. The diamond bird was completely out of sight by the time the housemaid poked her head cautiously into Émilie's room.

"She's sleeping," Lucille whispered.

"Oh, is that what she's doing?" whispered Sophie, who went to Émilie's closet, found a dress that needed mending, and brought it into the parlor. She had no idea what Émilie could be doing with such a costly bauble in her possession. She could have pawned it and paid a year's rent in a beautiful town house. Although she still didn't have all the facts assembled, Sophie was beginning to get a sense that things were even more complicated than Charpentier had told her.

Twenty-six

We would gain more by letting others see us as we are,
than by trying to appear as we are not.
Maxim 457

Madeleine hunched over her embroidery frame and unpicked the petit point it had taken her an hour to do. Her mind was not focused on her task, and she found that she had inadvertently given the shepherdess in her pastoral scene a green face. She could not imagine how she had allowed herself to work the entire one-inch square patch without noticing. It was all so vexing. A waste of good silk thread. She was in a foul mood when her little maid, who now wore a new serge gown with no tears or patches and had learned to keep her hair neat and her fingernails clean, entered the parlor.

"Beg yer pardon, Madame," she said, and then curtseyed somewhat after the fact. "There's a gentleman here."

"Does he not have a name, you—" Madeleine stopped herself from calling the girl something vile. It was a bad habit, to save up all her anger and unleash it on the poor, ignorant creature, who really did not deserve it. Except that she was so unbearably stupid sometimes. Madeleine had told her and told her, just saying someone had come to call was not enough. She had to announce the person, like they did in the best houses. The girl was about to leave the room and ask the visitor his name when Madeleine stopped her. "Oh, don't bother! Show him in." She put away her work and tried to look calm and complacent.

To Madeleine's complete amazement, the gentleman who walked into her parlor was none other than le Comte de St. Paul, who had not come to visit for several months—not since he had told them the news of Émilie's death. At first she was so confused that she neglected to stand. But Madeleine soon remembered herself, stood, and curtsied, relinquishing her best chair to her distinguished caller.

"To what do I owe this honor?" she asked. "Tea, girl . . . Or would you prefer some wine?" Madeleine turned on her most practiced smile for St. Paul's benefit.

"It has simply been too long since I was a guest in your . . . home," he said. "I believe these are new curtains?"

"Why, thank you, sir! They are indeed! I hope you are well?" Madeleine felt a little flush of pleasure. She knew that she had been impolite to the count when he was last there, that she had been unable so much as to look at him for fear of losing control of herself, of giving in to a grief that was completely private, and she was happy to have this chance to show him that she could be gracious.

"I am in excellent health. But of course, I did not come here to talk about my health or your furnishings!" St. Paul said, giving Madeleine a knowing look.

She felt herself blush. The man was presumptuous, and she knew he was toying with her: after all, she was several years older than he. It annoyed her that she could not help responding to his provocative behavior. "Where is that girl with our tea?" she said, rising from her chair and starting toward the kitchen.

As she passed by St. Paul, he reached out and caught her by the wrist. "I am afraid that I must open a subject that may give you pain. You see, I look upon you as a friend of a particular sort . . ."

The luthier's wife looked at the fine gentleman who did more to raise the tone of her parlor than all the upholstered furniture in the world and wondered what on earth he could be talking about. She gently but firmly withdrew her wrist from his grasp. She was not so blinded by flattery that she could not tell when she was being worked on.

"It concerns your daughter—your late daughter."

Madeleine said nothing but waited for him to continue.

"I fear that all was not as it at first appeared," he said, pausing as the maid put the tea tray down on the table and Madeleine poured them each a dish.

"How so, Monsieur le Comte?" asked Madeleine, bringing St. Paul his tea. The memory of Hortense's revelation was fresh in her mind. She realized that she must be careful. She did not want to give anything away unless she knew it was safe to do so.

"Well, simply that dear, sweet Émilie, whose voice held such promise, may not have taken her own life."

"What exactly are you suggesting?"

"I mean to say that it may simply have been an accident."

St. Paul's expression was damnably blank. Madeleine could not read it. "My poor, poor child," she said, taking a lace-edged hand-kerchief out of her sleeve and blowing her nose in it loudly. "What makes you suspect this?"

"Ah, there are mysteries in death, just as in life. One of the ladies at court—a very sober, trustworthy lady, you understand—had a vision, in which Émilie appeared to her."

Madeleine's mind worked furiously, although she did an excellent job of maintaining her outward composure. What if Hortense had really seen a ghost? Or what if St. Paul was trying to trip her up, to get her to confirm that Émilie was now in Paris?

"If only, if only my child would come back to me!" said Madeleine, standing and walking to the window. She felt a sudden need to have her back to St. Paul.

"I am so sorry to distress you," said St. Paul, who rose and approached Madeleine. When he reached her, he placed his hand lightly on her shoulder and then let it slide gently down her back. "If you, or anyone you know in Paris, should have any similar visions, it would help us greatly in our effort to clear Mademoiselle Émilie of the heinous charge of self-murder if you were to tell us about it, right away." His mouth was so near her ear that she could feel his warm breath as he spoke.

She turned abruptly and stepped away before St. Paul's hand reached her buttocks. "I can assure you, kind sir, that if I had seen, or if I do see, any vision of my daughter, you will be the first to know."

Madeleine's eyes met St. Paul's. Without speaking, he reached into his coat and drew out a small leather bag. He turned away from Madeleine and walked to the table, where he deposited the bag.

"I have long wanted to make you a special present to help you over the grief of your daughter's death," he said, bowing courteously.

Madeleine walked over to the table and picked up the bag. It was heavy. Before, his gifts had been mere tokens. This was something more troubling. She knew from her past encounters with the count that his flirtation was not serious. Nothing ever came of his whispered attentions. And in truth, although she had been flattered, she found his prissy foppishness a little repugnant. For all his rough simplicity, Marcel was much more to Madeleine's taste. She held the pouch out to St. Paul. "Now that I am in a more respectable position in society, I find it imprudent to accept gifts from men who are not my husband, even those who are as thoughtful and generous as you."

St. Paul stared at the pouch for a moment before taking it from her.

"Good day," said Madeleine.

Once the door had shut behind him, Madeleine went to the window and looked down at the street, watching as the nobleman climbed back into his coach while passersby stared. She was certain that she would never see that handsome young man again.

St. Paul settled himself in his coach, practically shaking with fury. "How dare that peasant refuse my beneficence!" he said to no one in particular, as he helped himself to a large pinch of snuff and indulged in a noisy sneeze. It was clear that Madeleine Jolicoeur knew something. She looked guarded. The woman was shrewd, there was no denying it. It would not have surprised him if she had seen her daughter, if she had even known all along where Émilie was hiding. In spite of himself, St. Paul had to admire her perception, her ability to realize the point at which she should back away. He had been too obvious; it would have worked better if he had kept up his visits, however distasteful, instead of arriving after all those months. A rare miscalculation.

"I don't need her," St. Paul said aloud, as his coach picked up speed on the road to Versailles. "Everything will turn out just as I plan."

∾

St. Paul's unexpected visit put Madeleine in a state. She didn't know whether to feel relieved, angry, guilty, frightened, or elated. Émilie must be alive. Why else would the count have tried so obviously to pump her for information? He must have thought she was stupid. Madeleine burned with shame to think she had been taken in by him.

The idea that Émilie had not died filled her with joy. But there was something about the whole mysterious affair, something that stopped her from rushing to the workshop that instant to tell Marcel. She knew he was devoted to their daughter and that to deprive him of the happiness of knowing she still lived was cruel. But Madeleine was afraid. Afraid that her daughter would involve them in some illicit activity that would endanger them both. She asked herself what good it would do for Émilie to return to them. She would not want to work, and it was dishonorable for a grown woman to live with her mother, unless she was a widow. Madeleine even had a fantasy that it really was only Émilie's spirit that had paid them a visit, that St. Paul had been telling her the truth. Although this was preposterous, still she could not understand why a man like St. Paul would lie about a poor young woman's fate. What was Émilie to him?

And how was she to tell her husband? What would he say if he knew that Hortense had seen Émilie a month ago, and she had said nothing? "Last week. That's it. I'll tell him last week."

"Did you want something, Madame?" The maid entered the room when she overheard her mistress, whom she knew to be alone.

"What? No. Nothing." Madeleine resumed her restless pacing, shaking her head, knotting and unknotting her hands in front of her.

~

"Is anything the matter?" Marcel had returned for their midday meal and could not account for his wife's behavior.

Madeleine continued her pacing. "There's something I must tell you."

"Yes?"

"It's just that, well, you see, Hortense . . ."

"Is Hortense ill? You want to go to her?"

"No! It's not Hortense, it's something that Hortense saw, you see, it's, it's . . ."

"It's what?"

"It's Émilie!" The words exploded from her mouth.

"Émilie's dead," said Marcel.

"That's just it! She's not!"

Once the statement was out of her mouth, Madeleine let loose a stream of words so fast that her husband could hardly follow them. He heard something about St. Paul, and a cloaked, mysterious figure, but he could not string her sentences together in a way that made any sense at all. He was still trying to figure out what exactly his wife was saying to him when the maid walked into the parlor and cleared her throat.

"What is it, girl!" shrieked Madeleine.

"Dinner's ready," she said, and then went back into the kitchen to fetch the stew.

Madeleine stood in the center of the room like a diver at the edge of a cliff, suspended between action and inaction for a moment too brief to measure. By the time Marcel covered the space between them, she began to sob, great dry, heaving gasps, so that she could not draw in her breath. He shook her gently.

"It's all right! We will find her. If you say she is alive, I believe you."

All at once Madeleine's tearless gulps became a torrent of weeping. Marcel wrapped his arms around his wife and let her collapse against his shoulder, allowing his own tears to fall onto her gray head. The young maid tiptoed around them and set their bowls of stew on the table, then returned to the kitchen, closing the door behind her.

Twenty-seven

*Reconciliation with one's enemies is nothing but a desire
to improve our condition, a distaste for war,
and a fear of some bad outcome.*
Maxim 82

Sophie arose early the next morning and let herself out of the apartment before Charpentier awoke and Lucille arrived. She walked through the misty Paris streets in the direction of the rue des Rosiers. She knew a merchant there who was adept at converting questionable assets into liquid cash. Although she had never had a reason to visit Monsieur Rothargent before, several of the other women who walked the streets with her had mentioned him. It was not uncommon for prostitutes to supplement their incomes by relieving customers of their gold snuffboxes at the moment when they were least likely to notice. One prostitute prided herself on being able to satisfy her customers so completely that they did not even twitch when, while they were sunk in a deep, postcoital sleep, she removed their gold teeth. Sophie hastened to the fence's establishment by a devious little route through the cellar of a house of ill repute. Although she had no reason to suspect someone was following her, she decided it was best not to take any chances.

The shop was closed, but Sophie knocked insistently until Monsieur Rothargent let her in. He was still dressed in his robe and nightcap. When Sophie placed the brooch on the table in front of him, he nearly dropped his loupe.

"Where did you get this, Mademoiselle?" he asked her.

"A friend gave it to me," she answered, knowing that it sounded like the lie it was.

Monsieur Rothargent picked up the bird, letting the light catch it and peering through his glass into the hearts of the precious stones. "Your friend must be very fond of you indeed," he said, as he continued his examination of the piece. After several minutes of silent contemplation, he blurted out, "Twenty-five écus."

"But it's worth much more than that!"

"Twenty-five écus, and I swear on my honor that I will never reveal whose hand this little bird flew from."

Sophie was torn. She knew that the brooch was almost beyond price, because of the stones, the workmanship, and because of what it could mean to anyone who wanted to cause problems for Émilie and Charpentier.

"Thank you, but I've decided not to sell it," she said, as she wrapped it up once more in the hankie and tucked it away in her bosom. She left quickly, taking a different route back. She stopped at a flower stall on the way, figuring she could use the errand as an excuse for her early excursion.

But her movements that morning did not go unremarked. Around the corner from the rue des Écouffes, St. Paul waited in his carriage for the spy he and Lully had engaged to let him know as soon as the couple made any move to flee Paris or as soon as the maid emerged so that she might be bribed. When instead of Lucille he saw Sophie leave the house at that early hour, the spy went immediately to St. Paul and informed him, so that by the time she returned from Monsieur Rothargent's, the count was waiting for her a discreet distance away.

"Well! If it isn't the pretty young maid with the delicate digestion!" Sophie's misadventure with the king five years before had been the talk of the court for weeks.

"Ah, Monsieur de St. Paul. What a surprise. I'm afraid I have no time for pleasantries this morning." Sophie walked on toward the house.

St. Paul grasped her arm. "I wonder if I might have a word with you? It could be well worth your while."

Sophie did not like St. Paul. But something told her he could be useful if she decided to pursue her course of revenge against Émilie. "I have only a minute, and then I must return to my employers."

"Let me guess. In the house you were seen to leave a little earlier, the only inhabitants who might be able to afford a lady's maid would be the Charpentiers."

"A lucky guess," said Sophie as St. Paul led her down the street, away from the front door and toward the river. So, they were watching the house, she thought. That was a bad sign. Sophie wondered if Charpentier had seen the count. Surely St. Paul would not be so bold as to accost Émilie in her home. The image of Émilie helplessly waiting, weakened from her recent ordeal, suddenly loomed before Sophie.

"I wonder why you would do such a thing as go to work for a couple who are in hiding. Although it must be more pleasant than spreading your legs for all and sundry. I heard that you were dismissed from the Hôtel de Guise because of a pair of slippers."

How did he know? Sophie said nothing, but she remembered that the count had been there when she returned with the "borrowed" slippers for Émilie. And doubtless he had his ways with the other servants at the Hôtel de Guise: that Mathilde would have been only too happy to tell him the story.

"I too have a score to settle with Mademoiselle Émilie. I thought, perhaps, that we could work together to achieve the result we both wish for."

"And what result is that?" Sophie asked.

St. Paul stopped walking. "Riches, respect, and the utter annihilation of the little songbird and her milksop of a husband."

"What, pray, did she do to provoke you?"

"Two things, really. She slipped through my fingers at a most inopportune moment. But that is not to the point. She has absconded with a certain valuable trinket, the possession of which could send her to the Bastille. We both know about her propensity for thievery."

"And if you discovered this trinket in her possession?"

"She would be apprehended by the forces of the law and taken to the Bastille—to teach her a lesson, you understand, before her return to Versailles to fulfill her destiny."

"What destiny is that?" Sophie was curious as to why St. Paul was so concerned with something that, on the surface, had nothing to do with him. She knew how poor he was, so it was obvious that the brooch could not be his.

"That is for the king to say. Now, if you were able to locate this item in Mademoiselle Émilie's possession, it could be worth, say, twenty-five louis?"

It was five times what the merchant on the rue des Rosiers had offered Sophie. But still she held back from just turning over the brooch to St. Paul there and then. In any case, it would surely be better for anyone who wanted to incriminate Émilie if the diamond bird were actually discovered in the apartment. Sophie told herself that this was why she did not reach into her cleavage and produce the item for St. Paul. "Your offer is very enticing."

"Do we have a bargain?" St. Paul put his hand out to Sophie.

"I need time to think about it," she said, curtseying to him politely before turning and walking back to the Charpentiers' apartment with the diamond brooch jabbing uncomfortably into her left breast.

Sophie locked the door behind her when she entered the parlor. She was surprised to see Émilie up and seated at the table, drinking a dish of tisane.

"I feel so much better. Those flowers are lovely! Lucille never thinks of flowers."

She looks pale, Sophie thought.

Charpentier came out of the bedroom, dressed for work at the

Hôtel de Guise. "Are you certain you do not want to stay in bed one more day?" he asked his wife.

"No. With Sophie here I shall have someone to talk to. And really, I feel fine."

"If she is tired, please make her go back to bed," Charpentier said to Sophie. "I would stay here, but there is a soirée this evening at the Hôtel de Guise." Émilie looked up at him. He saw the expression in her eyes and wished he had not said anything about the party. Charpentier kissed his wife on the forehead.

"Monsieur Charpentier," said Sophie in a low voice, stopping him as he put his hand on the doorknob to leave.

"What is it?"

Sophie looked back and forth from Émilie to her husband. She was tempted to say something about St. Paul, that he was outside, waiting and watching. But to do so would close off her options. "I'll take care of Mademoiselle Émilie," she said.

Charpentier left.

Once she was alone with Émilie again, Sophie picked up her mending. Her mind worked furiously to think of a way to replace the brooch in Émilie's drawer undetected.

"A cat! How wonderful!" To Sophie's surprise, Monsieur le Diable walked right up to Émilie and rubbed against her legs. "Listen to him purr! He is singing, I think. I long to sing. You know," she said looking up at Sophie, "my husband has written some beautiful airs for me."

"So sing them," Sophie said, breaking the thread in her teeth.

"I can't."

"Why not?"

"I thought you knew," Émilie said.

Sophie peered through the eye of a needle and pulled the thread through. "Clearly I do not."

"You see, no one is supposed to know I'm alive. If I sing, they will recognize me."

Sophie did not lift her eyes from her work. "Who will hear you sing, all alone in here? And anyway, don't they know now? About you?"

"You don't understand," said Émilie. "You know, I was thinking about something. About how to make it up to you, about the slippers."

Sophie stopped what she was doing for a moment and glanced in Émilie's direction.

"I don't own much; there is little of value here. But there is something I could give you. I think it's worth a lot. I'm afraid it might get you in trouble, though."

"What's that?"

"Something I carried away with me from Versailles, by accident."

"Like the shoes, which you ruined by accident!" Sophie sniffed.

"Well, no. It was a gift, from the king. But still, I did not mean to take it."

"A gift?"

"For singing. For singing, and for what he expected, later."

Sophie put down her mending.

"I'd like to give it to you. I don't need it. You'll find it at the back of my handkerchief drawer, in my dressing table. My husband does not know I have it, so it won't be missed."

Sophie stood, preparing to go into the bedroom. But instead of doing what she knew would have been very easy, leaving Émilie in the parlor and pretending to reach into the back of the drawer to find the brooch, she stayed where she was, put her hand into her bodice, and pulled out the handkerchief with its concealed treasure. "You mean this?"

Émilie's eyes widened.

"I found it, yesterday, while you were asleep." Sophie sat down. "I was going to sell it this morning, but I couldn't get enough money for it." That's it, Sophie thought. There's no going back now.

She resumed her mending while Émilie sat in shocked silence. If Émilie's enemy had been anyone beside St. Paul, Sophie might conceivably have decided to carry out her plan for revenge. But her intuitive dislike of the count was stronger by far than the anger born of the slipper fiasco. Had it not been for that episode, things between Sophie and Émilie might have been very different. They might have become friends, and perhaps Émilie would have engaged her as a maid and taken Sophie along on her rise to success at court. It seemed all wrong, suddenly, to be on opposite sides.

"I see," Émilie said. "If you still want it, it's yours."

"If I could take just one of the stones, I could live for a year. As it is, I think it is a dangerous piece of property. Not just for me, but for you. You shouldn't keep it either. Did you know that St. Paul was here? And that he asked about this?" Sophie held the treasure up to the light, and she thought the diamonds looked as though there were tiny fires burning in their hearts.

~

Charpentier was worried about Émilie. Although she seemed better, he'd never seen her so pale. He didn't like to leave her, and yet he knew he had to perform his duties for the princess that evening or the alarm would surely be raised. He had done everything else François had told him to do. The doctor had warned him not to move Émilie, but clearly it was more dangerous for her to stay where she was. The carriage was arranged: all that was necessary was to go around to the stand after the soirée and show the driver the way to the rue des Écouffes. He would go with Émilie and Sophie out to the hamlet where a farmhouse stood, and where he had been assured no one would ever look for them. Then he was to return to his life at the Hôtel de Guise as if he had never been married, never fathered a child who perished before it was old enough to live. Charpentier did not know how long he would have to remain apart from his wife.

"Let us start with the second part, gentlemen, the courante. Now, not too fast. It's not a gallop!" A low chuckle went through the ensemble. Charpentier began to beat the time.

"Pardon, Monsieur, but there is a gentleman here to see you." A footman spoke quietly into Charpentier's ear.

"Take a few moments' rest," said Charpentier at the end of the movement, and then he went to see who had come to visit him at such an awkward time.

When he entered his apartment, he was shocked to see Marcel Jolicoeur standing in its midst, his large frame dwarfing the small space. "Marcel! How may I help you?" Charpentier tried to sound casual, unconcerned.

"I am sorry to trouble you, Monsieur Charpentier, but I am here because my wife, Madeleine, believes—you will think us crazy, perhaps!—but she believes that Émilie did not die, that our daughter is alive."

Charpentier went to his desk and pretended to shuffle the mess of papers into some sort of order. This he had not expected. He turned to Marcel.

"What made her think such a thing?"

"It is foolish, I know. A friend of hers thought she saw Émilie. And then, when Monsieur de St. Paul came to visit yesterday, and asked so many questions—"

"Please, be seated," Charpentier interrupted Marcel. He had heard enough. "I know I can count on your discretion. You would never do anything that might harm Émilie."

"Then it's true! How long have you known? Why did you not tell us?" Marcel looked as though he might cry.

"I'm sorry. Truly I am. But when I tell you everything, I think you will understand. First I must finish the rehearsal. I will be no more than half an hour. Wait for me here. If you want tea, just ring for it."

Before Marcel could protest, Charpentier left and returned to the ballroom to rehearse the final movement, and figure out how to tell Marcel what he needed to know without endangering him, and without jeopardizing Émilie's safety.

Twenty-eight

*There are few faults that are less pardonable than
the means one uses to hide them.*
Maxim 411

"I have an idea. About the brooch."

Émilie and Sophie sat at the table in the Charpentiers' parlor
drinking hot chocolate and eating bread. Lucille was out doing the
laundry at the river.

"You see, it cannot be found in your possession or in mine, now
that St. Paul has gotten hold of me. They will use it to accuse you of
stealing, and then you will have no power to defend yourself."

"Surely they cannot be so wicked," Émilie said, still shocked
about everything Sophie had told her. What did it matter to all those
important people where she was, or whether she lived or died?

"Oh yes, they can! I'm surprised you don't see that, after everything that happened. But that is not to the point. Let us package it up
in a box, and send it to Madame de Maintenon."

"Why to the widow Scarron? Why not Madame de Montespan?"
Émilie preferred to trust the king's official mistress, who had helped
her get away, and who must have sent François to warn her husband
that they were trying to bring her back.

"Because the widow Scarron is your enemy. If she has the brooch and cannot trace where it came from, she will be unable to pin it—so to speak—on you." Sophie smiled and took a gulp of cocoa.

"I see your point. But I am afraid of her. I think she is capable of anything."

Sophie stood and walked slowly around the room, talking aloud but to herself. "If we send it to Madame de Montespan, what happens? Does she know that the king gave it to you? Or will she think it is a gift from a distant admirer? She may keep it, or it may never reach her. Or if it is discovered in her possession, they may think you somehow gave it to her for helping you escape. That would make her cross, to be incriminated by you, and would not do us any good."

Émilie marveled at Sophie. These subtleties would never have occurred to her. "I don't know. Truly."

"And, Madame Charpentier, what makes you so certain that the marquise is your friend? She is not known for taking kindly to potential rivals for the king's affection, even—or perhaps I should say especially—those who are only acting as instruments of the widow Scarron."

She had to admit, Sophie had a point. Émilie realized that she could not say for certain exactly what either Madame de Maintenon or Madame de Montespan felt about her or how they would respond about the brooch, and about her continued existence. She wondered if they already knew. If all Sophie said about their spies and their ability to plot and scheme was true, it seemed likely. "So what do you suggest?"

"Just leave it to me."

With that, their discussion ended. It was a relief to Émilie, in a way, to turn over the brooch and all it represented to Sophie, just as she had trusted the maid to help her prepare for her first performance.

Hour by hour, Émilie felt better. Her cheeks were a little pink again, and she could walk around the apartment with little pain. She had no doubt that being in the country, away from all these intrigues and uncertainties, would be good for her, although she wished that

Marc-Antoine could stay with her. It would be worth it, though, in the end. One day, they would be together and she would sing his music again. She was certain of that, more certain than she had ever been of anything.

"I must go see about getting this precious item delivered into the right hands, and so I shall leave you for the present. I'll be back before night." Sophie stood and drained her dish of cocoa.

"Sophie," said Émilie, looking up. "Thank you."

Sophie waved her hand at Émilie dismissively, took her cloak off the peg by the door, and left the apartment.

I can't believe I'm doing this, thought Sophie, as she went in search of someone to help her get the brooch to Versailles by the next day. Was it only that morning that she had thought of selling it? Of claiming its value as compensation for all that she had suffered since the day Mademoiselle's slippers were discovered missing? It wasn't at all like her, she thought, to change her mind like that. Perhaps it was all because of St. Paul. She had never liked him; no one did. In the instant that he accosted her, she could see a life of deception and treachery stretch out before her. It was not what she wanted. Mischief, flirtation—that was harmless and fun. The life that St. Paul led put others at risk. Sophie was afraid she would lose her ability to sleep soundly at night, and she did enjoy her sleep.

Besides, she had seen quite enough of the base side of human nature. Something refreshed her about Émilie's protected naïveté. It was easier, in fact, to believe that the matter of the slippers had all been an unfortunate accident than to harbor a grudge that had grown stale over the period of a year. Sophie preferred to be in service, especially with someone whom she could dominate so easily.

As to the problem at hand: she decided to stick with her first instinct and send the brooch to Madame de Maintenon. Her own past experience with Madame de Montespan's vindictiveness did not give her confidence that the marquise would ally herself too closely with Émilie's cause. Something told her that the brooch would end up in the widow Scarron's hands anyway, and so the preemptive gesture seemed the safest at the moment. In no other circumstance, she thought, could she possibly derive some benefit from her intimate acquaintance with the Parisian demimonde. If she had remained a lady's maid at the Hôtel de Guise, she would never have known how to find a person to undertake the task ahead, someone who was willing (for about half of her savings—now that she had a job, she didn't need them immediately, and something told her that Charpentier would willingly reimburse her if her efforts were successful) to see that the parcel was transported to Versailles and given into Madame de Maintenon's hands by the next morning. It was a tricky business. If she gave any hint as to the value of the contents of the box, she knew it would simply disappear. She decided to pretend that it was a paste copy of a brooch. The courier she had in mind would not be able to tell that it wasn't.

On her way back to the rue des Écouffes, the brooch safely on its way to Versailles, Sophie heard a carriage draw up next to her. She continued walking, pretending not to notice.

"Mademoiselle Sophie, a word."

St. Paul. Again. Best to play along for the moment, she thought. "Ah, Monsieur! Forgive me, I was somewhere else entirely."

"Will you join me in my carriage?"

"The day is so fine, and I am enjoying my walk. Perhaps *you* would join *me*?" Sophie did not want to find herself enclosed in a moving vehicle with St. Paul.

"I think I would prefer to talk to you in private," he said.

Before Sophie took another step, the coachman leapt from the box and lifted her off her feet, then threw her inside the coach, where she hit her head on the floor. By the time she recovered from being stunned, the coach was moving along at a sprightly clip.

"Forgive me, Mademoiselle. Our business was too sensitive for the open air." St. Paul held out his hand and helped Sophie onto the seat next to him in the carriage.

Sophie rubbed her head.

"Now, about the precious object we spoke of this morning . . ."

"Ah yes, Monsieur le Comte. I'm afraid it is nowhere to be found. Mademoiselle Émilie possesses no jewelry that I could discover."

"Then she has hidden it, or sold it. Or . . ." St. Paul looked Sophie up and down. "Tell me, Mademoiselle Sophie. What could possibly be worth more than twenty-five louis to you?"

"I'm sure I don't know what you mean!" Sophie drew herself up and did her best to look prim and proper.

"Perhaps you have hidden this object on your person?"

"No, Monsieur, I have not."

"Prove it." St. Paul pulled his velvet coat back just far enough to reveal the gilt handle of his dueling pistol.

Sophie looked at the fields flying past. They were going too fast for her to jump out of the carriage. As to staying where she was and continuing to bluff her way out—well, there was a chance it would work, and it did seem unlikely that St. Paul would take such a drastic step as to shoot her. On the other hand, she knew how desperate his circumstances were. "And just how would you like me to prove that I do not have this item?"

St. Paul took the pistol out of his sash and cocked it. Then he reached over to Sophie's bodice and pulled one of the laces that held her dress together. "You can do the rest. It's rather difficult with one hand."

With a sigh Sophie continued to untie her bodice. Before long she was completely naked except for her shoes, and her clothes were in a heap on the floor.

"Yes, I see that you do not have it. It does not matter. I shall take care of Charpentier this evening, and you, I believe, will be in no position to cause me any trouble." St. Paul rapped on the ceiling of the coach with his walking stick. The coachman pulled up the horses in front of an inn a few miles outside of Paris. "Get out."

"Monsieur le Comte!" Sophie was genuinely horrified that she was expected to descend from the coach in the middle of nowhere without a stitch of clothing on.

"I said, get out."

The burly coachman appeared at the door of the carriage with an enormous grin on his face.

St. Paul opened the door and the coachman dragged Sophie out. While she tried to figure out which parts of her body to hide with her hands, the coach took off, raising a cloud of dust that made her cough.

Within moments a small crowd poured out of the inn.

"Mademoiselle, this way," said the innkeeper's wife, who was just as glad to get the pretty woman out of her husband's sight.

Sophie sat by the fire, wrapped in a blanket, drinking a beaker of wine, and trying to explain how she happened to have been tossed naked out of a nobleman's coach.

"I must return to Paris, immediately!" she said after she finished her explanation.

"Paris is only five miles down the road. If you walk, you might reach the city gates by nightfall." The innkeeper stroked his beard.

"She cannot walk! It's too dangerous. Do you ride, Mademoiselle?" The woman cast a scornful look at her husband.

"All the horses are needed here." He glared at his wife.

We're wasting time, thought Sophie. "It's all right. I shall walk. Perhaps you could lend me some clothes, and a knife, so I may protect myself."

"I don't like it. A lady is not safe on the roads these days."

Sophie's eyes lit up. "A lady is not, but a man—" She turned to the innkeeper. "Perhaps *you* have some old clothes I can borrow?"

∽

It was dark, and Sophie had not returned. Lucille was gone for the day, Marc-Antoine had to stay late because of the soirée, and Émilie found herself entirely alone. She had spent a lot of time by herself before, but knowing, now, that St. Paul was determined to take her back to Versailles and that he had been seen just outside the house that morning, she was frightened.

Émilie picked up her embroidery and tried to focus on the delicate work, but she kept making mistakes. After a while she put it away and walked around the apartment, searching for something to take her mind off her fear. On the mantelpiece was the notebook of songs that Marc-Antoine had given her. She took it down, sat by the fire, and started to learn them, one by one. She hummed the tunes very quietly to herself. When she felt she had each one, she closed her eyes, and repeated the words over and over. There were about forty airs in this one notebook. Learning them all would keep her busy for a long time.

Twenty-nine

⁓⁓⁓

Nothing is more rare than true goodness.
Maxim 481

Marcel was in a fiacre outside the Hôtel de Guise waiting for his son-in-law to finish directing the music at the princess's soirée. The plan was to hasten to the rue des Écouffes at the end of the evening and pick up Émilie and Sophie. From there, they would flee to the country. He wished he could return to the Quai des Mégissiers and tell his wife what was going on, but he agreed with Charpentier that he had better not risk it. And so here he was, waiting.

The luthier reached into his pocket and pulled out a scrap of velvet ribbon. He had carried it everywhere with him since the day Émilie left them, about a year and a half ago. He threaded it through his fingers like a rosary. More than anything, he just wanted to see his daughter, to know she was safe.

While he waited for the moment when they could leave and fetch Émilie, Marcel watched a stream of elegant coaches approach the Hôtel de Guise and discharge their glittering cargoes. The tinkling sound of laughter reached him, and when the great doors opened, the roar of many people talking interspersed with snatches of music spilled out into the Paris night. He was a patient man—it took patience to make violins and lutes—but he thought he might go crazy just sitting there, doing nothing.

The arrivals gradually slowed and became intermittent, and the rue du Chaume was now choked with coaches. The sounds of revelry were replaced with those of harnesses squeaking, horses whinnying and snorting occasionally, and once in a while conversations between coachmen and postilions, who passed the time as best they could before being summoned to take the weary partygoers home at the end of the evening. If he and his son-in-law had to get away quickly in this mess, it would be almost impossible. Marcel leaned back and closed his eyes.

All at once, he heard voices just outside the carriage. "Wait here. I'll go and pull the rug out from under Monsieur Charpentier, and then return. Be ready for me."

"What about the police?"

"That's all taken care of."

Marcel sat up, suddenly completely alert. He recognized the voice of St. Paul and knew they must be talking about his son-in-law. Once he heard their footsteps pass by the fiacre and fade away, he slowly opened the door of the coach and crept out. The driver had nodded off on the box and did not notice that his passenger alighted. Trying to make as little sound as possible, Marcel walked toward the great iron gates that led into the main courtyard. He approached one of the liveried footmen who stood at attention at the front gate.

"Big crowd?" he said.

"Oh, nothing more than usual," answered the footman, looking Marcel up and down.

"It's boring, waiting for my master to come out again. He just arrived, though, so I expect I'll be here a long time."

"You mean le Comte de St. Paul? He just came in, yes, but he usually doesn't stay so long."

"No, no, I don't work for Monsieur le Comte. I'm coachman to Monsieur de Brouilly."

The footman looked at Marcel skeptically. Before the man had a chance to ask why he wasn't wearing Monsieur de Brouilly's livery,

Marcel walked away from him, back to the fiacre. His fears had been confirmed. He must warn Charpentier. Must get a message to him. How he wished he knew how to write!

Just as Marcel was about to climb back into the waiting coach, he saw a small figure pressed against the stone wall slip around the corner into the rue des Quatre Fils. There was something odd and furtive about this. Perhaps it was a thief, come to try his luck with all the bejeweled folks who attended Mademoiselle de Guise's party. Marcel flattened himself against the same wall and inched his way to the corner. When he got there, he stepped out quickly. The young lad was too surprised to run, and Marcel grabbed his arm.

"Ow! Let me go!"

It wasn't a boy's voice, it was a woman's. "Who are you? What are you doing here?"

"That's no business of yours. Let go of me! I'm here on a matter of life and death. I have an important message for Monsieur Char—" Sophie checked herself.

"For whom? For Monsieur Charpentier?" Marcel took a closer look at his captive. The woman was very pretty, and young. "I too need to get a message to that man. You'd better tell me what you're up to." Marcel dragged Sophie to the fiacre.

"Oh no!" she said, pulling away as hard as she could.

"I'm not going to hurt you. Please, don't make a scene. It's dangerous."

Sophie climbed into the coach. "Oh my God, it's good to sit down," she said, leaning back, "I've been walking for miles."

"Let me ask you again," said Marcel, "who are you, and what do you want with Monsieur Charpentier?"

"No, first, tell me who you are. Then I'll speak."

The two of them sat in silence for a minute or two.

"Very well, I am Marcel Jolicoeur, Monsieur Charpentier's father-in-law."

"Émilie's father! Thank God."

"You know Émilie? Have you seen her?" Marcel almost shouted, he was so excited.

"*Sssshh!* St. Paul is here. I saw his coach. We must get Charpentier away as quickly as possible. I think the count means to kill him."

"What makes you believe so? What can we do? How can we get inside?"

"I saw his pistol. It's a long story. Perhaps it won't be necessary to go in. Do you have paper or quills?"

"I have no need of such things, since I cannot read or write."

"Damn!" said Sophie. "I can't get in easily. They know me." She drummed her fingers on her knee while she thought. "Wait here."

Before Marcel could ask what she was going to do, Sophie let herself out of the coach and ran around the corner. He realized that he still had absolutely no idea what this young woman was doing there, why she was wearing ill-fitting men's clothes, and why she had any interest in warning Charpentier about St. Paul. When after about twenty minutes she did not return, he was afraid something had gone terribly wrong.

~⌒~

The soirée started just as it should, with a great fanfare and the entrance of Mademoiselle de Guise, with her "maids of honor" scattering white flower petals like snow in front of her as she arrived. Then Monsieur de La Rochefoucauld, who was so elderly he could barely stand, read aloud a beautiful sonnet he had written for the occasion, in which he flattered his patroness obliquely as the embodiment of eternal springtime—although she was a very old lady. Charpentier could not help thinking of the night that Émilie had made her début at a similar occasion. If only she could be there now.

The musicians had played a dance suite at the beginning of the party and were now preparing to accompany a singer, a tenor who was having something of a vogue in the Paris theaters. Charpentier stood to one side, taking in the carefully choreographed magnificence of the scene, lost in his own thoughts. A voice at once familiar and jarringly out of place spoke quietly in his ear.

"Ah, how I recall the evening of Mademoiselle Émilie's first triumph," said Monsieur le Comte de St. Paul.

Charpentier started and turned to face him. He fought to suppress the anger he felt toward this man who he knew was trying to take his wife away from him. At least, thought Charpentier, if he is here, then Émilie is safe. "Madame Charpentier is no concern of yours," he said, turning away from the count.

But St. Paul gripped his arm and pulled him back. Charpentier submitted. He had no desire to make a scene in his patroness's drawing room by wrenching himself free.

"Are you enjoying your little songbird, my friend?" St. Paul chuckled quietly. "The question is, how many were able to enjoy her before you? It is hard to imagine a minstrel being able to compete with a king!"

At that, Charpentier's self-control deserted him. He broke from St. Paul's grasp, wheeled around with his fist clenched, and struck him on the chin.

The practiced courtier, in addition to dodging scandal, had somewhere learned to dodge blows, and this one was not serious enough to cause his body much distress. Charpentier saw him stagger a little, but the shock in the count's eyes was very soon superseded by something that resembled smugness.

Silence enveloped the drawing room. Everyone had turned to face the two men. Charpentier glanced around himself. People were frozen in mid-gesture, their faces arrested in mid-expression. The only movement was that of a canapé plopping messily onto the floor from the fingers of a bishop.

"My honor must be satisfied." St. Paul's voice held the slightest suggestion of a quaver.

"I shall meet you wherever you like," said Charpentier.

"My man will call on you directly."

Charpentier turned and left the room. He could hear what at first seemed like a dull roar, but as it grew in volume, he realized that it was the noise of two hundred people all talking at once.

"Marcel!"

Marcel sat forward and opened the carriage door. "Monsieur Charpentier! Are you ready to leave?"

Charpentier climbed into the fiacre. "Not yet. I can't."

"Why not?"

Charpentier took a deep breath and let it out slowly. "That deuced blackguard! I must meet him, in the fields, halfway to Montmartre."

"I don't understand. A duel? Why?"

"He challenged me."

"But duels have been outlawed!"

"How can I not answer him? If I kill him, perhaps all our troubles will be solved."

"I see! And so murder is the way out of your difficulty? Listen to yourself! To be caught means death for both of you!"

"You're right, of course. But how can I face Émilie if I am not willing to defend her honor? I have said I will fight him, and so I must." Charpentier looked into Marcel's eyes. "I need you to come with me. When it is over, we will get Émilie and leave Paris forever."

Marcel put his hand on Charpentier's shoulder. "I don't like this, but you're my son-in-law. My family. I will not let you face the count alone. Are you a decent swordsman?"

Charpentier sighed. "No. Hopeless."

"Can you shoot?"

"I've never used a pistol."

"We have some work to do before dawn." Marcel knocked on the roof of the fiacre and told the driver to leave Paris by the Porte St. Martin.

～

Sophie waited outside the servants' entrance for her opportunity. She knew that there would be many comings and goings on a night like this, and that she might just be able to slip in and find her way to Monsieur Charpentier. If her borrowed clothes had fit her better, she would have been a little more comfortable, but she had to make the best of the situation.

"Come on out here and give us a kiss!"

It was Mademoiselle de Montmorency's coachman, already

drunk. He had one of the parlor maids by the hand and was trying to drag her outside to take advantage of her. It did not take long for them to be completely involved in their own business, and Sophie crept past and through the door that stood open.

Once she was inside, Sophie realized she had not thought very clearly about how to find Monsieur Charpentier. Getting into where the guests were would not be so easy, especially dressed as she was. After checking to make sure no one was around, she went up to the third floor, to the attic where the servants slept that was larded with a network of passages leading to all the rooms in the Hôtel. It was dark but mercifully empty. Everyone was working hard downstairs making sure that the party seemed effortless. Sophie found her old room easily enough. It led to a back stairway that opened on the floor below just at the princess's bedchamber. Trying not to make a sound, she descended, listening all the time. Once she had assured herself there was nobody in the corridor, she opened the door to Mademoiselle de Guise's bedchamber, then, so that it would not make too much noise, just pushed it until it was almost closed.

The room was empty, but the candles were still lit and the fire crackled in the marble fireplace. Sophie remembered the care she used to take of the princess's elegant belongings, how she had cleaned her brushes and polished the silver pots of rouge and scent. She went through to the dressing room and opened the armoire, which the new maid had not locked, doubtless having had to rush and scamper to prepare her mistress for the evening before going to attend to numerous houseguests. Inside were gorgeous gowns of English silks in beautiful, rich colors. Sophie dug through and found her favorite one, a yellow damask with gold trim. Quickly she stepped out of her borrowed men's clothing and into the dress. Without stays, the fit was not perfect, and it was a little too short for her, but the cut was very good and so it did not matter. She threw her doffed garments into the armoire.

"Oh dear! I must have forgotten to close up mademoiselle's bedroom!"

Sophie froze in place. It was undoubtedly Mademoiselle's new maid. Without another moment's hesitation, she climbed into the armoire and buried herself behind the mass of fabrics. She heard the girl humming, heard the sound of things being straightened and dusted off, heard her enter the dressing room.

"Hmm." The maid was so close, Sophie could hear her breathing. "Thought I closed this before."

To Sophie's horror, the maid pushed the armoire doors firmly shut, then locked them. Sophie hated tiny spaces. She wanted to cry out, to scream. But if she did so, they would simply assume she had returned to continue the business of thieving she had started when she presumably stole the slippers. Sophie bit her knuckle and hugged herself hard. She heard the chamber door shut with a resounding slam, then set about trying to unlock the armoire from the inside. But the mechanism was clever, and there was nothing she could do.

Thirty

*We all have enough strength
to withstand the ill fortune of others.*
Maxim 19

By the time Marcel and Charpentier arrived at the appointed spot, a faint light illuminated the outlines of the landscape. Charpentier could see the contour of St. Pierre and the abbey of Montmartre against the lightening sky in the distance and heard the mournful tolling of the bell calling the nuns to lauds. Another coach already waited for them there. Charpentier recognized it right away as Monsieur de St. Paul's. The count and his second lolled nonchalantly against a jagged stump, taking aim through the gold-handled pistols.

The formalities were accomplished, and Marcel and St. Paul's friend loaded the guns. Charpentier's hands shook.

The duelists paced apart as agreed, and then turned.

At first Charpentier did not know what had happened. He could not see anything when he tried to aim, and thought that St. Paul was dancing around in merriment at the spectacle. The report of the pistol deafened him for a while, and he felt as if he inhabited a bizarre twilight of existence. Suddenly he found he was lying flat on the ground and staring at the now pale blue sky. Marcel's face appeared over him wearing a look of concern, and then the world went black.

~~

Every now and again Sophie tried anew to pick the wardrobe lock using her fingernails, but to no avail. After about an hour, she gave up altogether, and sat crouched in the corner behind a muslin slip. She began to weep, using the slip to dab her eyes.

In what must have been the early hours of the morning, Sophie heard the door of the room open.

"Just help me out of this gown, and you may go. I'm too old for these festivities. It will take me a week to recover."

It was the princess. Sophie barely breathed.

"Yes, Mademoiselle. But the party was a great success, no?"

"It was. But fancy that nephew of mine, challenging poor Monsieur Charpentier to a duel! What can have possessed him?"

"I understand the fellow hit him on the chin, Mademoiselle."

"I'm sure he deserved it. I hope they have the good sense to cool off and forget their argument. Such a waste. Thank you, Jeanne. Just put the gown away and then you may go."

Sophie heard the maid's steps approach, and she pressed herself into the back of the armoire. The metallic grind of the lock disengaging was followed by a flood of fresh air. It was all she could do to prevent herself from leaping out and filling her lungs. The girl put the dress in its place, pushed the doors shut again, but did not lock them. Sophie breathed a quiet sigh of relief. She would wait until Mademoiselle was asleep and then steal away. She knew now that she had missed her opportunity to warn Charpentier. All that was left was to get back to Émilie as quickly as she could.

Once the princess was snoring, Sophie pushed open the armoire door and crawled through the room. She heard a seam tear when her toe caught in the hem of the gown.

"Oh my poor Alençon!"

Sophie stopped. The snoring commenced again. The princess was talking in her sleep. Sophie made it to the door, opened it quietly, and slipped out of the house unseen.

~

Émilie awoke with a start at dawn. The notebook lay open on her lap, and the fire was almost out. She closed the book, rose, and tried to poke the fire into life again, but there was no wood left. Lucille had not yet arrived. She looked around. Sophie was not there, nor was Marc-Antoine. Émilie's heart began to beat fast. She searched around the apartment, as if she might find her husband hidden somewhere, until the silence and emptiness were almost unbearable.

The stillness was broken suddenly by loud knocking at the door below.

"Émilie! Open up!"

It was Sophie's voice. "Thank God!" Émilie said as she went as quickly as she was able down the stairs to let her in.

When Émilie threw the door open, there stood Sophie in a state of disarray, wearing a beautiful gold gown that was rumpled and torn. "What happened?"

"I don't have time to tell you. We must get away this instant. Leave everything behind, just come with me. I can hide you!"

"But Marc-Antoine! I cannot go without him. He will worry if I do not leave word."

Before Sophie could explain, two police officers sprang out from the alley next to the house. "Madame Émilie Charpentier, née Jolicoeur?"

Émilie was about to open her mouth to say it was she, when Sophie stood in front of her and spoke. "That's me! I'm Émilie Charpentier."

"Sophie!"

"Shut up!" she whispered.

One of the police officers grabbed Sophie roughly by the arm. "You're under arrest, by order of His Majesty the King."

"On what charge?"

"Theft of property belonging to the Crown."

The other police officer began to tie Sophie's hands together behind her.

"No!" screamed Émilie. "I'm Madame Charpentier! It's me you want!"

The two policemen looked at each other, then at Sophie and Émilie.

"Don't listen to her," said Sophie.

"She's lying!" insisted Émilie.

"Look, we only need one of you. We're looking for Madame Charpentier, the singer."

"That's me! I'm the singer. Listen!" Sophie began to belt out one of her comic songs for all she was worth. The policemen looked at each other again and grimaced.

While Sophie was still howling, Émilie began to sing in earnest, one of the new songs her husband had composed for her and that she had learned during the long night before. After a moment Sophie fell silent. For several minutes the little group on the pavement stood completely still. Émilie's voice rang out in the clear morning, echoing off the buildings. They stayed there, a reverent audience, until Émilie finished her song.

The policeman let Sophie go and instead tied Émilie's hands behind her.

"No!" cried Sophie. "Émilie, you fool! I know how to get away! Don't you see? They would have ended up with no one, and now they have you!" Tears streamed down Sophie's face as she watched the policemen put Émilie in a cart that waited down the street. Within moments, they took her away.

Sophie turned and went into the house, making no effort to stop her sobbing. She would have to stay there, to tell Charpentier that Émilie had been taken. "Why did she do it?" she asked the empty parlor.

She wiped her nose on the sleeve of Mademoiselle de Guise's gown and flopped into a chair. Next to her, Émilie's embroidery lay abandoned, and the notebook of music was open on the floor. Poor Émilie, she thought.

After no more than a quarter of an hour, Sophie heard the door below squeak on its hinges and then slam shut. What sounded like a wild beast grunting was making its way up the stairs to the apartment. She stood up and pressed herself against the wall next to the parlor door so that she would be hidden when it opened.

"Émilie? Sophie?"

It was Marcel. Sophie came out from behind the door and gasped. Marcel supported Charpentier, whose shirt was awash in blood.

"What happened?"

"A duel. I tried to stop it."

"Let's get him into bed," said Sophie, coming to support Charpentier on the other side. Together they laid him down. "He is feverish; he needs a doctor."

"Can you stay with him? I must go tell my wife what has happened. Where is Émilie?"

"They took her. The police."

Marcel collapsed onto a chair. "The police! What has she done?"

"I'll explain it all later. Go home, bring Madame Jolicoeur here to help. We will get Émilie back," Sophie said, putting her hand on Marcel's shoulder.

Marcel nodded and left without saying another word.

∽

"Help me up. I must go immediately!"

"But Monsieur le Comte, you are not out of danger!" St. Paul's valet fluttered about rearranging the count's hairbrushes and making a great show of pouring a dish of tisane.

"I might as well be dead as let Mademoiselle Émilie come to any harm before I get her to Versailles. Fetch my coat!"

St. Paul flicked his hand at the bowl of tisane, which flew across the room and smashed against the wall. When he tried to stand, a sharp pain stabbed through his right leg, and he collapsed on the edge of the bed. "And my walking stick," he said through his clenched teeth.

All the way to the Bastille, St. Paul's leg throbbed. He had not counted on Charpentier's being able to wound him at all. Although it was not a fair fight, the count had not aimed to kill. He intended only to render Charpentier ineffective at preventing Émilie's arrest, which he had arranged just before his godmother's soirée. Now she had no doubt spent the night in prison. That would not gain him any favors with the king.

At that moment the blood started to seep through the dressing and into his last pair of good breeches. St. Paul wondered what excuse he could think of for asking his godmother to lend him another fifty écus.

~

The large, dark chamber where Émilie and about a dozen prostitutes, thieves, and other petty criminals were thrown together had a thin layer of straw on the floor. Everyone defecated in the corners, and rats ran around freely. Her wrists were rubbed raw from the ropes they had tied around them to bring her there, but once she was in the prison, the ropes were removed. The massive stone walls and the iron bars were adequate measures of restraint for the motley assortment of troublemakers who had been put in prison for a month or two to teach them a lesson. The few accused of heavier crimes would eventually be led from that place to their execution. They were those who, although guilty of capital offences, were not considered dangerous enough to take up space meanwhile in the more secure and still more inhospitable Châtelet.

No murmur from the outside reached Émilie where she was, so she assumed that the king had discovered the diamond brooch missing and had ordered her arrested. A part of her felt that she had gotten what she deserved for having ruined the slippers, for having carried off the diamond brooch, and most of all for having lost her baby. She thought perhaps if she just closed her eyes, she would die, that all the time she had spent since the day she tried to leap out of her window at Versailles would be as if it had never occurred. But life was not so simple. Émilie comforted herself by imagining all the music she had learned from Marc-Antoine's notebook, creating a concert in her own mind as she rocked back and forth on her heels, crouched down in the middle of the cell.

~

Madeleine Jolicoeur brought her son-in-law a bowl of broth. She had removed the lead slug from his shoulder and cleaned the wound. Her mother had taught her how to deal with injuries, assuming that she would never be wealthy enough to afford a doctor if Marcel should have an accident while working with his sharp implements.

Lucille arrived at her usual hour, just in time to miss all the excitement. She screamed when she saw Monsieur Charpentier wounded. Madeleine sent her out for food.

Once Charpentier was resting comfortably, Sophie looked through Émilie's clothes.

"What are you doing?" demanded Madeleine.

"I can't go around in Mademoiselle de Guise's dress. I thought I could just borrow one of Émilie's for now."

Madeleine did not trust Sophie, for no other reason than that she was too pretty. "Very well. But not one of the silk ones."

Sophie changed her clothes and joined Marcel and Madeleine in the parlor. "Where do you think they've taken her?" Marcel asked.

"Probably the Bastille. It's close to here, and she's not a known criminal." Sophie paced back and forth. Marcel and Madeleine followed her with their eyes. "In which case, someone needs to go there and bribe the guards. That's the way to get her out."

Marcel shook his head. "We have little money. Probably not enough."

"I have some," said Sophie. She went into Émilie's room and fished out from her small valise the leather pouch where she kept the remainder of her savings.

"Why would you do this?" It was Madeleine. She did not understand what Sophie had to do with her daughter, what possible ties she could have that would link her to Émilie.

"It's a long story, and we don't have any time. Monsieur Jolicoeur, take this, and go to the Bastille right away."

"Wait!" said Madeleine. She had brought her workbox over with her from home, not wanting to waste any time if she had to stay and nurse Monsieur Charpentier. She opened it and groped around in the bottom, retrieving two scraps of satin with tiny jewels embroidered on them. "These might be worth something. You could sell them, get a little more money."

Sophie looked at the bits of fabric Madeleine gave her. "Where did you get these?"

"They were all that was left of a ruined pair of slippers Émilie wore. I cut them out before throwing the rest of the slippers into the fire."

"When was this?"

"Oh, more than a year—yes! Of course. It was the night Émilie sang at the Duchesse de Guise's salon."

Sophie smiled weakly and shook her head, and then before she knew what was happening, tears began to flow down her cheeks.

"I'm afraid I don't understand," said Madeleine.

The words came out all squeezed and breathless. "You see, it's the shoes! I've found them!"

Madeleine was completely mystified. It never occurred to her to wonder where the ruined slippers had come from: like the dress, she assumed they were a gift from Monsieur Charpentier. Sophie, unable to speak, waved her hand at Madeleine and went out to see if she could turn the scraps into ready cash.

Thirty-one

Men do not seek death.
They die only because they cannot prevent it.
Maxim 23

The next morning two uniformed guards entered Émilie's cell. All the other inmates cowered in the corners. Guards generally took prisoners out of that particular cell for one reason only: to escort them to the gallows. Anyone who was to be released was simply called upon by the jailer and allowed to walk through the door. The guards found Émilie easily enough, because she was alone, crouched in the middle of the dark room, her arms wrapped around her knees, still rocking back and forth on her heels. They dragged her roughly from the floor. The other women all crossed themselves and spat, at once pitying her and feeling glad for themselves that they were not being led to a similar fate, at least not yet.

Émilie was certain she was being taken to her death. Indeed, she wished for it. And since this was her last hour on this earth, her last opportunity to leave something of herself behind, she started to sing. At first she could not make her vocal cords obey her commands. But as they warmed up, the sound of her voice swelled and echoed through the cold, dank mass of the Bastille.

Émilie continued to sing as she was led out of the dark prison into the midst of a gorgeous June afternoon in Paris. Her eyes had grown accustomed to the obscurity of the cell, and she had to close them against the flat, brilliant sunlight, unmitigated by shade. So she did not realize that rather than being shoved into an oxcart for the trip to the Place de Grève, she had been bundled into St. Paul's coach. For several minutes she kept her eyes tight shut against the glare of daylight, convinced that with every revolution of the wheels, she grew closer to the hour of her execution.

But the rue St. Antoine seemed unnaturally long. Her throat became tired, and she stopped singing. When the trip continued beyond the short distance from the Bastille to the Place de Grève, Émilie opened her eyes. She saw the interior of the coach, and through the window the houses and shops of Paris passing by. Sitting across from her, with a hankie to his nose and mouth because of the stench that Émilie gave off after sitting amid the detritus in the Bastille, was St. Paul. He looked just the same, but a walking stick leaned on the cushion next to him, and there was a dark stain on the right leg of his breeches.

Too shocked even to speak, Émilie assumed that all would become plain to her in due course. After the recent events, she had relinquished any idea of being able to control her own destiny and simply watched with detached curiosity as things happened to her.

"Well, aren't you going to say anything? Don't you want to know what is going to become of you?"

St. Paul's smile sickened Émilie. Her eyes had become enough accustomed to the light to notice that his coach, on first appearance so elegant, showed signs of wear, that the edge of the silk cushion was threadbare, and that the gold leaf was wearing off around the door. They sat in silence for the remainder of the trip.

∽

Moments after Émilie had been shoved into the coach, Marcel arrived at the Bastille. He had his pouch of money ready and was prepared to lay it all out to bribe the guards and get his daughter out of prison.

"I've come for Madame Émilie Charpentier," he said to one of the guards.

The man said nothing but consulted a large book. He closed it, and then went through a door to another room. After about an hour he returned.

"Your daughter's not here anymore."

"What do you mean? She was brought here yesterday."

"Yes, but she's gone, I tell you."

Marcel instantly feared the worst. He knew Émilie had just had a miscarriage, that she had not fully recovered from it. His legs began to give way beneath him, and the guard reached his hand out to steady him, realizing that Marcel had jumped to the wrong conclusion.

"I mean, she's just been taken away, released from prison, and gone in the Comte de St. Paul's coach."

It took Marcel a moment to comprehend how completely he had misunderstood. As he did so, his face underwent a miraculous transformation. Although he feared St. Paul, at least Émilie was out of the Bastille, and perhaps they could get to her. He clapped the guard on the shoulder, then practically ran all the way home.

"She is out of prison! Émilie is saved!" Marcel could not contain his joy when he arrived back at the Charpentiers' apartment, where his wife and Sophie sat in the parlor. Charpentier was in the other room, propped up with cushions in bed.

"Thank God!" breathed Madeleine. "But where is she?"

Marcel told her his story, leaving out nothing. "All that remains is to find out where St. Paul has taken her, and she will be home!"

"She is at Versailles. I must go immediately and get her back," came a voice from the bedroom doorway.

Marcel, Madeleine, and Sophie all looked over to see Charpentier, who stood before them, wearing only his shirt and breeches. His bare calves and feet looked thin and unsteady, and his face was the color of bleached parchment. At first no one moved a muscle, but then Charpentier began to sink, slowly, to the ground, as though his legs were made of sponge. Marcel and Madeleine reached him at the same moment and helped him back to bed.

~

Madame de Maintenon stood at her window and watched a flock of geese lift off from the surface of a fountain and fly away in perfect formation.

"When Madame Charpentier awakes, bring her directly to me," she said to Marie, who stood silently by. "You may go."

Marie curtseyed and left.

"So, St. Paul, you have brought her back from the dead."

St. Paul paused with his dish of tea halfway to his mouth. "She fooled us all. She deserved to be apprehended."

The widow Scarron turned and looked at the count, whose walking stick leaned next to him on his stool. "How did you hurt yourself?" she asked.

"A hunting accident," he said, blowing on his tea to cool it off.

"Perhaps it would have been better if you had left her where she was."

"Better for whom?" St. Paul put his dish down and stood.

"For everyone, I think." Madame de Maintenon extended her hand to St. Paul, who bowed over it and left.

Almost as soon as the door closed on St. Paul, Lully was announced.

"Madame de Maintenon. You truly set an example for the court, living in such modest retirement." Lully had heard that the widow Scarron was none too pleased about Émilie's return to court, and knowing that her influence with the king was now beyond dispute, had decided to take preemptive action.

Madame de Maintenon held her hand out for Lully to kiss. "Good of you to come and visit me, considering your busy schedule composing a new tragedy for the king."

Lully was surprised that she knew about it. He generally discussed these things with no one but His Majesty. "Yes, the premiere is in two months."

"Your message said that you had something important to tell me, about the singer?"

"Yes. I thought you would want to know. My position is so delicate here. I must sometimes pretend to go along with things just to keep my neutrality." Lully then proceeded to tell the widow Scarron that St. Paul had approached him to plot for Émilie's return. "Naturally, I did not agree to this."

"Strange. That is not what I have been told by Monsieur de St. Paul."

"I can have no way of knowing what lies the count has chosen to spread about me. You know what a desperate state he is in."

"He must have had some hold over you, to feel that he could even suggest such a treacherous action. And he brought me this, which he claimed to have gotten from you." Madame de Maintenon retrieved François's letter from her desk. "If I did not know the handwriting, I might have believed him when he told me that you wrote it."

"I assure you I did not! And when it came into my possession because the luthier could not read, I endeavored to keep it from disturbing His Highness's tranquillity. Otherwise I would not be speaking to you so openly now." Lully took a pinch of snuff. She was a devious creature, and St. Paul was—St. Paul.

Madame de Maintenon smiled. "Your candor is quite unexpected. But I imagine you are not sorry to have such a talent returned to court? And surely you must take some pleasure in having thwarted your rival so effectively."

"But, as I said, Madame, I have done no such thing!" Lully drew himself up. He would not have gotten where he was without the ability to act.

"Do not trouble yourself, Monsieur Lully. I shall make sure that His Majesty understands your position completely."

*   *   *

What a pity, thought Madame de Montespan. Why could they not just leave the poor girl alone? She never liked St. Paul much. He always had a desperate air about him. Even if he really was practically starving, it was very unseemly of him to let anyone else notice.

The marquise hoisted her legs up onto the divan. She was far along in her pregnancy. Too far along to upset herself over something she could not change. And what if the king finally enjoyed Mademoiselle Émilie—or Madame Charpentier, rather? She herself would be out of commission for a while. He had strayed before. Yet she was always able to draw him back. Sweet as she was, beautiful though her voice was, that little peasant would never be a substitute for the most desirable woman in the realm.

The marquise smiled. She knew that Madame de Maintenon was extremely vexed that the pretty young singer was back at court. She had heard, through her spies, that little Émilie's death had been presented to the king as divine retribution for his sinful longings. For a time Louis forbore to indulge his carnal appetites. He must have been frightened. And then he had sent her to the rue Vaugirard, to put the evidence of his immoral behavior out of sight of the court.

But he was the king, and the greatest one that ever lived. The rules were different for him—for both of them. The marquise gently stroked her swollen belly. She knew that her beauty, her fertility, gave her as much power as the queen. And Madame de Maintenon could never take that away from her, no matter what she did.

After a short while Madame de Montespan turned her mind to other things. She set about planning her next meal, ordering her favorite delicacies, as the mental exertion had given her a prodigious appetite. After all, the baby, the royal baby, needed to be nourished in a manner befitting its station in life.

～

Colbert closed the enormous ledger book and stood from his stool. "You have heard, Your Majesty, that the little singer has returned?"

"Yes, extraordinary that. Seems she didn't die after all. Divine justice, don't you think?"

"A bizarre affair, apparently."

"Madame de Maintenon tells me that she is very contrite and wishes to be taken back into court."

Colbert scratched his ear. "It would be a nice gesture, I think, to forgive her. She has done you no real harm. And she is so young."

"Yes, that's what I thought. Lully will be pleased to have her, I imagine. Shall we go to chapel?"

King Louis XIV and his finance minister left the room.

⁓

As soon as Émilie arrived at Versailles, she was stripped, bathed, and scrubbed. It was the first time she had ever been completely immersed in water in her life, except for once when she was a little girl and fell into the river. Then the servants put her in a muslin shift and sent her to bed in her old room, which now had two bars on the outside of the window, positioned so that she could not open it wide enough to fit her body through the gap. She was to lie still for three hours—the time the medical men thought necessary to allow her internal organs to settle into their correct places once again, since water must have been absorbed by her skin, and Émilie's liver, kidneys, and stomach would float around dangerously until she had dried out completely. Émilie was by this time so exhausted that the forced rest was not forced at all, and she instantly fell into a deep sleep. Except for opening her eyes once or twice, she did not fully awaken for sixteen hours.

When she at last became conscious of her surroundings, her first thought was that what had happened over the last eight months had been nothing but a dream, that she had never left this place. But the scratches and bruises on her arms and legs from rough handling in the prison soon disabused her of that impression. She was conscious of pain that spread over her entire body. It was a mighty effort to move, but she sat up, very slowly, and then swung her feet over the edge of her bed until they rested on the cold wooden floor. Within seconds of doing this, Émilie heard a knock on her door.

"Come!" she said, in a voice that sounded oddly strangled, as if she hadn't used it for a very long time.

Marie, the same silent servant who had waited on her before, unlocked and then opened the door and entered with a court dress for her to wear, and all the materials necessary to arrange her hair in the manner preferred by the king. She was followed by another maid Émilie had never seen before, who carried a light breakfast on a tray. This young girl placed the tray on the little desk, then curtseyed and left. Marie stayed to help Émilie dress. Just as in previous times, the two women said nothing to one another.

When the process was complete and Émilie had eaten a little of the food, Marie indicated that she was to follow her and led her through the endless corridors in the direction of Madame de Maintenon's apartments. It was only then that Émilie began to tremble. She would have given anything to be on her way to Clagny instead.

All too soon, they arrived. The widow Scarron looked exactly the same, almost as if she had not moved from her spot since the last time Émilie was brought to her apartments.

"You have grown. And suffered, I can see, which was only to be expected when you so flagrantly ignored the wishes of His Majesty." Madame de Maintenon gave Émilie time to reflect on what she had just said, walking slowly around her austere parlor and letting her fingers touch the spines of the books ranged neatly on the shelves. "You caused many people pain. When we thought you had taken your own life, we wept for you as if you were our daughter."

"I beg your pardon, Madame, but it was not my wish to deceive anyone by not dying," Émilie said.

The widow Scarron ignored Émilie's remark, and turned from her to get something that was on the table beside her. Émilie recognized it as the velvet box the king had given to her, the box that had contained the diamond bird. So the widow had received it. And yet here she was, no doubt prepared to accuse Émilie of stealing anyway. Sophie would be upset if she knew.

"You remember this, of course?" said Madame de Maintenon.

"You thought, perhaps, to profit by the king's magnanimous gesture?"

Émilie was about to contradict her, but she could see that it would be futile. The lady had prepared her lecture and was not to be deflected from delivering it.

"The king was greatly wounded by your behavior when I told him the entire story. Indeed, your removal of this precious object," she opened the box and held it out to Émilie so she could see the glittering bird, "and your betrayal of his hospitality is a breach that is punishable by the most severe means. But the king has a generous heart." Madame de Maintenon closed the box, replaced it on the table, and turned toward Émilie again. "His Majesty has decided that he will allow you to determine your own fate. I assure you, this is something he does not grant to many."

Émilie remembered, now, how deliberate everything about this woman was. She never did anything quickly. The widow Scarron judged the exact measure of each of her gestures, planned every syllable and its proper inflection, and probably already knew what the eventual outcome of it all would be. Any hint of emotion, any chink in the armor Émilie thought she detected would have been revealed to her purposefully, as a trap, to catch her off her guard. The idea that she, Émilie, was to have any say in her future was absurd, when Madame de Maintenon was involved.

"His Majesty has instructed me to give you two choices. Once you choose, you must live by your decision, which will determine how you pass the remainder of your days on this earth."

Émilie could not take her eyes off the widow Scarron's fingers, which played with the pearls of her rosary, bunching them up and then letting them fall in soft clinks against each other.

"The first of the two choices the king offers you is the usual punishment for such treachery as yours, treachery that results in calling the good name of our divinely appointed sovereign into question. Many whose crimes were less serious have suffered that fate, and, should you choose it, you must consider yourself fortunate not to have forfeited your life. The punishment I speak of is to have your tongue cut out of your head so that you can spread no more lies that portray His Majesty as anything less than he is, the supreme, infallible ruler of France."

Émilie went pale and swallowed. She pressed her lips together protectively, suddenly acutely aware of the tongue that lightly touched the backs of her teeth.

"You may choose this fate," continued Madame de Maintenon, "after which you would be allowed to return to your husband and live in peace for the rest of your days."

Émilie's head began to buzz. She could feel the blood rush to the tips of her fingers and the ends of her toes. *Run!* her body said to her. But there was nowhere to go. And besides, her legs felt like posts that were stuck into the floor. Her muscles were stiff and weak at the same time from resting for so long, and she was having trouble simply standing.

"In his great magnanimity, and in recognition of your extraordinary gift, His Majesty the King offers you another choice, which would not deprive you of the ability to speak—or to sing. You may choose another path." Madame de Maintenon drew closer to Émilie and looked her directly in the eyes. "Be aware that this is a very great privilege, to be allowed to choose your punishment for such a grave offense." She backed away from Émilie again and then turned so that she no longer faced her and said, "You may join the Carmelite sisters, where you will live in seclusion and silence, save on those occasions when you raise your voice to the glory of God. You will then be required to sever all ties with your family and friends, living only to serve the Lord."

Émilie looked down at the floor. The frantic pace of her heart began to slow. So that was it. The battle was over her voice.

"You have twenty-four hours to consider your decision. At the end of that time you will come to me and inform me what that is. After you have done so, I will take you before the king, to make your apologies to him. It was his special wish that no mention be made of this choice, else others would expect to be so handsomely treated." At that, the widow Scarron nodded to one of her footmen, who left the room. A moment later Marie came and took Émilie back to her chamber on the floor above.

*　*　*

Once more alone, the widow Scarron knelt at her prie-dieu. "Please, my Lord, make her choose the right path. Make her choose to be your servant, to enter the convent, and preserve that voice which is so delightful to His Majesty. If you bear me any love at all, hear me now. Amen."

Thirty-two

◦◦◦

True eloquence consists of saying everything
that is necessary, and nothing that is not.
Maxim 250

Émilie stood in the middle of her room under the eaves in the old château. At first she opened her mouth and tried to make the muscles in her throat work without producing any sound. But she had forgotten what happened when she sang—or perhaps she had never really noticed before. Very quietly and slowly, she hummed one of Charpentier's melodies, drawing out each note as long as she could, feeling how it was to let the sound resonate in her body. Émilie closed her eyes, concentrating on the back of her throat, on the precise feeling of the opening that was only achievable with the full use of her tongue. Her mouth tingled, her lips buzzed.

After a few minutes of this quiet, blind practice, Émilie went to her mirror. She formed words without making any sound at all, just to see if she could tell what they were simply by looking at the shapes her mouth made. She looked ridiculous.

Still gazing at her image in the mirror and making not a sound, she pretended to sing. Her mouth opened in a parody of speech, holding its shape for unnatural stretches of time. She tried to make the right expressions to go with the music she heard in her mind but which did not emanate from her body. She looked like a child pulling faces.

The idea of not having a voice—it was inconceivable. But the alternative. How would that be? Separated from Marc-Antoine forever, never to see his loving eyes, never to feel his gentle embrace. She gazed at herself in the mirror. She was pretty. Her eyes were clear and blue, her cheeks soft and round, but firm. She ran her fingers gently over her forehead, her eyebrows, her eyelids, her cheekbones, down her nose, along the line of her chin, noticing how everything fit together, harmonized. And the warm cast of her skin was set off perfectly by her light blond hair.

Slowly, she let her hands continue down from her face. Émilie stroked her throat, feeling the place where music came from, then measured the narrow circumference of her swanlike neck with her fingers. Gently, tenderly, she let herself enjoy the softness of her own skin, just as her husband had on those nights they had been together.

And what of the days? What of their dreams to sing together? It pained Émilie to think of how sad Marc-Antoine would be. She knew that her voice was important to his career, but she also knew that, even if she could not sing, he would still love her. If only she could have had her baby. That would have given their life together some purpose, some meaning. If she chose the first punishment, how would it be if she were unable to talk to him, unable to make music, and, as the doctor had told her, unable to have his children? Would a life like that be enough for either of them?

Émilie lost all track of time. After a while she heard a light tap on the door. She called out, "Come!"

Marie entered with her supper on a tray.

"Where is François?" Émilie asked. The girl curtseyed politely and made a gesture indicating that she did not know.

Still she did not speak. Here I stand, Émilie thought, a woman condemned, with less freedom than she has. I am less than she, and yet still she does not speak. "Can you not talk?" Émilie asked.

The girl's downcast eyes and expression of sadness answered the question.

"Why not?"

In some part of her, Émilie did not really want to have the answer, not now, when there was nothing she could do about it. But her morbid curiosity got the better of her. She waited, patiently.

Marie opened her mouth. Inside was the jagged stump of a tongue.

Émilie made it to the washbasin just in time to vomit into it. Marie picked up the bowl and then left Émilie alone once more.

~

François was not surprised that the blame for all that had happened landed on him. He did not really expect Madame de Montespan to leap to his defense, although he knew it was because of her that he had been sent to Pignerol and not the Bastille or the Châtelet. Although he was confined, the room was hardly less comfortable than his quarters at Versailles, and he didn't have to work. True, the food was not as good, and already he had developed a nasty cough because of the damp, but they let him have books, and paper and quills and ink.

He had expected this, after he wrote the letter to Marcel, and after he went to see Charpentier at Madame de Montespan's behest. He had even packed a little bag with his most important belongings, because he had not known if he would have time to think about it when they eventually found him out. It was all very civilized. The guard bowed to him, he remembered. It was that young Hugues Martin, whom he had known since he was just a boy. They had a nice chat in the coach on the way to the prison.

François did not regret his actions. In fact, he felt very much at peace, knowing that, for once, he had done as his conscience dictated.

"Monsieur, your letters."

They gave him a valet too—which was more than he had ever had at Versailles. "Thank you, Henriot." Probably the usual petty gossip from court. One of the lady's maids wrote to him daily, glad of the opportunity to spread the dirt about everyone. François unsealed and opened the letter.

Cher François,

It grieves me to tell you this. I know how fond you were of the little singer. She is here, and they say the king—or at least, Madame de Maintenon, which is even worse—is livid with her. There was something about a stolen brooch, and treason. My friend, I am truly sorry to have to say it, but . . .

François covered his eyes with his hand. In his retirement, the tears came very easily.

It was evening, and the one candle he was allowed each day had almost burned down. François held the paper over the flame and watched as it caught fire, suddenly illuminating his cell, casting his shadow against the stone walls.

It had not been worth it, after all. He had not saved her. And now there was nothing else he could do.

◦───◦

What really rankled in St. Paul's stomach was that Madame de Maintenon didn't even have the courtesy to give him the news in person.

"Will you want your pistols, Monsieur, or just the sword?" The valet, Jacques, was busy packing up as many of St. Paul's belongings as would fit in a small, wooden trunk.

"The pistols are not very practical where I'm going. Perhaps I can sell them."

St. Paul was stretched out on the small bed in his quarters at Versailles. If he hadn't been sent away—banished, really, although they didn't call it that—his godmother would have taken him in. At least they were giving him twenty-four hours to make his arrangements. He had to leave the country. The image of Colbert's unyielding face was still vivid. The finance minister told him that he could either go on a mission on behalf of the king to the colonies in the New World, or spend the rest of his days in prison. All for trying to please his sovereign!

The mistake, thought St. Paul, was in thinking he could outwit the widow Scarron. He wondered if everyone at court realized how much she had the king under her thumb with all her pious nonsense. It was all so much easier when God wasn't brought into the picture.

"Forgive me, Monsieur, but what of my own things ought I to bring?"

St. Paul sat up. "You? You're not going with me, Jacques. What would you do in Louisiana?" They had bought his passage on a merchant ship and kitted him out with a musket. Other than that, all he had to fend for himself with was a piece of paper that entitled him to some property in America. Doubtless some useless tract of swamp, infested with poisonous snakes.

The old valet stopped his packing and looked at his master. "But Monsieur, the gentlemen in my family have served the gentlemen in your family for five generations."

"I'm told there's no need of valets in the New World." St. Paul frowned when he thought about dressing himself and taking care of his own personal needs. "They only booked passage for one." That was a lie; he was told he could bring one servant, and he chose his strapping coachman instead of old Jacques.

With his arthritic hands, the aging servant carefully folded St. Paul's brocade waistcoat and laid it on the top of the pile of clothes already neatly stacked in the trunk.

"You'll find another position. The Duc du Maine told me the other day that he was looking for a valet. With any luck, you might even get paid." St. Paul stood, reached into his waistcoat, and took out a small pouch of coins. "This should tide you over until you're settled."

The valet took the pouch and bowed, then turned and walked out of the room. When the door closed behind him, St. Paul let out a long sigh. The light poured in through the window, revealing only the absence of belongings, and the wooden trunk that held everything he owned. At least there would be no interfering marquises in Louisiana, he thought. By all accounts it was a man's world. And there were fortunes to be made, he had heard.

The door opened and three palace guards entered. One of them hoisted the trunk onto his shoulders and led the way. The other two stood on either side of St. Paul and walked him out of the château.

* * *

Among those looking out of the windows when St. Paul climbed
into his carriage attended by the guards was Lully. He watched the
men tie the trunk onto the back of the coach, and then St. Paul and
one of the guards climbed inside. The other guard sat on the box
next to the coachman, who urged the horses to a trot right away.
Lully stayed at the window until the vehicle was out of sight of the
château. Then he stepped away from the window and walked to his
desk. He took a fresh sheet of paper from the tidy pile and, using a
straight edge, drew staves on it carefully. At the top of the sheet, he
wrote the title, *"Psyche,* Act IV." It was his new *tragédie lyrique,*
and now Émilie, not Mademoiselle St. Christophle, would be the
lead.

The court composer smiled and sat down at his spinet. After writing a few notes on the paper, he picked them out on the keyboard.
Back and forth he went, from quill to ebony and ivory, until in about
half an hour he had covered one of the sheets of manuscript paper.
When this was accomplished, he replaced his quill in its rest, put the
cover on the inkwell, and stood.

After placing his best wig on his head, Lully rang a little bell that
was answered by Pierre. When the valet arrived, he ran to the composer and wrapped his arms around the man's thick waist.

"Not now, my love," said Lully, pushing him away. "I have an
appointment, with the king." He extended his arms directly in front
of himself and waited while Pierre placed six rings on his fingers.
When this process was finished, the young man held the door open
and Lully passed through it. It was time to go and lead the ensemble for a minuet, something to take the king's mind off pressing
issues of foreign policy. That was his job, after all. None of this was
for him. King Louis XIV was the only person alive for whom Lully
would gladly have died. Or for whom he would, without hesitation,
betray another.

Thirty-three

*The mercy of princes is often nothing more than a policy
to win the affection of the people.*

Maxim 15

During the twenty-four hours that Charpentier drifted in and out of delirium, Marcel, Madeleine, and Sophie tried to think of a way to find out what was happening to Émilie at Versailles. But Sophie's sources had proven unreliable in the past, and without being able to read or write, Marcel and Madeleine could only pray that their son-in-law would recover quickly and help them get information about their daughter's whereabouts. Just under two days after Émilie was removed from the Bastille, Charpentier's fever broke and he insisted on getting dressed and taking a fiacre to Versailles. Each step of the process exhausted him, and it was difficult to put his chemise, waist-coat, and coat on over his still wounded shoulder. He stood up, and then had to rest for a while. He dressed, and then had to sit quietly in the parlor for about an hour. It would be difficult to disguise the fact that he could not move his left arm.

"You must not go so soon! What good will it do for Émilie if you kill yourself?" Madeleine argued with Charpentier.

"You don't know what they—St. Paul especially—are capable

of. Émilie has no one to protect her. I must go. They must see that I am not simply going to let her be taken from me without a murmur."

There was a knock on the door below. Both of them froze, listening intently. They heard the landlady's voice. She mounted the stairway and tapped on the Charpentier's door. Lucille opened it for her, and when she had gone, came into the parlor with a letter in her hand. She gave it to Charpentier.

"What does it say?" asked Madeleine.

It was on very heavy paper and sealed with a large quantity of red wax and a stamp that bore the fleur-de-lys. "It says I am to appear before His Majesty. Today."

"Does it mention Émilie?"

Charpentier let his hand drop, as if the piece of paper were instead a lead weight. "No, it does not. And now it is no doubt too late. But still, I must go."

He looked up from the letter to face Madeleine's level stare. It had been a year and a half since Émilie's parents had seen her. Charpentier found himself wondering whose fault it had all been. It was they who had consented to send Émilie to Versailles. It had been he who had removed her and made it necessary for her to hide away, to risk the king's wrath. They were in this together. Although he did not know what would happen, and he suspected that his attendance at Versailles would alter nothing, he had to keep hoping that at the end of the day, Émilie would be sitting beside him with her arm through his, and her head resting on his good shoulder.

"Heavens! You're dressed," Sophie said to Charpentier, having returned from her errands, which included gathering the remainder of her belongings from her shabby room.

Madeleine embraced her. The maid had proven her loyalty and gained the respect of both Marcel and Madeleine. "He has been summoned to Versailles," she said.

Charpentier held out the letter for Sophie to read.

"Where is Marcel?"

"Gone to fetch a coach," said Charpentier.

The luthier came back a few moments later, and Madeleine and Marcel helped Charpentier stand. From the top of the stairs they watched him take each step with his wobbly legs. "Bring me my daughter," Madeleine said, and then looked away before he could turn around and see the expression on her face.

All the way to Versailles Charpentier tried to work out what to say when he was brought before the king. Should he be indignant? Respectful? Pleading? Desperate? He had no way to know what was appropriate. Besides, Lully had been spreading lies about him, so Émilie told him, and for all Charpentier knew, the king thought he was a traitor. Perhaps I am going to be sent to prison, he thought. Matters were complicated by the fact that he felt very ill. He cradled his bad arm in his good one, but still every bump, every jolt of the carriage sent a searing pain through his shoulder. Charpentier wished that he could fall into a deep, interminable sleep, nestled up to Émilie. But ever since he had recovered enough to understand the entire sequence of events, he had barely closed his eyes.

By the time the carriage arrived at the main gate, Charpentier was in agony. He climbed out of the coach and crossed the Cour Royale on foot, remembering so clearly the night he had entered on horseback. How everything had changed since then. But he did not have time to dwell on the past. A servant led him away, not to the king's apartments, but to the office on the ground floor of the château occupied by Monsieur de Lully.

"Welcome, Monsieur Charpentier!" said Lully with a smile that limited itself to his lips. "At long last we meet."

It was odd, thought Charpentier, to look into the eyes of the person who had done more to thwart his career than anyone else alive. He noticed that they were overshadowed by folds of skin that gave them an almost slanted look, and that Lully's nose was pinched and narrow at the top and splayed out at the bottom. The cheeks were sallow and flabby. Altogether, it did not look like a French face.

Also in the room was a valet, who stared angrily at Charpentier.

"But I forget myself," said Lully, noticing that Charpentier leaned on the back of a chair. "Please, sit down."

Charpentier took the chair gladly.

"I am a great admirer of your sacred music, Monsieur Charpentier."

"You might perhaps also admire my music for the theater if I were permitted to make use of adequate forces to mount a production." Charpentier knew he was being rude, but he did not care.

"The king is very particular, what can I say? Is that perhaps your reason for coming here today, to persuade him to alter the ordinance?"

"I imagine you know the reason for my visit."

"Ah yes, it is quite an honor!"

"An honor to have one's wife abducted?"

"Come now, Monsieur Charpentier, that is an exaggeration . . . So, you thought you would come and reclaim your rights? I assure you, the king does not often relinquish conquered territory," Lully said with a chuckle.

"I do not see the cause for mirth." Charpentier was a little surprised by Lully's manner.

"Of course, how callous of me." Lully sat in a chair opposite Charpentier and looked at him, the hint of a smile on his face, without speaking for what seemed a long time.

"Tell me," he finally said, "when was the last time you heard Mademoiselle Émilie—I mean, Madame Charpentier—sing?"

Charpentier seethed. This game had gone on long enough. "I have not heard her sing for eighteen months, since I introduced her at a soirée at the Hôtel de Guise—and I do not see that it is any business of yours!"

Lully ignored him. "And how would it be, for you, if you were never able to hear her sing again?"

"I've heard enough. My appointment was with the king." Charpentier used his good arm to push himself to a standing position.

"Forgive me. I speak in riddles. But I simply wondered, as a matter of personal curiosity, one musician to another, whether you cared more about the woman or the voice?"

Charpentier clenched his fist so hard that he could feel his finger-nails dig into his palm. If he had full use of his limbs, he would have been tempted to wrap his hands around Lully's neck with the same deadly pressure. Instead he spoke, an icy edge in his voice. "Tell me, Monsieur de Lully. Are you married?"

"Why yes, I am. But that does not signify," he said.

Charpentier saw the servant cast a searing glance in Lully's direction, which Lully returned. So that was how it was. "The king is wait-ing for me."

"I see you do not want to answer me." Lully tore his eyes away from the pretty young man. "No matter. The outcome will be the same." He rose. "A word of advice, Monsieur Charpentier. The king does not like to be contradicted. You will get nowhere by telling him it is your right to have Émilie returned to you. Le Comte de St. Paul learned, greatly to his detriment, that it does not do to anticipate the king's wishes." Lully paused to brush some imagined dust off his coat.

"I am certain St. Paul received no more than he deserved."

"Perhaps. Who can say? When the king discovered that he had fought a duel, the count was banished immediately. Shall we go? I believe this was the appointed hour."

Charpentier's jaw dropped open and then clamped shut. "I was under the impression I was to have a private conversation with the king."

"Whatever gave you that idea? My dear sir, there is no such thing as a private audience with the King of France!"

Lully laughed as they made their way to the Ambassadors' Stair-case. Charpentier followed him up the marble sweep and through the apartments that had been the scene of Émilie's last night at Versailles a lifetime ago, and that she had described to him in her letters for all those months. Because it was not yet sunset, there were no candles lit, and the ornate hangings made the enormous rooms appear even darker and more somber than they actually were. Charpentier tried to imagine Émilie there, thinking about him, writing letters to him. He wondered if François was still at Versailles, and if he had been allowed to comfort Émilie again.

Although the Hôtel de Guise was a large house, the sheer scale of the Château de Versailles awed Charpentier. He felt small. Utterly insignificant. It took so long for the two composers to reach the room where King Louis held court that in his fever Charpentier almost forgot why he was there. When at last they arrived and the door opened before them, the raucous sound of men's and women's voices all chattering at the same time flooded out. The room was mobbed with courtiers trying to get into position to be noticed by the king. He and Lully hovered in the background of the crowded space, but Louis clearly anticipated their arrival and noticed them immediately.

Charpentier had seen his share of splendor before, but the king's robe of deep blue velvet embroidered with gold fleurs-de-lys and trimmed with ermine was magnificent beyond his wildest imaginings. The great monarch sat, raised above the tumult, looking like a father who indulgently permitted his wayward children to cavort noisily in his presence but who was capable at any moment of commanding utter obedience. Louis turned to a soberly dressed minister who stood by his side. The man motioned Charpentier to approach.

Charpentier's legs almost refused his command to move, and his wounded shoulder throbbed unmercifully. He was extremely tired after his long walk from Lully's apartment to this public reception room. With a mighty effort, he stepped forward. His slow progress had the effect of silencing the entire company, who practically held their breath as the composer made his way.

"Your Majesty," said Charpentier, bowing deeply, forcing his left arm into the correct position for a courtly bow. He almost fainted, but he took Lully's advice and did not say anything more, waiting for the king to address him. He had, after all, been summoned there.

"We hear that you have talent. It is our wish that you compose music to aid us in our devotions. For that purpose, we grant you a pension and the title of Chapel Master." The crowd applauded politely, and he waved Charpentier off, as if this was the only reason he had summoned him to come before him. The courtiers all began talking again, pressing forward to catch the king's eye.

"But Your Majesty!" said Charpentier. All chattering in the room ceased once more, and eyes focused on this nobody who had said "but" to the king after being granted a pension. "My wife, Émilie. Is she not here? Am I not to see her?"

Louis turned to a woman clad all in black, whom Charpentier had not noticed before. The king whispered something to her, and she nodded, then left. When she returned, a postulant of the Carmelite order followed her in. Because he was not expecting to see her in such garb, Charpentier failed at first to realize that it was Émilie. Her lovely blond hair had been cut short, and what was left of it was hidden beneath the short veil she wore. Her young face looked almost raw, almost indecently naked without the frame of her hair. He could not read her expression because her eyes were focused on the floor.

The king spoke again. "Your wife, Monsieur Charpentier, has chosen to follow the path of God. You may say your farewells."

At that Louis rose and left the room, and everyone who was attached to the court followed him out, except Lully and the woman who had led Émilie into the chamber. Lully strode up and stood right in front of that woman.

"This is your doing!" Although he did not shout, the fury in his voice was unsuppressed.

"Mine? No one can choose the convent who is not called."

Lully turned from her and stormed out of the room, leaving Charpentier and the two women alone.

"Émilie?" This creature, whom he knew to be his wife, but who seemed like a stranger, walked toward him with her eyes cast down.

Émilie raised her gaze to meet that of her husband. She stopped just out of his arm's reach. She could feel Madame de Maintenon watching to see if she did one thing wrong, one thing that violated the agreement she had been forced to sign. Émilie had been prohibited from touching her husband, from weeping, from calling out to him. She had been warned that she would forfeit her life if she even suggested the nature of the alternative to her choice to enter the convent.

Charpentier broke the silence. "Why?"

The question hung in the air, unanswerable.

The widow Scarron walked forward to join the couple, who, although not even close enough to touch if their arms were outstretched, were held within each other's orbit. "Sister Marcelline—as she is now called—has made her choice."

Émilie glared at her with an expression that made her back away slowly and turn to face out of one of the long windows.

"But why? There must be a reason! I must know!" Charpentier's voice was shrill with desperation.

Émilie spoke. "Please don't ask why. You must trust me. It was the only way."

Charpentier could not take his eyes from Émilie's face, searching there for something—anything—that would help him understand what had happened.

"If I had come back," she continued, "I would not have been—never—" Émilie's voice grew smaller as she spoke. She took a deep breath and tried again. "I have chosen to dedicate my life, and my voice, to God. It was you who showed me what it was to sing. I would be—am—nothing without you." There was the suggestion of tears in the tone of her voice, and she paused and took a deep breath before continuing. "But without my voice, I would be less than nothing." Émilie stopped. She could say no more. The muscles in her jaw tightened with the struggle to suppress her emotions.

"Émilie!" cried Charpentier. He lunged forward and took hold of his wife's left wrist, collapsing to his knees at her feet. The guards, who had to this point been nothing but ornamental to the room, quickly left their posts and approached him. Madame de Maintenon motioned them to stay back. She herself drew closer again, ready to intervene between the couple if necessary.

Émilie forced her arm to hang by her side. She could feel her husband's sweating, shaking hand, feel his rapid pulse through the serge sleeves of her habit. She backed away from him, pulling herself out of his grip. Just as he released her, she felt Madame de Maintenon's small, steely grasp on her shoulders. Slowly, the widow Scarron turned her around so that she faced the door. But Émilie kept her eyes locked with Charpentier's as long as she could, craning her neck as she walked away.

"Who are you to take my wife from me?" Charpentier cried, reaching out for Émilie, too exhausted to move.

"I am Madame de Maintenon," she said, not pausing, pushing Émilie through the door, which shut behind them.

Charpentier sat back on his heels and stared at the space where Émilie had been. He raised his hand to his chest and clutched it, pressing hard as if to stop some invisible bleeding. He began to tremble. Slowly he pulled himself to his feet and walked to the door.

He hardly remembered finding his way back to the Cour Royale. When at last he climbed into the waiting fiacre, Charpentier felt near to passing out. Everything seemed very far away and very close at the same time. The exuberant colors of the scenery were almost painfully vivid, and he heard every sound as if it were uttered just inches from his ear. The boisterous, mating birds seemed to sing with a single, insistent voice. The revolving coach wheels created a rhythm that tormented him.

"Émilie, Émilie, Émilie." The music of her name, the rhythm of it, a perfect triplet if it was pronounced correctly. And with a shift of the accent, it was in two, an insistent beat, a pulse. Of course, he thought. It had been there all the time. Why had he not seen it? Or, rather, why had he not heard it? Madame de Maintenon thought she could separate them, but she was wrong. The sentence was pronounced, on both of them. He accepted his own punishment with joy.

Epilogue

*Philosophy triumphs easily over evils past and
evils to come; but present evil triumphs easily
over philosophy.*
Maxim 22

It was Easter Sunday. The king and Madame de Maintenon walked
arm in arm down the aisle of the splendid new chapel he had built
just for her. All the courtiers were already in their places. A new
oratorio was to be performed. It had been written by the distinguished composer of sacred music, the chapel master Monsieur
Marc-Antoine Charpentier, who had already taken his position at
the front of the ensemble and the choir. Most of the performers
were seated in the choir stalls, but there was one, a soloist, whose
order made it necessary for her to remain behind a rood screen.
The beauty of her voice was legendary. It was this that drew so
many from far and wide to share the king's devotions in the chapel
at Versailles.

The orchestra began to play. The first sections were sung by the
choir and a tenor soloist. It was the story of the Resurrection, clothed
in magnificent music. Even those who only pretended to be devout
could not help being moved by its beauty. But everyone waited,

tensed, for the moment when the artist they had come to hear would begin to sing.

At long last the time arrived. After some introductory measures, a treble voice floated a high note above the accompaniment. To the congregation, it seemed as if an angel had chosen that moment to visit the earth.

The hush that descended on everyone present continued as the music wove its spell. A shared ecstasy hung just above the congregants' heads. Madame de Montespan, grown fat and no longer on an intimate footing with the king, closed her eyes and gave herself to the music. The courtiers all looked down at their clasped hands or up at the magnificent ceiling. In the back, the lady's maids and valets knelt, feeling keenly the privilege of sharing this hour.

But the most exquisite moment of all, the instant of sublimation, was yet to come. When the soprano finished her air, and the orchestra began the next movement, Monsieur Charpentier stepped away from his spot in front of the ensemble. He began to sing, and after a few measures, the voice of the hidden soprano joined his, following it, weaving through it, dancing around the same notes, holding dissonances together so long they were almost unbearable, and then melting into resolutions both anticipated and unexpected. Their voices blended so perfectly that they seemed to be one. The king placed his hand over his heart and looked heavenward. The chapel warmed to the sounds, absorbing and reflecting in perfect proportion the harmony created by the voices joined in song.

Monsieur Charpentier kept his eyes closed while he sang. He faced away from the nave, toward the altar. The voice that blended with his came from behind him, and washed over him, finding its way into his body, awakening his deepest memories. Time seemed to disappear. The union was perfect.

When the service was over two hours later, a priest gave the benediction and the devout listeners filed out of the chapel, led by the king and the widow Scarron. Charpentier kept his eyes on Madame de Maintenon. She walked with undisguised pride at her monarch's side, still clad all in black. Now, though, in addition to her pearl rosary, she wore at her neck a magnificent diamond brooch in the shape of a singing bird.

When the worshippers were all gone, he looked over to the rood screen. There, indistinctly, he could see the shape of a nun. She raised her hand and touched the screen, then turned away, following the other members of her order back to the convent.

The chapel was empty. Charpentier gathered up the music from the stands and returned to Paris.

Acknowledgments

My heartfelt thanks to Adam Chromy, my agent, who believed in me; to Amanda Patten, my editor, who worked with me; to Peg Haller, my copy editor, who saved me from a few embarrassing mistakes; but most of all to Charles Jackson, my best friend and partner in life, who put up with me.

Acknowledgments

A TOUCHSTONE
READING GROUP GUIDE

ÉMILIE'S VOICE

1. Émilie's mother, Madeleine, is reluctant to let her take singing lessons. In fact, for most of the story she has only negative things to say about Émilie's good fortune. Why do you suppose she is so gruff with her daughter? Do you blame her for what happens to Émilie?

2. Émilie is consistently portrayed as being very innocent and naïve. Do you think this is a positive character trait? Why or why not?

3. What is it about Émilie that Charpentier falls in love with? Or is he just enamored of her voice and beauty?

4. Why do you think François agrees to help Émilie write to Charpentier, when it could get him in serious trouble?

5. Madame de Maintenon purports to be a pious woman who wants nothing more than to save the king's soul. Do you think her scheming is truly for religious purposes? What other motives might she have?

6. When the Marquise de Montespan tells Émilie that she is obviously in love with Charpentier, how does Émilie react? Do you think she finally realizes the nature of her feelings for him, or is the marquise correct in assuming that Émilie is only in love with the *idea* of love?

7. *Émilie's Voice* portrays the royal court of King Louis XIV as a hotbed of scandal, scheming, and sexual mischief. How does this contrast with the concept of staid nobility, reverence, and religion? Does the royal court have a modern counterpart?

8. Imagine yourself living at court in Versailles, where "invisibility is worse than death." Do you think you would enjoy it? Could you survive in such a treacherous environment?

9. Émilie feels that she cannot tell Charpentier that she loves him, even when he says he loves her. Given her decision at the end of the book, do you think Émilie ever truly loved Charpentier? Do you think she loves her voice more?

10. Émilie makes very few decisions for herself in this story. How is she used by those around her? Do you think that, in his own way, even Charpentier uses her? Why do you think Émilie refuses, or is unable, to take charge of her own life?

11. The author has cleverly tied several subplots to create a slowly building sense of anxiety about Émilie's fate. What are some of the threads that threaten to entangle and ensnare Émilie? Do you think she ultimately triumphs or succumbs?

12. How did you expect the novel to end? Were you satisfied with the ending?

13. Music is at the heart of this novel. How does the author convey its importance and demonstrate its effect on the characters? Do you have an image of what Émilie's voice must have been like? Does the author succeed in making you "hear" the novel?

14. Could what happened to Émilie in the seventeenth century happen to someone today? Why or why not? What about Émilie is very old-fashioned, and what is not? Are there any characters that bring to mind modern-day counterparts?

An Interview with Susanne Dunlap

1. *Émilie's Voice* is a song as much as a story. What involvement do you have in the world of music?

I began studying music at the age of five, when I started piano lessons. I was a music major at Smith College, and eventually went to graduate school at Yale to study music history. Opera was my area of specialization, in particular early opera, because I have always been fascinated by the relationship of words and music. Beyond that, I have been working for the last four years at Connecticut Opera, a regional opera company, where I have come to know many singers and other artists and production professionals, as well as hear a lot of great performances.

2. What made you decide to become a novelist?

Ever since I was a child, reading has been one of my greatest joys, on a par with music. I have been a "writer" all my working life, first writing advertising copy, then scholarly papers and a dissertation. But my imagination was sparked by the music history I studied, and I felt a burning need to bring the stories and themes of that history to a wider public. The challenge of writing a novel was both inspiring and energizing, and I feel very fortunate to have several mentors who have helped me develop as a writer.

3. What gave you the inspiration for *Émilie's Voice*?

Actually, it was the study of an entirely different seventeenth-century work that brought to my mind the idea of an innocent young singer unaware of the power of her own voice. That work was an oratorio by the seventeenth-century Italian composer, Alessandro Stradella, called *La Susanna*. Susanna is a character from the Apocrypha who is virtuous and beautiful. But Stradella's music is seductive and powerful. I wanted to explore how music can transform the singer and the listeners, and not always in the way intended by the performer or the character.

4. Your descriptions of seventeenth-century Paris and Versailles make these locations (and their inhabitants) come alive. Did you spend time in France to research your setting?

It was my great pleasure to take two trips to Paris, during which I also went to Versailles. On the first trip, I hadn't even started the book. By the time of the second, I was polishing up a late draft, and I really walked around and thought about where Émilie and her father would go, what it would be like to live in Paris during the seventeenth century, and what life at Versailles must have been like. Apart from that, I read a great deal about Paris and Versailles and the period, including works by people who were alive at that time.

5. *Émilie's Voice* is a historical novel that blends fact with fiction. Can you point out some of the real persons and historical events that give *Émilie's Voice* its flavor?

The composers Lully and Charpentier are both real figures, and there really was an outdoor performance of Lully's *Alceste* at Versailles in the Cour de Marbre. Both Madame de Maintenon and Madame de Montespan are historical figures too, and the things they actually did are in some ways more shocking and devious than the fictional events of *Émilie's Voice*. Mademoiselle de Guise was also real, as are the singers in Lully's troupe, whose names are recorded in history. Very little is known about the details of Charpentier's life, but Lully really was a rather unsavory character with a preference for men and young boys, and a voracious appetite for power and influence. And, yes, he did make the king pass those ordinances. (King Louis XIV is, of course, historical too, as are the other members of the royal family and the illegitimate children of Madame de Montespan.)

6. First novels are often said to be very autobiographical. Are there elements of your own personality in Émilie? Do you identify with any of the other main characters?

Aside from the fact that my middle name is Emily, I don't really think I'm much like my heroine at all! I can't sing, and I'm rather ornery and outspoken. I suppose I might identify more with Sophie, who is a tough, hardworking survivor. I think the only part of Émilie that I really relate to is her dreaminess. I used to drive my parents mad with my ability to sit for hours and just daydream.

7. The ending of the novel is not what one might expect. Why did you choose such a bittersweet twist, as opposed to a more traditional happy ending?

I think that Émilie came to understand that, to everyone around her, she was truly just an embodied voice. She needed to do something dramatic to reclaim herself from the life she had been forced to lead. And yet, I wanted an ending that was true to the time: women really didn't have many choices then. Her voice, her expression, was the most powerful thing she had, and ultimately it's what kept her involved with Charpentier. Besides, there's no historical evidence that Charpentier ever had a wife, and while I have freely bent the historical facts when necessary, I always try to resist obvious falsehoods.